Thrilling reviews for

# RHYANNON BYRD's

## PRIMAL INSTINCT series from HQN Books

### Edge of Hunger

"Byrd successfully combines a haunting
love story with complex world-building."
—*Publishers Weekly*

### Edge of Danger

"Ms. Byrd had me first intrigued and then
spellbound from the first page to the last."
—*Joyfully Reviewed*

### Edge of Desire

"[Byrd] serves up plenty of action and passion
that won't be denied...Great stuff!"
—*RT Book Reviews*

# RHYANNON BYRD

## TOUCH OF
## SURRENDER

HQN™

Recycling programs
for this product may
not exist in your area.

ISBN-13: 978-0-373-77464-7

TOUCH OF SURRENDER

www.HQNBooks.com

Printed in U.S.A.

Dear Reader,

I'm so thrilled to present *Touch of Surrender,* the newest book in my PRIMAL INSTINCT series with HQN Books. Set within a world of passion and danger, the fifth installment in this dark, provocative series tells the story of Kierland Scott, a werewolf who finds himself in serious trouble when he's forced to track down his missing brother with the help of the woman he once wanted for his own...but lost to another man. For the past decade Kierland has hungered for shape-shifter Morgan Cantrell, hiding his searing desire behind a mask of bitter indifference. But now that mask is crumbling. Each moment he spends with the mysterious female soldier is drawing him closer to the fraying edges of his control—and when that control is finally shattered, nothing will stop Kierland's inner beast from claiming the one woman it has always craved.

I truly hope that Kierland and Morgan's wickedly seductive romance will capture your heart as strongly as it has captured mine, and I especially want to give a special thank-you to all the readers who have kept me company in the PRIMAL INSTINCT world! My characters and I are forever grateful. Kellan Scott is looking forward to having his turn next...so be on the lookout for another sexy wolf coming your way. ;)

All the best!

Rhy

To my dear friend and fellow author
Patrice Michelle.
Endless thanks for always being there to chat with
about everything under the sun, from music to
movies to our muses.

# TOUCH OF
# SURRENDER

# CHAPTER ONE

*Prague, Czech Republic*
*Saturday night*

THE CLUB REEKED OF SEX, DRUGS and rock 'n' roll.

*If you can call that god-awful noise rock,* Morgan Cantrell thought, wishing she'd brought along a set of earplugs. Though she was hardly an expert, the female Watchman doubted the techno trash blaring out of the club's sound system at one hundred decibels could even be classified as music. Torture seemed a more fitting description. Her eardrums—far more sensitive than a human's—were probably bleeding in protest, but she tuned out the pain, focusing instead on her target. On the man, or *werewolf*, that she'd specifically come to track down.

Filled with every kind of depraved vice imaginable, the dark, trendy establishment was the last place on earth she ever would have expected to find fellow Watchman Kierland Scott. And yet, Morgan knew the tall, auburn-haired hunk wedged between two willowy, scantily dressed swan shape-shifters was Kierland. Even with the distance of the massive, strobe-lit room between them, she recognized the hard, rugged angles of his gorgeous face. Recognized that racehorse-lean body that looked as lethal as it did delicious. He wore a faded pair of jeans that hung low on his hips, scuffed leather boots and a soft white shirt that perfectly showcased his sun-darkened coloring and muscled physique, though she knew he would have chosen the clothes solely for comfort. Despite his outrageous good looks, he wasn't vain or pretentious. He was just pure, mouthwatering male animal. Beautiful. Dangerous. And built for sin.

Morgan's breath shortened just as her pulse quickened, and she burned under her suddenly too-tight skin, feeling as if she'd swallowed something hot and thick. It didn't matter how they felt about each other. Didn't matter that they couldn't stand to be in the same room together. Despite how much she disliked him, he always made her feel as if she'd been injected with an overdose of sex hormones…or some kind of head-spinning aphrodisiac.

*Don't you mean how much you* wish *you disliked him?*

Pushing the heavy curtain of her hair over her shoulders, Morgan tuned out the irritating voice in her head and focused instead on her surroundings, instinctively searching for any signs of danger. The establishment was obviously geared toward nonhuman clientele, as it was packed with wall-to-wall clansmen. A dynamic, diverse collection of paranormal species, the ancient clans had lived hidden among human society for centuries, the secret of their existence guarded by the organization of shifters she and Kierland worked for, called the Watchmen.

When Morgan had first walked through the door, leaving the howling January winds behind her, she'd been overwhelmed by the strong, thick scents of the varying species all roiling together on the dance floor, their sweat-slicked bodies moving in a kind of hypnotic, sexual frenzy. There were Lycans, witches, various shifters and even a few Deschanel vampires, though they looked over the crowd with the same cocky expression as Kierland, as if they found all the writhing madness a bit beneath them.

Wearing jeans and boots herself, along with a tight black turtleneck sweater, Morgan had more skin covered than any other woman in the club, which suited her just fine. She hadn't come to join the meat market. She just needed to talk to Kierland and tell him why she was there.

*So get on with it, then. Don't just stand here gathering dust.*

"Right," she whispered under her breath, and yet, she didn't move, her heartbeat picking up speed while her skin went cold and clammy, even with that sensual burn of heat still smoldering inside her. There were too many people, and without enough space, she could feel that familiar flare of panic that had haunted her for the past decade creeping up on her.

Taking a deep breath, she struggled to maintain control. It would be deadly to lose her cool in a place like this. There were too many predators who might seize on the opportunity to bully her. See her as easy game and move in for the kill, for no other reason than she was weaker than they were.

Descended from a freethinking line of shifters who had bred with various species from generation to generation—lion with fawn, wolf with lamb—Morgan was unable to take the shape of any specific animal, and was therefore considered "lacking" by most of the shape-shifting breeds. The prejudice sucked, but it was the nature of the beast for many of the clans. And she hadn't let it hold her back from what she'd wanted, which was to become a Watchman like her paternal grandfather had been. She'd simply trained longer and harder than her peers, tirelessly honing her skills to compensate for the fact that she could only manage a small set of fangs and short claws, and had ended up a damn good Watchman as a result. She no longer even thought of her inability to shift as a weakness, but used it to her advantage, knowing her adversaries often underestimated her.

The only true weakness she had was this nauseating fear of being crowded in by people, the sensation worse when she was indoors, without the freedom of the skies over her head. She wanted so badly to turn tail and return to the wide-open spaces of the night, but there was no turning back. Though she hated the situation, she would have to fight through it. Would have to force herself into that massive, swirling crowd if she was going to make her way to Kierland on the other side.

"Just do it," she quietly growled, her hands flexing at her sides as she took a step forward, and then another. Her vision swam and her throat started to close up as a trickle of sweat slipped down her spine, but she pushed on, refusing to give in to her fears.

*Don't look at anyone but Kierland. Just stay focused on him.*

It was easy to follow the mental instructions, since the Lycan was so big. So...satisfying to watch, and she wasn't the only one who held that opinion. More than a few hungry, covetous stares covered his tall, muscle-sculpted form, drinking him in, coming from women and men alike. You could literally *feel* the power emanating from him. The strength and deadly potential that he held under such masterful control. It was mesmerizing, drawing you closer like a spell, until you just wanted to press up against him. Touch his dark skin with the sensitive tips of your fingers, just to feel that hypnotic power pulsing and buzzing beneath the surface.

As she watched, he leaned back against the long bar, his stance casual as the blond shifters pressed in close to his sides, their looks so similar Morgan figured they must be sisters. Maybe even twins. They were exceptionally beautiful, but then swans always were, their pale skin and nearly white-blond hair denoting their species. They were also, in Morgan's experience, all a bit birdbrained...and well-known for their jealous rages. They weren't going to like her moving in on their territory—and she knew, without any doubt, that the hardheaded Lycan would be less than thrilled to see her.

*He always is.*

It was odd, how much that particular truth still bothered her. After a decade of discord between them, during which they'd avoided one another as much as possible, she really should have gotten used to it by now. Frustrating that she hadn't been able to master that simple concept, no matter how hard she'd tried.

She'd last seen him a week ago at Harrow House, his family estate in England and the house where his Watchmen unit had recently relocated from Colorado for protection purposes. Though Morgan herself had been a part of the Watchmen compound in Reno for the past five years, she'd joined up with Kierland's unit a month ago, after his brother Kellan had called, saying that he and the others could use her help protecting a little girl named Jamie Harcourt from a group of Casus monsters who were hunting her. Together, Morgan and the others had made it to England, where they'd met up with Kierland. He'd stayed at Harrow House with them until all the necessary security upgrades had been made to the previously abandoned mansion, but the second he'd been able to leave, he'd run. Though his friends had wanted him to stay, he'd claimed he still had unfinished business in Prague, where he'd been in negotiations with the Consortium, the governing body of officials who ruled over the remaining ancient clans.

*Or maybe he'd simply been itching to get back to his girlfriends.*

Shaking off the disturbing thought, Morgan was trying to decide the best way to approach him, when Kierland's head suddenly shot up, and she knew he'd scented her. Strands of dark auburn hair fell over his brow, and the full, sensual shape of his mouth compressed into a hard, tight line the moment his pale green gaze zeroed in on her. Although severe irritation was carved into his fierce expression, it was that piercingly sharp, almost violently intense glare that made her shiver.

*What? Like I expected him to be happy to see me? Get real. He'd rather cozy up with a rabid chipmunk.*

"What are you doing here?" he demanded in a low rasp, the instant she was within hearing distance. "Are you alone? Where are the others?"

She wasn't surprised by the rapid sequence of questions, considering how dangerous it was for the Watchmen at the moment to be out on their own. After all, they were at war.

Although the Watchmen weren't meant to interfere in the world of the clans, unless ordered to do so by their superiors, times had changed with the return of the Casus—and the awakening of the once formidable Merrick clan.

Though the Merrick had once been one of the most powerful of the ancient clans, their numbers were decimated after years of war, and they eventually took human mates. For centuries, the clan's unique traits had remained dormant within their human descendants—until the recent return of the Casus and the beginnings of the war.

A sadistic race of immortal creatures who were imprisoned over a thousand years ago for their crimes against humanity and the Merrick, the Casus had finally discovered the means to escape from their metaphysical holding ground. Needing the power that came with feeding upon their longtime enemies, they began to hunt down the awakening Merrick, determined to destroy them once and for all.

Now the Watchmen were acting on their own orders and fighting to stop the return of the Casus, their efforts organized by Kierland's unit. They were being aided by three newly awakened Merricks from the Buchanan family—Ian, Saige and Riley—who each possessed a mysterious power that had helped them in the search for a collection of ornate crosses called the Dark Markers. In fact, it was Saige Buchanan who had discovered the set of encrypted maps that led to the Markers' hidden locations, her unique "power" enabling her to decipher the code in which the maps were written. As the only known weapons capable of killing a Casus and sending its soul to hell, the Dark Markers were invaluable in the fight against the Casus—and time was of the essence, because the Casus wanted them, too. They'd even managed to steal the maps for a short time, no doubt making copies while they had them in their possession. Copies everyone had hoped would prove impossible for them to decipher.

The war, to that point, had been bloody, and the Casus hadn't taken kindly to their defeat in England the month before, when the monsters had attacked Kierland's unit in an attempt to get their hands on three-year-old Jamie Harcourt. Since then, they'd assaulted several members of the unit who had left to search for the Dark Markers, and there'd been some close calls, a few of the injuries serious enough that they could have turned fatal.

And then there were the Death-Walkers. The Watchmen had wondered what effect their war with the Casus would have on the world, and now they knew. The gypsy legends that had foretold the return of the Casus and the awakening of the Merrick clan had been based on the fundamental belief that everything in the world was interconnected—and they were only now realizing just how true that belief was with the arrival of this newest enemy.

Each time a Dark Marker was used against one of the vile monsters hunting the Merrick, a portal would open into hell. Unfortunately, as the Casus's soul was forced through, something else was able to crawl out. Thanks to one of Kierland's sources, the Watchmen now knew that these strange, corpselike creatures were called Death-Walkers, and they were bad news. Once the condemned souls of clansmen and -women who'd been sentenced to hell for their crimes, they were now maddened creatures driven insane by their time in the pit. Their only goal seemed to be the creation of chaos among the clans, for no other reason than they wanted to watch the world slip into madness along with them. And their first order of business was to destroy the Watchmen, since the highly trained shifters acted as the eyes and ears of the Consortium.

Kierland might not like Morgan, but he wouldn't be keen to lose another soldier, especially when so many Watchmen had already fallen victim to the Death-Walkers, another streak of deaths taking place in the past few weeks, which brought the toll to nine. The Lycan and his friends had been arguing for a month now about what was considered an acceptable risk when it came to leaving the safety of Harrow House—which was protected from Death-Walker attack because of the surrounding moat that had its waters salted and blessed by the village priest, making it impossible for the creatures to cross—and Kierland was constantly stressing the need for safety in numbers.

Which meant that he was going to be pissed as hell at her for coming alone.

"I'm not a child, Kier. I don't need a chaperone," she told him, surprised by the huskiness of her voice as she finally got around to answering at least one of his questions.

"So you're here by yourself?" Kierland asked, the steely note of frustration in the graveled words testament to just how pissed he really was. Known as a master of self-control, it wasn't often that the Lycan lost his temper—but when he did, it was always a dangerous, yet fascinating sight, like watching a natural disaster erupt right before your eyes.

"I came alone for the same reason you did. The fewer of us who leave the safety of Harrow House at this point, the better," she replied, the sickly sweet scent of the swan-shifters burning her nose as she stepped closer. Morgan might not have been able to completely shift, but her senses were even more highly developed than a predator's, which meant that her sense of smell was exceptionally acute. It was a great asset in the field, but sucked when forced to breathe down the cheap stench of Kierland's dates.

He opened his mouth, looking as if he was about to

say something ugly, but the blonde on his left beat him to it. "You actually know this woman, Kierland?"

"Yeah." He turned as he muttered the word, and reached for a thick glass that sat on the bar just to his right, its glistening amber contents smelling like Scotch. As he gripped the glass in his large, battle-scarred hand, Morgan had to admit that she liked the way his cuffs were casually rolled up a few inches, since it revealed the thick lines of sinew that roped his powerful forearms, his skin darkened to a warm gold from the countless hours he spent training beneath the sun.

"How...unfortunate," the other blonde said with an exaggerated pout, her free hand playing with the gilded tips of her high ponytail, while she inspected Morgan with a cold, calculating gaze.

"Funny," Kierland offered in a tight voice, staring into the contents of his glass. "I was thinking the same thing."

"Then let's just ignore her," suggested the one on his left again.

"If only it were that easy," he rasped, throwing back his head as he took a long swallow of the whiskey. His hair was damp at his temples, making the red seem almost black, his body throwing off a scorch-ing wave of heat that made Morgan feel burned. Her own body temperature was on the rise, but she honestly couldn't say if it was from the temperature in the club...or the searing intensity of Kierland's gaze as he stared at her. Eyes that were such a light shade of green should have looked washed out and cold, but they didn't—and within the dark fringe of his lashes, the outer rim of his irises were already beginning to glow with a bright, unearthly light, signaling the rise of his beast.

*Oh, he's pissed all right.*

"So what exactly are you doing here?" Clipped, hard-edged words, but she still enjoyed the way they rolled off his tongue, the barest trace of a British accent molding the individual syllables. There was something inherently male about the way his mouth shaped words when he spoke, the almost cruel curve of his lips adding a wicked, sinful element to his rugged masculinity. What made it even sexier was the fact that it wasn't an act or something he worked for. It was just Kierland.

"We need to talk," Morgan said, wishing her voice didn't sound quite so breathy.

The blonde with the ponytail slid her a haughty, condescending smile. "Actually, he's here with us tonight, so you'll have to run off and find your own. I should think something like a poodle might be more your style."

"Or maybe a guinea pig," the other one snickered. "She might have a chance of keeping it interested."

Ignoring the women, Morgan kept her gaze focused on Kierland. "We have a problem."

"Wrong," he bit out, the deep shades of his auburn hair gleaming beneath the club's pulsing lights as he tossed back the rest of his drink, his strong, corded throat working as he swallowed. For a split second, she had a fantasy flash, imagining how good it would feel to press her mouth against that hot, male skin and scrape him with her fangs, but then she quickly shook herself back to sanity as he said, "You and I have nothing, Morgan. Never have. Never will."

The caustic words would have stung, if she'd been stupid enough to let them. But she'd prepared herself to hear that and worse tonight, knowing he was going to get nasty. He always did…*with her*. It was just the rest of the world who thought he was one of the most righteous, charming badasses around.

Crossing her arms over her chest, she took a deep breath and tried talking some sense into the jerk. "Look, I get that I'm not your favorite person, Kier, but do you really think I would have come here if it wasn't important?"

"If there was a problem," he argued, setting his glass down, "the others would have contacted me."

"We decided this was something best explained in person." So that he couldn't go running off before she had a chance to find him. "And you're acting like a real bastard."

"What could possibly be so damn important that they would send *you*?" he suddenly growled, pushing away from the bar so quickly that his two companions toppled on their spiked heels, forcing them to clutch onto his powerful arms for support. Despite his attempt to appear casual, he was obviously seething with fury, all of it directed at Morgan. "What the hell do you want with me?"

"It's not what I want that brought me here." She craned her head back so that she could still see his face as he came closer, looming over her. "It's what you're going to need. *From me*." His expression darkened with rage, but she held up a hand, speaking rapidly, before he could cut her off. "It's about Kellan."

He made a thick sound in his throat, and scrubbed one hand over the bottom half of his face. "What? You finally break his heart? Did guilt send you scurrying after me so that I can put him back together again?"

Frustration drew her brows together. "No matter how many times we tell you, you refuse to listen. But I'll say it again anyway. Kellan and I are just friends." It was the truth, not that Morgan expected him to believe her. He accused her of sinking her claws into every man she came into contact with. His brother was no exception.

"It's time you ran along now," the blonde on Kierland's left snapped, pulling ineffectually on his arm.

Tired of their bitchy interference, Morgan slanted each woman a hard look of warning. "And why don't you try minding your own business?"

Arrogant blue eyes narrowed with outrage. "You'd better watch how you speak to me," one woman hissed. "My family owns this club. I'll have you tossed out on your ass before you know what hit you."

Morgan arched her brows and smiled, a warm jolt of satisfaction flaring through her system when she saw Kierland's eyes widen a little, as if he knew what was coming. "Is that meant to impress me?" she asked in a soft voice. "Because you should really let them know that the place could do with a bit of class. I could smell the sleaze the instant I stepped inside."

"You bitch," the woman sneered. She almost surprised Morgan with a swift, openhanded slap, but instinct kicked in and Morgan's hand whipped up, her fingers wrapping around the woman's wrist.

*Rule number one. Never underestimate your enemy.*

She smiled grimly as the words played through her mind in Kierland's deep baritone, a memory from the days when she'd been a young, idealistic Watchman trainee and he'd been her instructor. But she wasn't that awkward, gangly teenager anymore—and she sure as hell wasn't going to let Blondie here get the better of her.

"*What* are you?" the blonde snarled, yanking her hand from Morgan's grip and giving her wrist a shake.

She smiled wide enough to bare her fangs. "A little bit of everything."

Silicone-injected lips curled with disgust. "Mongrel."

Morgan lifted her brows. "Make that a mongrel who can kick your ass," she offered in a dry tone, almost hoping the blonde would try to hit her again.

"Enough!" Kierland growled, grabbing hold of Morgan's arm and yanking her back around. She crashed into his chest so hard that her breath rushed out, her senses suddenly overwhelmed with hard, hot, aggravated male. "What the hell are you doing?"

"Me?" she gasped, blinking up at him. "The swan started it!"

Though the music continued to blare through the room, the dancing had stopped, everyone moving closer as word of the "almost" catfight spread like a flame lapping at trails of spilled gasoline. From the corner of her eye, Morgan could see the blondes talking with their heads close together, and listened as one of them told the bartender to summon their bodyguards from downstairs. Judging from their prima donna attitudes, she thought it figured that the Barbie twins would have their own professional set of bullies. She also figured it was time they got out of there.

Locking her gaze with Kierland's, she stated the obvious. "We should go."

"You mean before you cause any more trouble?" he snapped, glaring down at her, six and a half feet of pure, enraged male.

"Don't sound so bent out of shape," she muttered. "You were just worried that I might break one of your new playthings."

"Save your ridiculous jeal—" Morgan heard him say, but she lost track of the words when a beefy hulk of a guy broke through the crowd and launched himself at her, slamming her to the ground. She could hear Kierland's indignant shout, followed by an eruption of sound as more guards showed up, attacking the Lycan, and chaos broke out all around them. The brute lying on top of her, who smelled like a sweaty cross between a grizzly and a badger, was obviously one of the blondes' bodyguards. The swan-shifters were goading him on, shouting things like "She's the one!" and "Show her a lesson, Frankie!"

"Oh, yeah. I'll show you a lesson," he sneered, his stale breath nearly making Morgan gag. His beady eyes focused on the shape of her breasts, a lascivious smile curling his damp mouth as he crouched over her, trapping her arms against the floor. Deciding to fight dirty, Morgan hiked her knee and watched his expression turn to one of comical horror as he clutched his abused testicles with both hands. She'd just started to shove him off, when Kierland was there, already having dispensed with the guards who'd jumped him. Growling a deep, guttural sound that was pure animal, he hauled the guy off her, his expression one of savage outrage as he tossed the heavy bastard behind the bar.

"Thanks," she rasped, moving back to her feet, but Kierland had already turned, exchanging blows with yet another thick-shouldered grizzly-shifter, and Morgan began to wonder just how many bodyguards the blondes carted around with them. Then again, considering their personalities, they probably pissed a lot of people off, so maybe she shouldn't have been so surprised.

"God, you still know how to cause a scene, don't you?" Kierland muttered, once he'd managed to knock out the guard.

She grimaced, knowing he was referring to the time when he'd taken her academy class out to celebrate after they'd completed their combat training. They'd been having a great time at a local pub, when a group of Regan—one of the ancient clans who were well-known for their troublemaking—had shown up and started hitting on Morgan and the other girls in her class. When one of them had groped her backside, she'd responded with a cracking punch to the guy's long nose that had resulted in a huge bar fight that Kierland had been forced to drag her out of.

"Wasn't my fault then, and neither is tonight," she argued, sounding suitably insulted. "All I asked for was a chance to talk to you!"

She doubted he even heard that last part, since

another guard came after them, though Kierland knocked the guy out with one powerful blow to his jaw. Unfortunately, she could see that five more behemoths were right behind their fallen comrade, pushing their way through the crowd. Calls of encouragement were coming from the drunken, drugged-out, bloodthirsty group of onlookers, and the blonde with the ponytail shouted, "What are you guys waiting for? Rip her guts out!"

"Wow, those are some classy chicks you've got there," Morgan drawled when Kierland moved closer to her side.

At the edge of her vision, she watched a flat smile twist the corner of the Lycan's mouth as he rolled his head over his shoulders, his narrow stare locked on the approaching guards. "What can I say? After spending the last few weeks around you, they fit my mood."

Before she had a chance to respond to his comment, she was busy defending herself again. Although Morgan didn't have a lot of meat on her bones, what she did have was pure, lean muscle that had been trained for combat. She was used to fighting opponents who were bigger than she was, as well as stronger—but it was the crush of people that was messing with her mind.

She pressed her lips together and tried to control her growing sense of panic as the crowd seemed to pull in closer around them. While Kierland took on the brunt of the guards, two of the massive shape-shifters separated them and drove her back, coming at her hard and fast, their claws and thick, deadly incisors fully extended as they forced her deeper into the crowd on the dance floor.

"We don't have to fight, little one," one of them called out over the music, leering at her with a slick, sharp-toothed grin.

"That's right," the other one snickered. "We can go somewhere and play instead."

As they began to circle around her, Morgan's sense of fury finally overrode her panic. She wasn't going to let these assholes bully her. Knowing she could take them off guard with some offensive moves, the female Watchman flew into motion, whipping her right leg around with a high, powerful roundhouse that cracked against the jaw of the stockier guard. She immediately pivoted, driving a swift side kick into the other one's groin. The first had already recovered from the jaw strike, and she swung her body in a graceful dip to miss the sharp slash of his claws, then struck him with a hard jab to his kidneys that brought him to his knees. Breathing hard, damp with exertion, she then parried a savage onslaught of blows from the one she'd just nailed in the groin, nearly losing her footing as he got in a cracking backhanded hit across her face. The metallic taste of blood filled her mouth, the inside of her lip broken open where it'd been smashed against the sharp point of her fang.

"You little bitch," he growled, grabbing her while she was still reeling from the blow to her face. Damn it, she was screwing up, the effort it took to hold back her panic making her slow, making it too easy for this jerk to overpower her. She could no longer hear the

music or the waspish shouts of the blondes, the
thundering of her heart and racing pulse the only
sounds that filled her head, as loud and thrashing as a
ground-quaking storm. The shifter pulled her too close
for her knee to be effective, and her lungs constricted
at the feel of his heavy body mashed against hers.

*Oh, hell. Here I go...*

Her vision darkened...going hazy, the panic growing, swelling, just seconds away from crashing over
her in a black, suffocating wave. Morgan opened her
mouth, ready to scream for Kierland, her pride willing
to take the blow if it meant getting free...getting out
of that closed-in hellhole and away from the jerk-off
who was about to do God-knew-what to her, when a
fist suddenly shot past her head, connecting with a
hammering blow against the bastard's thick nose. Her
assailant immediately let go, sprawling unconscious
on the floor, his partner crawling away with the rest of
the guards, and a new pair of hands grabbed onto her,
spinning her around. In her confusion, she continued
to struggle, but the muscular chest she was suddenly
pulled up against smelled warm and delicious, the gaze
that snared her wide eyes burning the brightest, most
breathtaking green she'd ever seen.

*Kierland.*

His big hands were like manacles around her biceps,
nearly lifting her off the ground, his body so close that
she could feel the violent pounding of his heart pressed
hard against her breasts. For a split second she was
trapped in the scalding, fiery violence of his focus,
thinking he would shake her or shove her away in

anger. But he did neither of those things. Instead, he made a rough, animal-like sound low in his throat, and then he was…kissing her.

*Kissing? Me? Oh my God…*

## CHAPTER TWO

MORGAN FOUGHT TO MAKE SENSE of her dazed, disorienting thoughts, but it was no use. Her abilities to reason or apply logic to the situation had been obliterated, first by the encroaching panic attack...and then by the shocking, searing touch of Kierland Scott's mouth against hers. She knew he could taste the blood from her smashed lip as he deepened the devastating invasion, and it was an explicit kind of intimacy that made the carnal kiss even more than a physical melding of mouths. A scintillating wash of anger and hard male aggression hovered at its edges, but its main force came from something even more potent...more savage than fury, though it eluded her. In that moment, trying to grasp any kind of thought was like trying to hold on to an ethereal wisp of smoke.

His breath came in sharp pants as his mouth worked over hers, slanting for a deeper penetration as he licked inside, past her lips, seeking and tasting with dark intensity, pulling up an unwanted, frightening wave of pleasure from the churning depths of her body.

In a way, his effect on her—that magical, purely masculine way that he'd always mesmerized her—was even worse now than it'd been when she was that shy, gangly girl of eighteen. It didn't matter that he was a jerk and a jackass, her traitorous body still wanted him. That part of her that had always hungered…always wondered what it would be like to kiss him, wanted so badly to get lost in the physical details of him. The heat of his skin. The rich, clean scent of his sweat. The hot, honeyed flavors of his mouth and the aggressively possessive way his fingers clenched around her arms, lifting her onto her toes. It was all beautiful to her, as painfully erotic as it was seductive.

Nearly out of her head with the accelerating burn of lust, Morgan was actually trying to crawl her way up his body, desperate to get as close to him as she could, when she caught a whiff of the blondes' perfume clinging to his clothes.

And just like that, the fire went out.

From one second to the next, anger rose up like a deep, boiling geyser, obliterating the pleasure haze in her brain. Wrenching her mouth away, Morgan jerked out of his hold, fully aware that she was only able to break free because he'd let her. Then her palm cracked against the side of his face before she'd even realized she was going to hit him, snapping his head to the side.

"Don't even think about kissing me when you smell like a couple of cheap hookers," she panted, working to get her breath back.

"Don't worry," he muttered, pulling the back of his hand over his wet mouth as he stared down at her through the thick veil of his lashes. "They weren't hookers. And they sure as hell weren't cheap."

Her lip actually curled. "And to think I honestly thought you had better taste than that."

"Don't sound so outraged." His drawl was smooth and lazy, but the color in his dark face was still fever high. "I wasn't looking to marry them."

She gave a soft snort and rolled her eyes, not wanting him to know just how deeply the kiss had affected her. "Yeah, I know exactly what you were looking for."

"Careful, Morgan," he murmured, clucking his tongue, his eyes suspiciously narrow. "You almost sound jealous."

"And you're obviously drunk," she shot back, looking away from that knowing gleam glittering in his eyes. With the fight over, the mass frenzy of writhing bodies picked up right where they'd left off, focused on sex again rather than fighting.

"Oh, come on. Is she actually calling the cops?" Morgan asked, noticing that the blonde with the ponytail was now holding a cell phone to her ear, the woman's scornful gaze locked onto Morgan with the ferocity of a rabid pit bull.

Kierland looked over his bloodstained shoulder, then cursed something crude under his breath. "Probably one of her brothers," he grunted with a thick dose of irritation. "We need to get out of here before her entire pack shows up."

Glancing at his hard expression, Morgan lifted her brows, the corner of her kiss-swollen mouth kicking up with a wry grin. "Wow. I never thought I'd see the day when the wolf was scared of a flock of birds."

"Stop trying to pick a fight with me," he muttered, grabbing her wrist and pulling her along behind him as he began elbowing dancers out of his way. "We don't have time for it." But as they broke through the last of the dancers and she got a clear shot of the wide double doors that led out to the street, Morgan could see that they were already too late.

THE ONLY THING STANDING between Kierland and Morgan and the freedom of the street were five massive jackal-shifters, unless more happened to be waiting outside the club's entrance. Another quick look over his shoulder showed Kierland that retreat wasn't an option, since the bodyguards he and Morgan had been fighting—at least the ones who'd managed to get up from the floor—had huddled together at the rear exit.

The tallest of the jackals, a barrel-chested brute with a shaggy head of black-and-brown hair, looked hungry for blood, his ham-size hands fisted aggressively at his sides as the others fanned out around him.

"Call me crazy," Morgan murmured out the side of her mouth, "but those guys don't look like swans."

He blew out a tense breath, keeping his attention focused on the one in the center as he said, "That's because the blondes are adopted."

"By a family of jackals?" she croaked.

He gave a tired sigh. "Yeah."

"Wow." Disgust laced her tone, but he couldn't blame her for it, considering the circumstances. "You really know how to pick them, don't you?"

"You have no idea," he muttered under his breath, while she moved to stand at his side.

Wearing expectant looks of aggression, the jackals came forward, spreading out in a wide arc. Like the one in the middle, they were all tall, with thick, stocky shoulders and square jaws, their eyes already glowing with preternatural fire. "Get behind me," Kierland said in a low voice, fully expecting the order to be followed.

Of course, he should have known better, considering who he was dealing with.

"Behind you?" she snorted. "Yeah, right."

"This is no time to argue, Morgan." He released his long, razor-sharp claws, allowing his hands to transform into that deadly phase that existed between man and wolf—the ones humans called "were"—then allowed his fangs to slide from his gums. Kierland was fully prepared to fight as dirty as he had to in order to get Morgan out of there alive, ripping out a few throats if that's what it took.

*Just like I do for any of my fellow Watchmen,* he silently growled, obscenely irritated by his beast's rumbling pleasure at the idea of protecting this particular woman.

"Looks to me like the *perfect* time to argue," she shot back. "I'm a soldier, Kier. Same as you. I don't need to hide behind your back."

Kierland knew it was true, especially after seeing how fiercely Morgan had fought during the battle in England the month before. But he was still…concerned. That grueling confrontation with the Casus had simply been too close. He and his friends had left the fight barely standing, and they'd been lucky they hadn't lost anyone. Another minute and someone from their group would have undoubtedly gone down with a serious injury, if not worse. But they'd fought with the sheer determination to do whatever it took to keep their friends and loved ones protected, and Kierland knew that the fortitude and strength that could be tapped into when fighting for the ones you cared about was something that the Casus would never understand.

The jackal in the center of the group had obviously been given their description over the phone, because he scanned the crowd with slitted black eyes before pin-pointing that feral gaze on Kierland. With a curl of his lip, the shifter said something to the man at his right, jerking his chin in their direction. Though the crowd had stopped dancing for the second time that night, the music continued to blare through the speakers. Just as a heavy, bone-jarring drumbeat began to blast through the club, the jackals rushed at them like a great battering wall of fury. Kierland took a deep breath, then gave himself over to his natural instincts as the bloodthirsty battle began.

From the corner of his eye, he could see Morgan fighting with the graceful poise and agility that he'd come to expect from her. He still didn't understand how the guards had been able to get the better of her just before he'd lost his mind and kissed her. He'd seen her fight enough times to know that it didn't matter if she was outnumbered and outsized. She was always fast and wily enough to avoid the brunt of blows directed at her, while delivering a maximum amount of damage. For whatever reason, she'd faltered earlier, but she was in prime form now, ripping through her targets with an efficiency that he couldn't help but admire.

And it was strange, how fluidly he and Morgan had always fought together, when they chose to stop bickering long enough to actually focus on the other's actions. Still, it was a bloody, messy brawl, and the bastards got in some good shots against them both, though Kierland tried hard to put himself in the way of any slashing claws that were aimed for the female Watchman.

He didn't know how long the fight might have gone on, if the sudden sound of distant police sirens hadn't filled the air. Though no one from the crowd had bothered to offer them any assistance, someone had apparently thought to call the police.

Obviously in no mood to tangle with the local human authorities, the jackals snarled their intent to "finish them off later" and disappeared through the front of the club. Kierland waited until the bastards were out of sight, then shifted his hands back into human form and wrapped his fingers back around Morgan's delicate wrist. "Let's go," he grunted, quickly moving with the exodus of patrons who were heading for the rear exit and choosing escape from the police over the chance for another dance.

Shuffling out with the others into the cobblestoned street, Kierland instantly looked to the skies to ensure that nothing was preparing to swoop down on them from above. There were too many damn dangers for Morgan to be out on her own, and the Death-Walkers were especially a problem, considering the ones they'd encountered so far were able to take a vaporous form that enabled them to fly.

"You got a flask on you?" he asked. They'd started carrying flasks of salted holy water after learning that the combination could be used to scare off the Death-Walkers. Unfortunately, they still didn't have a clue how to kill the creatures, but Kierland was hoping his sources would be able to come up with something soon.

"I've got my flask," she told him, sticking close to his side as he pulled her through the crowd.

"It was stupid for you to come here," he grumbled, keeping his hold on her wrist. "Too much of a risk."

"Yeah, well, a phone call wouldn't have done the trick. You'd have just run off before I could finish what I've come to say."

Kierland couldn't imagine what that could actually be, but forced himself to be patient until they were someplace quiet and out of danger. And in the meantime, he still had plenty to say about what she'd done. "The point is that you shouldn't have left Harrow House for any reason," he growled. "It's the only place that's safe right now. I can't believe Quinn—"

"Your best friend doesn't have any say in what I do. God, Kier. I'm not a child."

Ha. As if he thought of her as a child, even with that new haircut she was sporting. She'd had long bangs cut into all that straight, shoulder-length brown hair since he'd left England. It made her look younger, like the girl he'd known all those years ago, and his gut clenched at the memory. But he sure as hell didn't think of her as a kid.

Itchy. That was how Morgan Cantrell made him feel, as if he had a million freaking ants in his pants, all of them skittering over his skin. Tall and slender, with shadowy gray eyes and a heart-shaped face that looked as if it'd been carved from fine porcelain, she was undeniably beautiful. She had the firm, lean physique of a woman who was a trained fighter, and yet, she still carried a sensual, earthy aura of femininity that was hell on any man's libido. Not to mention how it affected the predatory side of a male's nature. Kierland's wolf had always been mesmerized by her, to the point that it all but howled every time she walked into a bloody room.

In fact, it was the wolf's fascination—its incessant craving for a taste of her—that had finally sent him slumming tonight in the first place.

Kierland didn't resort to the club scene often, but these were desperate times. He'd been forced to be close to Morgan for too damn long and had needed to get away. Though he'd barely said two words to her in the past month, he'd felt her presence at Harrow House as if she were a part of him, plastered against his skin. When he'd slept, she'd filled his dreams, and his waking hours had been spent constantly wondering where she was…what she was doing. It'd driven him crazy, the way she got on with the others, her acceptance a given, as if she was already a part of their growing unit, when all he wanted was to be rid of her.

The sharp squall of the approaching police sirens filled the air, and he moved his grip to her hand, pulling her along behind him as he started running down the street. "Come on. I have a car parked a few blocks away."

They cut around the next building, ducking into a dark alleyway. He concentrated on looking for any potential dangers as they sped down the narrow passage, and tried not to think about the woman running along behind him.

"You're going to have one heck of a hangover," she told him, making a soft sniffing sound.

"Doubtful."

"Haven't you ever heard that liquor can get a man into trouble? It's stupid to get drunk," she lectured him, "especially these days. You need to stay alert."

Kierland snorted. "I'd agree with you, if I was actually drunk."

"Come on," she drawled. "You smell like a distillery. I'm getting high just from the fumes."

In a dry tone, he said, "That's because I had a bottle of whiskey cracked over my head back at the club."

"No way. Who did it?"

His tone was even drier than before. "I think one of the blondes objected to the way I was fighting her brothers."

She snickered, snuffling something that sounded like "Classic" under her breath. Then she said, "Still, that doesn't mean you're sober. I saw you with a drink."

"A drink. As in one. I weigh a solid 230, Morgan. It takes a helluva lot more than one drink to knock me on my ass."

They turned out of the alley and onto a sidewalk that bordered a wide, busy street. As they slowed to a fast walk, cars sped by, throwing slashes of color across them with their headlights.

After a moment, she coughed, then said, "Are you, uh, telling me that you're not actually sauced?"

"'Fraid not."

"Then what was that kiss about?" she burst out.

*Ah, so that's what has her so uptight,* he thought, running his tongue over his teeth. Damn it, he should've just gone with the alcohol-induced-stupidity plea when he'd had the chance.

Without looking at her, Kierland rolled his shoulder and answered, "I was just trying to get your attention. At the time, it seemed like the only way to get you to stop terrorizing my date."

She pulled her hand from his grip and crossed her arms. "You mean *dates*."

"I'd planned to settle on one," he said reasonably. And it was the truth. He'd just needed a female for the night to help him burn off some steam. Ironically, the swans had appealed to him simply because they were so unlike the woman currently giving him hell.

The woman he'd been trying hard to forget.

"One of them, huh? How noble," she offered with a heavy dose of sarcasm. "And like I said before, they started it."

Kierland slid her a curious glance from the corner of his eye. "You usually aren't so easily riled."

"And you usually don't go for the drug scene," she shot back, her slight shrug pulling the fabric of her sweater tight across her breasts. They weren't heavy or overly large, but a man would have had to be blind not to notice that they were...well, perfect.

And Kierland, unfortunately, had excellent eyesight.

"I wasn't there for the drugs," he muttered, ripping his attention away from her. He stared straight ahead, determined not to look at either her or her perfect breasts, because once he started, he couldn't be entirely certain that he'd be able to stop. She might be one of the most irritating individuals he'd ever known on the inside, regardless of their species, but he couldn't deny that on the outside she was exactly what he liked in a woman.

It was just one of those maddening anomalies in the universe that made it clear someone up there either had a really sick sense of humor...or just got a kick outta screwing with some people's lives—because there was no doubt that the world would've been a hell of a lot simpler for Kierland if he'd gotten off on short blondes, instead of leanly muscled brunettes with prickly attitudes.

"And at any rate," she murmured, "I wasn't terrorizing your dates when you kissed me. I was getting mauled by one of their bastard bodyguards."

He grunted in response, and walked faster, figuring he had a better chance of getting her to shut up if he kept her busy trying to keep up with him. "Get in," he ordered a moment later, jerking his chin toward the sleek black Spider that sat parked on the curb.

A soft whistle fell from her lips as she ran her hand over the cold, shiny roof. "Nice. When'd you pick this up?"

"A few days ago." She climbed into the passenger seat, and Kierland slid behind the wheel. It was a testament to his mood that not even the low purr of the V6 could soothe his nerves when he started the engine.

"How'd you get the Consortium to approve the purchase?"

"Actually, I paid for this one myself," he explained, and she accepted the news with a quiet nod, since she knew he and Kell had inherited a near fortune from their grandfather.

"You always did like fast cars," was all she said in response, before fastening her seat belt.

He waited for her to make some scathing comment about how he liked fast women, as well, but she seemed too absorbed in checking out the Spider's sleek interior, a low, almost sexual kind of murmur falling from her lips as she ran her hands across the butter-soft leather of her seat.

Kierland ground his jaw, knowing he was in trouble when he got off watching a woman fondle his car. Pulling out into the traffic, he blurted out the first words that came into his mind. "You handled yourself well back there against the jackals."

MORGAN SEARCHED FOR ANY hidden sarcasm in the gruffly spoken words, but couldn't find any. It was a reflex reaction, since most people, aside from her family, treated her like she was something inferior. Kierland was one of the few exceptions. At least when she'd first met him. He'd pushed her harder than the others in her class, expecting her to be better than her peers, because in the field she would *have* to be if she wanted to survive. And then he'd demanded that she go above and beyond even the highest expectations of the academy. It'd made her feel foolishly special, until she'd discovered that he'd secretly harbored doubts about her abilities. The knowledge had been one more pain on top of many, and she had never forgotten.

Clearing her throat, she finally decided to be magnanimous and said, "You weren't too shabby yourself."

In fact, she'd been mesmerized by his viciousness. Though she'd seen Kierland fight on numerous occasions, it never failed to amaze her how dangerously beautiful he was during combat, his body moving with a powerful, animal-like grace that rendered him invincible. Tonight, he'd slashed through the group with a ferociousness that she'd never seen from him before, and it had been nothing short of breathtaking, her soldier senses still humming with pleasure.

He seamlessly slid the car up a gear, speeding down the street, and rumbled, "Maybe now would be a good time to tell me what you're doing here, before we get attacked again. Which, considering the way this night has gone so far, could be any second now."

"Like I said before, it's about Kellan."

"Did he send you here?" Everyone knew that Kellan had been furious when Kierland had left Harrow House alone, arguing that his brother was taking too great a risk by staying in Prague by himself.

Wetting her lips, Morgan wondered how best to ease into what she had to say. "Not in so many words."

He shot her a quick, hard glance. "Meaning?"

"Look." She took a deep breath, and wrapped her hands around the strap of her seat belt. "There's no easy way to say this, so I'm just going to spill. Kellan has gone missing."

Silence, and then his low, graveled rasp. "What do you mean 'gone missing'? He's in Norway, searching with Noah for the next Marker."

Noah Winston was a human who had the rotten luck of carrying Casus blood in his veins—and it was bloodlines like Noah's that were being used as "human hosts" for the Casus shades that escaped back to this world from Meridian, their name for the metaphysical holding ground where they had been imprisoned over a thousand years ago. Not wanting to end up being used as a "body suit" by the Casus, Noah had joined Kierland's unit a few months ago, determined to help the Watchmen and the Merrick find a way to stop the monsters before it was too late.

"This is kind of a long story," she began to explain, "so just bear with me for a minute. When Kellan and Noah came back from Finland a few weeks ago, Kellan took me into his confidence and told me that he had a lead he was going to follow, if things panned out for him. While he and Noah were in Norway, they panned out."

"A lead on what?"

"On where Chloe Harcourt is being kept."

"Olivia's stepsister?" he asked, shaking his head.

Once a small-town kindergarten teacher, Olivia Harcourt was now engaged to one of Kierland's colleagues and best friends, a tiger-shifter named Aiden Shrader. Although Olivia was human, her father had married into a family of half-Merrick, half-Mallory witches, giving Olivia two stepsisters. Her eldest step-sister, Monica Harcourt, had been murdered by the Casus several months ago, after her Merrick awakening, leaving Olivia to raise Monica's daughter, Jamie.

But that wasn't the entire story. For a time, Monica Harcourt's ghost had been able to communicate with a psychic in Kierland's unit named Molly Stratton, warning them that the monsters were coming after her daughter. She'd also been able to tell them that Chloe Harcourt, Olivia's youngest stepsister, who had been feared dead, was actually being held prisoner by the Casus at their secret compound. But Monica hadn't been able to give them a location, and now it was too late. Once they'd reached Harrow House and she'd known her daughter was safe, Monica's spirit had moved on from this world.

"That's right," Morgan said softly, in response to his question about Chloe. "Kellan has gone off on his own to follow the lead, determined to rescue her."

"That doesn't make any sense. Why would he take such a risk for someone who means nothing to him?" The raw, sharp-edged words were thick with frustration, as well as fear. "I mean, it's tragic that this girl's been taken, and I want her found as badly as everyone else, but that's no reason for Kellan to go on a damn suicide mission to get her back. She's a bloody stranger, for God's sake!"

"Kell feels differently. I'm not even sure how to describe it. But there's some kind of connection be-tween them."

He made a derisive sound, changing gears with a

violence that could've ripped the gearshift out.
"Bloody idiot. He's never even met her."

Morgan had known that trying to make him understand was going to be the hard part, or at least one of
them. "He carries her picture around in his wallet,
Kier. He's...I don't know, obsessed with—"

"You mean he wants to screw her," he growled,
scrubbing his hand down his face. "Christ. His
goddamn dick is going to be the death of him."

The youngest of his Watchmen unit at twenty-six,
Kellan had a questionable reputation when it came to
sex and duty and trouble. Morgan understood Kierland's anger, and yet, she also believed that something
was happening to Kellan. That some kind of...change
was taking place in his life, and even though she
couldn't explain it and didn't really understand, she
loved her friend enough to know that this was something he'd had to do.

"I understand how you feel, Kier, but I think there's
something more to it than just sex or physical attraction," she tried to explain.

"And does the idiot have a plan?" he asked, shaking
his head. "Or is he just going to waltz up to the Casus
and ask them all sweetly to hand her over?"

"Kellan told me that if the opportunity presented
itself, he was going to allow Westmore's men to
capture him. He thinks they'll take him to the secret
compound where they're keeping Chloe, and once
inside, he plans on rescuing her."

Ross Westmore was yet another name on the long
list of enemies they had going at the moment, and he

probably resided right at the top. He appeared to be the
mastermind behind the Casus's return, though they
still didn't understand his motivations. For a time they
hadn't even been sure of the guy's species, either, but
then they'd discovered that he was a Kraven, the offspring of a female Deschanel vampire who had been
raped by one of the Casus monsters before their imprisonment. Within the vampire hierarchy, the Kraven
were considered an embarrassing secret and treated
little better than slaves. It was hardly surprising, then,
that Westmore had turned against the Deschanel, con-
vincing the Collective Generals to partner with him in
exchange for the location of several Deschanel nesting
grounds. A militant organization comprised of fanati-
cal humans who were intent on ridding the world of
all preternatural life, the Collective Army should have
wanted the Casus dead, but their greed had gotten the
better of them, and the information they'd received
from Westmore had resulted in horrific massacres.

"And did you tell Kell that he was out of his
goddamn skull?" Kierland rasped, the warm, provocative scent of his body rising with his anger.

"No." She turned to look at him, staring at his
hard profile.

"Of course you didn't. Because you're such a great
friend, huh?"

Calmly, she said, "Sarcasm isn't going to help
the situation, Kierland. But you already know that,
don't you?"

He growled, scrubbing the palm of his hand over the
bristled surface of his jaw again, the faint shadow of

his ginger-colored beard coming through, adding to his rugged appeal. "How did he get away from Noah in Norway? Noah isn't an idiot. He wouldn't have let Kell just walk away."

They made a sharp turn, and Morgan had to brace herself. "There was a fight when Kell told him that he was leaving," she explained, while they crossed over the Vltava River. "It got pretty rough, and according to Noah, Kellan actually went wolf on him."

"Jesus," he responded. "I'm surprised they didn't kill each other."

"Noah came back this morning pretty banged up, but I'm sure he got in some good shots on Kell, as well." She coughed, then carefully said, "Actually, there's something else you should know. They didn't find the Marker in Norway."

He cursed a string of coarse, ugly words under his breath, his strong profile carved with grim lines of worry and frustration. "Was there a note?"

"Yeah. Same as before."

Another blast of stifled, graveled curses filled the interior of the sleek sports car, not that Morgan blamed him. The situation was dire, to say the least. In the past few weeks, members of Kierland's Watchmen unit had gone out to retrieve three Markers...and had only come back with one. After Noah and Kellan had found one of the ancient crosses in Finland, Saige Buchanan had quickly named Spain as the next location, and Noah had gone with Michael Quinn, another Watchman and Saige's fiancé, to retrieve it. But when they'd found the cross's hiding place, a note had been left waiting for them, claiming that the Casus had already discovered the Marker and taken it for themselves. Then they'd been attacked, and Quinn, a raptor-shifter, had suffered a serious injury to one of his wings.

"Why wasn't I called when Noah arrived solo at Harrow House?" Kierland demanded. "Quinn knows better than to keep this kind of crap from me."

"Because we knew exactly what you would do when you heard about Kellan, and he doesn't want you running off on your own. It's bad enough that you're staying here in Prague without anyone to back you up. The last thing he wants is you *and* Kellan running around unprotected."

More of that grim silence seethed around them, like a physical presence inside the car, until he said, "What is Kellan even thinking? If Westmore and the Casus can read the maps, which is looking damn likely at this point, considering they've taken two Markers right out from under us, then what will they need him for? It's not like they're going to exchange him for the code. They're more likely just to kill him on the spot than to take him into custody and back to their compound, wherever the hell it is."

"Kell believes they'll use him to demand the other Markers from us. The ones that your unit has already found."

"Shit," he muttered. From the way he thumped the steering wheel with the flat of his palm, Morgan figured he obviously agreed.

"I'm pretty much of the same opinion, but Kellan is set on doing this. As his friend—"

"As his friend," he snarled, cutting her off, "you should want what's best for him."

"And what if what's best for him turns out to be this woman?"

He made one of those thick, sarcastic sounds that only a guy could pull off. "Spare me the romantic drivel, Morgan. It's hardly your style."

"Don't go there, Kier," she warned in a low voice, narrowing her eyes. "Because you have no idea what my style is."

This time, the sound surging up from his throat was sharp and explosive, and as he shoved the dark, windswept fall of his hair back from his brow, she could see that a tic had started in his temple. "Chloe Harcourt is *not* going to be anything but another notch in my brother's belt." He ground out the words, forcing them through his clenched teeth. "And that's *if* he manages to get in the compound and back out again without getting his ass killed."

Another wave of silence settled between them, and Morgan almost wished for more of the arguing, since it was in those charged moments of waiting that his presence began to overwhelm her. It was painful, being trapped inside the confines of the Spider with him. One of those devastating little pains that you couldn't reach with a careful, soothing touch. A physical ache inside her blood and her bones that made her want to throw open the door and run out into the cold, chilling freedom of the night, just so she could escape it. He was too much—*everywhere*—the warm, mouthwatering scent of him covering her skin…filling her head…sinking into her pores. He smelled like something that Morgan wanted to take inside her mouth and sink her teeth into, the dizzying effect of his scent making it difficult for her to sit still, and she bit her lip, doing everything she could to hold in an embarrassing moan.

God, she'd rather die than let the Lycan know she was affected by his presence, the idea sending a cold, sickening shiver down her spine. It reminded her of how she felt when she was having an attack, and she frowned, unable to believe that she'd almost broken down while fighting the guards. The only godsend to her panic disorder was that she'd never actually freaked out during a battle. It was only afterward, if she'd been forced to fight in an enclosed space, that the thick, suffocating blanket of leaden anxiety would sometimes overcome her, squashing her down like a bug.

Strange, that she'd panicked tonight in the middle of the fight. And stranger still that she hadn't suffered any of that choking fear during the fight against the jackals. But then, she hadn't been in that second battle alone. She'd had an enraged wolf fighting to keep the jackals away from her, leaving her room to breathe… and work. It had been a truly impressive sight, watching Kierland slice his way through the jackal-shifters. He hadn't even fully shifted to "were" form, and yet, he'd still cut a path through their ranks like a tank plowing through a field of bodies.

Sliding a look toward him in the darkened interior of the car, she watched the pulse of another tic begin in his strong jaw, and knew she had to make him understand for Kellan's sake. "Your brother isn't a child,

Kierland. You may not like his decision, but he knows what he's doing."

"Like hell he does."

After the death of their parents, she knew they'd been sent to England to live at Harrow House with their grandfather. From what Kellan had told her, it was Kierland who had taken over the care of his younger brother, giving him the love and affection that he needed. "You've been taking care of him for a long time, but he's a man now, Kier."

"A man who acts like a damn child. There are a million things that could go wrong. Chloe could already be dead for all we know."

Morgan knew it was a testament to his fury that he could utter those words without wincing. "According to her sister's ghost, she's still alive."

"*Was* still alive. God only knows if she still is. You know damn well that Monica is no longer communicating with Molly. And what was the point of sending you here in person, anyway? It isn't going to stop me from going after him, and Quinn knows that."

Quietly, she said, "You're not thinking it through, Kierland."

"I'm thinking just fine," he argued in a raw voice. "Where did you leave your bags?"

"At your hotel."

"Call the front desk and tell them to have your things brought to the airport. Your ass is going back home to Nevada. I'm going after Kellan alone."

She started to respond, but he cut her off, saying, "It's for your own good, Morgan. This is only going to get uglier from here on out. I don't want someone who's not part of the group put in danger."

"No, you just like to call me in to act like the professional piece of meat."

He slid her a quick look before focusing that glowing green stare back on the road. "You still pissed about Ian's awakening?"

Ian Buchanan was not only a friend of theirs, but he'd also been the first to have his dormant Merrick blood awakened by the return of a Casus named Malcolm DeKreznick. Worried that he might accidentally take the life of the woman he loved, Ian refused to give his awakening Merrick a proper feeding, which could only be done by taking blood during sex. Kierland had asked Morgan to come to Colorado and offer the use of both her body and her blood to the stubborn Buchanan, so that he could finally face the Casus who had been preying on innocent human victims, and she'd agreed.

Morgan could only thank God that Ian had refused to touch another woman, knowing he would lose Molly forever if he did, since Morgan had had no desire to go through with it. Ian Buchanan was a gorgeous alpha male, but she wasn't the kind of woman who did one-night stands, much less the kind who jumped into bed with a man she didn't even know.

Though that was obviously what Kierland thought of her.

She knew that of all the female Watchmen in his acquaintance, he'd specifically asked her because he believed she was the type of female who could easily give herself to a stranger. And the soldier in her had seen the rightness of the plan. Had known that giving the Merrick what he needed to defeat the Casus was the "right" thing to do. But deep down, Morgan strongly suspected that the woman in her would never have been able to see it through.

Wrapping her arms around her middle, she turned her face to stare out the passenger-side window. "To be pissed about anything that you do, I would have to actually care, Kierland. And I know better."

"If you knew anything," he muttered, "you never would have come here."

"And you're wrong about my not being part of the group," she said, still not looking at him. "I might as well tell you now, I've transferred to your unit for the time being."

Stunned silence, and then a low, hoarse rasp. "You can't do that."

"It's already been done," she murmured, rubbing her arms. "Quinn put in the request for me, and the Consortium approved it yesterday."

"Quinn is going to get his ass kicked," he growled, dropping the Spider into a lower gear.

She snuffled a soft, bitter laugh under her breath. "Yeah, he said you would say that."

He didn't say anything for a heart-pounding span of seconds as they sped through the foggy streets of Prague, the old-world architecture of the city lending a ghostly edge to the night. And then the eruption came, blasting against her like a hot, dry wind. "Fine. Don't go back to Reno. I don't care one way or another.

But you're going back to England, Morgan. We are *not* going after Kellan together."

Blowing out a tense breath, she said, "Actually, you can't go without me, Kierland."

"Wanna bet?" he grunted, the low, guttural words sounding more animal than man.

Morgan turned to look at him. "Name the stakes. Because I'm not going to lose."

He turned his head toward her as he stopped at a red light, eyeing her with such a violent dose of rage, she almost flinched. Holding her ground, she said, "You might never find him without me."

"What are you saying?"

"Bread crumbs."

He glared, not comprehending. "Bread crumbs?"

"Before Kell left for Norway, he came to see me. Said to tell you that if things worked out the way he wanted, I was his trail of bread crumbs. Because he doesn't think you'll be able to find him otherwise."

Morgan knew the instant he realized what she was saying. The instant all the dots clicked together in his head to form a complete, coherent picture. A shudder moved through his long body, and she braced herself for the storm she had no doubt was about to hit. "He fucking didn't."

"Actually, he did."

The sudden blaring of the horn from the car behind them made her jump, and he hit the gas, accelerating through the intersection at a dangerous speed. "You linked with him?" he asked in a hard, gritty voice.

Thanks to her eclectic bloodline, Morgan had been gifted with the unusual, but not unheard of gift for some breeds of blood-tracking, which enabled her to "track" the location of a person once she'd taken their blood.

She nodded in response to Kierland's question, watching him warily from the corner of her eye as she said, "That's why you can't leave me behind."

# CHAPTER THREE

THE LOOK KIERLAND CUT IN Morgan's direction was one of pure, savage fury. "Are you telling me that you took his blood into your body?"

With a frown, she explained, "Stop making it sound dirty, because I didn't sleep with him. Not that it's any of your business, but I've *never* slept with him. I took his wrist, and Quinn was in the room with us the entire time."

His mouth twisted with an expression that was too mean to be a smile. "And I'll bet Kell just hated it, huh?"

True, blood-taking tended to arouse the one being bitten, but that hadn't been the case with Kell. The idea made Morgan cringe. God, she thought of the Lycan as a brother, for crying out loud. But she didn't waste her breath trying to explain it, when she knew Kierland wouldn't believe her anyway. Instead, she simply said, "He did it for you."

His laugh was low and ugly. "Like hell he did."

"Kellan said that if he found the lead to follow, he knew you'd want a way to find him, but that it would be nearly impossible. So I made the connection."

"Yeah," he rumbled, rubbing his hand over the grim shape of his mouth. "It was all just for my peace of mind."

"Well, for Chloe, as well," she reminded him. "From what Kell's learned about the compound, the only way to get her out alive is going to be from the inside. Security's said to be too tight to sneak in, which is why he's going to allow himself to get caught by Westmore's men. Once we're close enough, I'll be able to pinpoint where he's being kept, but we're not meant to take any action. At least not until he's expecting it. Kell figures it's going to take him nearly a week before he gets close enough to be captured, and we're meant to give him no more than a week on the inside, which would mean his time limit runs out two weeks from yesterday. If he hasn't gotten Chloe out by then, we're to call in the others and launch an attack."

"And save his ass."

"Actually, Kell was very clear about the objective. It's doubtful we could breach their defenses, but if we do, we're to get the witch out first, even if it means leaving him behind."

He didn't say anything more as they turned down Third Avenue, the luxury hotel where he was staying just a block down the road. Morgan had been there earlier that night, when she'd picked up Kierland's scent and followed it to the nightclub. Strange how the event seemed like ages ago, rather than a mere handful of hours.

Pulling the car into a parking space in the hotel's underground garage, Kierland cut the engine and shifted in his seat, facing her. "Tell me where he is, Morgan."

"I'm not trying to be a bitch or to manipulate you,

Kier. But I can't just tell you the location. It doesn't work like that, and you know it. My best guess is somewhere in Scandinavia, probably northern Norway, since that's where he was heading out from, but that's all I can give you until we get closer. So you *have* to take me with you. If you don't, you might never find him. It'll be all but impossible to track him by scent in that climate."

He climbed out of the car, pacing back and forth in the row of empty parking spaces, then turned and slammed his fist into the brick wall. The violent blow split his knuckles open, the warm scent of his blood filling her head as she got out of the car. Morgan wasn't afraid of him. For all his jealousy and his anger, she knew he would never harm her. Kierland would rather gnaw off his own arm before hurting a woman.

No, she wasn't afraid. But she knew better than to offer him comfort.

He braced his hands on his hips, his head hanging forward, and took slow, deep breaths. Then he tilted his face up and locked his glowing green eyes with hers. "I'm going to kill him for this," he rasped, his lips barely moving as he formed the quiet, guttural words.

"I knew you weren't going to like it, but you're—"

"I hate it," he snarled, cutting her off. "I bloody hate it, Morgan."

"Well, you can hate it all you want," she told him, straightening her spine, refusing to look away from his angry, hate-filled stare. "But until we find Kell, you're just going to have to live with it."

AN HOUR LATER, THOSE WORDS were still ringing through Kierland's skull as he sat on the edge of the bed in his hotel room. He leaned forward and braced his elbows on his parted knees, while his nerves itched for a cigarette so badly he could taste it. Locking his jaw, he listened to the roar of his pulse thrashing inside his head...and stared at the closed door.

Not just any door. No, this one led to the room where Morgan Cantrell would be sleeping that night.

"Christ," he groaned, as he fell back onto the bed. A sharp curse slipped from his lips when he wondered for the millionth time why he'd ever given up cigarettes to begin with. At the moment, he needed the burn of smoke in his lungs so badly it was a physical ache. Needed the acrid taste in his mouth to destroy the lingering remnants of that bloody kiss. Needed to get his hands on more of Morgan's soft, smooth skin....

*Shit*, he thought, snarling so loudly that the savage animal sound echoed through the spacious room.

He couldn't believe what he was going to do. That he was actually going to take her with him. Blood-tracking or not, he had to have lost his freaking mind. His heart hadn't stopped beating like a jackhammer since he'd set eyes on her in the club, and it was still taking all his willpower not to go hard with lust.

*No shock there. I'm always like that around Morgan.*

His lip curled at the thought, disgust flavoring each shuddering breath that he pulled into his tight lungs. Kierland despised his body's weakness, wondering how there could be such a disconnect between his brain and his cock. His damn body parts were all working on the same team, so why the hell couldn't they agree on this one simple thing?

Morgan Cantrell was bad news. Always had been, and she always would be.

They'd arrived back at the hotel an hour ago, picked up the luggage that Morgan had left at the front desk and gotten her a room of her own for the night. A room that was right next door to his. Then they'd parted ways to clean up, agreeing to meet again in his room within the hour—which meant that she would be walking through the doorway that connected their individual rooms any second now. And then the real battle would begin as they continued to bitch each other out, same as they always did, their wills clashing like two opposing forces of nature.

His relationship with Morgan had always been a nightmare in the making. The teacher falling for his pupil, though only a handful of years had separated their ages when she'd come to complete her final stage of training at the academy in England. But in terms of experience, they'd been light years apart. Kierland had seen her as the shy, innocent eighteen-year-old he'd had no business lusting after, and he'd been...well, a far cry from innocent.

He'd known he had no business getting involved with her. So he hadn't. And it'd still led to disaster.

But it wasn't the past that worried him now. No, what worried him was the future. All those new opportunities for disaster. The possibility that his brother could well be on the way to his death. Not to mention the news that another Dark Marker had fallen into the hands of Westmore and the Casus. And last of all... the chilling fact that spending any amount of time with Morgan Cantrell was dangerous, perhaps even deadly.

No matter what kind of spin you tried to put on it, Kierland knew the facts. He'd made mistakes because of this woman. Unforgivable mistakes that had resulted in tragedy, that had cost lives and he was still dealing with the consequences ten years later. If he wasn't careful, he could too easily see himself heading down that same path again, and he knew damn well where it would lead. Someplace he wasn't willing to go. *Not now...not ever.*

It should have helped that he now knew her for what she was. That the truth had finally shattered the illusions he'd built up around her into a million fractured pieces, but lust wasn't always a logical thing. It didn't reason or listen to advice. It just wanted, hungered...craved.

But that didn't mean that he had to give in to it.

*Rap...rap...rap.*

The soft knocking pulled him out of the dark, tangled web of his thoughts, and he rolled up into a sitting position. Clearing his throat, he called out, "It's unlocked."

The door opened, and then she was walking into the room, shutting the door behind her. She leaned against it with her hands behind her, freshly scrubbed and wearing a light gray T-shirt with a picture of some modern rock band on the front and loose black sweatpants. She'd showered, but not even the lingering perfume of her shampoo and soap could disguise the sensual scent of her body. It had always reminded Kierland of a rain-drenched jungle in the spring, deliciously warm and provocative.

Taking a deep breath, he finally said, "If you're right about Kellan being somewhere in northern Norway, we could have a problem."

Her soft gray gaze stopped its casual perusal of the luxurious room decorated in dark wood and pale creams, and settled on his face. "We *do* have a problem."

He flicked her a shuttered look from beneath his lashes. "So then you think he's in the Wasteland."

The graveled words were delivered as a statement, rather than a question, though Kierland wished to God that she was wrong. The Deschanel Wasteland was where exiled "nests" or family units of vampires were forced to live, once the Consortium passed judgment against them. Most vampires resided in "nesting grounds," which were located throughout Scandinavia and Eastern Europe. The grounds were ancient, sprawling castlelike communities where extended families lived for security, the lands protected by spells that kept them hidden from the outside world. But the exiled Deschanel families were forced into the Wasteland—a cold, desolate, dangerous region that had been created by powerful magic—where it was every man, or vampire, for himself.

"I can't be sure of the exact location until we're closer," Morgan told him. "But that was our best guess the last time we talked. It's also why Kell was so determined that I link with him, since tracking him by scent would be virtually impossible in that region."

She sent a look toward the cell phone lying on the bed beside him, and shook her head. "You tried to call him, didn't you?"

Kierland let out a short, explosive breath. "I'm his brother and he's in trouble. Of course I tried to call him."

Cocking her head a little to the side, she continued, "I doubt he would have taken your call, since he knows you would just try to talk him out of what he's doing. But if he's headed where we're assuming, then his phone is probably already dead. Technology doesn't work in the Wasteland. The spells used to keep the exiled nests inside its borders have a strange effect on most forms of modern technology, rendering them useless."

"I know that, damn it." He took another deep breath, which was stupid, since it just filled his head with more of her mouthwatering scent. "I also know that two shifters can't just go waltzing through the Deschanel Wasteland," he muttered. "If we wander outside of the neutral zones, which will be damn easy to do, we'll be ambushed within an hour."

"Actually, I've already put in a call to Ashe. As a Förmyndare, he's well acquainted with the region. He'd be the best guide we could find. I'm just waiting to hear back from him."

Kierland was so stunned that a gruff bark of laughter rumbled up from his chest. He stared at the delicate, fine-grained beauty of her face, into the almost silver depths of her eyes, and hoped like hell that she wasn't serious. "Is that some kind of joke?"

Quietly, she said, "I know it's not a solution you would have chosen, Kier, but Ashe is our best option."

From a purely unemotional standpoint, he could see the logic in what she was saying. Förmyndares were otherwise known as Deschanel Protectors, and it was often their duty to track down rogue vampires who tried to find refuge in the Wasteland. As such, Ashe would have firsthand knowledge of the dangerous no-man's-land they were going to cross, just as she'd said.

Unfortunately, emotion was very much a part of the situation.

"Like hell," he muttered, the raw force of his tone making her eyes go wide.

Ashe Granger was the reason so much animosity continued to brew between him and this woman. Kierland hated that she trusted the arrogant vampire who had worked with them from time to time during her training at the academy. Always had. Always would. It wasn't just that the girl Kierland had wanted had run off and fallen in love with the vamp, though he was honest enough with himself to admit that the sharp, explosive burn of jealousy had always been a key factor. But he and Ashe had never been on friendly terms even before Morgan had come between them, both of them too used to being in control and doing things their own way.

Granger had been living near the academy when Kierland had been an instructor there, and had reluctantly agreed to help train the students to best defend themselves against rogue Deschanel. Then Ashe's reluctance had fled when he'd met Morgan, and the true hatred between the two men had begun as the vampire made his interest in Morgan clear. Kierland could still remember how badly he'd wanted to dismember the vamp the first time he'd realized that Ashe was pursuing her. The destructive burn of jealousy had been so strong, it'd pushed him to make the first of what had proven to be an unforgivable series of mistakes that had simply fueled his hatred for Granger over the years, the passage of time doing nothing to lessen the way he felt.

And he'd have been lying if he said there wasn't a healthy dose of loathing directed at his own ass for the part he'd played, as well.

"What's wrong with Ashe?" she asked, the notch between her brows attesting to the fact that she truly understood nothing about men. "I mean, I know you two can't stand each other, but this isn't a social outing, Kierland. I would think you'd be willing to stomach having him along, if it means being able to give Kellan help if he needs it. And it's not like we're going to have a lot of other options here."

"You still sleeping with him?" he rasped, taken by surprise by his own question. He hadn't meant to ask her that, damn it, but it was too late now to take back the graveled words.

Morgan blinked at him, and he watched as surprise spread like a slow, thick syrup through her gaze. "Honestly, Kierland. I can't see how my current relationship with Ashe Granger would be any concern of yours."

He narrowed his eyes, moving to his feet as he

paced to the far side of the room, where a well-stocked bar had been situated against the wall. He was pissed at himself for asking the stupid question, and even more pissed at her for not answering it. Without looking at her, he reached for the bottle of single-malt Scotch and said, "For all I know, he'll be too busy screwing you to be any help. And I couldn't promise that I won't kill the son of a bitch if I see him."

Her breath made a short, irritated sound, and he could feel the force of her gaze burning curiously into his back, his neck prickling and hot as he twisted the cap from the bottle and poured. "If you're going to be childish and refuse to work with Ashe," she said after a moment, "then I'm assuming you have a better idea?"

He turned and rolled his shoulder, anticipating her reaction. "Gideon," he grunted in a low voice.

Her eyes went wide with comical surprise. "Gideon Granger? Ashe's *brother?*"

"Yeah," he muttered, tossing back a much-needed swallow of Scotch. "He has an apartment here in Prague, so we can pay him a visit in the morning."

With a thick note of incredulity in her voice, she stated, "I know you've made some kind of deal with Gideon, but I didn't realize you trusted him enough to ask him for help with something like this."

Kierland understood her reaction, considering how he'd felt about vampires since one of his girlfriends had been killed by a rogue nest of the bastards. Nicole was a human who'd lived near the academy when Morgan was a student there, and Kierland had started dating her in order to keep himself away from Morgan.

After Nicole was brutally attacked by the rogues, because of her association with Kierland, he'd been unable to stomach being near any of the Deschanel.

Knowing all this, Kierland's friends had been amazed that he'd made the deal with Gideon. But he hadn't been able to say no when the Deschanel had approached him the month before. Gideon and Ashe had lost family during the recent massacres carried out by the Collective. They knew that Westmore was the one who had given the nesting ground locations to the human soldiers, and they wanted revenge. In exchange for handing over Westmore, if Kierland's unit got their hands on him, Gideon had agreed to find out everything he could about the Death-Walkers—and he'd already delivered with the information about the salted holy water.

"I still find it hard to believe," she whispered. "I mean, that you actually made that deal with him. You're not one to trust easily, especially a stranger who happens to be a vamp."

"I didn't have much choice, did I? And Gideon has kept his word, providing us valuable information."

"But you really think Gideon will agree to help us navigate the Wasteland?" she asked, her tone doubtful. "I've never met him, but the impression I have from Ashe is that he's a man who enjoys his luxuries. I can't see him trudging through those cold, dark forests out of the kindness of his heart."

"He's helped before," Kierland said, taking another long swallow of his drink. "And the odds are high that Chloe is being kept at Westmore's compound. Considering how badly Gideon wants Westmore, I don't think it'll take much to convince him to help us out."

"If you're feeling so magnanimous, then I feel compelled to point out that Ashe has helped, as well. If it weren't for him, we might have never been able to destroy the vampires who killed Nicole. You know that as well as I do." Her fondness for the arrogant Deschanel was obvious, making Kierland's stomach turn. For years, he'd tried to understand what drew them together. Was it just sex? Or did Morgan honestly like the conceited son of a bitch? "He's not the villain you make him out to be," she added softly.

"I don't care if he's a goddamn saint, Morgan. If this is going to work," he ground out in a rough, hard-edged voice, his contempt twisting his expression, "then that bastard's name is not going to be brought up again. Is that clear?"

She arched one slender brow, the corner of her mouth twitching as she shook her head. "Are you truly operating under some kind of insane misconception that I actually take orders from you? Because I can assure you that I don't."

"You damn well will," he rasped, slamming his glass down on the bar.

Still leaning against the door, she crossed her arms over her chest. "I know Kellan and the others often choose to follow your lead, because you've proven to them that you're capable of making the hard decisions, as well as the right choices. I might respect that, Kierland, but until I see it for myself, I won't consider you any more capable of leading this project than I am."

By the time she was finished with her fiery little tirade, a reluctant grin had worked its way into the corners of his mouth, his irritation momentarily receding. "At times like these, it's hard to believe you were ever that shy, unsure little eighteen-year-old I used to know."

"I haven't been that girl for a long time." Her head tilted a little to the side as she said, "In fact, I'm surprised you even remember her."

"I remember lots of things," he murmured in a slow drawl, his grin melting into a lopsided smile as her cheeks turned a wild rose color. He knew she was thinking about the way she'd used to blush crimson every time he'd touch her during combat training, her hunger impossible for her to hide in her inexperience. "Such as the fact that you weren't nearly so good at controlling your shields back then as you are now. Your pheromones were especially easy to scent."

"Trust me when I say that you don't want to go there." The quiet words had an underlying thread of steel that he couldn't help but admire, even if their trembling edges touched a place inside him that he didn't want to think about. And just like that, the moment of easiness was gone, replaced by the familiar swell of discontent and aggression.

Holding that pure gray gaze, he started to walk across the room, closing the distance between them. "And what about us, Morgan? What about our little problem?"

Kierland knew he'd surprised her again by the tightening in her shoulders and arms. Her expression was a mixture of wariness and alert focus, as if she were trying to identify the danger in the situation. "Since we don't have a problem, I'm not exactly sure what you mean."

A rough, gritty bark of laughter rumbled in his chest as he crossed his arms and propped his shoulder against the front of a massive mahogany armoire, leaving no more than a handful of feet between them. "You honestly think we're going to be able to spend this much time together and not kill each other?" he asked, lifting his brows.

*Either that…or screw each other to death,* he thought. Both were a possibility. Though he was strongly leaning toward the second, given the fact that it was all he could think about. All he could *ever* think about when he was close to her. And God did that piss him off.

What made it even worse was that she usually did her best to ignore him, acting if she wasn't affected by his presence at all. He couldn't even use his heightened sense of smell to detect her arousal, like he'd used to, knowing she'd become a master of control over her body these days. She'd worked hard to perfect her masking skills, since she'd known she would need every advantage if she was going to survive as a Watchman.

And yet, there were times, every now and then, that Kierland could have sworn she wanted him as badly as he wanted her. At least for a good, hard, sweaty go between the sheets, though she buried it beneath the sparks and anger that always flew between them, their encounters forever laced with bitterness and frustration.

*But it hasn't always been like that.*

Popping his jaw, he hated that those silent words

were true. There'd been a time when he and Morgan had been…hell, he didn't know what to call it. Friends? In a way. For a while, he'd have even been willing to bet his soul that she might feel more for him than hunger and lust, but then she'd gone and hooked up with Granger, on orders from the Consortium, since they'd thought the headstrong vamp might be more willing to follow their orders when under the influence of Morgan's tender, sensual persuasion. The affair had started just days after Nicole had been murdered, and Kierland had been forced to struggle with his rage at the same time guilt was tearing him apart. To see the girl who'd fascinated him in ways that no other woman ever had—the girl he should have already claimed as his own, if he'd had that choice—all but whoring herself out with the arrogant vampire had been too much for him to handle.

The months that followed had only deepened his resentment, as he'd been forced to watch her fall in love with the bastard. It'd been like having a knife dug into his heart, over and over and over. As a result, his emotions where Morgan was concerned had become a crazy, chaotic blend of anger and guilt and loss that continued to rage within him to this day.

Of course, she'd never had any idea how he'd felt about her. He supposed he should have been thankful for that little triumph, but it left a bitter, sour taste in Kierland's mouth.

"Well?" he prompted, anticipating her response.

The uncomfortable rise of color along the delicate crest of her cheekbones would have been a satisfying sight, if he hadn't found it so damn alluring. "I've never really understood why you hate me so much, Kierland. But I'm willing to put our differences aside for Kellan's sake. Are you?"

"You're not leaving me much choice, are you?" he asked, sliding her a hard smile.

"I could have just taken someone else with me and left you out of the loop completely," she drawled, almost as if purposefully goading him. "So why don't you drop the jackass routine and be thankful that I'm letting you come along?"

"Thankful?" he choked out, amazed she had the audacity to stand up to him. Not that he could fault her for it, since he would have reacted the same way. He also couldn't deny that it was sexy as hell.

"Yeah, thankful. As in you should be appreciative of the fact that I'm willing to take your crap for Kellan's sake. You might try out the concept of gratitude sometime. And now, if you'll excuse me, I'm out of here."

She turned to leave, her hand already on the door handle, when he said, "Damn it, Morgan. Stop."

"Send me a text if you want to meet for breakfast," she threw over her shoulder.

"Christ, will you just stop? You're bleeding." Kierland chalked up the gruffness of his voice to anger, because it sure as hell wasn't concern.

*And just who am I trying to fool?*

Shaking his head, he watched as she stopped in the open doorway and looked over her shoulder. "Bleeding? Where?"

"Below your left shoulder blade. It's already soaked through your shirt."

"Crap." She frowned, her voice soft as she said, "I love this shirt."

He shook his head again, torn between exasperation and the fact that she was utterly adorable in that moment, though he'd have cut out his tongue before he admitted it. "You're bleeding like a stuck pig, and it's the shirt you're worried about?"

"I'm a woman," she grumbled. "I care about my clothes. So sue me."

"The jackals must have gotten you with one of their claws. You need to have it bandaged."

She turned her head to the side, but not before he caught the warm flush that crept up her face. "Don't worry about it," she said huskily. "I'll live."

"I've got my first aid kit," he told her, heading toward his bag. He'd left the leather bag sitting on the bench at the foot of the massive bed that was covered in acres of raw silk, and his kit was always stored in a side pocket whenever he traveled. "Take off your shirt and I'll put something on the cut."

She snorted, her voice choked as she responded, "I don't think so."

With his kit in the battered, but healing hand that he'd smashed against the brick wall of the garage, Kierland walked toward her. "Either you do it, or I'm doing it for you."

"Over my dead body," she drawled, lifting her brows.

"Damn it, I'm not coming on to you." Gruff, controlled words that made her eyes go wide again. "I just want to see your back," he added, motioning for her to turn around. "Go into the bathroom."

"I'm hardly going to be felled by a scratch." She didn't sound happy—sounded embarrassed, even— but she did as he said. He followed her to the opulent bathroom, the warm midnight blue tiles and marble counter and sinks seeming to fit her style a hell of a lot better than they fit his. Kierland didn't know why he chose to stay in this particular hotel, since he always felt out of place, afraid he was going to accidentally break something if he wasn't careful.

Pulling the heavy length of her hair over her opposite shoulder, she turned and gave him her back, then began to lift her shirt. Kierland knew he should offer to help her, since the action was no doubt pulling on the wound. But he was locked in place, held transfixed by the sight of her naked back as she lifted the shirt higher...higher. Smooth muscles flowed up the length of her spine, supple and lean, the delicate lace band of her bra almost the same color as her flesh. The slice from the jackal's claws was long and shallow, slashing across her left shoulder, the crimson line making him wish he could tear into the bastards all over again.

Finally shaking himself out of his daze, Kierland helped her pull the shirt over her head, then tossed it onto the counter. "That was the dirtiest I've ever seen you fight tonight," she murmured, a slight tremor moving through her body as she lowered her head, waiting for him to get on with it.

"I didn't have time to be chivalrous," he rasped, holding a thick washcloth beneath the hot-water faucet. "Those assholes would've liked nothing more than to get their claws into you."

She gave a soft, feminine snort. "One of them did, actually."

"You must be masking pretty strongly to have covered the scent of your blood from me." He wrung the washcloth out, laid one hand over her shoulder to hold her steady, then pressed the cloth against the bleeding wound as gently as he could. "If you weren't, I would have picked up on it the second you walked into the room. What're you trying to hide?"

"It's habit. That's all." She drew in a deep, shuddering breath, and surprised him by saying, "Do you realize this is the first time we've been alone together in...God, it's been years."

Kierland grunted in response, not trusting what might come out of his mouth at that particular moment. The skin beneath his hand was soft and silky, and as he carefully cleaned the edges of the cut, it occurred to him that this hadn't been his brightest idea. He wasn't some green-eared innocent, for God's sake, and had seen far more than his fair share of naked female bodies in his lifetime. But they hadn't been Morgan, damn it, and that seemed to make a hell of a difference.

Tossing the bloodstained washcloth into the sink, he reached for one of the plush hand towels to dry her back. Then he took some bandages from the first-aid kit and began applying them to the slice in cross sections so that it would stay closed. As he finished the last bandage, his gaze wandered over her smooth shoulder, up to the feminine curve of her throat and his mouth watered like a starving man standing before a banquet of succulent food. Though he didn't need blood for feeding, in the way that the Merrick and Deschanel did, he still wanted the taste of it. The feel and the warmth of it sitting in his mouth. Wanted to know what it would be like to sink his long fangs deep into that pale, petal-soft flesh and have the warm rush of her blood spilling over his tongue.

Kierland locked his jaw and tried everything he could think of to keep his gaze from shifting to that bathroom mirror, where her reflection was just waiting for him. Calling to him. He thought about her and Ashe together, his stomach knotting as he imagined them wrapped around each other, going at it hard and fast. Thought about the fact that she was no doubt still in love with the bastard. Thought about how she had thrown herself at the cocky vamp, when Kierland had needed her most.

But in the end, none of it was enough, and he lifted his gaze, staring with hot eyes over the top of her head, his gaze locking onto the mouthwatering sight of her breasts encased in that sheer, flesh-colored lace. If he'd ever seen anything more erotic, he couldn't remember it. He must have made some kind of hungry, guttural sound, because her gaze shot up. She caught him staring at her reflection in the wide mirror, the soft wash of golden light spilling from the overhead lights lending an amber glow to her skin. His jaw clenched as he waited for her to say something cutting or snide, but she appeared speechless, her breath coming in sharp, jerky bursts that made him think of how she would sound when he was covering her with his weight, pressing her down, driving his body into hers with a hard, relentless rhythm.

"You might be a kick-ass little soldier, Morgan. But the lace suits you," he managed to choke out, the husky words scraping his throat.

She opened her mouth, but still didn't say anything. Or maybe she couldn't. Her chest rose and fell with the rushed, hectic cadence of her breathing, her gray eyes swimming with confusion.

Kierland allowed his greedy gaze to drift lazily over her front, sliding it down the smooth plane of her stomach, the gentle flare of her hips, the feminine curve of her hip bones, and the hard-on that had started the instant she'd stepped into his room thickened, straining against the fly of his jeans. He flicked his gaze back up, snagging her drowsy, heavy-lidded stare, and the corner of his mouth pulled into a tight, wry smile. "Still gonna stand here and tell me we don't have a problem?"

"I…" She broke off, swallowing, her pupils so dilated they eclipsed the gray, leaving her eyes dark with a hot, feral look of hunger. She took a shivery breath and licked her lips. "I don't know wh—"

The sudden rapping of knuckles against his door cut off her words, and they both flinched, taking hasty steps apart from one another.

"That's gonna be room service," he said, sounding like he'd gargled with gravel. "I ordered us some dinner, thinking you might be hungry."

She grabbed her shirt and turned away, quickly pulling it back over her head. Kierland waited until she was dressed, made sure his shirttails were covering his fly, then went and opened the door. The waiter wheeled in the food cart, and Kierland handed him a tip before shutting the door behind him.

"What would you like to drink?" he asked, thinking that Morgan had followed him into the room, but when he turned around, there was no one there. He walked over to the bathroom, but it was empty, so he tried the door that separated their rooms…and found that the handle wouldn't budge.

The woman had gone back to her own room.

And she'd locked the bloody door behind her.

"Shit," he muttered, pushing his fingers through his hair while he tried to make sense of the strange, almost edgy feeling in his gut. His stomach growled, reminding him that he hadn't eaten since earlier that day, and he made his way over to the table, sitting down in one of the leather chairs. As Kierland began to eat, he didn't even taste the food, his gaze sliding to that locked door, again and again, while a single thought kept working its way through his mind.

She could run, but she couldn't hide.

# CHAPTER FOUR

*Prague, Czech Republic*
*Sunday morning*

NEARLY EVERY MAN IN THE ROOM turned his head and watched as Morgan entered the hotel's busy café. Kierland had sent her a text asking her to meet him for breakfast, but now he regretted the public setting. It made no sense, but his possessive instincts were kicking into overdrive. He wanted to grab a damn bag and throw it over her head, then wrap a heavy blanket around her sumptuous body, just to keep other men from noticing her.

There was no justification for the Neanderthal urges. They were stupid, ridiculous, destructive. But the jealousy seething inside him was impossible to ignore, flavoring the thoughts in his head, as inexorable as his need to breathe.

And yet, if he were forced to be honest, Kierland knew it wouldn't be this way if the past had played out differently and he'd followed his instincts, going after Morgan, instead of running to Nicole. The simple fact of the matter was that if Morgan was *his*—her beautiful body marked with his bite—he wouldn't want to hide her away. Instead, he would have been proud to show her off as his woman.

It was the "not having her" that made him want to shove his fist through a wall in a juvenile act of frustration. The fact that he had no claim on her. No right to object if another man caught her eye and approached her. Touched her. Seduced her into his bed.

Not that Kierland wanted that right, damn it. Even if he didn't have his father's blood flowing through his veins, he would never bind himself to a woman whose affections could be bought and sold by the Consortium. Or who could flirt with him so innocently one moment, then turn and slide into bed with an arrogant son of a bitch like Granger in the next.

Being his father's son simply closed the deal.

Which meant that nothing was going to happen between him and this woman.

*Not now. Not ever.*

His beast growled in reaction to the familiar phrase, the low, visceral sound rumbling through Kierland's body like a fault line breaking open in the ground.

The problem, he'd finally concluded at about 3:00 a.m. that morning, when he'd been tossing and turning in the hotel's bed, was that he'd never gotten Morgan Cantrell out of his system. He might hate the choices she'd made in her life, but the wolf still craved her, wanting a taste of what it'd never had. Like a festering wound, he still carried the hunger pangs of a gnawing, lingering need that had never been satisfied.

*Then maybe it's time to lance the wound, and bleed her out of our systems.*

He tensed in reaction to the wolf's treacherous words, because he knew damn well what his beast was suggesting. And he didn't trust it. The animal had always been too possessive of Morgan. It knew how he thought, how to manipulate him. It would fight dirty to get what it wanted. It had no morals, driven solely by its primal, animal instincts.

*Keep thinking we're different, but what I am, you are, as well. Same wants. Same hungers. Same needs.*

Kierland's hand curled into a fist on the tabletop until the veins beneath his skin stood out in stark relief, but he took a deep breath, forcing a look of bored indifference to his face as Morgan approached, unwilling to give anything away.

She wore another pair of hip-hugging jeans with her boots, but her sweater this time was a soft gray that nearly matched her eyes. The thick curtain of her dark hair was straight, falling like silk over the feminine curve of her shoulders, the bangs making her look too young...too innocent. She didn't wear any makeup except for a berry-colored gloss on her full mouth, but then she didn't need any.

The cake, as Kellan would have said, was already mouthwatering. It didn't need any icing.

Morgan murmured a quiet greeting and took the seat across from him. "Any news this morning?" she asked, reaching for her linen napkin. There was a nervous edge to her movements, though he could tell she was trying hard to hide it.

"I had a call from Seth. He's leaving England and heading back to the States."

Seth McConnell was a former Lieutenant Colonel in the Collective Army, and as such, he should have been their enemy. Fate, however, had other plans, and in an ironic twist, Seth was now fighting alongside the Watchmen and the Merrick in their war against the Casus. The disillusioned officer had broken ranks with the Collective when he had learned that his commanding officers had made a deal with the Casus and their allies, causing him to question the very beliefs that the Army had been founded on. Although the others in Kierland's unit had been fully prepared to despise the man who had once hunted those like them, Seth, who looked more like a California surfer than a soldier, had turned out to be a hard man to hate, his smile too easy and warm…and his regret for his past mistakes too genuine.

The last time Kierland had seen him, the shadows under Seth's dark green eyes had been proof that the guy was running as ragged as the rest of them. Before coming to Harrow House for a brief visit, the former Collective officer had been doing his best to find Westmore these past weeks, as well as to uncover whatever information he could about the whereabouts of Chloe Harcourt. But so far, Ross Westmore had done an excellent job of covering his tracks and Seth, along with the soldiers who'd remained loyal to him from his Collective unit, hadn't been able to get their hands on any useful information. Until now.

"Why is he going back?" she asked.

Kierland kept his voice low as he explained. "Seems his men have scored a bit of a coup. Finally got their hands on one of the high-ranking Collective officers who's been working with Westmore and the Casus."

She lifted her brows. "And the officer talked?"

Kierland nodded. "Seth's not sure how much this guy knows, but he thinks he might be able to get more out of him. From what the officer's said so far, it seems he was never all that keen on working with the monsters." He took a sip of his coffee, and tried like hell to ignore how good she smelled as he went on. "I guess the guy's already told them there's a rumor spreading that the Generals are having second thoughts about the deal they made with Westmore. Some of the soldiers are even threatening to revolt, since they don't like the way things are going down."

"Has he told Seth's men where Westmore's compound is?" she asked. "Or anything about Chloe?"

"If the guy knows, he hasn't shared anything." He leaned forward and braced his crossed arms on the table. "But like I said, Seth is hoping he can get some more out of him when he gets there."

After the waitress came and took their breakfast orders, Morgan turned her head, staring out the café's front window. "I can't believe we're actually sitting here, having breakfast together." Her voice was tight, strained. "It's so surreal."

"If you're ready to run, Morgan, then go ahead. It's probably the smartest thing you could do. Just try to give me the loc—"

"You're not going to talk me out of going," she

muttered, cutting him off. "So you might as well give up, Kierland."

They sat there in heavy silence for a few minutes—her staring out the window, Kierland staring at her—until the waitress came back with Morgan's coffee and then their food. As he ate his omelet, Kierland found himself torn between frustration over the fact that she either wouldn't, or couldn't, give him Kellan's location…and the unwanted reaction of his beast. The bastard was all but howling with satisfaction, eager for this chance to spend time with her, thinking that Kierland's willpower would eventually crumble and he'd finally give the animal what it wanted. Which was a taste of this one exasperating, complicated, thoroughly delectable woman.

"About last night," he murmured, just to see how she would react. And he wasn't disappointed.

Morgan's face turned bright red, her cheekbones darkening with color, and Kierland found himself wanting to drag his mouth along that warm, smooth skin, just so he could taste the heat of her blood blooming beneath its surface.

"Not. A. Word." Keeping her gaze locked on her plate, she forced out each word with slow, careful precision, as if she was afraid he wouldn't get the point.

Kierland pushed his empty plate aside and braced his arms on the table again. Quietly, he asked, "So we're just going to pretend that nothing happened in that bathroom?"

Her nostrils flared. "You bet your ass we are."

He didn't know why her refusal made him so angry, but it did. "Damn it, Morgan. That's not going to solve any—"

"I don't care if it solves anything or not," she snapped, gripping her fork so tightly he was surprised it didn't snap in two. "Please, just leave it."

The waitress returned at that moment to refill Kierland's coffee cup, and he was forced to sit there, seething with frustration, while Morgan chatted with the woman about the hotel and the city. Then, the instant the waitress had walked away again, she asked, "Are we still dropping by Gideon's apartment this morning?"

"Yeah," he replied, deciding to let her get away with the evasion. For the moment. "That's the plan."

She took her last bite of scrambled egg and picked up her coffee. "Have you tried calling him?"

He nodded as he leaned back in his chair. "His phone is switched off. Knowing the vamp, he's probably sprawled in bed somewhere with a horde of women. We might very well have to track him down, but his apartment will be the best place to start."

Her phone started to buzz, and she pulled it from her pocket, glancing at the screen. "Anything important?" he asked.

Without looking at him, she said, "It's a text from Olivia."

Kierland found himself sitting there with his gaze locked on her face as she read the message, thinking about how easily the group back in England had embraced her. She'd become good friends with all of the women, and the men loved her, as well. "Everything okay?" he pressed.

She glanced up at him with a lopsided smile. "That's exactly what Liv wants to know."

"Have you told them anything about where Kellan is?" he asked, as she started to type in a response on her keypad.

She shook her head, still typing. "All they know is that he's in Norway."

"Good. Don't tell them anything more."

Her fingers stilled, and surprise showed in her gray eyes as she lifted her gaze, locking it with his. "You're not going to tell them where we're going?"

"Not until I know what's going on. I'm not going to risk the whole unit following after us if they get worried because we haven't checked in with them." Before he'd finished the last word, his own phone began buzzing in his pocket.

"Is it Gideon?" she asked.

Kierland shook his head as he glanced at the screen. "It's Quinn," he told her, answering the call. Keeping his voice low, he said, "I can't believe you've got the nerve to call me, you son of a bitch."

Quinn's deep voice rumbled over the line. "Don't be that way, man. You know why I did it."

"I know I'm going to kick your ass the next time I see you."

"You can't kick your best friend's ass," Quinn offered in an easy drawl, and Kierland would have bet money that the shifter was smiling. "I'm sure there's some kind of law against that."

"Then trust me when I say it's a law that's gonna get broken," he shot back, while Morgan stared into the depths of her coffee cup with a slight grin tucked into the corner of her mouth, listening to every word. "Was there a reason you called? Or did you just want to bug me?"

Quinn sighed. "I just heard from Seth. He told me you said something about heading into the Wasteland."

Rubbing his hand over his eyes, Kierland choked back a graveled curse. "Nothing's positive at this point. What about it?"

He could feel Morgan watching him as he listened to Quinn say, "I don't think it's a good idea for the two of you to go alone."

"We won't be alone. We'll have a guide."

A surprised pause, and then Quinn asked, "What kind of guide?"

"Can't get into it now," he said in a hard voice. "I'll explain later."

"Well, I still think one of us should come over."

"And I think you should all damn well stay where it's safe," he snapped. "There's nothing out here that Morgan and I can't handle."

"Like hell there isn't," Quinn argued. "We still don't even know what those Death-Walkers are capable of."

Quinn was right, but it wasn't going to change his mind. If he was going to be stuck dealing with Morgan, Kierland didn't want one of the others there, watching them constantly. He'd had more than enough of that in the past month back at Harrow House. "We've gotta get going," he grunted, "but I'll be in touch."

"Damn it, Kierland. Don't hang—"

As KIERLAND DISCONNECTED THE call and slipped the phone back in his pocket, Morgan studied his expression, trying to gauge his mood. "Looks like our friends are worried about us," she murmured, taking a sip of her coffee.

He shot her a wry look, another one of those crooked grins kicking up the corner of his mouth. "Or worried we're gonna kill each other before we find my impulsive brother."

She gave a soft laugh. "Haven't killed each other yet."

"Don't be too hasty," he drawled. "The morning's still young."

"Hmm. I'm starting to feel like you're going to off me when I'm not looking," she drawled back, arching a brow. "Should I be worried?"

A slow, lean wolf's smile hovered at the edge of his mouth, his green eyes glittering with humor. But then the humor gradually faded, and she could see the tension as it crept back into him, hardening the sensual shape of his mouth. Beneath the soft black cashmere of his sweater, powerful lines of muscle coiled across his broad shoulders and in his ripped arms.

Morgan took another drink of the hot coffee, stared down into her cup for a moment, then forced her gaze up to his. She wanted to be staring him right in the eye when she asked her next question. "Exactly why do you hate me so much, Kier?"

His expression became guarded, and there was an underlying thread of caution in his deep voice as he said, "That's a hell of a thing to ask a man over breakfast, Morgan."

"I've been wanting to ask you for ten years," she told him, curling both hands around the warmth of her cup. "Might as well get it over with, seeing as how we're going to be spending so much time together."

He muttered something under his breath and looked away, staring out the café's front window, and pushed one long-fingered hand through his hair. The overhead lights caught the crimson tints threaded through the deeper, richer auburn strands as he raked the thick mass away from his face, the blend of colors as mesmerizing as the glittering depths of a jewel.

When he finally spoke, the words came in a gritty, halting rhythm. "I don't...hate you."

A husky burst of laughter fell quietly from her lips. "Tell me to go to hell, Kier, but please, don't lie to me. I can't stand a man who tells lies."

Casting her a sideways glance, he arched one of those dark, arrogant brows. "What about a woman who tells lies?"

Pushing her coffee away, she leaned back in her chair. "Depends on her reasons."

"Isn't that a bit of a double standard?" he asked dryly.

She rolled one shoulder, saying, "I'm just being honest. And you're avoiding the question."

He shook his head a little, the corner of his mouth twitching with something a bit too grim to be humor. "I'm not lying. You pissed me off, but I...I've never hated you, Morgan. I think..." He took a deep breath and paused, staring at her so intently that her pulse quickened, then slowly continued, "I've wanted to hate you for a long time now. But I can't seem to do it."

A frisson of something dangerous and warm skittered through her system, and she snuffled another soft laugh under her breath to cover her unease. "Well, if you don't hate me, you've spent a decade doing a damn good impression of it."

"It's difficult to explain," he said in a low voice, rubbing his hand against his hard jaw, his eyes burning a bright, turbulent green. "I was messed up after Nicole was killed. And then to see you with Ashe, who I couldn't stand... I couldn't believe that you'd done it. That you'd let the Consortium use you like a piece of meat just to get cooperation from a guy like him. You were worth so much more than that."

For a moment, all Morgan could do was stare back at him, unable to believe what he'd said. And then the familiar burn of frustration and bruised, wounded pride began to rise within her like a great, swelling wave. She didn't know what she'd expected to hear, but that wasn't it. She'd known he believed the worst about her relationship with Ashe, but she hadn't realized that it continued to form the basis for his contempt.

"So that's your answer? All this ugliness and rude insinuation because of what happened with Ashe?" She took a deep, shuddering breath, and then went on, the words ripping out of her with quiet, rushing force. "I don't know what I was thinking to actually hope that there might be some relevant accusations you could hurl at me. I mean, that's it? You've treated me like dirt because you're still pissed at me for something that had *nothing* to do with you? Because you believe I sold *myself* short? You were my instructor, Kierland. Not my goddamn father. Who I chose to go to bed with was never any of your bloody business!"

If she'd been hoping to get a reaction out of him, she shouldn't have bothered. By the time she'd finished with her quiet tirade, he was wearing his emotionless mask again. The one that made Morgan want to do something outrageous, like slap him again.

Sounding as if they were discussing nothing more interesting than the fashion trends in winter footwear, he explained, "You asked me a question, Morgan. And I gave you an answer. It's not my fault if you don't like it."

"Yeah, well, call me picky, but I was hoping for a better one."

Watching her closely, he asked, "What exactly were you hoping to hear?" and she shivered, hating how easily the deep, hypnotic timbre of his voice could cause chills to break out over her skin. "You want me to accuse you of following similar orders over the years? Don't think I haven't thought about it. But I've always hoped you were smart enough to have learned your lesson with the vamp."

"Just forget I ever brought it up," she muttered, thankful that their waitress arrived with the check. "It was a bad idea."

*There's an understatement.*

God, she didn't know what she'd been thinking, maneuvering him into a conversation that she really didn't want to have, its purpose to find answers that she really didn't want to hear. So the sexiest man on earth—the man she'd once thought was the most amazing person she'd ever known—still thought she was a whore. So what? It ticked her off, but it wouldn't kill her.

And Morgan knew it was her own fault for pressing the issue. It wasn't as if the stubborn Lycan was suddenly going to see the light and change his beliefs, no matter how wrong they were. He'd think what he wanted, same as he always had, and if she had half a brain, she wouldn't waste time worrying about it. She knew the truth—knew that she did the same damn job as a Watchman that he did, with just as much pride and integrity. She had nothing to be ashamed of. And she sure as hell didn't owe Kierland Scott an explanation.

She didn't owe him a damn thing.

He paid the bill, and she was still irritated enough to let him without putting up an argument. As they walked down to the underground garage, where the Spider was parked, he got a text message from Gideon saying that the vampire had something for them at his apartment that they needed to pick up. There was also a short apology for the "catastrophe" they were going to find. But that was it. Neither of them knew what to make of the strange message, but they figured they'd learn what was going on soon enough.

When she pulled her seat belt across her chest, Kierland asked her how the shoulder was doing, and Morgan told him that it was healed. But she didn't look at him as she spoke, keeping her head turned toward the window, and he didn't say anything more. They made the drive to Gideon Granger's apartment in silence, the purr of the Spider's engine the only sound other than the distant murmur of the city. Only a few beams of weak sunlight managed to battle their way through the dull, pewter-colored sky, a sense of heaviness in the air that made Morgan feel tired and cold and restless.

As she would have expected, Gideon's apartment spoke of wealth and prestige, located in a beautiful nineteenth-century town house that had been converted into spacious, high-priced flats. They took the elevator to the top floor and knocked on the wide set of dark wood doors, but there was no answer.

"I guess he isn't home," she murmured. "Maybe we should—" a quiet creak echoed through the sleek, wood paneled hallway, and she glanced down to see that Kierland had forced open the door "—just let ourselves in," she finished wryly.

The Lycan gave her a crooked smile. "Don't worry. The lock was already broken."

"What do you mean 'already broken'?"

He pointed his finger toward the handle. "The lock's been busted. Which means that somebody broke in before us."

"And how do we know they're not still here?" she whispered, while he pushed open the door and walked into the apartment.

"Intuition?" he offered over his shoulder.

"Intuition my ass," Morgan muttered, sniffing at the air. There was only a faint trace of a rich, tantalizing scent that reminded her of Ashe, so she figured it belonged to Gideon. Made sense, since it was his apartment. But that was all she could pick up.

"This must have been what he meant by that 'catastrophe' comment," she called out, stepping over a sofa cushion. Though the apartment had obviously been gorgeous at one point, it now reminded Morgan of something that'd been caught in the middle of a stampede. Furniture was overturned, covering the floor, along with upended drawers and shredded upholstery. "Since Gideon mentioned it in the message, he must know about it. Which means that he's come and gone since the place was wrecked. What do you think happened?"

"Either someone was looking for something," Kierland grunted, turning in a slow circle in the middle of the thrashed room, "or the vamp has really pissed someone off."

Morgan pushed her hands into her pockets and shrugged. "From what I've heard about Gideon, there's no telling. He's considered the 'wild one' in the Granger family, and knowing what I do about Ashe, that's some distinction."

Kierland raked his hair away from his forehead and said, "Just look around and see what you can find."

Walking into the kitchen, Morgan almost laughed when she spotted the envelope stuck to the stainless steel surface of the fridge. It was held in place by a magnet that read "Mind your fingers, I bite…."

"Hey, Kier. There's an envelope in here marked WOLFMAN. I'm thinking that means you."

He came into the kitchen, opened the envelope and gingerly pulled out a small glass vial. Inside was a shimmering, pearlescent liquid, but there were no identifying labels to say what it was. With a deep notch etched between his brows, he pulled out a piece of paper next and scanned the handwritten lines of script.

"What's it say?"

He muttered something under his breath that sounded like "Bloody idiot," then handed her the note so that she could read it for herself.

Kierland,

Got your message and sorry I can't be of assistance. My advice is to ask Ashe. I can imagine how you're reacting right about now, which is why I left you this note instead of calling. Plus, I wanted you to have the "sparkler." Thought it might come in handy where you're headed. If you don't know how to use it, Ashe can explain.

Don't know how long I'll be gone, but I'm following a lead on the Death-Walkers. Could be something big, but I hope to hell it's not true. If it is, we're going to have a problem. Like we need more of those, eh?

Haven't been able to get in touch with Ashe for you, but I'll keep trying. Not sure where he is at the moment…. I'll let you know when I find him.

And don't worry about locking up when you leave. Got someone coming to fix the door this afternoon. I'd have waited for you, but time is tight and I knew you were too much of a nosy bastard not to go ahead and let yourself in. Can you hear me laughing?

Gideon

Morgan slid a curious look toward the vial that Kierland still held in his hand. "Do you know what a 'sparkler' is?"

He closed his fingers around the object and shook his head. "You?"

"Not a clue." Propping her hip against the small island that stood in the center of the kitchen's granite floor, she braced herself for the inevitable argument that was sure to come with her next words. "So I guess this means we're going with plan B, then."

He snorted, crossed his arms over his wide chest, propped his shoulder against the fridge, then snorted again. "I thought I already told you that lame-ass joke isn't funny."

"You got any other bright ideas?" she asked, knowing damn well that he didn't. "Face it, Kier. Ashe is our best option."

He made a thick, guttural sound in the back of his throat, while a muscle began to tic below his left eye. "And how exactly are we meant to find him?" he muttered, the scent of his fury rising, making her feel as if his anger was a living thing there in the room with them. A deadly predator, dark and impossibly danger- ous. "Christ, Morgan. His own brother doesn't even know where he is, and he isn't returning your calls."

She took a deep breath, then quietly said, "Actually, that won't be a problem, because I can track Ashe, as well. Even more easily than I can track Kell."

FEELING AS IF HE WAS ABOUT TO burst the confines of his skin, Kierland walked out of the kitchen and headed for the full-length wall of windows that covered one entire side of the apartment, thankful that Morgan couldn't see his expression. He felt too raw, as if a layer of skin had been peeled away, leaving nothing but blood and bones and this visceral, destructive burn of fury clawing against his insides.

He could tell by her footsteps and her scent that she'd followed him into the room, though she was careful not to get too close.

"So you bit him, too?" He ground his jaw, unable to get the infuriating image of Morgan sinking her fangs into Ashe Granger out of his head. And she must have done it more than once, if she had a better "track" on the vamp than she did on Kellan. The thought of it made Kierland want to put his hands around something and squeeze. And by something, he meant Granger's throat.

Huskily, she said, "Don't you think that falls under the category of 'We really shouldn't go there'?"

"I'm starting to think that maybe we should." He shoved his hands into his pockets and turned to face her. "If we're going to be stuck using Ashe as a guide—" just saying the words made him feel like killing something "—then I need to know exactly where things stand between the two of you."

She gave him a hard, steely stare. "We're friends, and that's all you need to know."

Cocking his head a little to the side, Kierland studied her expression. "No lingering resentment after what he did?"

"You mean dumping me?" she guessed, surprising him with a soft laugh.

"Yeah."

"Nope."

She said it so easily—almost too easily—and his eyes narrowed with suspicion. "Unless that's not how it really happened."

With a quick, startled blink, she asked, "What are you talking about?"

Watching her closely, he said, "I've always assumed that he got wind of what you'd done, going after him on orders the way that you did, and his pride demanded he break it off with you. That even knowing you'd fallen in love with him, he couldn't get past what you'd done. But considering the way he would still watch you, unable to take his eyes off you…I don't know. There's always been something that didn't quite add up. So now I'm thinking that maybe that wasn't how it happened, after all."

With a soft, feminine snort, she shook her head and smiled. "Why would any woman in her right mind dump a guy like Ashe? And for that matter, why would you even care?"

"Like I said before, you were worth more than the Consortium realized. Hell, Morgan, you had more natural talent than any other student I'd ever had."

The roughly spoken words produced an immediate effect in her, the confident smile replaced by a look of almost vulnerable emotion that seemed completely unlike her. The slender column of her throat worked as she swallowed, and then she tore her gaze away from his, her hands pushed back into her pockets as she said, "If that's true, then you'll be happy to know that they've changed their minds about my worth. I've been offered a place on the Consortium's Private Guard."

Kierland stared, stunned by what she'd just said. Being offered a place on The Guard was one of the highest honors any clansman or -woman could receive, the position one of both wealth and prestige. Comprised of the most highly skilled warriors from all the clans, The Guard provided special security not only for the Consortium, but also to any persons of importance who were put under the Consortium's protection. If the circumstances were different and the Consortium leaders were supporting their fight against the Casus, Kierland had no doubt that Guards would already be stationed at Harrow House. But the Consortium had become too bogged down in bureaucracy, corruption and their own egos to take appropriate action, and were now doing their best to ignore the problem.

"So unless the Consortium's stance on your conflict with the Casus changes, this is the last time you'll be stuck working with me, Kier. In a few months, I'll no longer even be a Watchman." Her mouth twisted with a tight, bitter smile, and she suddenly looked back at him, locking her luminous gaze with his. "And after that, you and I won't ever have to see each other again."

# CHAPTER FIVE

*Kladno, Czech Republic*
*Sunday afternoon*

IT WAS HELL FOR KIERLAND, sitting there in the trendy coffeehouse, watching Morgan zone out as she stared at a snapshot of Ashe Granger that she'd tucked into the photo flap inside her wallet. To make it worse, it was a photograph of the two of them together. Morgan was sitting in the bastard's lap at what looked like some sort of Christmas party, a sexy red and black Santa hat on her head, her slim arms wrapped around the vamp's wide shoulders. They were both smiling, looking happy to be together, and Kierland wondered for the millionth time what the guy had been thinking to walk away from her.

Or maybe the vamp hadn't been thinking at all. Maybe he'd just been a dumb, arrogant jackass who hadn't realized what he'd had until he'd lost it.

Whatever the reason, Kierland couldn't help but wonder if Ashe wished for a different relationship with Morgan now. And if so, how the hell was he going to deal with that when the three of them were trudging across the effing Wasteland together?

Though he was a werewolf, Kierland had always considered himself a rational, civilized male. One who had remarkable control over his baser, predatory instincts. But he knew his limits. Knew exactly how much he was capable of handling...and what would push him over the edge. He was already worried sick about his brother. Not to mention the war. Throwing the Morgan problem on top of that worry was like letting an arsonist play with matches. Sooner or later, something bad was going to happen...and then the whole thing would end up in hot, fiery flames.

"How long is this going to take?" he muttered, sounding like a recalcitrant old grump. He wondered if that was how Morgan thought of him, and grimaced as he shifted in his chair, his long legs cramped from sitting at the table for so long. "We've been here almost two hours now. If I have any more coffee I'm gonna be bouncing off the friggin' walls."

"I'm almost done," she murmured, transferring her gaze from the photograph to the map of Europe that she'd laid out across the table when they'd first sat down. She ran her fingertip lightly over the surface, reminding Kierland of a scene from a movie he'd seen that had portrayed a group of teenage girls playing with a Ouija board. Except in Morgan's case, the magic really worked, her ability to blood-track an extraordinary gift that had been handed down from her ancestors. When they were closer, she didn't need a map to follow the signal, but when too much distance separated her from her target, she said that the maps helped her to "zone in" on a specific area.

"Okay," she finally whispered, slipping the photograph back into the small leather backpack that she carried like a purse. "I think I've got him, but he's not as near as I'd hoped."

When they'd driven out of Prague that morning, after leaving Gideon's apartment, she'd told Kierland to head west, since that's where she'd "felt" Ashe's pull coming from. As they'd traveled down the motorway, her directions had gradually become more specific, until they'd found themselves heading north, toward the German border.

"I'm thinking Hannover," she told him, slipping the backpack onto her shoulder. "But I won't know for sure until we get closer."

As they left the café, walking down the busy market street, Kierland found himself thinking back to the news she'd delivered that morning about the job with The Guard. It'd been impossible to hide his shock at the stunning announcement. He'd demanded to know the details, and she'd explained that the reassignment to his Watchmen unit was only temporary, until March, when she would be taking her first special protection assignment in southern Australia. It seemed that one of the Guards on the detail was retiring at the end of February, and Morgan would be taking his place.

When he'd laughed and told her that she'd be bored out of her mind within a week, she'd just shaken her head and smiled. Apparently, she was going to be assigned to an eccentric family of human scholars who were studying ancient scrolls from the lost civilization of Atlantis, which had always been a topic that fasci-

nated her. Then she'd gone on to say that it was the
perfect job for her, because of the freedom and space
it would afford her. *A sprawling ranch house in the
middle of nowhere, with nothing but wide open skies
and red sand that stretches as far as the eye can see,*
was how she'd described the family's home, and he
could tell that she was genuinely excited about the
relocation.

Kierland, on the other hand, was still trying to come
to terms with how he felt about it. Though he'd been
working the idea over in his mind throughout the long
hours of driving that they'd already done, he hadn't
come to any sort of conclusion. All he knew was that
the relief he would have expected still hadn't made an
appearance...and he was starting to wonder if it ever
would. A month ago, if you'd asked him how he'd felt
about the prospect of never seeing Morgan Cantrell
again, he'd have instantly responded with some smart-
ass comment about his prayers finally being answered.
And at the time, he would have meant it.

Only...now, he was beginning to realize just how
wrong he would have been. He still wasn't comfortable around her...and yet, he wasn't entirely comfortable with the idea of never seeing her again, either.

It took forever to make their way down the busy
market street, some kind of local bazaar drawing an
eclectic assortment of shoppers. Kierland stayed alert
to their surroundings, too seasoned a soldier to
overlook the possibility that their enemies could be
watching them, waiting to attack as soon as they got
the chance.

"Let's cut through here," he indicated, curling his fingers around Morgan's upper arm as he guided her through the crowd, heading for a covered shop arcade that led to the street where they'd parked. "It'll save us time."

She said something in response, but he lost the words beneath the hundreds of overlapping voices. As they headed farther into the arcade, the crowd became horrendous, bodies pressing in close until it was difficult to breathe. At first Kierland was just focused on keeping his hold on Morgan's arm, making sure they didn't get separated—but then he looked over his shoulder and caught sight of her panic-stricken expression.

Stopping in the middle of the crowd, he turned and took both her arms, pulling her close. "What is it? What's wrong?"

She was shivering, her eyes clouded with fear, but she only stammered, "N-nothing. It's…nothing."

"You're lying," he growled, hating that shattered look on her beautiful, sweat-misted face. "Damn it, Morgan. You're as white as a ghost. Did you see something?"

The crowd surged around them like a violent ocean current, pressing into her back, shoving her against him, and she gasped, her eyes going huge. "Can't… can't breathe," she choked out, and it scared the hell out of him.

Swinging her up into his arms, Kierland ignored the outraged shouts of those around them and started shoving his way through the mass of shoppers, snarling at anyone who didn't get out of his way fast enough.

When they were finally outside, he headed straight

for the nearest truck he could find parked on the curb of the road and carefully sat her on the hood. Standing between her long legs, he ran his hands over her upper arms in what he hoped was a soothing, calming touch. "Are you sick, honey? Come on. Talk to me."

"I'm fine," she mumbled, looking down, her hair shielding her face. Kierland reached up to push the heavy strands behind her ear, but she flinched. He stepped back a little, taking his other hand from her shoulder, sensing that she needed the space.

Rubbing his hand over his mouth, he wondered what the hell had caused her to panic like that, while a strange surge of protective instincts flooded his system, creating chaos in its wake. Suddenly everything seemed to be shifting on him, turning wrong side up, the perceptions he'd always held about this woman twisting and flipping. Despite the hard-ass persona she tried so hard to project to the outside world—tough, fearless, independent—he was starting to realize that there was a core of something tender and soft in her. And maybe something even a little bit broken. Something Morgan was trying hard to hide from him…that she didn't want him to know about.

"I'm better now," she whispered, still keeping her face averted. "Can we…can we just get to the car?"

Kierland wanted to demand an explanation then and there, but knew she wasn't going to give him one. "Are you sure you're ready to move?" With the edge of his fist, he lifted her chin and studied her pale, drawn features. "You still look a little green around the gills."

"Probably just too much caffeine, but I'm fine."

She wet her lips, and took a deep breath. "Really. Let's just go."

The Spider was parked about a block down the road, and after walking close by her side to make sure she didn't pass out on him, Kierland opened the passenger's door for her, waiting until she was settled with her seat belt on before shutting it. He drove through the town, vaguely familiar with its layout, since he'd done some work there for the Consortium several years ago. Wanting to avoid the traffic, he headed for a two-lane, less populated road that wove around the outskirts of the town, cutting through thick evergreen woodland, the ground still covered with the lingering remnants of the last snowfall.

As they left the town center behind them, Kierland couldn't stop thinking about the incident in the arcade, turning the event over in his mind like a puzzle that he needed to solve. He couldn't help wondering if the reason Morgan was looking forward to the "freedom and space" awaiting her in Australia was because she couldn't handle being surrounded by people. The bodyguards had almost managed to get the better of her in the packed club the night before, which should have never happened. And she'd recoiled from the people pressing against her in the arcade. He couldn't remember her ever suffering from claustrophobia during her time at the academy, but he supposed she might have just done a good job of covering it. Still, the back of his neck prickled with an uneasy sensation, and he knew that wasn't the answer. Neither was too much caffeine.

But if those weren't the answers, then what was?

Glancing up at the rearview mirror, a flicker in the distance caught his attention, and he tensed as he spied a sleek silver sedan behind them coming at a dangerous speed. "Shit."

Morgan had been sorting through some things in her backpack, but she looked up at the rough expletive. "What's wrong?"

Sliding the Spider into a higher gear, Kierland floored the gas pedal, but the burst of speed wasn't enough. "We're being chased," he forced out through his gritted teeth, knowing they weren't going to be able to outrun their pursuers.

"What? Are you serious?" she gasped, twisting around in her seat to look out the back window. The silver sedan was still gaining on them, which meant that it must have been equipped with a hell of an engine.

Damn it, he should have been prepared for this. If Kierland had noticed that they were being followed sooner, they might have had a chance to ditch whoever was in that bloody car. But he'd been so focused on Morgan, he'd stopped paying attention to what was happening around them—and now it was too late.

"Hold on," he growled, realizing the sedan was about to ram them. The jarring impact came just as they were taking a curve in the road, knocking them into a spin. Kierland fought for control of the car, and managed to turn the wheels so that the vehicle took the brunt of the next hit on the driver's side. Still spinning, the Spider slammed sideways into two massive pine trees, and both air bags deployed from the force of the

impact. Using one of the knives he carried to deflate
his air bag, Kierland turned and swiftly did the same
to Morgan's. Her face was turned to the side, away
from him, her body motionless in the seat, but he
couldn't see any blood or obvious injuries. Breathing
in hard, ragged gusts, he found her pulse at the side of
her throat, which was strong and steady, and prayed
that she'd only been knocked out. He wanted to take
her into his arms and check her from head to toe to
assure himself that she was okay, but they weren't out
of danger yet.

No, from the looks of things, as he glanced out the
passenger side window, they were still right in the
thick of it.

The silver sedan had stopped in the middle of the
road, its front bender crumpled from where it'd
rammed into the side of the Spider. Four men were
climbing out of the car, each of them tall and muscular,
with thick shoulders and dark sunglasses. Since a
tangle of broken branches and limbs blocked his side
of the car, Kierland opened Morgan's door and
climbed over her body as carefully as possible.

Positioning himself in front of Morgan, Kierland
had to fight his natural instinct to shift into "were" form
as the bastards approached. They were out in broad
daylight on a public road, which meant that turning
animal for the coming battle was out of the question.
Left with no other option, since he didn't have a gun
on him, he pulled out a second knife, glad he'd spent
the first part of the last month training with Noah.

Although Noah Winston had Casus blood running

through his veins, it was too diluted to have any impact on his physiology—other than his ice blue eyes—and as a result, the human didn't possess any supernatural fighting abilities. No claws or fangs or preternatural strength. To compensate, Noah had trained long and hard with his knives, and his skill was impressive. So impressive that Kierland had asked for some pointers while he'd been stuck at Harrow House during the past month.

Thanks to Noah, Kierland had been practicing with the blades until they felt like an extension of his hands, almost as natural as his claws, and as he palmed the hilts, he didn't care that he was outnumbered by the men coming toward him. He'd do whatever it took to take the bastards down and get Morgan out of there.

As the group drew closer, decked out in black T-shirts and jeans, he squinted against the bright glare of sunlight shining into his eyes, and tried to figure out what they were. They smelled human, but in human form, the Casus always did. The same could be said for the Kraven. And since they were wearing dark sunglasses, making it impossible to see the color of their eyes, they could have been Casus, Collective soldiers, or some of the Kraven who were working for Westmore. There wasn't going to be any way to tell until the fight started and he had a chance to determine their strength and skill.

"Lycan," the one nearest to him sneered, a long blade gripped in his meaty fist, and Kierland stepped forward, an instant away from slashing out, when the grinding screech of brakes filled the air. The next sixty seconds passed by in a blur as he watched a small commuter bus swerve to miss the sedan that'd been left in the middle of the road. The driver lost control, the bus tilting on two wheels as it sped straight toward them. His attackers scattered, but Kierland didn't pay attention to where they went, turning instead to reach into the car and rip at Morgan's seat belt.

He cursed, aware of the bus bearing down on the Spider, his heart pumping so loudly it sounded like thunder roaring in his ears. Continuing to snarl a guttural string of curses under his breath, he managed to get Morgan's limp body into his arms and jumped onto the car's hood, leaping into the trees just as the bus slammed into the passenger side of the Spider. The force of the impact hurled them into the woods, and Kierland twisted his body, sheltering Morgan from the branches and hard ground as they came to a bone-jarring stop against a tangle of roots and undergrowth. For several seconds afterward, the air continued to echo with the deafening sounds of metal crunching into metal, followed by frantic shouts from the passengers on the bus.

With a low groan, Kierland shook his head, thinking it all seemed so surreal, the strange sequence of events that had left him lying on a cold forest floor, surrounded by the smells of hot rubber and hydraulic fumes, cradling an unconscious Morgan against his chest. His heart didn't beat during the long seconds it took him to roll to his side and lay her down as gently as he could, fear having shocked his body into a hard, deathly stillness. Then her head turned toward him, one hand lifting to her temple as she gave a soft groan, and he took a deep, shuddering breath, the wave of relief so sharp it actually hurt.

Her eyelids fluttered, and she slowly opened her eyes, blinking up at him as Kierland knelt over her. "What happened?" she croaked.

"The car was hit." Taking care not to hurt her, he reached up and pushed back her hair, finding the swollen knot at her hairline. "You took quite a knock to the head. Probably hit it on the door frame."

Trying to sit up, she said, "My bag. Did you get my bag?"

"You don't need it," he told her, steadying her shoulders. "Damn it, stop trying to get up. Just lie still for a second."

She locked her gaze with his, a frown pulling at her soft mouth. "I want my stuff, Kier. And the 'sparkler' that Gideon gave us is in my backpack. You have to go back and get it."

Sensing that she wasn't going to give in, he muttered under his breath about stubborn, hardheaded women as he moved to his feet, then gave her a stern warning to stay where she was. Leaving her sitting on the ground, Kierland moved through the tangle of broken branches until he reached the pitiful remains of the Spider now wedged completely between the two massive pine trees.

The bus leaned against the trees at an odd angle, and Kierland could see the road through the long row of windows that ran along the side of the vehicle. The scene out in the street resembled nothing but sheer chaos. Passengers were still piling out of the bus, others wandering around the tarmac, their voices raised as they exchanged their versions of the event. And the silver sedan was already speeding away with its four occupants, the group clearly deciding to bug out in the presence of so many witnesses.

Although the Spider resembled a twisted piece of metal, Kierland was able to find Morgan's small leather backpack wedged under her crumpled seat. The passengers from the bus were too busy checking on each other—none of whom had serious injuries, just some cuts and bruises—to take notice of him digging inside what was left of the sports car. He grabbed their bags from the back, having to force the mangled trunk open, and slipped the shoulder straps over his head, then quickly made his way back to Morgan. He found her sitting with her head propped against a thick tree trunk, eyes closed, her complexion waxen, and without giving her a chance to protest, Kierland leaned down and scooped her up in his arms, cradling her against his chest.

"What are you doing?" she asked, resting her head on his shoulder.

"Carrying you. And before you waste your breath arguing about it, don't. It won't do any good."

"Okay," she agreed with a quiet sigh, and his jaw clenched at her easy acquiescence. Not that he'd wanted her to argue, damn it. But he knew the fact that she hadn't put up a fight was testament to how much pain she must be in.

As a pure-blooded Lycanthrope, Kierland wasn't easy to kill. The simplest, most foolproof way to end his life was to slash his stomach open, spilling his insides. His body could easily handle most other injuries, mending itself quickly, although gunshots and stab wounds could take him out of commission for a while if they were severe enough.

But Morgan was different. Her family's eclectic bloodline made it difficult to be sure exactly which traits had been passed on to her...and which hadn't. During her physical examinations at the academy, the medical officers had been able to ascertain that her healing powers were better than human, though nowhere near as effective as most shape-shifters. They were, however, completely clueless as to how she could be killed, which meant that she had to be a damn sight more careful than her colleagues.

Kierland had been walking for about fifteen minutes, heading deeper into the thick woods, before she stirred again. "Your car?" she asked, still resting her head against his shoulder, her body light and relaxed in his arms.

Ducking to avoid a branch, he said, "Totaled."

"Sorry," she whispered, breathing the soft word against the side of his throat as she wriggled to get more comfortable, and Kierland damn near stumbled over his own feet.

He coughed to clear his throat. "Don't apologize. It sure as hell wasn't your fault." He took a moment to tell her about the bus, assuring her that none of the passengers had been hurt.

With her right arm pressed against his body, she lifted her left hand and placed it on the center of his chest, as if she were pressing her palm to his heartbeat. "But it was a beautiful car," she murmured.

"Yeah, well, the car can be replaced." The thick, gruff words scraped against his throat as he forced them out, and it took all of the Lycan's concentration to keep his breathing even—to control his physical response to having this provocative woman in his arms, her mouthwatering scent filling his head. "I'm more worried about you."

She took a quick breath, as if he'd surprised her with the words, and then she asked, "Who were they? The men in the silver car? Or should I say *what* were they?"

"Hard to say," he muttered. "They were wearing dark glasses, so I couldn't see the color of their eyes. Could've been Collective, Casus or even Kraven. Bastards all smell the same in human form. Or hell, it could have been a mix of them all, since they're working together now."

Lifting her head a little, she glanced around at the snow-misted trees. "And where exactly are we headed?"

"The train station's about a half mile through these woods, on the north side of the town. I think there's a northwest line that'll take us to Hannover."

"Good plan," she murmured, resting her head on his shoulder again. "It'll save time and get us there faster than driving." For a few minutes there was nothing but the sounds of their breathing and the wintry breeze blowing through the branches, and then she sighed, saying, "Can you say something to take my mind off this headache?"

Looking down, Kierland found himself drowning in

soft, luminous gray. "Is it bad?" he asked, concern roughening his words.

She started to shake her head, then winced, the action obviously making her headache worse. "Getting better, but I could use a distraction to keep from thinking about it. Because the more I think about it, the more it seems to hurt."

His mouth curled with a slow smile as he thought of something guaranteed to take her mind off the pain. "Okay," he said easily, looking ahead again. "I've been thinking about something you said last night, when you told me not to think about kissing you when I smelled like a couple of cheap hookers."

She tensed in his arms. "Sound advice from any woman, I would think. Your point?"

"I've just been thinking about the fact that you didn't say *not* to think about kissing you again. Just not to do it when I've been close to another woman."

She drew an unsteady breath. "That's not what I meant, and you know it," she argued, the soft words quivering with emotion.

"You were mad," he pointed out, his tone light and conversational.

"And?"

He shrugged his shoulders. "It's just that people are less likely to lie when they're pissed about something. More often than not, they don't take the time to filter their words when they're angry."

"Kierland."

"Yeah?"

"Shut up."

A low laugh slid lazily from his lips. "Hey. You asked me to say something."

"Yeah, well, I'll know better next time," she muttered. "And you can put me down now."

Teasingly, he asked, "Is it that bad, being in my arms? Are you worried I'll drop you?"

"I know those Lycan muscles of yours can easily handle my weight and the luggage, but it's probably best not to carry me into the train station. We'll draw too much attention."

"I'll put you down when we reach the station. Until then, you're staying right where you are."

"Have it your way then. But be warned. Your chivalry could turn out to be a dangerous move. I mean, I might actually start to like being this close to you, and then we'd really have a problem." They were soft words, almost lost to the wintry breeze. But they brought a wave of heat to Kierland's body that he couldn't ignore.

"Fine," he grunted, giving in and lowering her legs until they touched the ground. "We're almost there, anyway."

They walked side by side the rest of the way, and Kierland made sure to keep his gaze focused straight ahead, not wanting her to see the heat still smoldering in his eyes…or the hunger he was sure he couldn't disguise.

# CHAPTER SIX

"THAT WAS REALLY TOO CLOSE for comfort this time," Morgan murmured, the second they slipped into their seats on the 3:05 train that would eventually make a stop in Hannover, before turning north for Hamburg. "If those guys in that sedan were Casus, just how many do you think have escaped?"

"Too many," Kierland rumbled, tipping his head back as he stretched out his long legs. He'd purchased first-class tickets, and so far they were the only passengers in the high-priced section, which meant they had the privacy to speak freely.

After checking to make sure that the small glass vial Gideon had given them hadn't been broken during the crash, Morgan set her leather backpack by her feet. As she settled into her seat, she bit back a low groan, not wanting Kierland to know how sore she was from the accident. Her headache was gradually getting better, but she still felt like she'd been trampled by a horse. "They took some risks, attacking us in broad daylight like that."

"Our unit's becoming a thorn in their side, especially now that we're loaning out the Markers, giving the

Merrick better access to them. They've probably decided that they have no choice but to try and take us out. Which means it's only going to get more dangerous for us from here on out." He slid her a shuttered look from the corner of his eye. "Or it could have just been you."

Morgan's own eyes went wide. "What about *me?*"

Rolling his shoulder in one of those utterly male gestures that looked great with all those mouthwatering muscles, he said, "After the fight we had against them back in England last month, they probably think we wouldn't send out one of the females without a Marker on her for protection."

"Well, I wasn't about to take Jamie's from her," she said, frowning at the mere thought of it. "And the others are all out on loan."

After the fierce campaign the Casus had mounted to get their hands on Jamie, it'd been decided that the little girl should keep a Marker on her at all times. And the loaning out of the other Markers that his unit had found so far had been Kierland's doing. He'd tried to convince the Consortium to enable the crosses to be used by any awakening Merrick who needed them. But the Consortium was still dragging their feet on the issue of the Casus, and Kierland had finally lost his patience, organizing a system on his own.

"Who are you calling?" she asked, watching as he pulled out his cell phone and began to punch in a number.

Holding the phone to his ear, he said, "The main line at Harrow House. I'm not sure what kind of telephone reception we'll have once we get going, and I need to warn everyone to be on guard."

With her exceptional hearing, and their close proximity, Morgan knew she would be able to hear every word of the conversation. She briefly considered getting out her iPod to give him some privacy, then decided against it. If he was going to argue with any of his friends because they hadn't warned him that she was coming to Prague, she wanted to hear it.

The line rang three times, and then a deep drawl said, "Shrader."

Leaning her head back and closing her eyes, Morgan listened as the hunk beside her said, "Aiden, it's Kierland. We've had some trouble." The rumble of his voice sent a shiver of awareness skittering through her system, and the corner of her mouth twitched with a wry grin. The bloody world could be falling apart around them, and her body would still react to the sexy timbre of his voice.

"I was just getting ready to call and tell you the same thing." The tiger-shifter's normally easygoing drawl was unmistakably strained, and she opened her eyes, her breath held as she waited, dreading what the Watchman would say.

Kierland sat forward in his seat, one elbow braced on his knee, his voice thick with worry as he asked what had happened.

"Noah got attacked down in the village," Aiden explained. "Quinn and Riley ran down with Saige to get him. They only just got back a few minutes ago."

A rough curse, and then Kierland asked how bad the human's injuries were.

"They're working on him now, but it looks like he's going to be okay," Aiden assured him. "They've had to stitch up a few cuts, but that's about it. Looks like he was one lucky son of a bitch, because one of the wounds barely missed an artery."

"Has he been able to give you any details?" Kierland asked, the muscles in his broad shoulders bulging with tension beneath the soft cashmere of his sweater. "Who was it that attacked him?"

"Two men. He thinks one was Casus, the other probably Kraven. They caught him coming out the side door of one of the pubs. Wanted to know how to get past our security here at the house. Sounds like they still want Jamie," the shifter muttered, his fury evident in the hard, harsh words.

After murdering Jamie's mother, the Casus had discovered that the curse that plagued the Mallory witches actually increased the sadistic pleasures of their killers. Westmore and the Casus had already managed to kidnap Chloe Harcourt, but that wasn't enough for the heinous monsters, and they'd launched a desperate hunt to get their hands on little Jamie, as well. Working together, Morgan and the others had thwarted their attempts, but that obviously hadn't dampened the monsters' determination to capture the child.

Kierland cursed again in response, and Aiden said, "My thoughts exactly. But I'm already running a diagnostic on all the security systems that Kell installed. Those bastards aren't coming anywhere close to her."

"What the hell was Noah doing alone in the village?"

Aiden snorted. "What do you think he was doing?"

"Christ," Kierland growled. "Next time he feels the

need to go out and get laid, tell him to take some damn backup."

"So what was your news?" Aiden asked, changing the subject. "How's Morgan? You two kill each other yet?"

A tired sigh, and then Kierland explained about the crash. "I want everyone there on high alert," he added, after assuring Aiden that they were both all right. "No one leaves the house."

"You know we can't do that," Aiden argued. "There are Markers to find and the race is on."

"And a lot of good it's going to do us if we're all dead," he ground out, and from her position beside him, Morgan watched the pulse of a muscle ticking in his hard jaw.

Husky laughter rumbled over the connection, and Aiden drawled, "You actually worried about me and Quinn?"

There was a pause while Kierland pinched the bridge of his nose, and then he lounged back in his seat again, before asking, "How's Olivia?"

You could hear the smile in the Watchman's voice as Aiden said, "Keeping me on my toes."

"She's good for you, Ade."

Another wry snort. "Too good for me, you mean."

"Nah. You deserve a woman like her."

"And what about you?"

Though Morgan had turned her head away a little, she could feel Kierland's gaze settling against the side of her face as he spoke in a rich, wry rumble. "I think I've got my hands full as it is."

"You still playing that same old game?"

"What game is that?" Kierland asked.

"The one where you refuse to practice what you preach," his friend shot back, making Morgan wonder just what the shifter was getting at.

"I'm hanging up now," Kierland said dryly. "But keep me updated on Noah. And get the word out to the other compounds. They need to know what's going on."

Aiden said that he would, then told the Lycan to watch his back before he ended the call. "Did you catch all that?" Kierland rasped, not looking at her as he hitched his hip up and slipped the phone back into his jeans pocket.

For a split second, Morgan thought of denying it, but then realized it was pointless. He knew how exceptional her hearing was—knew how easy it would have been for her to hear Aiden's voice. "I got most of it," she told him, crossing her legs. They talked for a minute about Noah as well as how aggravated Quinn and the others were that they had to keep postponing their weddings, and then she said, "You know, in all the commotion, I forgot to tell you about Ian's latest dream."

Like his brother and sister, the eldest Buchanan sibling possessed a unique gift that had proven useful during his Merrick awakening. While Saige could "hear" physical objects and Riley could control them with his mind, Ian had the ability to experience moments of precognition in his dreams.

"He had another one?" Kierland asked, his gaze focused on her face with a searing intensity that would have scrambled her wits if Morgan hadn't had the sense to look away.

She nodded in response, saying, "It happened the night before last, so I only just heard about it yesterday. Quinn asked me to tell you, but with all the madness, it slipped my mind."

From the corner of her eye, she could see him scrub his hands down his face, then scrape them both back through his hair. "What the hell did he see?"

"He saw us all standing together at a gate, trying to get through, but we didn't have the key."

"A gate?"

Morgan waited while news of the train's departure was announced over the speakers, then said, "We thought it might be the gate to Meridian."

"What did it look like in the dream?"

"Massive. Thick. Some kind of black, gleaming metal, with markings all over it that reminded him of the symbols etched into the Dark Markers. Which got me thinking during my flight to Prague. One of the things that Saige said, just before I left Harrow House yesterday, was that the crosses are the 'key to everything.' I could be way off base here," she said, pulling one leg beneath her as she turned in her seat to face him, "but the more I think about it, the more I think that Saige might be more right than she realizes. Ever since we learned that Westmore's desperate to get his hands on the Markers, we've been trying to come up with a reason why. One of our guesses is that he wants them to somehow bring about the flood, busting all of the Casus out at once, right? So what if they really *are* the key? Or keys? What if that's why he wants them?"

"You mean the keys that will unlock the gate?" His voice was rough with surprise.

Morgan nodded, and he asked, "Have you said anything to the others?"

"No." She gave a soft laugh and shook her head. "To be honest, I didn't want to sound like an idiot."

"No, it's good," he told her, sounding as if he actually meant it. "When we get back, we need to sit down with everyone and talk it out with them. I think you've got a hell of an idea, Morgan."

A slow smile curled her mouth, a strange flutter of warmth in her belly as their gazes held, and in the next instant, something changed. The air between their bodies became charged...heavy with expectation. Time became slow. Thick. They both shifted in their seats, their movements uneasy...restless, as if it'd suddenly occurred to them that they were sitting together, having a conversation...and actually getting along.

They had another fifteen minutes until the train was scheduled to pull out of the station, and when the refreshments cart went by, Kierland bought them both a soft drink and candy bar. But the caffeine from the sodas didn't keep them from crashing after the adrenaline high they'd been riding since the accident. By the time the train finally got on its way, Morgan was exhausted, but too nervous to sleep. Instead, she curled up in her seat, resting her face on her folded hands... and kept watch over the wolf.

Kierland's head had tilted toward her as he dozed, leaving her free to stare at his gorgeous face. She'd never realized how boyish he looked when tension wasn't hardening those tough, bold features. And yet, it was definitely a man's face. Strong jaw. Long nose that had seen its share of violence. But there was softness, as well. The full, sensual lips, slightly parted for his slow breaths. Long, burnished lashes that any woman would have loved to possess. For slowly passing minutes, Morgan studied the pattern of stubble darkening his jaw, the soft hair at his temples and the dark slash of his brows. She couldn't get enough of the details, soaking them in, dazzled by them in a way that she'd never thought was possible.

And he smelled so damn good. Logically, Morgan knew that scent didn't have a flavor; only...she would have been willing to bet her life that Kierland's did. She could taste his scent under her tongue, on her lips, filling her mouth, drugging and rich, reminding her of their kiss from the night before. In the interest of self-preservation, she'd been trying not to think about it— but it was like trying to convince her body that it didn't need air.

Then there was the way he'd carried her out of the crowded arcade. And the car crash. When she'd finally come to, his warm mouth had been pressed to her forehead, a low, husky whisper of words falling from his soft lips. Morgan had strained to hear them, but he'd gone silent the instant he'd realized she was awake. For just a fleeting moment, though, she'd felt herself transported back to that brief period of time when they'd been friends and he'd been the person in the world who'd made her feel the most safe. When she'd been so certain that he had cared for her and she'd believed the future would turn out so differently.

Of course, Morgan could just as easily remember the day all that had changed, when he'd introduced her to his girlfriend. God, she could still recall the moment she'd first met Nicole with such crystal clarity, it was as if she was watching it happen in real time. The human had been the complete opposite of her, with pale blond hair and a petite little body that was all softness and curves. She'd beamed at Morgan, glowing with bliss as she'd confessed that she'd been chasing after Kierland for years…and had finally caught him just weeks before. As the happily spoken words had filled Morgan's head, the pain in her chest had been so excruciating, she didn't know how she'd stood there and smiled and exchanged pleasantries. But she had.

And then she'd run. Straight into Ashe Granger's arms.

Though Morgan still didn't understand how it'd happened, she'd somehow managed to catch the gorgeous Deschanel's eye shortly after he'd agreed to help out at the academy. He'd been the devilish darkness to Kierland's golden light, making her impossibly nervous, and yet, she and the vamp had become friends during her training. Ashe had made it clear that he wanted to be more, but up until the day she'd met Nicole, Morgan's entire focus had been on the Lycan. And when she'd run to Ashe afterward, needing him to hold her and take away the wrenching pain, he hadn't laughed at her or treated her like a conquest. In truth, he'd been unbelievably tender with her, which had been surprising, considering his sordid reputation for one-night stands.

Morgan had never understood why Ashe had been so different with her, but he had. And she had no doubt that he'd been faithful to her during their brief affair. Despite his dark, devastating sexuality, it wasn't that Ashe *couldn't* commit to a woman—simply that he'd never wanted to.

In fact, Morgan still believed that she might have even had a chance with the beautiful, charismatic vampire, if her life at that point hadn't been filled with such turmoil. First there'd been her broken heart over Kierland, and then everything had slipped into madness when Nicole had been killed by the rogue nest of vampires Kierland and his trainees had been hunting. A few days after Nicole's death, Kierland had found out about her relationship with Ashe...and the Lycan had drawn his own sordid, hateful conclusions.

And after that, things had never been the same between them.

Morgan was still lost in the wrenching memories, her eyes heavy, drifting in that languid state of half sleep, when Kierland's low groan suddenly jerked her back to awareness.

"Kierland?" she whispered, reaching for his face. At the touch of her fingertips against his bristled jaw, he groaned again, the low sound pulling at her heart. It made her uncomfortable, this soft burst of worry taking shape inside her at that purely masculine sound of distress. Foolish, and yet, Morgan couldn't help but remember the unmistakable concern that had sharpened his rugged features as he'd carried her through the woods.

Leaning close, she brushed the dark, silky strands of auburn hair back from the damp heat of his brow, and said his name again. *"Kierland..."*

KIERLAND WAS DREAMING, trapped in cloying, oppressive layers of sleep that were impossible to break, like an insect trying to fight free of a spider's web. He knew it was a dream, and yet, he couldn't pull himself back to consciousness. The nightmare was sucking him under, despite how hard he was fighting against its inexorable pull. Despite how badly he didn't want to watch the scene playing out before him. It was too sharp, the setting as clear as it'd been all those years ago, when he'd been standing in his kitchen at home, witnessing the impossible happen.

"Don't leave me," he'd whispered in a small voice, watching his mother's life drain away.

As his father had stood over her bleeding body, he'd said, "Never love, Kierland. It'll rip even the toughest bastard to pieces." Then his father had torn his bloody claws across his own gut, spilling his insides out over the floor. Kierland had stood there, his small body frozen in horror, while the pool of crimson around their crumpled bodies had spread like a stain, coming nearer...and nearer, inching toward his toes.

"Kierland, damn it, wake up!" The harsh words were followed by a set of feminine hands gripping his shoulders and shaking him violently. His eyes snapped open, and instead of that blood-covered kitchen, he found Morgan leaning close, those soft gray eyes filled with stark concern.

She lifted her cool, slender hand to stroke his cheek, her voice so soft and soothing as she said, "You were having a nightmare. That's all. Just a bad dream."

His throat was tight, his breath jerking in panting gasps. He could still smell the coppery scent of the blood, but he ground his teeth, not wanting to think about the dream or his father or the past. He just wanted to keep staring at Morgan, breathing in lungfuls of her warm, mouthwatering scent. She made more of those soft little soothing sounds, like you would to a child, but instead of calming him, his heart thundered, pounding faster…harder, something primal and wild rising inside him, demanding release. Demanding the things it'd wanted for so long. It was like a tidal wave crashing through him. A violent force of nature that couldn't be constrained or controlled.

Kierland knew the instant she realized what was coming. She started to back away, but he reached up and curved his hands around her skull, pulling her mouth against his. His fingers were tangled in her silky hair, her lips tender and sweet as he licked his way inside with a rough, explicit kiss—and suddenly the most delicious scent he'd ever known was filling his head, churning a thick, guttural sound from his chest. In that moment, the Lycan knew that he'd caught her by surprise and she'd forgotten to put up her shields. He could scent her desire rising from her warm skin, mesmerizing and lush, telling him how much she wanted him, and it damn near blew the top of his head off. He wasn't thinking, was acting purely on instinct, and it felt good. Better than good.

Damn it, it felt incredible.

Keeping one hand on the back of her head, Kierland fed his ragged breaths into her mouth, while his other hand slid down the supple length of her spine, curving around her ass as he pulled her against him, her breasts crushed against the solid wall of his chest.

She gasped his name, and he kissed her harder, ravaging her mouth, terrified she was going to tell him to stop. The Watchman was grateful for every ounce of his strength as he suddenly flipped their positions, pushing her deep into the corner of her seat, his body angled over hers, his hips wedged hard between her thighs. With one hand still cradling her head, he used his other hand to grip her hip as he thrust against her, and he'd never been so thankful for privacy in his entire life as he was in that moment, the rest of the car still blessedly empty of passengers.

With a deep growl rumbling in his chest, he held her close as he ate at her mouth, feeding on the pleasure gasps that spilled from her lips, his cock so hard he could feel the imprint of his zipper biting into his rigid flesh.

"Come for me," he rasped, his voice ragged with lust and excitement as he pulled back enough to stare into her eyes. Rolling his hips, he ground the hard ridge of his cock against her clit, his chest heaving as he watched her face turn deliciously pink, becoming damp with heat. "I want to watch your eyes when you go over."

She sank her teeth into her bottom lip, shaking her head, fighting it. "I can't," she groaned, her eyes flashing like silver sparks of fire, wild with need.

"You *can*." His voice dropped, the guttural chords of the wolf bleeding through. "Damn it. I *need* this."

She shivered, staring up at him, and though he could sense her caution and confusion, the look in her eyes turned vulnerable...soft. "I need it, too," she whispered, shocking him, the quiet words wreaking havoc on Kierland's control. She lifted one slender hand, and cupped the side of his face, her other hand curling around the damp heat at the back of his neck. Pulling him down to her, she said, "Just don't leave me."

*Don't leave me....*

The whispered words, reminiscent of his dream, struck like a hammer, battering him back to his senses. "Shit," he cursed, suddenly pushing her away from him, his hands hard on her shoulders.

She blinked up at him, her expression a mixture of shock and hurt and disbelief. "What? What is it?"

Kierland shook his head, unable to explain, his breaths jerking so hard that it felt like his chest would crack open. Words bottled up in his throat, but he choked them back. He wasn't going to spill his veins, damn it, opening those old wounds—and even if he did, there would be no point to it, because the past could never be undone.

"Please. Talk to—"

"Don't." The rough blast of the word made her flinch, and she lowered her hands, the heat draining away from that burning silver in her eyes, leaving a chilled slate gray in its wake. He pushed himself out from between the seats, and stood in the aisle, staring down at her, while a thousand expressions worked their way across his face, reflected back at him in the endless depths of her eyes.

Curving his fingers into the tops of the aisle seats, Kierland opened his mouth, wanting to apologize. To tell her that he was sorry for acting like a bloody madman. But he couldn't get the words out. All he could do was shake his head again, mutter another sharp curse, and then turn…and walk away.

# CHAPTER SEVEN

*The Casus/Kraven Compound*
*Sunday night*

AS HE STOOD OUTSIDE THE SMALL cell located behind a set of ancient iron bars, Ross Westmore pushed one hand through his light brown hair and smiled at his good fortune. For a Kraven—a species that had been treated as little better than slaves for their entire existence—he was making quite a name for himself. A few cells down, the Mallory witch, Chloe Harcourt, was sleeping fitfully, and before him was his newest addition to his collection. She was slim and rather plain, but she was priceless.

They both were.

In fact, these two little females were his metaphorical "ace in the hole," and Westmore valued them as he valued his intellect, which had always served him as well as his ruthlessness. Thanks to the little gem before him, he'd been able to steal two of the coveted Dark Markers right out from under the Watchmen's noses. It was so sweet, he couldn't help but laugh every time he thought about it. In fact, he was enjoying himself so much that he'd been willing to hold off going after those Markers that the shape-shifters had already found, for no other reason than he enjoyed messing with their minds. Making them wonder and second-guess themselves.

But recent developments had caused Westmore to change his plans. Now that the shifters were sharing the dangerous weapons among their brethren, making them readily available for the awakened Merrick to use against the Casus, he'd decided to take action. They might have thwarted his attempts so far, but he'd given orders that the entire Colorado unit of Watchmen, along with their recent Buchanan additions, be killed. Although his enemies had had a string of good luck so far, sooner or later they were going to slip up, and when they did, the Kraven and the Casus were going to be there to seize the opportunity.

And as far as Westmore was concerned, he still had the upper hand. After all, the Watchmen and Merrick were clueless as to why he wanted the Markers, as well as to why he was so determined to facilitate the return of the Casus. And that was how he wanted it, for now. When the time was right, all would be revealed, and they'd be left broken and bleeding on the battlefield, while he and the Casus ushered in a new era of leadership over the clans…and eventually the world.

And all thanks to the precious little crossbreed in the cell before him.

She lay on her small cot, shivering beneath a pile of blankets. Clearly, she was cold, the hearth on the far side of the compound's underground level doing little to ease the snap of chill from the air. Half-psychic, half-Deschanel, she was also hungry, but Westmore knew better than to give her blood. He needed her weak enough to control, keeping her just on the edge of survival with the bits of food he allowed her to have.

Sensing his presence, she lifted her head from her pillow, staring at him through the most unusual color eyes he had ever seen. The pale pure gray of the Deschanel, but with threads of dark blue woven through, creating a mesmerizing effect, reminding him of lightning flashing through a warm summer sky.

"You know why I'm here," he murmured, stepping closer to the bars. It was time for his little psychic to use her powers and tell him where the Watchmen would be searching for the next Dark Marker.

Lowering her head again to the pillow, she rolled over, giving him her back. "And you know my answer," she responded, her English perfect, without any trace of an accent. "I have nothing to tell you, except that I wish you would die and go to hell, where you belong."

Keeping his voice gentle, he said, "Come now, Raine. Can we not be civilized in this exchange?"

"From what I've seen, there's nothing civilized about the Kraven. You're as monstrous as the Casus."

Yes, she knew what he was—but then she was part Deschanel, and it was the vamps who had kept the existence of Westmore's race a secret for so many years. A secret that had been so well preserved, not even the Consortium and their little Watchmen had learned about the Kraven until Westmore had launched his campaign to bring back the Casus.

Walking along the front of her cell, he ran his hand along the iron bars, his light tone completely at odds with the warning his words imparted. "If you force my hand, Raine, you know what will happen. Do you really want to be the Casus's plaything again? You barely survived your last punishment. If you're not careful, your impertinence is going to be the death of you."

He watched as her slender back stiffened and knew he'd hit home with his threat. He didn't dare allow those under his command to lay a hand on the Mallory witch imprisoned a few cells down, since she was being saved for Anthony Calder. A powerful Casus who was leading his brethren within Meridian, Calder was working with Westmore to coordinate their return.

But while Chloe Harcourt was to be protected, this little psychic vamp was free game, so long as they didn't kill her.

"Tell me where it is," he commanded in a soft, intimate rasp.

"Go to hell," she groaned, huddling beneath the covers. "I told you yesterday, the Merrick female hasn't finished deciphering the next map."

It'd taken Westmore months to find a psychic with Raine's unique gift of seeing into the past and the present—but as powerful as she was, there were still certain limitations to her abilities. For one, she could only "see" within a living subject's lifetime. So while she could mentally "watch" as Saige Buchanan deciphered the encrypted maps that led to the hidden locations of the Dark Markers, she couldn't simply "see" the Markers being buried, since the one who had buried

them was already deceased. As a result, she was forced
to wait until Saige had determined the location. Then,
once Raine passed that location on to Westmore, as
she'd done twice before now, it was a race to see who
could uncover the Marker first. The Kraven and the
Casus…or the Watchmen and the Merrick.

After a brutal session with four of his Casus
soldiers, Westmore was confident that Raine had
learned her lesson and now knew better than to feed
him false information—and yet, he didn't trust her not
to drag her feet when it came to imparting her mental
findings. Which was why he'd made sure to procure a
new incentive that would earn him her cooperation.

Pushing his hands into his pockets, he propped his
shoulder against the cold metal bars, proud of the
fact that he was the one standing there, delivering
threats, wielding all the power. He wasn't the best-
looking of men, or even the most physically impos-
ing, but then, when you were the one in control, those
things didn't matter.

And when it came to the insolent little twentysome-
thing in that cell, he was definitely the one in control.

Casually, as if he weren't about to break her heart,
he said, "By the way, have I mentioned that we found
your little brother?"

She sat up so fast that the cot nearly toppled, her expression stricken with fear as the blankets fell away
from her pale body, exposing small breasts that hadn't
quite healed from her punishment, the tender flesh still
bruised and marked with fading bite wounds. "You
didn't!" she cried. "That's not possible! He's in hiding!"

"Yes, well, you'd be amazed what information can be bought when you offer the right inducement. Luke wasn't so hard to find, once the right numbers were mentioned." Giving her a small smile, he relayed, "You should be proud of him, Raine. He's quite brave, for an eight-year-old. Threatens to kill me every time I see him, which is more than I can say for that sniveling sister of yours who would never stop whining."

"You bastard!" she shouted, trying to lurch to her feet. But her naked body was too weak, and she fell to the floor, smashing her bare knees against the cold gray stone. "He's just a child," she said in a broken voice, the soft words ravaged by despair as her shoulders hung forward, her small hands wound into tight fists.

Westmore made a crooning sound under his breath, then shook his head, his tone deceptively mild as he demanded, "Pay attention to the Merrick bitch and tell me when she has a reading on the map, Raine. If you don't and they find the next Marker before we do, I'll bring your baby brother to you in pieces, just like I did with your sister. Do you understand me?"

She nodded, her body trembling as she rocked back and forth, her long, honey-colored hair hanging in tangled, dirty waves over her shoulders, nearly reaching the floor.

"Good girl," he murmured, enjoying the sight of her on her knees, cowed by his ruthlessness. It was the kind of image that Westmore relished, and as he turned to walk away, his smile found its way back into the corners of his mouth. Whistling softly under his breath,

he made his way along the winding stone staircase
that led to the upper floors, the raw sounds of Raine's
grief keeping him company along the way.

# CHAPTER EIGHT

*Weesp, Netherlands*
*Monday afternoon*

"THERE'S SOMETHING WE NEED to talk about."

Despite his outward appearance of calm, Kierland had to push the low words past his lips, forcing them out, while his heart beat like a cornered animal trying to pound its way through his chest.

He was sitting with Morgan in a pub in the Dutch town of Weesp, a twenty-minute drive east of Amsterdam, their booth surrounded by a slew of chattering customers. By the time they'd arrived in Hannover the previous night, Morgan could sense that Ashe Granger had already moved on. They'd been tired—and Kierland had still been worried about the knock that Morgan had taken on the head—so they'd decided to get some rest and booked two rooms at a local hotel. He'd made some calls before heading to bed, checking in with Aiden again to see how Noah was doing, and had learned that three more Merrick deaths had been reported, as well as the deaths of two Watchmen who were believed to have been killed by Death-Walkers.

He'd also talked to Seth, who'd finally gotten back to the States and hooked up with his men, but there hadn't been any new information for the soldier to share.

After taking a long, scalding shower, Kierland had spent the night tossing and turning, twisted by worry and restless frustration, the memory of those scorching moments on the train with Morgan completely screwing with his mind.

For hours, he'd replayed that blistering kiss over and over, analyzing and observing, trying to figure out what had happened to make him go after her that way. Yeah, he'd been caught off guard by the dream, but the visceral surge of need he'd felt when he'd opened his eyes and found Morgan's face so close to his had been...uncontrollable. In that moment, he hadn't cared about the past or the future. He'd just wanted her, more than he'd ever wanted any other woman before.

And he still did.

When he'd finally returned to his seat and had tried to scrape out a lame-ass apology, she'd refused to talk about what had happened. Her tone had been distant as she'd blown him off, murmuring something about how it'd been nothing more than a "stress reaction" to what they'd been through. Then she'd completely ignored him and buried herself in a paperback she dug out of her bag, barely saying two words to him as they'd made their way to the hotel.

They'd met for an early breakfast that morning, and after poring over her maps, Morgan had determined that Granger was now in Amsterdam. So they'd altered their course again, heading west from Hannover. It'd been a stressful day of travel on the crowded trains, and they'd finally decided to get off at Weesp so they could grab a hot meal.

The waitress had already cleared their lunch plates and the bill had just been paid, which meant it was time for Kierland to say what needed to be said.

A part of him sat aside, slack-jawed at what he was about to do, but he didn't see any other way. As he'd lain in bed during the long, sleepless night, he'd finally come to a conclusion.

He *had* to have her. It was as simple as that.

And yet…there was nothing simple about it.

The remnants of his nightmare still lingered in his mind, causing twinges of horror and grief, but he had to face the facts. Sooner or later, the lust that constantly fought to pull him and this woman together would have to be dealt with. And he'd rather deal with it on his own terms.

Warnings from the grave or not, this was his only choice. Kierland couldn't be near her and *not* touch her, as last night had proven. If he was going to survive the coming days as they continued the search for his brother, then he needed some kind of temporary claim on this woman. It was the only way he could keep himself from losing his freaking mind. But he would have to be smart. Would have to approach it in an objective, rational way, making it about nothing but the physical release, since to get involved with a woman like Morgan Cantrell on any emotional level would be the greatest act of idiocy he could ever commit.

Leaning back against the padded booth, Kierland

watched as Morgan applied a quick sheen of that berry-
colored gloss she always wore over her lips, then
pushed up the sleeves of her violet sweater to her
elbows. As she took a quick look at her cell phone,
scrolling through her text messages, he thought about
the proposition he was about to suggest...and knew
that he wouldn't have been able to make it before,
when she'd been a trainee at the academy. The "quick
sex" option simply wouldn't have been possible then,
because he never would have been able to touch her
without losing control and claiming her with his bite,
marking her as his mate. Her effect on him had simply
been too strong.

When he'd first met her, the physical attraction had
been immediate, but it'd been more than that. Once
he'd gotten to know her, Kierland had found that he
liked everything about her. Her strength. Her smiles.
Her laughter. He had no doubt that to touch her would
have been to put a permanent claim on her.

But now they had the past between them. His
mistakes. Nicole's death. Her relationship with Ashe.
All the bitter, nasty years of anger and cutting remarks
that had been designed to push her away and make
her hate him.

*But she still wants you,* the wolf whispered through
his mind. *If nothing else, her reaction to that kiss last
night is proof that she still lusts for you.*

It wasn't much, but Kierland would take it. Hold on
to it with everything that he had, until it was time to
let her move on and they went their separate ways.

Closing her backpack, she looked over at him, a

quizzical expression pulling her brows together. "Didn't you just say that you had something you wanted to talk about?"

Kierland nodded, and she lifted her brows, waiting for him to get on with it.

"I need a woman," he growled, and would have laughed at the bluntness of that statement if he weren't drawn so damn tight, his body knotted with tension and hunger and barely restrained lust. There wasn't any space for humor in the primal, volatile mix. Hell, there was barely even room enough for him to remember what it was he needed to say.

Her eyes went wide, and she leaned back, her dark hair sliding across her cheek as she slanted him a sideways look. "You had two women on Saturday night. I would've thought that was enough to keep any man going for a few days. Even a Lycan."

"You know damn well I didn't sleep with them. It was—"

"Not my business," she said quickly, holding up one slender, delicate hand. "So stop right there and spare me the details."

"Damn it, Morgan. I didn't touch eith—"

"If that's true, then it's only because you didn't have the chance," she stated, cutting him off. She looked around the inside of the pub, as if trying to find something to focus on that wasn't him. "So is this your way of telling me that you need to go off on your own tonight to pick up a woman?" she eventually asked, rolling her lips together. "Because if so, you certainly don't owe me any explanation, Kier. I'll be fine on my own."

"Christ, I'm not looking to leave you alone," he muttered.

She sent him a look of comical disgust. "Well, I'm sure as hell not going to tag along!"

"Damn it, Morgan. I wasn't asking you to!"

She crossed her arms over her chest and eyed him warily, her gaze shadowed by a heavy weight of suspicion. "Then spell it out for me, because I have no idea what you want from me, Kierland."

"You," he growled, and it was easy to hear the graveled edge of the wolf's voice in the guttural word, the beast stretching within him, irritated by the human constraints of his body. "You're the one that I need."

She blinked, staring at him as if he'd just grown a second head...or lightning beams had just shot from his eye sockets. With one hand pressed against her chest, she wheezed and managed to splutter, "Is that meant to be some kind of *joke?*"

A thick sound of frustration broke from his throat, and Kierland pulled a hand down his face, hating that he could feel a damn blush burning beneath his skin. "I'm not telling you that I want to go out and find another woman," he muttered, before looking away to stare out across the crowded pub. "I'm telling you that I want *you.*"

"Me?"

"Yeah." His gaze came back to her, and whatever she saw in his eyes made her own face flush with heat, a wild bloom of color burning in her cheeks and along the bridge of her nose.

"I don't understand." Slow, careful words, as if she

was talking to someone who'd lost their grip on reality. And hell, maybe he had.

Kierland rubbed at the knotted tension in the back of his neck, then made a quiet, gritty confession. "The truth is, I haven't been with another woman since you came to England with the others."

WORRIED THAT SHE MIGHT actually be dreaming, Morgan reached under the table and sank a short claw into her thigh. As the sharp sting of pain faded, she could only marvel at the fact that she hadn't awakened in her bed, alone, to find that this was all some kind of fatigue- or stress-induced fantasy. But Kierland was still sitting across from her, looking like he wanted to eat her alive, the provocative scent of hunger pouring off his big, ripped body making her light-headed.

"What exactly are you saying?" she asked, choosing her words with care. She was still mortified by the things she'd said to him on the train. No way in hell was she going to compound her embarrassment by misreading the situation.

He took a moment to respond, his head angled forward and a little to the side as he stared at her through his dense lashes, his gaze touching upon her individual features—eyes, nose, mouth—before returning to her eyes again. Finally, he answered her question. "I'm saying that I haven't been with another woman in the past month, because you're the only one that I've wanted under me. No one else. And I'm saying that there's still lust between us, just like there was ten years ago." The husky words shook with a raw force of emotion that she could hardly believe was real. "It doesn't matter how misplaced it is," he went on to say, "or how badly we wish it didn't exist. I think it's finally time we got it out of our systems, once and for all."

Blinking, Morgan took a slow, careful breath and wet her lips, while her blood slipped through her veins like hot, thick syrup. "Are you...actually admitting that you wanted me back then, Kier?"

He turned his head farther to the side, and slid her one of those wry male expressions that managed to look both sardonic and sexy as hell. "I would have thought it was pretty obvious."

"And what makes you think I wanted *you?*"

The corner of his mouth twitched, as if he was fighting back a smile. "Are you really gonna try to deny it?"

"No," she whispered, shaking her head. "But...I was a girl with her first adult crush. I had stars in my eyes. Then I got a heavy dose of reality, and I grew up."

From the look on his face, she could tell the quiet words had revealed more than she'd wanted. Morgan thought he would question her, digging for answers, but he didn't. Instead, he blew out a rough breath and said, "I want you under me, Morgan, and I'm tired of pretending I couldn't care less if it ever happens. Because it's a lie. I care a hell of a lot about wanting you. I always have."

God, she couldn't believe this was Kierland sitting across from her, speaking so...openly. The man had never so much as even attempted to kiss her all those years ago, and now he was claiming that he'd wanted her. A lot. It made her head spin, knowing that she hadn't just imagined the hunger she'd sometimes thought she'd caught in those beautiful green eyes.

But if that was true, then why had he gotten involved with Nicole? Why had he never told Morgan how he felt?

"You really think this is a good idea?" she croaked, too wary to ask the questions that she really wanted answered.

"I'd give you an easier option if I had one, but I don't." The raw force of his gaze made her flustered and hot. "The fact is, I've given this a lot of thought, and there's only one way I'm going to be able to stomach working with Granger."

*Oh...hell.*

Morgan dropped her head forward and covered her face with her hands, holding perfectly still, even though she was shaking apart inside. God, she should have known where this was leading. That it would turn ugly, the way everything always did between them.

Slowly, she lowered her hands to her lap, a wry, self-deprecating smile curving the corner of her mouth. "This isn't about me at all, is it? It's about Ashe. Some weird jealousy thing." There was a soft edge of anger to her words as she said, "One of those 'You don't want me, but you don't want anyone else to want me, either' situations."

His voice slid over her like dark, crushed velvet, his heavy-lidded stare smoldering with lust. "Trust me," he reiterated slowly. "Wanting you has never been a problem."

"Some sort of vampire prejudice, then?" she shot

back, trying hard not to melt beneath the primal heat of his stare. "You can't stomach to see someone in your unit cozying up with a vamp?"

Frustration rode the hard, muscled lines of his body, blasting against her like a physical force. "Don't ask me to explain it, because I can't. But it's not a vampire thing. I'm just... Damn it, I hate this," he muttered, taking a deep, shuddering breath, as if willing himself to calm down. The fisted hand on the tabletop slowly relaxed, and he flexed his fingers, laying his palm flat. For a moment, all he did was stare down at the back of his hand, with its long fingers and thick veins, while the pub continued to provide a noisy backdrop to their quiet conversation. Finally, he lifted his head and stared right into her eyes as he said, "I don't want to fight with you anymore, Morgan. I just want to have sex with you."

Madness, how much those rough words turned her on. Not to mention how badly she wanted to believe him. How desperately she wanted to throw herself across that table and attack him, right there in the middle of that bloody pub. But the doubts and fears were nearly impossible to ignore.

She swallowed, and fought to make sense of the words crashing around inside her skull. "If you're doing this to keep me away from Ashe, it isn't necessary, Kier. Like I've told you before, Ashe and I are just friends."

He snorted, clearly not believing her.

"That's the truth, Kierland. He was a friend when I needed one. And then he was...he kept me together at a really bad time in my life. Kept me from falling apart, and I owe him more than I can ever repay. I know the two of you have never gotten along, but he's not the villain you've made him out to be."

"He's hardly a saint," he muttered under his breath, and she could tell that he was trying hard to control his temper.

"No, he isn't a saint," she agreed. "But he isn't evil, either." She lowered her gaze, staring at the polished surface of the table. "Still, I meant what I said. I won't be sleeping with him."

"Then so long as we're on this assignment, you'll be sleeping with me."

The husky, devastating words jerked a short, nervous laugh from her chest, and she looked back up, mesmerized by the hard, determined expression cut into the rugged angles of his face. With the burnished rays of sunlight spilling in through the pub's high, stained-glass windows, pouring splashes of color across that lustrous hair and powerful body, he really was the most gorgeous thing she'd ever seen.

Wetting her lips again, she shook her head a little to break the spell, and tried to remember all the reasons why this was such a bad idea. "What in God's name makes you think I'm going to agree to this?"

"We've been putting this off for years, Morgan. Don't you think it's time we finally did something about it?" he asked in a deep, rich rumble. "Whatever else might be between us, we've always wanted the hell out of each other, and it's even worse now than it was before. These past two days have proven that. And as much as I figure you'd like to deny it, the truth is that you want to know the answer to the question as badly as I do."

"And the question would be…"

He focused on her hot face with a visceral, predatory intensity, and replied, "What it's going to be like when I'm inside you."

Need spiked through her body, molten and warm and aching, her expression no doubt giving away every damn thing that she felt, but it couldn't be helped. Morgan wished she could be cool and sophisticated about the intimate topic, but that just wasn't her. Put her on a battlefield, and she could fight like a ruthless bitch with the best of them. But land her in the middle of a conversation about sex, and she blushed like a schoolgirl, her heart beating so heavily she knew he could probably hear it over the clatter of the pub.

Nerves were so ridiculous at her age, and yet, there seemed so much to be nervous about. For one, this was Kierland saying these outrageous things to her, which would have been enough to rattle any woman. And for another…she'd never been intimate with a wolf before. And from the things Morgan had heard, it wasn't an experience a woman could ever forget. Lycans were known to be insatiable lovers. Wild. Ravenous. As aggressive as the Deschanel, when their beasts were awakened.

With those thoughts tumbling through her mind, she couldn't quite look him in the eye as she said, "I've heard things about Lycans, Kier. They're rumored to be some of the most…aggressive of the breeds when it comes to sex."

A heavy pause. A rough breath. Then he finally responded. "You've slept with a Deschanel, Morgan. I wouldn't have thought you'd be afraid of aggressive sex."

He was right about the Deschanel's reputation, but the truth was that Ashe had always been incredibly tender with her, mindful of her age and innocence...worried that he'd scare her if he got too rough. But she wasn't going to admit any of that to Kierland. "I'm not saying that I'm afraid. Maybe I just want to make sure you won't hold back and act differently with me. Because of my bloodline."

He waited until she'd slid her gaze back to his before saying, "I've always considered you one of the strongest women I know, so there'd be no reason for me to go easy on you." His chest shook with a gritty bark of laughter that seemed to take him by surprise, and a slow grin crossed his mouth. "I doubt I could lighten up even if I wanted to. And I don't. I plan on doing everything I can to make sure the experience is one that makes an impact. One you won't ever forget."

Morgan bit back a telling moan, so aroused she could barely sit still. He'd spent so many years hiding this part of himself from her, and though she'd imagined it in her fantasies, seeing the sexy redhead in full hunger mode was too delicious to be real.

But he was lying, and she knew it.

"What?" he asked, arching a dark brow as he spotted the sparks of accusation glittering in her eyes.

"It's just that I know that's not true," she told him, shrugging her shoulder. "Ashe told me what happened with that nest of rogue vampires. That you refused to attack with the full unit of trainees, the way you'd been ordered to, because you didn't want me involved. The only explanation I can think of is that you were worried I would jeopardize the mission, because I wasn't as pure-blooded as the rest of you."

"Granger talks too much," he grunted, shoving one hand through his auburn hair.

"You don't deny it, then?" she asked in a soft voice. "That you thought I was weak?"

"I've already told you that I considered you the most talented student I ever had," he growled with a blast of impatience. "And I don't want to sit here wasting time talking about the past. I'm done with the past," he muttered, and then he suddenly shook his head, a grim, breathless burst of laughter spilling from his lips. "Hell, I know I sound like a madman, but I just...I need to put the past behind me somehow and go on from here. Only, I can't do that with this...with what's between us still hanging over my head. I swear to God, Morgan, I'm gonna go out of my mind if I don't get this out of my system."

She scowled at his words. "You make me sound like some kind of illness."

"You're *my* illness. And I'm just trying to get my hands on the cure." He sent her a deep-grooved grin that was unbearably beautiful, and said, "Or maybe addiction would be a better word for you."

"And you're just trying to get your fix?" she asked, surprised to find herself grinning back at him.

"Yeah. Something like that."

It was so tempting just to fall under the spell of that

devilish, lopsided smile he was giving her, but she knew what could be waiting for her on the other side. "If I say yes," she whispered, shifting her gaze away again, "I know how you'll act, Kierland. Belittle me. Call me a slut."

"No," he said in a rough voice. "That's not going to happen."

"You—"

He cut her off, his voice ragged as he interjected, "Morgan, I'm ready to get down on my knees and beg. If that's what it's going to take, just tell me. I'll do it."

"*If* I agreed," she murmured, trying to hide the fact that her stomach was doing somersaults, "when did you want…to do this?"

His answer came hard and quick. "Right now."

Unable to hide her surprise, she jerked her head around, her stunned gaze colliding with his. "You can't be serious."

"You say yes," he rasped, "and we're gonna be lucky if we make it to a bloody bed."

Again, she lowered her gaze, which was so unlike her. But she couldn't help it, damn it. The raw heat and hunger on his gorgeous face was melting her down. Turning her brain to mush. Making her feel stripped and bare and completely exposed.

*Which is exactly what's going to happen if I say yes to him.*

Suddenly, Morgan found herself staring at the way his big hands rested palm down on the table, imagining what those rough, masculine hands would feel like on her body. Imagining those long fingers inside her, touching all those intimate places that had always hungered for this man's touch. He had beautiful hands. Not pretty, but hard...rugged. Battle-scarred and dark. Powerful...strong. She knew, without any doubt, that they were more than capable of making her scream with pleasure.

And oh...God, was she actually thinking of agreeing to this insane idea?

With her breath coming in sharp, embarrassing pants, Morgan lifted her gaze, staring deep into those heavy-lidded eyes, and knew that she didn't have any other choice. Her lips felt numb, but she somehow managed to form the words she wanted to say. "I... Okay." A soft, shaky whisper. Almost too silent to be heard. "I...I think you're right. We should...clear the air, so to speak."

She'd half expected him to gloat or burst out laughing or tell her it had all been some kind of sick joke. But he didn't say anything. Not a word.

Instead, the Lycan stood up and grabbed their luggage from under the table, hooking the straps over his broad shoulders. Then he reached down, took her wrist...and pulled her out of the pub behind him.

"Where are we going?" she gasped, squinting at the bright rays of afternoon sunlight as they stepped onto the busy street, his hold on her firm and solid and strong.

"We're getting a room."

That was all he said. Just those four gritty words.

But as he headed down the bustling sidewalk and she ran to keep up with him, Morgan knew they were the most exciting, terrifying, breathtaking words she had ever heard.

# *CHAPTER NINE*

IT WASN'T UNTIL THE DOOR TO THE hotel room—the room Kierland had just walked in off the street and paid for—was closed with a hard, solid thud that Morgan understood just how tightly he'd been holding himself together. But with the closing of the door, he stopped fighting it and allowed the hunger to fill him. The fury-tinged lust and craving he'd confessed to in the pub was suddenly staring her right in the face...and she almost panicked.

She stumbled back, not running from him, but needing some space to breathe...to think.

Misreading her intention, Kierland rasped a single, desperate word as he dropped their bags on the floor. *"Don't."*

Then he moved so fast, Morgan couldn't even remember seeing him cross the room, but suddenly he was there, on her, crushing her into the mattress, crawling over her, his hard weight pinning her down. For a split second Morgan worried that the panic which sometimes came when she felt crowded or confined would rush over her, ruining the moment. It'd happened before during sex. Ever since the awful night when things had gone so horribly wrong ten years ago, she hadn't been able to take all of a man's weight on her. Not the times she'd been with Ashe, after the incident, or with the few other lovers she'd had over the years. The feeling of being trapped always threatened to take her back to memories she'd worked hard to forget.

But Kierland's weight didn't make her feel frightened or suffocated. It made her hungry…greedy, and she wound her arms around his broad, tough shoulders, clawing at his sweater, wanting more of him…needing everything he had to give.

His lips found hers, at once hard and tender, the heat of them after being out in the cold making her gasp. With his long fingers shaped around her skull, he held her trapped, kissing her like he was making love to her mouth. Then he pushed his hips between her thighs, forcing her legs to part, the hard ridge of his erection grinding against the slick, damp heat of her sex. With a thick sound, he pushed his jeans-covered cock against her in a move that would have driven him impossibly deep, if not for the frustrating layers of clothing separating their flesh, and she arched in reaction, clutching onto his powerful shoulders.

*It's too good,* she thought, wondering if it was possible to spontaneously combust from lust.

He groaned her name, fed a feral growl into her mouth, and pulled one hand from her hair. His fingers touched the curve of her cheek, trailing across her jaw, the sensitive side of her throat and down the front of her sweater before curving around her breast, his thumb finding her beaded nipple and rubbing it with a strong, aggressive touch. Shivering, Morgan curled her hand around the back of his neck, where hot, silken skin met the short, damp layers of his hair. The heat of him burned her palm, and he shuddered beneath her touch, thrusting hard again, his hand shaping her breast. His tongue slid suggestively against hers, the kiss turning savage and raw, and then he tore his mouth away with a low, guttural curse.

Pulling back, he shot off the bed, his hands fisted at his sides. His chest heaved as he stood at the foot of the mattress, staring down at her with the force of all the fires in hell. He looked tormented...in pain, his voice a graveled rasp as he said, "Gotta slow down."

Morgan pushed up onto her elbows, her hair hanging over one side of her face. "What? Why?"

"Because I've waited too long for this to have it be over in a matter of seconds," he said between hard breaths, his hands fisting and flexing, his muscles hard and thick beneath his sweater and jeans.

Morgan wanted to see him naked. Desperately. And Kierland apparently wanted the same thing, since his next words were, "Take off your clothes."

She started to sit up, but he shook his head, saying, "No. Right there. Lying down. I want to watch you strip like that."

Her breath caught, but she lowered her back to the bed, and began to do as he said, reaching for the hem of her sweater and pulling it over her head. Her movements were clumsy with nerves, no practiced striptease to lure him with her feminine grace, but he didn't seem to mind. He didn't move, except for that flexing of his hands, as if he was fighting the urge to reach down and grab her, and Morgan had never, in her entire life, felt more desirable than she did in that powerful, intensely provocative moment.

Crazy, to think that she would experience this height of feeling with the one man she'd been so sure would never lay a hand on her.

"You on the pill?" he grunted, his molten gaze locked on her fingers as she began to open the button fly on her jeans.

"Yes."

He didn't have to ask about tests or blood work, and neither did she, since sexually transmitted diseases didn't affect their species. So with the question of birth control out of the way, they were free to indulge. As Morgan pushed her jeans down her thighs, kicking them away, she thought she might die if he didn't get started. She felt charged, like some kind of electric current was surging through her veins, unable to take her hungry stare off the startling, mesmerizing sight of his heavy erection bulging against the denim of his jeans.

Reaching for the front snap on her bra, she said, "I want your clothes off, too."

He gave a sharp nod, his gaze glued to her breasts as she bared them. He reached for the hem of his sweater and all but ripped it over his head.

"Lose the underwear," he rasped, jerking his chin toward her black bikinis.

Pulling her lower lip through her teeth, Morgan hooked her fingers in the waistband of her panties and started shimmying them down her thighs, her attention focused on his hard, bare torso. She took a moment to drool over the outrageous beauty of his chest, dazzled by the golden skin stretched tight over solid slabs of muscle, the scattering of scars only adding to his rugged perfection. She loved his dark brown nipples and the jut of his hip bones, but his abs were her favorite. She wanted to run her tongue over the deep grooves, kissing her way down that silken trail of hair that arrowed toward his groin, disappearing beneath the ragged waist of his jeans.

She tossed her panties over the side of the bed at the same instant his strong hands began undoing his fly, and Morgan simply forgot how to breathe.

It was impossible to look away from him—not that she wanted to. Her pulse roared in her ears as he shoved the denim down his hips, along with a pair of white cotton boxers, and all she could do was stare at the thick, heavily-veined length of his cock as it rose up high against his stomach, her mouth hanging open, her face burning with heat. She knew she shouldn't have been so surprised by his size, considering Kierland was *massive* everywhere. That dark, mouth-wateringly male part of him was merely in proportion to the rest of him, but even so, she was fairly certain she was having some kind of awe-induced heart attack.

"Get higher on the bed," he rasped. "Right in the middle."

He gripped himself with a rough hand, stroking the heavy length of his cock as she clumsily scooted back, sliding along the quilted comforter. Morgan licked her lips, wanting to touch her tongue to the dark, bruised color at the head of his shaft. Wanting to take him into her hand and feel that hot, velvety skin against her palm. Feel the pulse of his blood in that thick knotwork of veins.

He jerked his chin toward her again, and said, "Now spread your legs. Let me see it."

"You like to give orders, don't you?" she whispered, shaking, unbearably aroused by his aggressive attitude. Morgan never would have thought it possible, but it seemed that getting bossed around in bed by a gorgeous Lycan really did it for her.

Or maybe it was just getting bossed around in bed by the outrageously sexy Kierland Scott. Which meant that she had some serious issues. He might be staring at her like he wanted to eat her alive—like he couldn't wait to find out how she tasted, *everywhere*—but she needed to remember that this was just sex for him. A way for him to satisfy his curiosity about what he'd never had, so that he could put it behind him and move on. She couldn't afford to get lost in emotion. She couldn't afford any emotion at all.

"Do it, Morgan." His husky, rough-edged voice slipped into her system like a drug, mesmerizing her senses. "Spread your legs for me."

Her breath hitched with some kind of soft, embarrassing girlie sound as she lifted her knees in an explicit pose, showing him the wet, pink flesh between her thighs. His eyes narrowed, his thick lashes leaving spiky shadows on his carved cheeks. His body seemed to expand, his skin stretched tight over all those hard, coiled muscles.

The way he stared...it was like she'd shown him something priceless. Something precious and dazzling.

Needing to say something before she started crying, and God would *that* have been embarrassing, she told him, "I'll let you boss me around for now. But I get my turn eventually. Just be warned, you're not the only one who likes to take control."

The corner of his mouth twitched with a grin. "Strong women happen to turn me on," he rasped, the husky words feeling like foreplay. "I'll let you have your turn."

He settled onto the foot of the bed then, and Morgan tried to stay calm. But God, it wasn't easy. She hadn't done this in a long time, her interest in sex waning over the years. Not that she'd ever been a prude. She'd just been...picky about her partners. And when they wanted to get serious, that had been her clue to walk away. Unfortunately, that meant that she now felt shaky and out of practice, everything he did shocking her to a bright, nervous awareness. The intimacy of having Kierland Scott pressing his mouth to the inside of her bent knee, and higher, against the pale skin of her inner thigh, had her shivering and strung tight with breathtaking excitement.

He moved higher, crawling over her body like something stalking its prey, and Morgan made a sound that she'd never made before. Something low and thick, like a purr, the erotic hum making him pause. It was obvious from the heat in his eyes as he slid a blistering look up at her face that he'd liked it. A lot.

As he lowered himself over her, she felt his shocking heat and his hardness, and knew, in that moment, that there was no going back. He was all over her, his hands, his mouth, the delicious weight of his huge body pressing her down, while his male scent made her head spin. Her breath was jerking so sharply it made her chest hurt, but she didn't care. All that mattered was getting more of him...all of him.

His fingers shaped themselves around her skull again as he kissed his way into her mouth, his body so hard and hot and strong, his taste rich...drugging, making her writhe. The strangest sensation of bursting from the confines of her body spread through her, and yet, she was still there...still whole. But it was like a switch had been flipped inside her mind, and Morgan could suddenly feel everything he did, every touch... every brush of his fingers and his lips, more sharply than she'd ever felt anything before.

He fisted his hand in her hair and pulled back her head, dragging kisses along her arched throat, his breath uneven and loud in the quiet shadows of the room, same as hers. And then he started to kiss his way down the front of her body. He flicked his tongue against the rapid flutter of her pulse in the base of her throat, his mouth warm against her skin as he placed kisses across her chest, then lower. As he ran his lips along the curve of her breast, stroking the damp heat of his tongue across one painfully tight nipple, she cried out, the sharp sound becoming a low moan as he reached between her legs with those long, wicked fingers, knowing just where to rub and stroke and tease. She was already drenched, burning for him, trembling with need.

Lifting his head, Kierland locked his gaze with hers as he pushed two fingers inside the tight, slippery clench of her sex, gently thrusting the hard knuckles back and forth within the small, swollen opening. "You're tight," he grunted, his hot breath brushing against a sensitive nipple. "Feels incredible. My hand's in heaven."

Aware of the warmth beneath her skin, Morgan turned her face into the rumpled bedding. God, it was crazy, how shy she felt. She wasn't innocent, for God's sake—and yet, she felt like they were going someplace she'd never been before. That something unfamiliar and unknown lay on the other side, waiting for her, and she was…worried. About what she would find when they got there.

About being left there alone.

And what was truly frightening was how easily he seemed to read her, as if he was right there inside her mind, picking his way through her thoughts.

"Stop thinking," he rasped, his warm lips moving against her nipple as he spoke. "Stop worrying. I don't want anything else in this room but the two of us. Not the past. Not…anything."

*Not the future, either,* she thought, but she bit back the words. She wasn't an idiot. She craved him…and if this was all she could have, she was damn well greedy enough to take it.

He moved farther down, placing kisses and gnawing bites against her skin as he worked his way along her body, until he was kneeling between her thighs, his shoulders solid and broad and roped with muscle. She could feel the press of his hot gaze as he spread her with his thumbs, his breath warm and moist against the slick, sensitive folds.

"Beautiful," he whispered, just before he lowered his dark head and took a long, lingering lick. Her groan blended with his deep, guttural growl, and her back arched as he went at her again, licking and lapping as if he'd found something delicious to devour. Something he needed to get more of. Squeezing her eyes shut, Morgan figured she should have known he'd be amazing. He gave oral sex in a way that left no doubt about the fact that he was enjoying it, taking as much pleasure from the erotic act as he gave. His strong hands pressed her knees to the bed, holding her open in a blatantly explicit pose, while his mouth ate at her like he was starved for her taste, his tongue lashing against her clit with hot, wet strokes, before thrusting inside her. She choked out broken, sobbing phrases that didn't make any sense, her hands finding the damp, silken locks of his hair and holding tight.

Kierland muttered something dirty and gruff and impossibly sexy about her taste, the provocative words buzzing in her ears. Then he pushed two thick fingers as deep as she could take them, and Morgan was gone. Flying. Screaming. Completely destroyed, the violent pulses thrashing her with pleasure, leaving her damp and pink and wrecked, her arms and legs flung wide, while she struggled to draw in a decent breath. It took a few seconds, but when she finally managed to crack open her heavy eyelids, she saw him lifting his glistening fingers to his mouth...and licking them with his tongue.

His throat worked as he swallowed. "Like I said before. Incredible." He sounded drunk, though he'd had only one beer with their meal. But his husky words were pleasure slurred at the edges, his eyes drowsy and hot with fever as he looked up at her, a fine sheen of sweat covering his face and shoulders and throat. A single lock of auburn hair fell over his brow, and Morgan reached down to push it back, threading her fingers through the warm, silken strands.

"I think that's my line," she said unsteadily, horrified to feel the moisture on her face, the salty taste of tears at the corner of her mouth.

"So strong," he murmured, leaning over her as he stroked one callused palm along the inside of her thigh, then over her hip, up along her side. When he reached her face, he rubbed his thumb against the edge of her trembling mouth, and leaned down, pressing the hot silk of his lips against the corner of her eye, where the tears were flowing freely. "But you're not as hard as you pretend to be, are you?"

BEFORE MORGAN COULD GIVE him an answer, Kierland pressed the straining head of his cock to her warm entrance, and pushed deep, shoving hard, with all his strength, unable to wait a single second more to be a part of her. Her scream instantly filled his ears, her body clasping him in the tightest, sweetest hold he'd ever felt. She was smaller than he'd expected, almost virginal, though he knew damn well that she wasn't.

But Morgan obviously hadn't done this in a long time, and he didn't know what to think of that. He'd have pegged her as having a different lover every week, but...he'd have been wrong, and he cursed something hot and gritty under his breath, hating that he might have hurt her.

Lowering his head, he nuzzled his mouth beneath her ear. "You okay?"

"F-fine," she whispered, and though her voice shook, he could tell that she was trying to sound strong. "I'm fine."

"Did I hurt you?" he asked, lifting his head so that he could see her face.

"Just caught me a little off guard," she murmured, and he smiled, knowing she'd rather cut out her tongue than admit a weakness to him. But the smile fell as she lifted her hand to his damp face, her fingertips lingering against his hot skin. "I should've known you'd be a lot to handle," she said huskily, widening her knees with a voluptuous little movement that took him even deeper.

"Damn it," he growled, shaking, shocked to realize that his control was already shot to hell.

Kierland managed to hold still for all of another ten seconds, letting her get used to the feel of him...and then he lost it.

With a primal, animalistic snarl on his lips, he covered her mouth with his, swallowing her sharp cry of surprise as he pulled back his hips, dragging his shaft through the drenched clasp of those tight inner muscles. Then he drove back in with a powerful thrust, putting all his strength, all his power behind it, shoving into her the way he'd spent the past decade dreaming of entering her, penetrating her, the pleasure so intense it was a sharp, physical ache.

He couldn't get over how it felt to be inside her. A part of her.

*Incredible* didn't do it justice. Nor did *amazing* or *wonderful* or any of the other adjectives Kierland had heard people use to describe good sex. He loved how the slightest brush of his mouth against her damp skin made her clench around him. How the barest brush of his callused fingertips over her nipples brought the most sensual arch to her back. She was so responsive…so sweet, that he couldn't control it. He gave it to her rough and raw, pumping into her with more hunger and aggression than he'd ever shown with any other lover. But then, this was Morgan. The one he'd always wanted. The woman he thought about every time he took another female beneath him. He couldn't control his body or temper his body's craving. He was too far gone, completely strung out on the bliss-drenched feeling of shoving himself into her hot, slippery little sex.

Release was bearing down on him, unstoppable and huge, but he forced it back, needing to feel her coming around his cock—soaking him, sucking him in, all those cushiony muscles fluttering around his shaft in strong, voluptuous pulls. He needed to be buried inside her, thick and deep, when she crashed over the edge. But she was fighting it…straining against release, doing everything she could to hold it back.

"Let go, damn you." He licked his thumb and reached down, between their bodies, rubbing the callused pad against her clit, and she trembled, writhing, her short claws digging into his arms, drawing blood. "Don't you dare try to hold back on me."

"I won't," she gasped, her eyes heavy-lidded and dark with passion. Kierland took his thumb from her clit and caught her behind her knee, pulling it up so that he could sink even deeper, and suddenly her mouth-watering scent was becoming even richer, filling the air, and he knew her shields were dropping as she lost control. With his next thrust, he buried every thick, rigid inch of his cock inside her, grinding against her clit, and then she was coming, convulsing around him in strong, gushing pulls. It was all he could do to keep from following her over.

*Not yet, damn it. Not yet.*

Gritting his teeth, the Lycan fought it down, determined to make it last. He was spellbound by the tears he could see glistening in her eyes. She looked so soft...so fragile, the toughness of the warrior ripped away to reveal the tenderness of the woman she always tried so hard to hide. It was beautiful, breathtaking, and now that he'd found it, he wanted more.

Burying his face in her silken hair, Kierland admitted to himself that while he was damn proud to fight beside her as a colleague, it was this deliciously soft female that he wanted in bed with him, and he knew he'd do whatever it took to get her beneath him again.

She whispered his name, and he lifted his head, staring into her eyes as he rolled his hips, moving in slow, lunging thrusts that drenched him in pleasure, her body tight and warm and impossibly tender.

She swallowed, ran her tongue over her top lip, and quietly said, "I want...I want to bite you."

At the sound of those hoarse words, Kierland got even harder...thicker, and her eyes went wide as she felt the difference in him—felt his wolf rising within him, making the change in his body. He'd have never been able to fit inside her like that if she wasn't so wet, the tight, silken friction too good to be real.

"Can...I?" she asked, wetting her lips, her gaze fastened hungrily on the pumping of his jugular in the side of his throat. Although she didn't "need" blood for feeding, it wasn't uncommon for female shifters to hunger for it when their animal instincts had been aroused. It wasn't the first time Kierland had been asked the question by a lover—but it *was* the first time he'd ever wanted to say yes.

With his wolf punching against his insides, desperate for what was coming, Kierland turned his head and offered her what she wanted. There was a small whimpering sound of excitement, and then she licked the heavy vein with her tongue, scraping her small, delicate fangs against him in a way that was sexy as all get out. The prick of her sharp teeth against his flesh made him shudder, his control slipping as he rammed into her, giving her everything that he had.

The Lycan hadn't been concerned about controlling his beast...but now he wondered if maybe he should have been—because he wanted nothing more than to sink his fangs into her, as well. Gritting his teeth, Kierland reached down with one hand, anchoring it under her bottom to hold her in place, then wrapped the other around one of the wooden slats in the head-board. She started pulling on the wound, taking his hot blood into her throat, and he went even further over the edge, slamming into her with a desperate, primal urgency. The wooden slat snapped in his hand, and he reached higher, grabbing the thick crossbeam at the top of the headboard, his fingers making deep hollows in the wood as he felt himself starting to come.

The orgasm was so strong, it made him shout.

So good, it damn near killed him.

The devastating blast of pleasure rolled through him in thick, blistering waves, breaking out of Kierland's body in such a violent rush that it made him growl and groan and shout again, and he buried his face in the fragrant tangle of her hair spread out over the bedding, muffling the harsh, guttural sounds. She shifted the angle of her head, still feeding...still pulling on his vein. He kept driving into her with hard, heavy lunges as his body unloaded, his fingers biting deep into her ass and the top of the headboard, his heart doing everything it could to batter its way out of his chest.

"Again," he growled, releasing the headboard so that he could push his arm under her shoulders, holding her beneath his body as he pumped into her harder... heavier, forcing his way into the narrow, cushiony, de-liciously liquid depths of her body. "Damn it, I want to feel it again. I want to feel you come."

She gasped, pulling her fangs from his throat, her arms thrown tight around his neck, and then her husky cries were filling his ear, her body arching sharply beneath him as pleasure jolted through her like an explosion. Her tight little sex convulsed around him in a series of lush, drenching spasms that damn near made his eyes roll back in his head, milking his cock, draining him completely.

When the last shocking pulses of pleasure had finally faded away, Kierland managed to pull in a deep, shuddering breath, feeling as if he'd just experienced something that he never would have even believed was possible, if it hadn't happened to him. He wanted to kiss her. Hold her. Put his mouth between her legs and feel the heat of her clit against his tongue. Lap at those smooth, slippery pink folds. He wanted a thousand different things that he didn't know how to put into words, damn it, his head spinning with confusion and a drugged-out feeling of aftermath that he'd never known before. But when he pulled out, moving carefully so that he didn't hurt her, she turned her face away, one forearm drawn over her mouth, her eyes squeezed shut, and so he dropped onto his back beside her.

It was...unsettling, how badly he wanted to hold her...kiss her...get inside her all over again, but Kierland breathed it down, forcing himself to be patient. To wait and see what she would do.

FEELING WRECKED AND SORE AND unbelievably wonderful, Morgan took a deep breath, and finally opened her eyes. She rolled toward Kierland, and found him lying beside her, one arm under his head, his other hand at his throat, his long fingers rubbing against the small bite wound that she'd made.

"I'm sorry," she whispered, shocked at what she'd done. "I...I shouldn't have asked for your blood."

"S'all right." A lazy smile crossed his mouth as he turned his head toward her, his eyes crinkling sexily at the corners. Then he reached over, catching what must have been a smear of blood at the corner of her mouth with the pad of his thumb. "I'd be lying if I said I didn't enjoy the hell out of it."

She caught a soft laugh under her breath, and wished she knew what to do...what to say.

"I guess this means you'll be able to find me now, too," he said in a low, sex-roughened rumble.

Biting her lip, she nodded and asked, "Does that bother you?"

"Nah." He turned his head so that he was staring at the ceiling, working his fingers against the bristled edge of his jaw. The seconds stretched out, filled only with the quiet sounds of their breathing, and then he said, "Did he ever feed from you?"

Morgan knew, without even asking, that he was talking about Ashe. She wouldn't have even bothered to answer, if he'd posed the question with his usual sarcasm—but his tone struck her as merely curious, without any judgmental criticism. "Not when we were...intimate."

"Why not?" He rolled toward her, the dark auburn hair falling over his brow making him look younger, the strain in his face somehow lighter than it'd been before.

"You don't know much about the Deschanel, do you?"

"I guess not, since I thought they fed from their lovers," he said in a low voice.

"They can. But when not mated, it…can be dangerous if they feed during sex with someone who's not of their race, so they usually don't risk it. At least, not with someone they're not in love with."

He didn't say anything—just stared at her with those beautiful green eyes—and Morgan suddenly heard herself asking, "Has there ever been anyone special for you? Anyone you could have loved?"

"What makes you think I haven't?" he asked with a lift of his brows.

Softly, she said, "I know you. You would have married any woman who held your heart."

"Think you know me that well, huh?" There was a teasing edge to his smirk, but she could see something brittle lurking beneath its surface, and could tell that he didn't like knowing she could read him so easily.

Pushing her folded hands beneath her cheek, she said, "Kellan told me that for a time you were…that he thought you might be interested in Molly."

Surprise showed in his eyes, but then he shook his head, the corner of his mouth twitching with a wry grin. "Kellan should learn to keep his mouth shut."

With a quiet laugh, she guessed, "Is that your way of saying you don't want to talk about it?"

A deep breath, and then he rolled to his back, one hand scratching lazily at his chest. "I'd thought, hoped, that I might be able to feel something for her," he finally responded, the rhythm of the words halting, as if he was struggling to put his thoughts into words. "But I didn't. We're friends, and I couldn't be happier for her and Ian. He needs her."

"And you don't need anyone?"

"Something like that." He turned his head toward her again and grinned a little, but then the grin faded as he reached over, pushing her hair back from her face. "On the train..."

"Yeah?" she asked, her body flushing with heat as she noticed that he was already getting hard again.

"What did you mean when you told me not to leave you?"

The heat of embarrassment burned beneath her skin, but Morgan forced herself to give him an honest answer. "I didn't want to get played." Seeing the question in his eyes, she continued, "You know what I mean. You make me come, then pull away and cut me down. Make me feel like I'm an inch tall."

His mouth twisted, and he gave a rueful shake of his head. "You don't have a very high opinion of me, do you?"

She opened her mouth to explain, but he cut her off, saying, "I know I deserve it. Hell, I've been a real bastard, treating you like shit for a long time now, Morgan." Quietly, he added, "Whatever my faults, I'm sorry that you think I could ever do something like that to you."

Shock made her brain feel hazy, and she lowered her gaze to his chin, not knowing what to say. "I...um, we're less than an hour from Amsterdam by train. We should probably go soon."

"Probably." He waited until she was looking him in the eye again before telling her, "But I want you again."

The smart thing to do would have been to smile, make some light comment and climb off the bed, cutting her losses while she still could. Before the damage could get any worse than it already was. But she couldn't do it.

Instead, Morgan moved closer to him, brushing the warm silk of his mouth with hers, and he groaned, pulling her against him in a hard, aggressive hold as he rolled to his side. It seemed like they kissed for hours, his hands running over her body, his mouth on hers, feeding her his breath, his growls, the predatory sounds filling her head while something that went beyond pleasure rushed through her.

"I told you that I wouldn't go easy on you," he warned in a rough voice, his strong hands suddenly turning her body, pushing her to her front, one arm wrapped around her hips, the other across her chest, caging her beneath him. Then he drove in, shoving his rigid cock into the tight clench of her sex, and his next lunging thrust touched places inside her that jerked hoarse, breathless cries from her throat.

Morgan chanted his name as he knelt in the middle of the bed and pulled her up, her back to his front. Bracing her on his taut thighs, he pumped into her harder…deeper, his hand coming around her front to rub more of those wet, erotic circles into her clit. She couldn't control the needy sounds that poured from her trembling lips. Every time she tried to choke them back, he just pushed her harder, driving her wild with his raw, savage aggression, until she finally gave him more.

"I'll give it to you as hard and as rough as you need it," he growled, his breath hot against her ear when she started to come, the sharp convulsions of pleasure dragging him right along with her. He shoved impossibly deep while she trembled and screamed, his open mouth warm and damp against the side of her throat. His arms were like steel bands around her body as he shuddered and tensed and cursed, filling her with violent, searing pulses of heat.

They lay in a tangle of limbs and sweat-slick skin afterward, pretending to doze, though neither was fooled by the other. Morgan didn't know what to say, the mind-blowing orgasms leaving her drowsy and dazed. Kierland seemed content with the silence, but at least he didn't leave her in that strange, unknown place all alone. He wrapped his muscled arms around her, and pulled her into his chest, his hands stroking every part of her that he could reach, as if he took pleasure in the simple touch of his skin against hers. As if he were trying to memorize the shape of her body. Every hollow. Every curve.

Squeezing her eyes closed, she had to accept that it had been an even worse idea than she'd feared. But she wouldn't regret it. No, if this was all she could have from him, then she was going to find some way to shove her heart into a box and enjoy him while she could.

She'd deal with the fallout later, when he walked away.

But until then, Morgan was going to take as much of Kierland Scott as he was willing to give.

# CHAPTER TEN

*Amsterdam*
*Monday night*

KIERLAND HAD THAT RAW FEELING again, and it wasn't a sensation that he cared for. The time he'd spent with Morgan in that hotel room in Weesp had been about nothing more than sex. About slaking a physical hunger that had seethed within him for too damn long now. He should have been experiencing some measure of peace...of finality, but if anything, his craving for her was now stronger than before. Tighter. Deeper. Twisting him into tangled, frustrated knots.

One taste...and all he could think about was having another. A dangerous temptation, and no doubt stupid as hell, but Kierland knew it would happen again. Even now, hours later, as they were heading into a smoky blues club in downtown Amsterdam, he couldn't keep his hands off her. Couldn't stop touching her. Just little, innocent touches. His hand on the small of her back. His fingers brushing her arm. He could feel the rise of her nerves shivering through her as they moved through the well-dressed crowd, and though he didn't understand her anxiety, Kierland sought to soothe her by staying close to her body, letting her know he was there if she needed him.

They hadn't talked about what had happened in that hotel room in Weesp, but every time Morgan turned to give him another surreptitious glance from the corner of her eye, Kierland knew she was thinking about it. Her lips were still swollen, her cheeks flushed warm with color, her body moving in that languid way of a woman who's been thoroughly satisfied—though he could feel her tension increasing as they moved deeper into the crowd. Slipping his hand beneath the heavy fall of her hair, he rubbed his thumb along the back of her neck, trying to calm her.

It was strange, this newfound sense of awareness surging through his system, as if he could sense her moods and emotions on a different level now that he'd been inside her—a part of her.

*Nothing more than sex...*

Yeah, right. He'd tried to convince himself of that little lie, but who was he trying to fool? He was searing with need, the taste of her in his mouth only making him burn hotter. Her skin, tears, sex. The mouthwatering flavors were driving Kierland mad, making him crave more, and he wanted to ask her if it'd been the best she'd ever had. Because it had for him—to the point that he should have been worried as hell. But he held back. He didn't know what to make of the strange emotions coiling him up inside. All he knew was that he'd never experienced that shattering sense of connection with any of his other lovers, but then, he'd never had sex like he and Morgan had had that afternoon, either.

Over the years, he'd had hard sex...raunchy sex...fun sex—but Kierland had never felt like he was going to die if he didn't get inside a woman. Never felt like he'd just created a miracle when he'd made her come. But he'd felt like that with Morgan—and he still didn't know what to think about it.

He also didn't know how to help her relax inside the packed club.

Deciding it was time they finally addressed the subject, Kierland lowered his mouth close to her ear and asked, "You don't like crowds much, do you?"

She frowned, slanting him a look that was equal parts unease and irritation, as if she didn't like how easily he could read her—though he'd have had to be blind not to have noticed the problem. Especially after her reaction in the crowded arcade of shops in Kladno, just before they'd been involved in the car crash.

"If you don't want to talk about it," he said in a low voice, looking away from her, his gaze sliding over the crowd as he searched for Granger, "that's fine. I'm not looking to start a fight. I just thought it might be good to get it out in the open."

"If it's all the same," she murmured, "I think we've gotten enough out in the open already today."

While his chest shook with a gruff bark of laughter, Kierland guided her toward the ornately carved mahogany bar that took up one entire side of the club. Settling onto an empty stool, Morgan sat with her back to the bar, so that she was facing the jam-packed room.

Although he could sense a large presence of Deschanel within the crowd, many of the patrons were human, almost all of whom would have no idea that there were vampires and werewolves mingling among them.

"And if we blow the lid on all our secrets," she went on to say, keeping her gaze focused on the men and women who were standing around high cocktail tables as they chatted with their friends, "we might run out of things to fight about."

Staring down at her delicate profile, Kierland couldn't help but shake his head, a slow grin kicking up the corner of his mouth. "Think about it, Morgan. If Granger agrees to come with us, we're going to be stuck with the bastard for days out in the Wasteland. I seriously doubt that 'not fighting' is going to be a problem for us."

She released a soft laugh under her breath, her tension seeming to ease now that they were no longer in the thick of the crowd. "You make a good point, Kier."

The bartender came to ask what they wanted, and they both ordered a Heineken. When the chilled green bottles were set on the bar, Kierland took one and handed it to Morgan, before grabbing his own. "You sure he's here?" he asked, watching her from the corner of his eye.

She lowered her thick lashes, took a deep breath, and her mouth curled with a warm, satisfied smile. "Oh, yeah. I'm sure," she replied, taking a drink of her beer before tilting her face up so that she was looking right at him. Kierland could see that her color was high, her soft gray eyes dancing with anticipation.

"You seem pretty excited," he grunted, his fingers tightening around the frosty bottle in his hand. He hated his inability to control the ugly burn of jealousy singeing through his veins, knowing it was only going to lead to trouble, same as it always had.

With a slight roll of her shoulder, she shifted her focus back to the crowd. "Of course I'm excited. I haven't seen Ashe in months, and he's one of my best friends."

"As well as one of your past lovers," Kierland added, his mouth twisting with bitter humor as he stared down at the icy vapor swirling around the mouth of his beer bottle.

She snuffled another one of those soft laughs and shook her head, her dark hair sliding like silk over her cashmere-covered shoulders. "Is this 'state the obvious' night," she drawled, "and nobody remembered to tell me?"

"Maybe I'm just wondering if you'll be sleeping with him on this trip, in return for his help, like you've done before." They were rough, huskily spoken words, barely audible beneath the din of music and voices, but Kierland knew from the tight set of her jaw that she'd heard him.

Though Morgan turned her body toward him on the stool, she didn't make eye contact. Her head was lowered, her gaze on the slender bottle in her hand as she said, "This is an issue for you, isn't it?"

Setting his beer on the bar, Kierland ran his tongue over his teeth, wishing he'd just kept his effing mouth shut. "What is?" he asked, knowing damn well what she meant.

She lifted her head, locking her curious gaze with his. "Jealousy."

The soft word made him cringe, and Kierland ground his jaw, figuring it safer not to say anything at all. Her head tilted a bit to the side, her eyes bright as she studied his expression, and whatever she saw there brought one of those strange, womanly smiles to her mouth that always left a man scratching his head, wondering just what in God's name she was thinking. "I won't be sleeping with Ashe," she finally told him. "In case it escaped your notice, Kier, I happen to be sleeping with you."

"And that means something?"

MORGAN FORCED DOWN AN instinctive burst of irritation, determined to keep her cool. On the one hand, the words coming out of the gorgeous Lycan's mouth belonged to a jackass. But on the other, there was something in his eyes that made her think Kierland was hiding something behind his jerk-of-the-year attitude. She just didn't know *what* he was hiding, and her brain was still too fried from the mind-blowing orgasms he'd given her to figure it out.

Setting her beer bottle on the bar beside his, she raised her brows and said, "One man is more than enough for me to handle, Kier. And before you start making ugly accusations, let's just remember that I wasn't the one with the psycho Barbie twins on Saturday night."

His eyes went narrow, while frustration hardened his masculine features. "I already told you that I didn't touch either one of those women," he rasped.

"Only because I pulled you away," she pointed out, shrugging her shoulders.

"And did I mention that I didn't even *want* to touch them?" he shot back in such a low voice, she almost didn't catch the words. Heat rose up in her body, prickling in her earlobes and behind her knees, her pulse suddenly rushing in her ears like an ocean surf. "They were just substitutes," he muttered, raking his auburn hair off his forehead as he looked out over the club.

Morgan wet her lips, unable to take her gaze off his rugged profile. "Substitutes for what?" she asked, her body still experiencing a series of delicious little aches and twinges from having been so thoroughly used.

A low, gritty laugh fell from his beautiful mouth, and he said, "Like you mentioned before, we've probably gotten enough out in the open already tonight." He ran a hand over the rough edge of his jaw, the rolled up sleeves of his white shirt revealing the long lines of muscle and sinew in his powerful forearms, and then slanted her a shuttered look. "Let's find Granger and get out of here."

With a nod, Morgan slipped off the stool. "I think he's in one of those rooms over there," she told him, pointing toward a far wall with several wooden doors leading to private rooms. They began making their way toward the closed doors along the edges of the crowd, and she noticed that Kierland kept his tall body positioned so that no one could get too close or bump into her. The protective gesture was so unlike him— at least where she was concerned—that it deepened the dreamlike sense of fantasy she'd been drifting in since that afternoon. Sooner or later, Morgan knew she was going to get a cold, hard slap of reality in the face, but for the moment she was still riding the high…and secretly enjoying the hell out of it.

"What now?" he asked, when they were standing outside the three mahogany doors, the rich brown contrasting sharply to the club's pale sage-colored walls.

Pushing her hands into the front pockets of her jeans, she did her best to ignore the couple making out at a table to their right, and said, "I guess we wait. I'm not exactly sure which room he's in, and since I have no idea what's going on in any of them, I'm not about to start knocking on doors."

He gave one of those gritty, wickedly sexy laughs in response, then propped his shoulder against the nearby wall. Morgan stood beside him, her attention focused on those three doors, trying to determine which one Ashe was behind, until she felt the blistering heat of a stare against the side of her face. Shifting her gaze toward Kierland, she found his eyes focused on her, instead of the doors. Her breath stuck in her throat, a thick, liquid heat spilling through her body as she spied the molten gleam that told her exactly what he was thinking about.

"Stop it," she whispered, her pulse racing as she remembered what it'd felt like when he'd pushed his cock inside her, stretching her, burying himself hard and deep. He'd been everywhere, touching every part of her, the pleasure burn still buzzing beneath the surface of her skin like a powerful current.

"Stop what?" His mouth kicked up in one of those lazy, crooked grins that made him look like a devil—

a gorgeous devil sent to earth to make all the good girls sin—and Morgan could literally feel her brain cells being melted down by lust.

"Stop looking at me like you want to eat me alive," she said unsteadily, pulling her lower lip through her teeth.

"Can't help that," he drawled in a low, husky rumble, the wine-dark strands of his hair falling back over his brow as he flashed her a wide wolf's smile. "Because it's exactly what I want to do."

Embarrassed by the schoolgirl's blush she could feel burning in her cheeks, she used a dry tone as she stated, "You've already gotten off once today. Or... twice, actually."

And she had a feeling he could have kept going, if they'd had the time.

His right eyebrow lifted in a slow, knowing arch. "What gave you the impression that once was going to be enough with you? Once didn't come anywhere close to being enough." A deep breath, and he looked away from her, a guttural edge bleeding into his deep voice as he said, "If anything, what happened in that hotel room today only jacked me up even tighter."

It would have been impossible to miss the tension in those graveled words, even if Morgan hadn't been watching him as closely as she was. "And that bothers you, doesn't it?"

Staring at the doors, he shrugged, saying, "Everything about you bothers me. It always has. But I still intend to screw your brains out the second we're back at our hotel tonight."

Morgan's breath caught on a sharp gasp, but before she could make any kind of response, the center door opened and Ashe Granger came through the doorway, his silver eyes widening with shock when he spotted her standing there with Kierland Scott. Dressed in black cashmere and jeans, the vamp was still as gorgeous as ever, his body long and lean and heavily muscled, his hair a rich, sable brown, the cut more severe than it'd been the last time Morgan had seen him. The short brush cut would have been too much for most men, but when you had a face like Ashe's, it didn't matter. In fact, it only accentuated the fact that his tall body and rugged face were...well, obscenely perfect.

It was said among the clans that the complex nature of the Deschanel was a delicate balance between the light and dark aspects of the world, and Ashe was a prime example. He was a thing of outrageous beauty, and yet...he was also a thing of sinister danger. The complex duality of his nature was a helpless allure to most women, and Morgan knew damn well that he never lacked for female companionship. But then, she also knew that none of the women who shared the vampire's bed ever meant anything to him. Though Ashe made sure his lovers enjoyed their time with him, he seldom even recalled their names once he'd left their beds, and Morgan couldn't help but feel sorry for her friend. After so many years on his own, she desperately wanted Ashe to find the love and peace and happiness that he deserved.

"Morgan," he purred in a low, decadent rumble, his smile a slow melding of sensual delight and hard-edged tension as he quickly snapped the door shut behind him and came toward her. "Stellar timing as always, sweetheart."

"You could sound a bit happier to see me," she murmured, her keen senses easily picking up on the predatory aggression she could feel blasting from the Watchman beside her. "I haven't seen you for almost three months."

"Happy isn't good enough to describe how I feel when I see you." His gaze slid to Kierland, and she could see him trying to figure out just *what* she was doing there with the Lycan. Ashe knew all about how Kierland had treated her for the past decade, and he wasn't shy about voicing his opinions on the subject. "I'm just not too keen on your company."

"Feeling's mutual," Kierland muttered, pushing away from the wall. His hands flexed at his sides, no doubt imagining how good it would feel to curl his fingers into a huge fist and knock Ashe clear off his feet.

"I've been trying to call you," she said quickly, moving a little to the side as she took a step forward, putting herself between the two primal, dominant males.

The corner of Ashe's mouth twitched, and he said, "I'm sorry I missed your calls, honey. But I lost my phone a few days ago."

Morgan grinned, since Ashe's inability to keep track of his cell phone was an ongoing thing with the sexy vamp. He might have had the IQ of a genius, but the guy was notorious for setting his phone down in public places and then forgetting to take it with him when he left.

Jerking his chin toward her, the Deschanel said, "I

imagine you've got something pretty important to say, seeing as how you've tracked me down, so let's get somewhere we can talk."

Surprised by the urgency she could sense in his husky words, Morgan started to ask him what was wrong, when the door behind him opened and four fair-haired Deschanel vampires came through, their pale eyes narrowing with fury when they spotted her and Kierland.

"What the hell is this?" the tallest of the group snarled, his gray eyes sliding over her face, before landing with a wrathful look of accusation on Ashe, who had turned to face the group.

Morgan didn't have a clue what was going on, but whatever it was, she had no doubt that it was going to be bad. Sensing serious danger, she was thankful that Kierland had moved closer to her side as she whispered, "Ashe?"

Under his breath, Ashe said, "Not now, Morgan."

"You working with these Watchmen?" the vamp on the far left growled.

"It's not what you think," Ashe told them, holding his hands up in one of those universal signals of *Let's just calm down and take it easy.* "I just ran into an old friend."

Dread turned cold in Morgan's veins, and she reached out, curling her fingers around Ashe's powerful arm. "What exactly were you doing in that room?"

"Shh," he whispered, shaking free of her touch as he stepped toward the blond vampires.

"I knew we couldn't trust him," snarled the tallest one again, looking around at his comrades. "Förmyndares are all the same. He wasn't interested in making a deal. He was just trying to set us up."

"Deacon's right," one of the others grunted, his face turning splotchy with rage.

"Morgan, get out of here," both Kierland and Ashe commanded at the same time, their deep voices shredding her pride. Obviously, neither of them thought she was strong enough to fight, expecting her to just turn tail and run. She wanted to tell them both off and stand her ground, but she could already feel the icy tendrils of panic clutching onto her throat at the thought of facing the vampires, the irrational fear like a set of murderous hands squeezing off her air supply.

Morgan turned on her heel, her vision swimming, knowing only that she needed to flee, to escape—but there was nowhere to go. Another half dozen golden-haired vampires were now blocking them from the rest of the club, their pale gazes focused directly on her.

*Oh, hell*, she thought, stumbling back a step, her heart all but pounding its way through her chest. As the sounds of battle broke out behind her, the wall of vampires moved closer, their eyes burning with hunger and rage. A screaming darkness crashed through Morgan's mind, her lungs burning, aching, desperate for air....

And then her world turned black.

# CHAPTER ELEVEN

AFTER MORGAN'S BLOODCURDLING scream caught their attention, Kierland and Granger finished off the four foulmouthed vampires who'd started the fight. Then they went after the second group who were taunting a clearly hysterical Morgan. The club's human customers had moved back, giving them a wide berth as they battled against the remaining blond vamps, all of whom looked to be related to the four that had followed Ashe out of that private room…and were now knocked unconscious on the floor.

Whatever Granger was mixed up in, Kierland would have been willing to bet his fortune that it wasn't good or legal or sane.

With the large human presence in the club, no one released their claws, talons or fangs, making the fight purely a contest of skill. The vampires were ruthless, but not as well trained as he and Granger. With a bone-crunching kick to the last vamp's jaw, the bastard went down…and stayed down. Pushing his hair back from his face, Kierland immediately turned toward Morgan, a low growl rumbling up from the depths of his chest at the sight of Ashe Granger already kneeling beside her. She sat on the floor, blood dripping unchecked from her nose, her eyes still hazy and unfocused with panic as she stared blankly into space. She'd obviously tried to fight the assholes, but hadn't been able to hold her own against them under the circumstances.

Not that he had any better understanding of what those circumstances were, except that she didn't do well when crowded in by people...or *vampires*.

With Ashe on her right, Kierland dropped to his knees on her left. He reached out to place a careful hand on her shoulder, and she flinched, shaking her head, her lashes fluttering. "It's over," he told her, keeping his voice as gentle as possible. She turned her head, blinking as she gave him a slight, shaky smile, and he started to reach for her, intending to lift her into his arms, when she turned to look at Ashe. In the next instant, she launched herself at the Deschanel, all but crawling her way up the guy's body.

"Get your damn hands off her," Kierland bit out, as Ashe clutched Morgan against his sweater-covered chest and moved to his feet.

The vampire rolled his gray eyes and started to step around him, but Kierland moved into his path, blocking his way, unable to control the rage that clawed through him at the sight of her in Granger's arms. He had no justification for it. No valid reason for objection, and certainly none that he would own up to, but it didn't stop him from saying, "If she needs to be held, then I'll do it."

Granger appeared torn between irritation and amusement. "It isn't sexual, you ass. I'm comforting her."

Baring his fangs, he repeated, "I'll do it."

Morgan's face burrowed deeper into the vampire's shoulder, her arms locked tight around his neck, and Granger slid Kierland a taunting smirk. "Call me crazy, wolf, but I don't think she wants you to."

"And you think you know what she wants?" he demanded in a quiet snarl, wanting to throw it in the arrogant vamp's face that Morgan had spent the afternoon in bed with *him*. That just hours ago, *he* was the man who'd been driving into her, making her scream with pleasure. The only thing that stopped him was the thought of how Morgan would react if he did it, which only pissed him off even more.

He didn't want to take her feelings into account, damn it. Especially when she was clinging onto the vamp like she wanted to slip under his freaking skin.

"I think I know her wants a hell of a lot better than you do," Ashe murmured in response to his question. "What were you thinking, taking her into a club full of vampires?"

"What do vamps have to do with anything?" he forced out through his gritted teeth.

"She can't stand them." Granger's head cocked a little to the side, his tone tinged with derision as he guessed, "Or didn't you know?"

Sweeping his gaze over the way she'd plastered herself against Granger's chest, Kierland made a thick, sarcastic sound in the back of his throat. "Yeah, she really looks like she can't stand you."

For a moment the Deschanel simply stared at him, and then a mocking smile slowly curled his mouth, re-

vealing the tip of a fang, and he pulled Morgan closer
to his chest. "I'm the rare exception to the rule. She
trusts me. Knows I'd rather die than hurt her." A pause,
and then he added, "Which is more than can be said
for the other men in her life."

"I'm not fighting with you now." Kierland ground
out the words, his rage and frustration like a physical
thing in his body, punching against his insides, his
wolf wanting the vamp's blood the way an addict
wanted his fix. "But as soon as she's calmed down, I'm
kicking your ass."

"I'll look forward to you trying," Ashe drawled,
heading toward the front exit as Kierland stepped
aside, then followed after them. No one bothered the
two tall, grim-looking males as they made their way
through the club, the human guests giving them a wide
berth. "Where are you staying?" the vampire asked,
once they were standing on the sidewalk, the bitter
January winds whipping at their clothes and hair.

Shoving his hands deep into his pockets, Kierland
told him they had rooms at the Whitney. Then he kept
pace at Granger's side as the vampire headed north
toward the hotel. "You gonna explain what you were
up to back there?"

His voice flat, Granger said, "Work."

"You're on assignment?" he growled, knowing that
the Förmyndares sometimes worked undercover for
the Consortium on special cases, infiltrating Deschanel
organizations whose illegal activities threatened the
security of the clans.

"It's not any of your goddamn business, but I'm not

working for the Consortium," Granger replied, his tone thick with scorn. "Not all of us care to sit around and wait for orders to be handed down. If there's a problem, we deal with it."

It wasn't the first time Kierland had heard that sort of insult levied against the Watchmen and their rules of engagement, and it wouldn't be the last. The highly trained shifters were never meant to interfere in the workings of the clans until their superiors said differently. They kept "watch" over the preternatural species and reported their findings, only acting when the Consortium ordered them to.

At least, that was how it was meant to work. The first time Kierland had broken the rules, Nicole had lost her life. His knee-jerk reaction had been to follow all future orders to the letter, to the point of obsession—until the Casus had returned and the Buchanans had needed his unit's help. And ever since Kierland and his friends had chosen to act on their own orders, waging war against the Casus without the consent of the Consortium, the Lycan had found himself breaking one rule after another. It was as if a chain reaction had been set into motion, culminating in those intensely erotic moments a few hours ago.

Suddenly, the Consortium's "golden boy" had become the biggest rule breaker of them all—not that Kierland would ever make such an admission to Granger. Instead, he curled his lip and muttered, "The rules that govern the Watchmen are there for a reason."

"And are you really going to lecture me about obeying those pompous bastards?" Granger questioned in an easy drawl. "From what I hear, wolf, you're no longer even on good terms with the grand ol' Consortium."

Kierland could have told him that the leaders now viewed him as a loose cannon that they couldn't control, but held his tongue. The last thing in the world he wanted to do was make it sound like he and the vamp actually had something in common. "My unit's fight against the Casus is nothing like your idea of vigilante justice, Granger, and you damn well know it."

"Sticks and stones," the vampire murmured, slanting him a wry smile as he lifted his dark brows. "And dare I ask what you're doing here? I've been trying to figure out what could possibly be dire enough to bring you and Morgan together, then send you coming after me. But I'm completely at a loss."

"We need a guide through the Wasteland," Kierland said in a raw, muted voice.

The Deschanel cut him a hard, swift look, all traces of sarcasm and humor dulled by shock. "What the hell for?"

Rubbing at the tension knots in the back of his neck, Kierland explained about his brother's plan to get captured by Westmore and taken to the Kraven's hidden compound, so that he could rescue Chloe Harcourt. Ashe shook his head the instant Kierland mentioned Kell's name, saying, "I should have known it had something to do with Kellan. No way in hell would Morgan risk something this insane unless someone she cared about was in trouble."

Kierland grunted in response, his thoughts suddenly

diverted by the strange realization that he hadn't reacted to the Deschanel's words with his customary possessive bite of jealousy. Two days ago, he'd have sworn that Morgan had, at some point in the past, been to bed with his brother, considering how close they were...and he'd have been wrong. She could have been lying all the times she'd told him that she and Kell had never been involved sexually, but for some illogical reason, Kierland actually believed her. He didn't trust her worth a damn, but he believed her. He had no proof. No evidence. And yet, as strange as it was, his gut instincts told him that they hadn't.

What was even stranger was the dawning discovery that even if they *had* screwed around together, Kierland would have still wanted her, and that thought was so bloody out of character for him that he wanted to retreat. Wanted to take ten steps back from the situation, from *her,* and give his mind the time to figure out what was happening to him.

Time, however, was something he didn't have.

He and Granger made the last block of the walk in silence, until they reached the Whitney and took one of the side elevators up to Morgan's room, avoiding any curious eyes in the hotel's lobby. "Is she asleep?" Kierland asked, unable to see her face beneath the heavy fall of her hair, her body relaxed in the vampire's arms.

"Barely," Granger murmured. "So keep your voice low."

It was impossible to conceal his worry as he asked, "Is this normal?"

Granger studied his expression with a mixture of

surprise and curiosity. "She reacts this way sometimes," he finally replied. "If the panic gets a strong enough hold on her, it pretty much wipes her out afterward."

As they exited the elevator on the eleventh floor, Kierland took out the extra key they'd given him at check-in and opened the door to her room. Stalking toward the huge window on the far side of the room, he stared out over the glittering city, listening as Granger softly pushed the door closed behind him. The fiercely possessive animal inside him writhed with the urge to turn around and rip Morgan out of the vampire's arms, but he locked himself in place, his every muscle coiled hard and tight with seething tension.

*Stay cool. Calm. And whatever I do, I can't let the bastard rile me.*

Kierland exhaled a rough breath of air, the predator in him enraged by the presence of a rival male...while the man in him struggled to make sense of the madness in his head. Finally, he locked his jaw, forcing himself to turn around, and had to bite back a sharp snarl at the sight of Granger sitting on the bed, another one of those crooked, mocking smiles curving his mouth as he returned Kierland's blistering stare.

The vamp sat with his back to the wooden headboard, Morgan's lean body draped across his wide chest, the side of her face resting trustingly against his shoulder. In that moment, with jealousy and hatred and raw aggression searing through his system, scraping him raw, Kierland could have happily driven his fangs into the bastard's throat without suffering a single moment of regret.

He didn't want to think about how good they looked together. How *right*. But he couldn't tear his gaze away, drawn to the sight of them the way a person's eyes were drawn to something horrible, like a roadside accident. Their hair was nearly the same burnished brown, and though Morgan's eyes were closed, Kierland knew they were almost the identical shade of gray as the vampire's.

As he watched Granger run his hand over her silken hair, cuddling her against his chest, it was painfully obvious to Kierland that the vamp still wanted her. That he still cared.

Holding Kierland's narrow stare, Granger spoke in a deep, quiet voice. "You're not going to tell them about the panic attacks, are you?"

The question caught Kierland off guard, and it took him a moment before he said, "Tell who?"

"The Consortium."

He slowly shook his head. "No, I'm not going to tell them. How often do they happen?"

"No idea," the vampire admitted with a grimace, his touch gentle as he looked down and pushed the stray strands of hair from Morgan's pale face. "She won't tell me."

Beginning to piece various fragments of the puzzle together, Kierland asked, "Is it because of the panic attacks that she wants to take the position on The Guard?"

A sharp nod, and Granger said, "She's not going to find the protection work nearly as exciting as what she does now, but she's looking forward to those wide-open spaces in Australia."

"Why?" He ground out the question, stalking toward the foot of the bed, unable to stand still. "I mean, why does she have the attacks?"

The vampire slowly lifted his head, his expression mocking as he held Kierland's burning stare. "What makes you think I know?" he asked in a laconic drawl, arching one of those dark brows again.

Kierland glared, a muscle ticking in his locked jaw, and the vampire sighed, saying, "Even if I wanted to tell you, wolf, it's not my secret to share."

"But she told *you,* didn't she?" he demanded, digging his fingers into the top edge of the footboard.

Another crooked smile, and the vampire conceded, "Actually, she didn't have much choice in the matter. I was determined to look after her. To be her friend when she needed one." A pause, and then he softly added, "Unlike some people."

The reins to Kierland's control slipped a little further out of his reach, and the wood of the footboard groaned as his fingers tightened their grip. In a raw, stifled voice, he said, "At least she's never had to fuck me for my help."

Instead of flinching at the crude accusation, Granger lowered his head, a slight half smile curving his mouth as he pressed a tender kiss to her smooth forehead. "Actually," he murmured, "you've never helped her at all. And I've always been willing to do anything Morgan wanted. All she's ever needed to do is ask."

"Is that right?" he snarled, no longer even sounding like a man.

Lifting his gaze, the vampire replied in a dry tone,

"I'm going to lead your ass across the Wasteland, aren't I? I should think that's answer enough."

"But when she came to you under the Consortium's orders, you didn't turn her down, did you?"

Granger slid him a laughing look. "No sane man would, I assure you. In fact, I've always wondered just where you found the willpower to keep your hands off her. It made me especially curious ten years ago, in light of the fact that you were so crazy about her."

Kierland found it impossible to hide his involuntary flinch, then realized that he really wasn't all that surprised that Granger had known how he'd felt about Morgan. It must have been obvious to anyone who had seen them together.

Granger shifted his focus toward the delicate bite wound on the side of Kierland's throat, barely visible above the collar of his dress shirt. "I'll tell you this, though," the Deschanel added, the low words roughened with a deliberate note of warning. "She's not always as tough as she pretends to be. Morgan needs loyalty. Not some jackass who's just going to use her and then toss her aside like yesterday's garbage."

Shaking his head at the bastard's audacity, he snapped, "If that's true, then why did you crush her by breaking things off with her? She was in love with you, you son of a bitch."

The vampire's lashes lowered, concealing the look in his eyes. "Considering how you've treated her for the past decade," he murmured, "I can't help but wonder why you would even care."

There was nothing that Kierland could say that wouldn't bury his ass ten feet into trouble, so he changed the subject. "Are you really going to be able to do it?" he demanded in a gritty rasp, shoving his hands back into his pockets. "Actually get us across the Wasteland? Or is this just some macho ego crap you've fed to Morgan?"

Laughter danced in the vampire's eyes, his smile cocky as he said, "You really don't like me, do you, wolf? Is it because of what I had with Morgan?" Pulling her tighter against his chest, his voice lowered as he continued, "Or is it because of what I have with her now?"

"Just answer the damn question."

"I can do it. It won't be pretty, but I can get you across."

For a moment, Kierland simply held Ashe's stare. "You screw this up," he finally warned in a quiet voice, "and there won't be anything left of you when I'm finished."

He turned then, heading for the door, unable to stomach the sight of Morgan in the vampire's arms for another moment. He'd just pulled open the door, when Granger called out to him. "Just one more thing."

Kierland looked over his shoulder, and in a soft voice, the vampire said, "Hurt her, and I'll have you gutted before you even know what's hit you."

A slow, feral smile twisted the Lycan's mouth. "I can't tell you how much I'd love to see you try," he shot back.

Then he stalked out of the room, determined to find a way to forget about the infuriating little Watchman wrapped up in his enemy's arms.

THE SLAMMING OF THE DOOR brought Morgan back to a jarring, aching awareness, a low groan spilling from her lips as she lurched upright into a sitting position.

"Easy there, sweetheart. You've had a helluva night."

Despite the lingering pains from her fight with the vampires, she managed a shaky smile. It was impossible not to love the sound of Ashe's voice, the husky blend of Eastern European and cultured British dazzling her senses. "I'm okay now," she told him, touched by the concern she could see tightening his beautiful eyes, the shadow of a beard darkening his jaw only accentuating his dangerous looks.

"You sure?" he pressed, using the sleeve of his cashmere sweater to dab at her bloodied nose, and she nodded in response, laying her cheek against his chest again. "What do you do when I'm not around?" he asked, his touch gentle as he pushed her hair from her face.

With a stiff shrug of her shoulders, Morgan gave him an honest answer. "I manage on my own."

"You shouldn't have to," he muttered, running his hand down her back.

"Yeah, well, you shouldn't be doing whatever it was you were doing in that club tonight," she argued.

His chest shook beneath her cheek with breathless laughter, and Morgan could hear the smile in his voice as he said, "Touché."

"So, um, where's Kierland?" she asked, trying to sound casual, though she knew the intuitive vamp could read her too easily.

"If I had to guess," Ashe rumbled, playing with the

ends of her hair, "I'd say he went downstairs to the bar after storming out of here. The wolf definitely looked like he could use a drink. Or three."

Groaning, she pulled back so that she could look him in the face. "Did you fight with him?"

"Not yet," he admitted, a lazy grin curving his lips. "But I relish the opportunity."

"Men," she muttered, her eyes narrowing as she noticed the dark shadows lurking beneath the vampire's silver eyes. "What's going on with you, Ashe?"

"Just the usual," he responded too quickly, his arms locked in an easy hold around her waist. "Work's been crazy. The Casus's return has caused every kind of madness. Seems like all the psychos and megalomaniacs are coming out of the woodwork these days, eager for their slice of the power pie. If the Consortium doesn't wise up, it's going to find itself toppled before this thing is over."

Crossing her arms over her chest, Morgan frowned. "I'm sure you're right, but I think you're involved in something that's…more personal to you than work. Or maybe to your family. When Kierland and I went to Gideon's apartment in Prague, someone had trashed it. Then I find you hanging out with those creeps tonight at that club, doing God only knows what."

She could see his brain working as he decided how much to tell her, weighing it against how much to keep to himself, and then with a tired sigh, he said, "Yeah, we've got some family troubles, but it's nothing that Gideon and I can't handle."

Watching him carefully, she asked, "Did you know that Gideon is working with Kierland?"

He answered with a nod, saying, "Gid told me the last time we talked." His mouth twisted with a wry smile as he added, "I guess it just goes to show that taste doesn't always run in the family."

She wanted to know if Kierland had told him why they'd tracked him down, and Ashe told her that he had. "As grateful as I am for your help, I want you to promise me that you won't start any fights on this trip," she told him, her firm tone warning him that she meant business.

Curiosity smoldered in his eyes, but instead of giving her the third degree about her relationship with the sexy Lycan, he just grinned at her, stating, "You still love to boss me around, don't you?"

"Promise me," she persisted.

With a theatrical wince, he cursed under his breath. "Come on, Morgan. That's just cruel."

"I mean it, Ashe."

"All right," he groaned, pulling a face. "I promise. But you're no fun, lady."

"Tell me about it." Sighing, Morgan leaned down, pressing the side of her face against his chest, and smiled at the heavy thumping of his heart—just one more thing that the human folklore had gotten so wrong about Ashe's species. "Was Kierland mad when he left?" she asked in a quiet voice, remembering how the Lycan had looked when she'd instinctively thrown herself into Ashe's arms.

A low, rugged laugh, and he answered, "He glared

at me like he wanted to rip my head off, but he wasn't mad at you, sweetheart. To be honest, he seemed worried as hell every time he looked at you. As well as confused." A pause, and then he quietly continued, "I take it you haven't told him about what happened to you with the rogues."

Sinking her teeth into her lower lip, Morgan shook her head. "I can't," she rasped, the husky words scratching her throat. "I don't want him to know about the past, Ashe."

"Why not?" They were gentle words, without any judgment or criticism, but she knew from past conversations that Ashe didn't agree with her.

"Because it wouldn't make any difference now," she told him, thinking about the situation. There was something odd about Kierland's actions that she couldn't quite put her finger on. If he was using her to get back at Ashe, like she'd accused him of wanting to do before they'd slept together, then why had the stubborn Lycan left her in the comfort of the vampire's arms? Why hadn't he used the opportunity to create a scene?

Morgan was still mulling over the question, when Ashe said, "So, you finally slept with him."

Her body jolted with surprise, an unsettling mixture of shock and hurt instantly ripping through her system as her brain zinged to the logical conclusion. "He told you that?" she choked out.

"No, he didn't say anything, honey. But...I can tell."

A piercing wave of relief made her light-headed, and she buried her face against his chest. "You're crazy, Ashe. Especially if you think I'm going anywhere near that subject with you."

"You can't lie to me, angel." His hand moved to her hair, stroking its length. There was nothing sexual in the soothing touch. It was simply comfort…caring. "I know you too well."

She closed her eyes, feeling as if her blush would burn its way through his sweater, and she knew he could feel the heat. "Please don't make me talk about this," she said in a muffled voice. "I can't explain, because I don't understand it myself."

Ashe seemed to ponder that for a moment, before saying, "So then there wasn't an undying declaration of love, I take it."

Bitterness flavored her low laugh, and it was a moment before she was able to swallow past the knot in her throat, somehow managing to state, "He wants to screw me out of his system."

He tipped her chin up and smiled down into her face, his eyes glittering with a strange blend of wicked humor and a shadowed kind of sadness. "Well, I could have told him that's not possible."

Morgan rolled her eyes. "You know you don't want me like that anymore."

Snorting, he said, "You know so much, do you?"

"Despite the heat burning in your skin right now," she murmured, placing her hand against the side of his warm throat, "you know I leave you cold, Ashe."

"It didn't have to be that way." His voice was low, careful…as if he was taking extra care with his words, but then he always did take care with her. Taking her hand from his throat, he held it in his and ran his thumb across her knuckles, his voice a dark, velvety rumble as he said, "I still believe that if you'd been able to give me your heart, I'd have started the burning."

The "burning" for Deschanel males began when they met the one woman who was meant to be theirs for all eternity. Although they could take or borrow "heat" for a time from their non-Deschanel lovers, only their life-mates could initiate the permanent change within their bodies that would banish the cold forever.

Softly, she argued, "I don't believe it would have worked that way, Ashe. Someday you'll meet a woman who sets you on fire, and then you'll understand the difference."

His lips twitched, a wry smile touching the corners of his mouth. "You don't know everything, Miss Smarty Pants. If you looked at me the way you look at the wolf, I'd probably go up in flames."

Morgan was still shaking her head when he asked, "Was he gentle with you?"

"What kind of question is that?" she spluttered, her face burning as she pushed away from his chest.

"Sounded straightforward to me," he rumbled, his grin turning wicked. "Now let's hear you give a straightforward answer."

A heart-pounding silence, and then she finally choked out a response. "Gentle is definitely not a word I would use to describe the experience," she told him, keeping her gaze focused on the strong shape of his chin, too uncomfortable to look him in the eye.

"Good."

Raising her brows, Morgan couldn't help but give an amazed laugh as she lifted her gaze to his. "And this from the vamp who treated me like something that might break every time he touched me."

Rolling one muscular shoulder, Ashe stated, "That was what you needed back then." He rubbed his thumb against the corner of her mouth, then teasingly brushed his fist against her chin. "But you're different now. Stronger."

"Not that strong," she groaned, any pleasure she'd felt in his words fading as she thought about what'd happened at the club. "I was a total wreck tonight, Ashe. And I seem to be freaking out on a regular basis now, even when I'm fighting, which has never happened before. The past few days have been so embarrassing."

"It's probably just the stress that you're under," he told her, his deep voice warm with concern. "And you know damn well that it's not something for you to be ashamed of. Christ, what you went through was a nightmare, Morgan. It's a miracle that you even survived."

With her stomach in knots, she argued, "I've been under stress before, and it's never been like this."

"Yeah, but these past few months have been rough. You've been worried about the war, and now you're worried about Kellan. Though I guess it could also have something to do with the wolf," he suggested.

Her eyes went wide. "What would Kierland have to do with it?"

A slow grin crossed Ashe's mouth. "Think about it, sweetheart. When you're around Scott, you probably use so much of your emotional energy fighting your feelings for him, you end up not having enough strength left to hold off your panic, the way you're usually able to do."

Morgan started to respond, thinking he just might be on to something, but her words got lost behind a long, exhausted yawn that caught her by surprise. "Sorry," she murmured, covering her mouth as she yawned again. The comforting combination of the warm hotel room and Ashe's strong embrace were lulling her to sleep, her system crashing now that she felt safe and secure.

The vampire's deep voice was hypnotically soothing as he pulled her against his chest. "Shh. Just try to get some rest, honey. We can work this all out later. Right now you need some sleep."

"You won't leave?" she whispered, her eyes so heavy she could barely keep them open, the emotional strain of the past few days suddenly catching up to her.

Stroking her back, he told her, "I'm staying right here."

"You've always been too good to me," she said sleepily, cuddling against Ashe's warm chest, his arms cradling her in a strong, protective hold.

But it was the Lycan's grim, gorgeous face that Morgan saw when she closed her eyes.

# CHAPTER TWELVE

*The Wasteland*
*Tuesday evening*

KIERLAND FIGURED IT WAS A TRUE measure of his madness that Morgan looked mouthwatering even when wrapped up in layers of winter clothing. Though most of the clan species could withstand the cold better than humans, the three of them had still needed sweaters and jackets for their journey through the severe climate of the Wasteland.

They'd begun their journey in the early hours of the morning and had headed north by train, making excellent time into Norway. Thanks to the humans who'd allowed him to take their blood the week before, Granger was able to travel in the sunlight, since the Deschanel could temporarily "assume" certain traits of those they fed from. Kierland didn't understand exactly how it worked, but apparently some species, like humans, could give the vampires the ability to walk in the sunlight for up to a week. And seeing as how it would never become lighter than a dusky twilight in the Wasteland this time of year, Granger's aversion to sunlight wouldn't be a problem once they were there.

Having never before traveled into the Wasteland, Kierland had been unsure how it would work, but Granger had known of the easiest, southernmost entry point, which had saved them hours of travel time. Protected by spells that made the region invisible to humans, the Wasteland was a vast, bitterly cold prison that "shared" physical space with the Scandinavian forests surrounding it. Kellan could have probably spouted a more elaborate, technical explanation, using words like "dimension" and "time/space continuum," but then that was Kell for you. His brother always had been too clever for his own good, and Kierland could only pray that Kell's keen intellect would be enough to keep him alive in the coming days.

And when he finally got his hands on him, Kierland was going to plant a kiss on the idiot…and then kick his ass for scaring the ever-loving hell out of him. Then, when his brother had picked himself up off the ground, he was going to kick his ass all over again for putting him in this untenable situation, where he was stuck with Granger and Morgan. His resentment towards the vamp grew with each step they took, while his hunger for the female Watchman seethed beneath his skin, turning him inside out.

Once they'd entered the Wasteland, Morgan had set the direction they would travel, following the "pull" of Kellan's blood that would eventually lead them to him. After hiking for five solid hours— Granger's knowledge of the dangerous lands keeping them in so-called neutral territory that had yet to be claimed by any exiled families—they'd finally stopped to make camp in a small snow-dusted glade, all of their tempers on edge, exhaustion already taking its toll. It was cold, dark and windy, flurries of snow whipping down from the slate-gray sky, the rugged terrain a combination of steep hills and thick forest, making it impossible to use any kind of mechanical transportation, such as snowmobiles. But even if the land had been clear and flat, the spells that made the use of cell phones impossible within the Wasteland had a similar effect on engines. As a result, they'd been forced to travel on foot, their equipment limited to what they could carry on their backs.

Though he and Granger had been doing their best to ignore each other, the Deschanel turned away from the small fire he'd just started in the center of the glade, leaving Morgan kneeling beside the crackling flames, and headed toward the place where Kierland stood. When the vamp came to a stop no more than a few feet away from the massive, towering pine tree that Kierland was leaning against, he met the Lycan's belligerent glare and muttered, "I got a weird feeling we were being followed a while back, but haven't been able to pick up anything specific. You?"

"I've had a similar feeling," he admitted, while part of him objectively observed, slack jawed, the fact that he was talking to Ashe Granger in a semi-casual manner. But he didn't want to waste time fighting with the bastard when they were in such hostile territory, the danger increasing with each step that they took into the vast wilderness. "You think we're just projecting?" he asked. "Looking for trouble because we haven't found any yet?"

A wry smile touched the vamp's mouth, and he laughed as he ran a hand over his short hair. "Could be. God knows this place has always given me the creeps," he murmured, casting a rueful look across their bleak surroundings, before locking his gaze with Kierland's again. "But I was wondering if you think it might be those Death-Walkers you've got coming after you? Gideon told me about them the last time we talked."

Kierland shook his head. "Unless they've managed to mask their scent, we'd know, because they smell like something that's been left to rot in the heat. Even out here, where the snow and the constant winds make tracking near impossible, we'd be able to tell if they were close. But, I'm not sure if they even have the balls to follow us too deeply into the Wasteland."

The vamp gave another gritty laugh. "Pretty sad when a bunch of rotting psychopaths have more sense than we do, huh?"

"Lately, it feels like everyone and everything has more sense than I do," he muttered dryly, surprised to find himself momentarily bantering with the guy.

"I know the feeling." Granger worried two fingers against his shadowed jaw, then gave a firm nod. "I'm going to run a perimeter and make sure there's nothing too close, just to be safe. Even without the possibility of Death-Walkers, Casus, Kraven and Collective soldiers coming after us, we've still got to be on the lookout for the vamps who live in this shit hole. With the way we Deschanel can mask our scent, they could be right on top of us before we even know they're there. And from what I've seen of them, the vampires imprisoned here are more trouble than we need at the moment."

The vamp made his way back to the fire and spoke briefly to Morgan, then headed into the thick forest, leaving them alone. Kierland remained against the tree, just watching her, while wishing he'd remembered to pick up some cigarettes before they'd set off. God only knew that he needed one, his system so jacked up it was a wonder he could stand still.

She had a tired, kind of tense expression on her face as she stared into the flickering flames, her mind obviously a million miles away, leaving him free to stare, soaking in the fine-grained beauty of her profile. As he stood there, fighting to hold himself away from her, he couldn't help remembering the phone call he'd had with Quinn when he'd left her room last night.

Left her room, and headed down to the bar by himself…leaving her in the arms of another man.

After choosing one of the booths in the far corner of the dark, wood-paneled bar, Kierland had just lifted his Scotch to his lips when his phone rang. A half-minute later, after he'd explained where he was and what had happened, he'd downed the contents of the highball and muttered, "What is this? The conference call from hell?"

Quinn and Aiden had given dark laughs at the other end of the line, then continued to accuse him of being a stubborn bastard, one who always refused to practice what he preached. Though he wanted to argue, badly, he couldn't. Kierland knew his friends were right. He had no problem dishing out advice to the men who were like family to him, but hell if he ever applied that advice to his own circumstances.

The conversation had continued with claims that he was being a "hypocritical jackass" and a few sharp, guttural warnings that he was going to lose her, for good, if he wasn't careful. Of course, Kierland's bitter response was that he couldn't lose something that had never been his to begin with. Then he'd added, for good measure, the fact that he had no desire to saddle himself with a woman like Morgan Cantrell for the rest of his friggin' life, to which his friends had responded with another round of biting accusations.

He'd shot back that she was probably still in love with Ashe Granger.

They'd argued that if Kierland wasn't man enough to fight for her, then he didn't deserve her.

Digging his fingers into his tired eyes, he'd finally snarled that they didn't know what the hell they were talking about, after which they'd both called him an uptight control freak—one who would never learn to be happy if he didn't get rid of the stick up his ass. Since the conversation was obviously going nowhere, Kierland had changed the subject, telling them of Morgan's theory about the Dark Markers possibly being the keys that would open the gate to Meridian. Their attention diverted, the Watchmen had grilled him for details, and they'd found themselves engrossed in a tense discussion about the war.

"The Death-Walkers are the element that worries me the most," Quinn had grunted, "and not just because they're coming after my friends. It's the fact that they don't give a rat's ass about anything. Once the humans find out about them—"

"The shit's gonna really hit the fan," Aiden had cut in, finishing Quinn's thought.

After he'd promised to watch his back and get in touch with them as soon as possible, Kierland had ended the call. He'd had another drink, and had tried to sit back and chill. Breathe. Relax. But it hadn't worked. All he could think about was Morgan in her room, lying in that bastard's arms. Anger and lust and jealousy were all twisted up inside him, coiling him in knots, his face hot, his grip on the highball so tight it was a wonder the glass didn't shatter in his hand.

Eventually, he'd given up trying to fight it and had gone back upstairs, letting himself into Morgan's hotel room. The vamp had fallen asleep on the bed with her, still cradling her in his arms. The urge to throw the dickhead out on his ass had been nearly impossible to resist, and yet, he'd held off, knowing she needed the rest…the peace. So he'd settled down on the sofa instead. He'd felt like an idiot, but he hadn't been able to go to his own room and leave her there with Granger.

It was becoming clearer to him that in so many ways, he didn't know the real Morgan Cantrell at all. He'd created an "image" of her in his mind, which he'd used as a target for his anger and frustration, but…that wasn't the real Morgan. She was tough and could be a hard-ass when she needed to be. She was strong and fierce and could stand up to him, refusing to take his shit. But she was also kind and soft and almost…

fragile. As delicate as antique lace or the furled, tender petals of a flower in bloom. As ethereal as a misty, lavender dawn...or the first glistening, shimmering rays of sunlight after a storm.

Embarrassing, the way he was waxing poetic about her, but it couldn't be helped. His friggin' head was spinning just from looking at her, remembering every moment of those blistering hours in that hotel room in Weesp, his damn dick so hard he could have hammered through a bloody wall.

She was, in reality, a complex blend of tenderness and strength—white-hot...dangerous...fascinating— and if there'd been a chance in hell he thought it could happen without ending in disaster, Kierland would have wanted to keep her more than he'd ever desired anything in his entire life.

*Aw, hell,* he thought, scrubbing his hands down his face, his beard stubble scratching against his palms. Who was he trying to fool with that line? Just because he knew he couldn't keep her didn't mean he wanted her any less. He knew it was madness, but he couldn't stop thinking about getting her under him again. And after the crazy, out of control sex, he wanted to cradle her in his arms and just hold her against his heart, telling her how precious she was...how beautiful...how brave.

*And just what in God's name is that about?* he silently snarled, digging his fingers into his eyes.

"You seem tired."

The soft words jerked Kierland out of his thoughts like a splash of cold water in his face. He lowered his hands, blinking, surprised to find Morgan standing before him, staring into his eyes…waiting for a response. Clearing his throat, he shoved his hands into his pockets and simply said, "It was a long night."

"LONGER FOR SOME THAN others," Morgan murmured, unable to disguise the bitterness in her voice.

He cocked his head a little to the side, obviously picking up on the strain in her words. "If there's something you want to say, just say it."

"Okay. Where did you go last night?" she whispered, the words tumbling out in a breathless rush. Morgan knew she was nuts for even asking him, but she couldn't stop herself. It had been driving her crazy all goddamn day. "While I was with Ashe? I know you came back to the room and slept on the sofa, but where were you before then? What were you doing?"

He drew his brows together in a scowl, the brackets lining his mouth deepening with anger. "Wait a minute. Are you serious?"

Pushing her hands into her coat pockets, she wet her bottom lip and nodded, her stomach twisting with nerves.

He narrowed his eyes, the pale green beginning to glow with an unearthly light as he asked, "What do you think I was doing?" His voice was deceptively soft, but Morgan could hear the undercurrent of anger sharpening the words to a lethal point.

"I think you went to the bar downstairs and…" She swallowed, unable to get the words out—but it didn't matter. She could see from the grim, shocked lines of his expression that he knew exactly what she was getting at.

He ran his tongue over his teeth, then forced out two low, guttural words. "I didn't."

The way Morgan's heart lurched in response told her how badly she wanted to believe him. Stupid, but she couldn't help it. Taking a swift breath, she turned her face to the side, staring at the tangle of snow-covered limbs in the surrounding forest. "I'd be an idiot to believe you," she whispered, shaking her head.

"Damn it, Morgan. I didn't screw anyone!"

She flinched from the brutal force of his words, her gaze whipping back to his, caught by the fierce burn of emotion smoldering in that pure, beautiful green. She wanted so badly to believe him, which just made her feel like a bloody fool.

"I could have had a woman under me, if I'd wanted one." Husky words, heavy with restraint, as if he was struggling to sound calm. "But the only woman I was interested in was cuddled up in bed with a vamp. So I had a couple of drinks and came back upstairs to sleep on your bloody sofa."

"Why?" she murmured, her gaze locked with his. She couldn't have looked away even if she'd wanted to. "Why did you come back to my room? Was it because you didn't trust me with Ashe?"

He pulled his hand from his pocket, shoving his long fingers through his windblown hair as he growled, "I was worried about you, damn it!"

Her breath caught on a gasp, and she pulled her bottom lip through her teeth, wanting so badly to touch him...kiss him, even though she knew it would be stupid. A mistake. She was already obsessed, unable to get him out of her mind. Any extra contact at this point was only going to make it worse.

In a soft voice, she asked, "What do you want from me, Kierland?"

"Something I can't have," he muttered, looking away. "Something that doesn't even exist."

Fighting the urge to reach out and touch his hard, shadowed jaw with the tips of her fingers, she whispered, "I don't know what that means."

A rough, gritty bark of laughter tore from his throat, and this time it was his turn to shake his head. "You don't want to know, Morgan. Trust me."

With a deep breath, she forced herself to take a step back, deepening the distance between them. "It doesn't matter anyway," she said in a soft rush, knowing she needed to turn around and walk away, before she did something stupid. "This was a bad idea. I don't know what we were thinking. What happened between us, it…it didn't make anything better."

His head shot up, nostrils flaring as he pushed away from the tree. "There's no going back now." He ground out the words, his eyes gleaming within the dusky shades of twilight.

"No, listen. Three nights ago you were picking up two women in a club. Despite what you think of me, Kier, that's not the speed I move at. I like sex, and I'm not ashamed to admit it. But I'm not…I don't play the field like you do. It *means* something to me. There may be no love lost between us. I mean, I know you were just looking for a physical release to burn out whatever it is…lingering between us, but I'm not wired that way."

For a long, strained moment, he simply stared down at her, his eyes heavy-lidded, the muscular wall of his chest heaving with the ragged force of his breath. And then he was standing right in front of her, his powerful body pressing against her, his big hands holding the sides of her face, tilting her head back. "I didn't want it to, but it means something to me, too." Gruff, thick words that vibrated with hunger. "So stop thinking I'm looking for another woman to score with, because that's not gonna happen."

Blinking up at him, she said the first words that popped into her mind. "But you don't even like me, Kierland."

He shook his head a little, a wry smile touching the corner of his mouth. "I never said that."

She rolled her eyes. "I think our history speaks for itself."

He blew out a rough, shuddering breath of air, and pressed his forehead against hers, his fingers shaping themselves around her skull. "My feelings are...complicated where you're concerned, Morgan. But if I didn't like you," he rasped, his voice low...raw, "I never would have given a damn about what happened between you and Granger."

"You are so confus—" she started to say, but the rest of her words were lost in his mouth. Stolen right off her tongue.

The deep, open-mouthed kiss was deliciously wild, hungry and gnawing, his body rubbing against hers in a way that made her breath get all stuck in her throat. He licked the inside of her mouth as if he was eating at her taste…her flavor, the sensual act one of the most erotic things Morgan had ever experienced, and her body answered with a startling, dizzying wave of heat.

She'd never have guessed that he would enjoy kissing as much as he did, but it was obvious in the way that he ravaged her mouth with deep, seductive licks and nibbles and thrusts. It was hypnotic, rich and drugging and achingly delightful, every rough breath and hungry stroke of his tongue pulling up sensations from the churning depths of her soul.

Growling low in his throat, he twisted around, switching their positions, a sudden urgency in his movements as he pressed her against the thick trunk of the same pine tree he'd been leaning against. She gasped, her pulse roaring as he tore open her jacket, shoving her sweater up and pulling the cup of her bra down until her pink nipple was bared to the elements, puckered from the cold. Morgan shivered, then cried out as his hot mouth closed over the sensitive tip, burning and wet. He suckled her greedily, working her nipple against the roof of his mouth, while he ripped at the button on her jeans, tugging on the zipper. Then he pushed his hand inside the opening, shoving those long fingers inside her panties, reaching deep until he was touching the hot, drenched folds of her sex.

"You're still swollen," he groaned, licking her nipple, then catching it playfully with his teeth. His eyes flicked up to her face, full of secrets and hunger and things she needed more brain cells to analyze, but all the blood was rushing to the place where his fingers touched her, pulsing in the swollen knot of nerves caught beneath the deliciously callused pad of his thumb. "Too sore?" he asked, pushing two thick fingers into the slick, tender opening of her sex, stretching her as he forced them deep, up to the knuckles.

Morgan shook her head, unable to keep her hips from shoving forward, seeking more of that intimate penetration. Snowflakes fell onto the dark spill of his auburn hair, catching at the tips of his long lashes. His eyes burned greener, as if they were soaking in the colors of the wintry forest.

Then he kissed her again, and she was undone by the hot silk and velvety softness of his mouth. Ways she'd never thought of Kierland before. He was so hard and aggressive on the outside, and yet, his kisses were full of lush, carnal promise. They were like foreplay all on their own, and she melted from the sensual onslaught, drowning in hunger and blistering sensation.

Curling his thick fingers inside her, he stroked the slick, sensitive depths of her body as he broke the kiss, his breath hot and fast against her cheek. Words tumbled out of his mouth, husky and rough. "I can't stop thinking about you. About how you feel, how you taste. How tight this sweet little piece of you is. How it holds me. Sucks me in." He pressed his warm mouth to the coolness of her face, rubbing pleasure into her skin. "I want to spend hours inside you, Morgan. I want to stay there until we can't remember our bloody names."

"Yes!" she hissed, going crazy at the thick, rigid pressure of him grinding against her hip. She was desperate to touch him. To hold his heavy shaft in the coolness of her palm. Breathless and aching,

Morgan reached for his fly, but he suddenly grabbed onto her wrist.

"Wait," he grunted, immediately pulling his other hand out of her pants. "Something's wrong."

"What?" She shook her head as if trying to wake up from a dream. "What's wrong?"

Kierland lifted his head, sniffing at the air. "Shit, something's coming. Don't move," he growled, drawing one of the guns they'd picked up that morning as he turned to face the clearing. She fumbled with the button and zipper on her jeans, oddly bemused by the fact that Kierland had situated himself in front of her, as if she was going to cower behind his back. His protective streak was kinda sweet, but she had no intention of allowing him to face the coming danger on his own, without her help.

No matter what was out there, she would fight beside him. Though the darkness was deepening around them, she had a wide-open sky over her head, and fresh air gusting against her face. No way in hell was she going to let the panic sink its teeth into her again.

A second later Ashe loped into the glade, his gun drawn, as well. "We have company."

"How many?" Kierland grunted.

"One Deschanel male for sure. Maybe more."

"How close?" Morgan asked, pulling her own gun from the pocket of her coat. Bullets alone weren't going to kill a vamp, but at least they'd slow it down.

Before Ashe could answer her question, a raspy voice came from the trees off to their left. "Not nearly as close as I'd like to be," challenged a tall, rangy male, his wild eyes glowing an unnatural silver in the flickering light cast from the fire. Morgan could tell from his scent that he was a Deschanel. He was dressed in boots, bloodstained jeans and a torn black T-shirt, his skin covered in a glistening sheen of sweat, as if he didn't even register the cold. "Do you know you're trespassing on my land?" he demanded, his English heavily accented.

Ashe's deep voice was calm, if not friendly. "This is neutral territory."

"Not anymore," the male argued in a rising voice, his gray gaze jerking over Kierland and Ashe, before flitting to Morgan's face, where it stayed. He was over six foot, his powerful body lean, making the definition of packed muscle sharper beneath his pale skin. Thick, chocolate-brown hair was brushed back from his flushed face, which would have been handsome if it weren't for the heavy, potent pulse of madness vibing off him. "I've claimed this land as my own," he added, "which means that everything on it belongs to me."

The vamp was clearly off his rocker, and Morgan's stomach knotted with tension, a slithering sensation coating her skin at the way he kept staring at her, his bloodshot gaze moving slowly over the front of her body, lingering on her breasts...her thighs. There was a dark, reddish smear at the corner of his wide mouth that looked like dried blood, and she wondered who or what he'd last attacked.

"We don't want any trouble," Kierland said in what she could tell was a forced effort at sounding reasonable. "We're not staying. Just passing through."

"You want across my land," the vampire snarled, cutting a dark look toward Kierland as he released his razor-sharp talons from the tips of his fingers, "then you're gonna have to fight me for the woman." He took a deep breath, and Morgan knew he was pulling in her scent. His tongue flicked against his lower lip, as if he could taste her there, and his voice roughened with lust as he added, "She smells good enough to eat."

"Oh, hell. This is the last damn thing that we needed," she whispered, checking her grip on the gun. "I thought you said you could get us across the Wasteland without any problems, Ashe."

"I never said one of us wouldn't have to fight for what we want," Ashe replied, his tone deceptively mild. "And by *want,* I do mean you, sweetheart."

"Damn it, Ashe. Did you do this on purpose?" she gasped, turning an incredulous look on him.

"Come on," he snorted. "Would I do a thing like that?"

Before she could respond, Kierland took an aggressive step forward. "If I find out you deliberately put her in danger," he growled, his deep voice vibrating with rage, "you're a dead man."

The corner of Ashe's mouth twitched with a wry smile. "I don't know what you're so upset about, Lycan. Now's your chance to prove to her how badly you want her."

She jabbed her finger against the center of Ashe's chest, her voice shaking. "Who said Kierland has to do the fighting?"

"Trust me, sweetheart." A lazy, laughing drawl, as if Ashe was actually enjoying the horrific situation.

"There isn't a chance in hell the wolf is gonna let me fight for you. Isn't that right, Lycan?"

Kierland muttered something ugly under his breath about Ashe's parentage, then handed her his gun. "You'd better hold on to that for me," he rasped, holding her worried gaze as he slipped out of his jacket, tossing it over a low-hanging branch.

"Don't do this," she pleaded, begging him with her eyes. "Please, Kier. Just…just shoot him and let's get out of here."

"You know I can't do that," he grunted, shaking his head.

"Why not?" she whispered, keeping a careful watch on the vampire from the corner of her eye. "Because he issued a challenge? Forget your freaking pride, Kier. This guy isn't sane. Something bad could happen."

"How about a little faith?" he muttered, making her want to grab his broad shoulders and shake some bloody sense into him. But he was already turning away from her, heading toward the waiting challenger. When he stood about ten feet in front of the restless vampire, he stopped and flexed his hands, his body held lightly on the balls of his feet, waiting for the vamp to make the first move.

"Be careful he doesn't bite you," Ashe called out. "Some of the exiled clans are poisonous."

"THIS JUST KEEPS GETTING BETTER and better," Kierland muttered under his breath, keeping a careful eye on his opponent as the vampire flexed his talon-tipped fingers. There was a glazed look of insanity in the guy's pale eyes, his skin slicked with a light sheen of sweat despite the bitter, biting cold.

"Come on, wolf. Let's see what you've got."

In the next instant, the vamp launched his attack, and Kierland gave himself over to his instincts, blocking a series of powerful kicks, then countering with a swift right hook followed immediately by an uppercut that jerked the vamp's head back with a sharp crack. The Deschanel roared, lashing out with his talons, and Kierland had to duck and weave to avoid the lethal swipes, before twisting around and nailing the vamp in the kidneys with a powerful roundhouse. Although the guy was obviously a hell of a fighter, he couldn't maintain his balance, and he stumbled, falling to his knees. Keeping his arms loose at his sides, Kierland bounced lightly on his feet, waiting for the vamp to get up, but he didn't. Instead, a sharp scream poured from the guy's throat, and he curled his arms over his head, his body shuddering as if he was in excruciating pain.

"What's the matter with him?" Kierland grunted, his brows pulled together in a deep scowl as he kept a wary eye on the vampire.

"He's been poisoned." The soft words came from the other side of the clearing, where a petite, dark-haired woman was stepping out of the thick forest, her pale face pinched with worry.

"Who the hell are you?" Granger demanded.

"My name is Juliana Sabin," she replied, then gestured toward the vampire who was now slowly dragging himself back to his feet, his body swaying, as if he'd been drugged. "And that's Micah, my brother. He's...unwell. I ask that you turn him over to us."

"Us?" Kierland asked, keeping a careful eye on his opponent.

"My guards," she explained. There was a rustling of leaves, and four males came through the trees, flanking her sides. "If you'll let us, we'd like to take custody of Micah."

"Stay out of this, Jules," the vampire slurred, and then he staggered forward, targeting Kierland with a savage slash of his talons. Kierland dipped back, then swept his left leg low, catching the vampire on the backs of his calves. With his balance already off, Sabin pitched forward, going down hard on his knees again, his body shaking with what appeared to be some kind of violent convulsion. Acting swiftly, Kierland trapped the vampire's hands behind his back and shoved him face first into the snow-dusted ground.

"Please, don't hurt him!" the young woman cried. As Kierland braced his knee in the center of Sabin's back, keeping his struggling arms pinned, she came closer, walking around the fire.

"Remember what I said about certain nests here being poisonous," Granger called out. "I don't recall anything about the Sabin nest, but I wouldn't let her get too close if I were you."

"We're not one of the infected families," the female argued, stopping a few feet away from where Kierland had trapped her brother against the ground. "But when we were exiled to the Wasteland several years ago, Micah was infected by a rogue female. We haven't been able to extract the poison or find a cure, but it isn't a contagious strain."

"Some of them are also liars," Granger murmured. For whatever reason, he'd clearly taken a disliking to the woman, his tone thick with derision. "So be careful what you believe. This is, after all, a prison. If the Sabins are here, there's a good reason for it."

Juliana compressed her lips, refusing to argue, though her eyes glistened with tears as her brother began to cry out in pain, another convulsion shuddering through his body.

Kierland could have easily gone for the kill, using his claws to remove the vampire's head, but he held back. If Juliana Sabin was telling the truth, then the man he was fighting wasn't in his right mind, which made killing him out of the question.

"Please," Juliana choked out, lifting her hands in entreaty. "Please, don't. If you'll hand him into my custody, I give you my word that I'll do everything I can to see that he won't escape again."

Kierland consented with a brief nod, and she called her guards forward, telling them to carefully bind her brother's ankles and wrists. Moving to his feet, Kierland made his way back toward Morgan, her expression a mixture of lingering fear and sharp relief as she stared into his eyes.

While the guards hauled a shouting Micah Sabin to his feet, Juliana came over and thanked them, apologizing for her brother's behavior.

"Have you heard any news of a high-security

compound in the Wasteland?" Morgan asked her. "One being used by the Kraven?"

"I've heard there's a Kraven who paid good money for the use of the Carringtons' land."

"Christ," Granger muttered, his expression grim.

"What is it?" Kierland demanded.

"The Carringtons are a marked nest."

Morgan lifted her brows. "What's that mean?"

"Rumor has it that they poisoned themselves by drinking the blood of innocents, draining them dry. Unlike Micah, the poison they suffer from can be passed on to their victims. Which means that traveling through their lands is going to be dangerous as hell. For Kellan and for us." Cutting a dark look toward Juliana, he said, "Do you know where the compound is?"

"I'm afraid not," she murmured. "The Carringtons have claimed thousands of acres as their own, stealing it from others. There's no telling where the compound is hidden."

"Come on," Granger rasped, jerking his chin toward Morgan. "We need to get going. No way in hell am I camping here for the night."

"There's a cabin in the east region of our land. You can stay there for the night, if you'd like," Juliana told them, her long hair streaming over her thin shoulders as she turned to watch her guards carrying her struggling brother from the clearing, her profile etched with strain. When they disappeared into the thick forest, she turned her gaze back to Granger. "The cabin is actually protected by a spell, so you'll be safe there."

"Thank you," Morgan murmured, and Juliana quickly told them the directions.

Eyeing the female vampire with a wary gaze, Granger asked, "Is there a password to cross the threshold?"

She nodded. "Yes, and it should be easy to remember. Just keep in mind that it's something we have very little of here in the Wasteland."

"Sunlight?" Morgan guessed, shivering as a gust of wind swept through the shadowed clearing.

Juliana shook her head, a sad smile tucked into the corners of her mouth as she told them the magic word. "Peace."

# CHAPTER THIRTEEN

*Tuesday night*

THOUGH MORGAN WASN'T entirely certain they could trust Juliana Sabin, she was beyond thankful for the use of the Deschanel's cabin. She needed a respite from the cold. Needed to feel warm, if only for a handful of hours, and the fire Kierland had started in the hearth already had delicious waves of slow melting heat spreading through the rustic room.

The Wasteland, Morgan had decided earlier that day, was even worse than she'd imagined it would be. You could literally feel the heaviness of the air there, the weight of the spell that entrapped the exiled Deschanel nests, like the Sabins, hanging over the land like a heavy shroud. She'd wondered, as they'd sat around the cabin's small table with their dinner of sandwiches and chips, if that was why Monica Harcourt hadn't been able to tell them that her sister was being held there. Perhaps the spell that protected the Wasteland was even strong enough to keep out a ghost.

The Watchman was still lost in her thoughts, worrying about Kellan and what the coming days would

bring, when the door to the small bathroom on the
other side of the cabin opened. Without turning away
from her spot at the window, she listened as Kierland
spoke to Ashe, who was resting in a chair by the fire,
telling him it was his turn to clean up. There obviously
wasn't any hot water on tap, but they'd been able to
heat some buckets of fresh water on the fire and use
them for sponge baths. Morgan had gone first, her hair
still damp from its recent washing, her body now
covered in sweatpants and a long-sleeved T-shirt.
She'd chosen comfort clothes, since they were plan-
ning to make use of the cabin's beds and rest for a few
hours. Though there was a double bed behind her,
placed close to the hearth, a doorway next to the
bathroom led to a small bedroom that housed another
bed, that one a single.

The second Ashe shut the bathroom door, Kierland
came up behind her, close enough that she could feel
the feverish heat of his body blasting against her. She'd
been staring up at the silver moon rising in the sky, and
wanted to stay lost in its peacefulness, but knew he was
waiting for her to turn around. As she lowered her
gaze, she could see the reflection of his gorgeous face
and broad shoulders in the window's frosted surface,
his larger frame towering over her.

"I heard you and Granger talking on the way to the
cabin." His voice was a low, provocative scrape of
sound. "About the last woman he was dating. Some
dancer in Paris."

Morgan lifted her brows, as if to say "And?"

Rolling one shoulder in a restless gesture, his tone held

an edge of impatience as he said, "Doesn't that make you jealous? Hearing about him and another woman?"

"Not at all," she replied, keeping her voice soft, neutral. "But I worry for him. He deserves happiness. Someone who will love him for who he is. Not an endless stream of bimbos who just use him because he's beautiful."

"He's not that bloody beautiful," he muttered with a heavy dose of disgust, curling his lip.

She smiled at his dry tone, but the smile fell as he ground out his next question. "What the hell did you ever see in the cocky bastard?"

Crossing her arms over her chest, she glared at his reflection through narrowed eyes. "I don't owe you an explanation, but let's just say that he was there when I needed him. If anything, I feel badly for Ashe. I used him when we were together just as much as you're using me."

His eyes darkened with questions and confusion, as if he could tell she wasn't talking about those infuriating orders he thought she'd followed. "What do you mean, you were using him?"

Shaking her head, she gave a weary sigh. "Do you really not know, Kier?"

"If I knew, damn it, I wouldn't have asked." A frustrated burst of words, punching against the quiet of the room, and Morgan flinched from their bruising force.

"Just forget it," she whispered, lowering her gaze until she found herself staring into her own weary, worried eyes. "It's not important, anyway. And I'm getting pretty tired of your mercurial mood swings, so I think I'll pass on this conversation, fun as it is."

Silence, so heavy and thick she could feel its weight draped across her shoulders...and then his slow, guttural rasp. "Yeah, well, at any rate, I'm sure Granger didn't mind being used. Not when screwing you was part of the bargain."

Trying to hold on to her temper, she took a deep breath, filling her lungs with the provocative, primal blend of burning wood and Kierland's own rich, mouthwatering scent—but it didn't work. Instead, she watched as her mouth curled with a slow smile, her words deceptively soft as she said, "Hmm, you're probably right, Kier. In fact, now that I think about it, he *was* awfully thankful for my virginity."

He jerked with a hard shudder, as if he'd been dealt some kind of blow, then went completely rigid, not even breathing. A second passed...and then another, and then a rough sound vibrated in the back of his throat, and he turned away from her. Looking over her shoulder, Morgan watched him quickly pull on his boots and jacket, before slamming out of the cabin.

A moment later, she could hear the sounds of destruction ripping through the forest, and knew the Lycan was taking out his need for violence on some unsuspecting tree, no doubt damaging his hands in the process. The Kierland she'd always known had been too controlled, too disciplined, for such a Neanderthal-type reaction, and she could only shake her head in amazement, shocked that she'd been able to get to him so easily.

Then again, maybe his violent reaction didn't really have anything to do with her. He had to be worried sick about his brother, as well as his friends back in England. Not to mention the danger surrounding them in the Wasteland. It could have been a whole combination of things, which meant she would be foolish to make too much of it.

God, she didn't even know why they'd been fighting.

"Whoa, honey. What'd you do to the wolf?" Ashe suddenly drawled near her ear, making her jump about a foot in the air. Pressing one hand to her chest, over her pounding heart, Morgan turned around, smacking her other hand against his shoulder.

"Damn it, Ashe. Don't do that!"

"Do what?" he asked with a lazy, innocent blink, though she could see the laughter lurking in his silver eyes.

"Don't sneak up on me like that. I swear you float over the ground like a ghost." For such a big, muscular male, Ashe had always moved with an effortless grace that was common among the Deschanel.

"You gonna answer my question?" he murmured, moving to her side so that he could prop his shoulder against the wall. He jerked his chin toward the window. "It sounds like he's trying to kill something out there."

Crossing her arms over her middle, Morgan explained that she'd said something to tick Kierland off…and he'd left.

Ashe hooked his thumbs in his pockets and playfully waggled his dark brows, his gorgeous mouth curved in a teasing smile. "If you really wanna drive him crazy, we could always jump into bed together."

She laughed, knowing he was only joking. They hadn't slept together in a decade, since the end of their brief affair, and she knew they never would again. After the long, intense years of friendship, it would have been like sleeping with her brother. "You get a real kick outta pushing his buttons, don't you?"

The vampire's response was almost painfully dry. "Seeing as how he'd love nothing more than to dismember me, I think a little button pushing is only fair."

"I seem to recall you having that effect on a lot of people," she murmured, arching her brow.

"What can I say?" His mouth curled with a slow, cocky smile. "It's a talent I've spent decades perfecting."

"I meant to ask you before," she said, changing the subject, "did you manage to get in touch with Gideon before we entered the Wasteland?"

He shook his head, his expression revealing his concern. "I couldn't get through to him, but I left a message for him with one of our cousins."

"I hope he's okay."

He sighed, saying that he did, too, then asked, "So seriously, what's the deal with the Big Bad Wolf?"

"There *is* no deal," she said flatly. "At least, not one I should want to be a part of. Like I told you last night, he's just using me."

Instead of agreeing with her, Ashe surprised her by saying, "You sure about that?"

Morgan snorted. "Pretty sure." The edges of her words were rough with frustration. "He just doesn't like to share his toys."

Watching her closely, he offered, "You know,

angel. It could be that his jealousy is born from something deeper."

"Not likely," she scoffed, knowing it would be emotional suicide if she allowed herself even the slightest shred of hope.

"Make as many arguments as you like, but I'm right about the wolf. He wants you."

"And you're starting to sound like a know-it-all," she muttered, slanting him a disgruntled look.

"It's a tough job," he drawled with a lopsided grin, "but someone has to have all the answers. Just think about what I said, Morgan. Because when a man chooses to fight against a psychopath like Sabin, I don't care what he might say. It sure as hell means *something*."

She rubbed her hands against her upper arms. "God. Just whose side are you on, anyway?"

He leaned forward to press a tender kiss against her forehead. "Yours, sweetheart. Always yours." Then he straightened and turned to walk away.

"Where are you going?" she asked, gripping his arm.

Ashe jerked his chin toward the door. "He'll be coming back soon. I'm going to make myself scarce."

"That's not necessary," she protested, but he lifted his hand, gently placing his fingers across her lips.

"Shh. Let's not waste time arguing, because I know my limits." A quick, crooked smile touched the corner of his mouth. "I'm afraid listening to you and the wolf might be more than I can stomach."

Grasping his wrist, Morgan pulled his fingers from her face, determined to protest his decision. "But that's hardly fair, Ashe. You hate the cold."

"I won't stay out too long. In an hour or so, I can climb through the window into the other bedroom and catch some sleep. And hell, it's not like the cold will kill me."

"You are so impossible sometimes," she breathed out, suddenly realizing that she was actually worried about being left alone with Kierland. Not because he scared her—but because of her desperate longing to find something in him that simply wasn't there.

"And just so you know," Ashe told her, pushing a lock of hair back from her face. "I'm willing to give him a chance to prove himself, for your sake. But if he hurts you, I'm killing him. No arguments. He's a dead man."

The sound of the door being jerked open made her jump, and she stiffened, her face burning from the force of Kierland's gaze as he came back into the cabin. Morgan didn't need to look at him to know he was glaring at her and Ashe.

The Watchman didn't say anything as the door slammed shut behind him. He just walked across the wood-planked floor, coming to a stop in front of the roaring fire in the hearth, his back to the room. But his silence spoke volumes.

Ashe took hold of her upper arms and gave her a gentle squeeze as he leaned down and pressed a soft kiss to her cheek. Then he gave her one of those slow melting smiles that would have made most women weak in the knees, and turned away, silently making his way out of the cabin.

*Okay*, she thought, pressing one hand to her hammering heart as she turned to look at Kierland. *Let's see what you've got.*

He still stood there facing the crackling flames of the fire, but now he leaned forward a little, his freshly scraped hands braced against the heavy mantle, long fingers digging into the dark wood. As she ran her gaze up the mouthwatering lines of his body, across the powerful shape of his broad, heavily muscled shoulders, Morgan couldn't help but remember how he'd fought for her just hours before. He'd been every bit the primal, savage warrior, his muscle-ripped body moving with the sleek, deadly grace of a powerful predator—which was exactly what he was—and it reminded her of how he'd moved when he'd been inside her. Although the ache that lingered in the intimate parts of her body had finally begun to fade, the memory still burned in her mind, making her restless...making her crave.

Clearing her throat, she swallowed a mouthful of nerves and carefully said, "I'd like to start over, if we can, and tell you that I'm sorry...about this afternoon. That you had to—"

"It wasn't your fault, so there's no need to apologize." He turned around, locking his gaze with hers, the look in his heavy-lidded eyes one of animalistic lust and aggression. "Where are you sleeping tonight?" he asked her, the rough, husky words slipping deliciously across her skin, leaving a wave of shivery sensation in their wake.

Morgan pulled her lower lip through her teeth, sucking in a deep breath through her nose. "I don't understand."

"I think you do." Soft, almost silent words, his eyes

smoldering with an unearthly fire that made her pulse
race, the frenzied sound rushing in her ears.

"You're still jealous, aren't you?" she whispered,
wetting her lips. "Even though I keep telling you that
there's no reason to be."

"What I am is starving." His big, battle-bruised
hands twitched at his sides, his long beautiful body
backlit by the flickering orange glow of the flames. "I
have been all goddamn day. So make your choice."

"There's no choice to make, Kier." She lifted her
chin, and took a step closer to him. "I'm staying
here. With you."

For a moment, all he did was stand there, watching
her with those predatory eyes, the long lines of muscle
and sinew in his magnificent physique straining
against the confines of his clothing. She started to
tremble, the fine vibration shivering under her skin,
and the fire in his eyes burned brighter. "If you want
to keep your clothes in one piece," he growled in a low,
guttural rasp, "then get them off. Now."

With shaking fingers, Morgan pulled the T-shirt
over her head and walked toward him. But instead of
putting her arms around his shoulders, she dropped
down to her knees, and knew she'd shocked the hell
out of him at the swift, indrawn sound of his breath.

She'd never seen his eyes as green as they were in
that moment, the flickering light from the fire gleaming on the wine-dark strands of his thick, unruly hair.
In a voice that sounded like churning gravel, he said,
"What the hell are you doing?"

"You don't have to be jealous anymore," she whispered, reaching up and pressing her palm over the hard, heavy length of his cock. "You're the only man that I want."

She leaned forward, scraping her teeth along that massive ridge constrained beneath tight denim, and a raw, fractured groan of pleasure tore from his throat, the erotic sound the sexiest thing she'd ever heard. His head fell back, his breathing loud...uneven, while his intoxicating scent grew warmer, drugging her senses.

*"Morgan."*

She'd never heard her name growled with so much longing...so much need, and her own breath became choppy as she shoved the denim and cotton boxers down his lean hips, and then he was there, surging from that dark patch of hair, more brutal and beautiful than any man had the right to be.

His breathing was ragged, the powerful muscles in his rigid thighs hard with tension, the air heavy with a sharp, seductive weight of anticipation. She could have played the tease, making him wait, but she was too desperate for his taste. There was far too much of him to fit in her mouth, but with a low moan of pleasure vibrating in her throat, Morgan took as much as she could, loving the salty heat of him, his sharp male energy blasting against her, hot on her face. With her hands wrapped around the broad base of his shaft, she licked and suckled, greedy for as much of him as she could take. In that moment, the only thoughts surging through her pleasure-dazed mind were of need and want and aching desire. Every voluptuous pull of her mouth on his hard, pulsing shaft was the answer to some burning question inside her heart. She needed his taste and his heat and his pleasure like she needed her next breath.

His fingers tightened in her hair, his hips punching forward in a hard, reflexive movement, shoving impossibly deep, while a harsh cry ripped from his throat. She smiled, licking up that heavy, throbbing length, his hot, suede-soft skin stretched taut over rigid steel, and realized that there was simply nothing in the world as sexy as making the master of control completely lose it. Aside from Ashe, who'd always been incredibly gentle with her, she'd never chosen an alpha lover among the few that she'd had, preferring betas. Men she could easily control. But there was a hell of a lot to be said for going head-to-head with a man who knew what he wanted, and wasn't afraid to take it. Demand it.

"Finish it," he growled in a raw voice, his blistering look one of primal command and savage desperation. He held her head compressed between his hot hands, his thumbs brushing the corners of her mouth. "Make me come, Morgan."

"Get the rest of your clothes off, first," she whispered, caressing his mouthwatering length with a strong, possessive grip. "I want to see you. All of you. Every inch of skin."

Color burned across the bridge of his nose and his sharp cheekbones, his skin fever hot to the touch, all but steaming with barely restrained hunger. "Damn it, Morgan. Stop dicking around with me."

"I'm not. I swear. I'll go down on you all night long," she promised, her voice trembling with excitement, husky and hoarse, the sound of it making his eyes go dark. "Give you as much as you can take. But I want you bare, Kier. I want to be able to look at your body."

His nostrils flared, but he didn't argue. He did as she said, though he didn't treat his clothes with any degree of kindness, his jaw locked as he cursed a foul string of words under his breath and began ripping them from his body with hard, urgent movements. Her lips curled in a slow, satisfied smile, her senses humming with decadent pleasure when he was finally standing before her, sublimely naked, his body all sleek, solid muscle and beautiful lines, with a *You're gonna scream when I get my mouth on you* look in his eyes.

"Damn it, I can't wait," he growled, suddenly reaching down and grasping her under her arms.

"I thought you wanted to come in my mouth," she whispered.

"Next time," he panted, ripping at the drawstring on her sweats and shoving them down her hips.

SATISFACTION THICKENED IN Kierland's veins as her eyes went glassy, glazed with hunger, and he wanted to howl.

Then she shocked the hell out of him by shoving at his chest, and they went toppling to the floor. He took the brunt of the fall on his back, the Navajo rug spread out in front of the hearth doing little to soften the impact, not that he cared. He could have been run over by a Mack truck, and he wouldn't have flinched, his entire focus on Morgan...and getting inside her. She landed across his chest in a soft heap of smooth skin and womanly curves, then wiggled to his side, latching back onto his cock with that lush, wet mouth, the suction so good his damn eyes nearly rolled back in his head.

"I told you next time," he rasped, lifting his head so that he could watch her going down on him, her pink tongue flicking against the dark head with a teasing swipe, before sucking him back in. "Damn it, Morgan. I need to be inside you."

"You *are* inside me," she muttered, her lips moving against the sensitive crown. "Face it, Kier. You just wanted me to stop because you didn't like that you were losing control."

"I lose control every goddamn time that I touch you," he growled. He hated it, but it was the truth.

Maybe it was what had happened with his parents. Or the hard-ass upbringing he and Kell had suffered at the hands of their grandfather. Whatever the reason, Kierland had grown into a man who didn't like situations he couldn't be in command of—and God only knew that he'd never been able to command Morgan to do a damn thing.

But he couldn't deny that he wanted her, now more than ever, the want deepening with every minute that ticked by. He needed his fill of her, needed more of her, until he'd found some way to burn her out of his bloody system.

*Never gonna happen. Not even possible.*

The husky words slithered through his mind, and he ground his jaw, determined to ignore them—and it was amazingly easy to do, with her lush, provocative scent growing stronger, filling his head, his mouth watering for another taste of her.

Reaching for her hips, Kierland pulled until she was lying on the floor beside him, her damp curls just inches from his mouth. With a feral growl, he shoved her legs apart, revealing the slick, candy-pink flesh of her sex, the scent of those glistening folds pulling a thick animal sound of hunger up from his chest. Spreading her open with his thumbs, he leaned forward, her mouth still wrapped around his cock, and lapped his tongue through all that sweet, melting honey, her taste hitting his system like a drug. One that already had him addicted, craving his next hit...and his next.

He could have lost himself for hours, days, in the warm, honeyed sweetness of her slippery juices, the flavor so perfect, it was like she'd been made for him. Lashing the tiny kernel of her clit with his tongue, he shoved two thick fingers inside the delicate, softly pulsing opening, and with a startled cry, she started to come for him. Hard and wet and achingly sweet. He shoved his fingers deeper, loving the way she clutched at him, the rhythmic pulse of her cushiony sheath as she screamed against his cock, taking him even deeper, nearly shoving him over the edge, the pleasure so intense it was like a physical pain.

Replacing his fingers with his tongue, he thrust into her, drinking her in, ravenous for her taste, while a dizzying spiral of questions kept working their way through his mind.

How could something so bloody good be wrong? Why couldn't he simply accept the past and get on with the future? Go down on his knees and beg this woman for a chance at what he'd always wanted...needed... craved?

Stupid questions, when he already knew the answers. For one, he didn't trust himself, and never would. And then there was the part of him that feared she was still in love with Ashe Granger. Hell, for all he knew, maybe she was only using him to make Granger jealous. Was he really the one that she wanted between her beautiful little thighs? Or was she just playing him? Would she go running back to the bastard if he asked her to? Kierland didn't know, damn it, and the frustration of it was driving him out of his goddamn mind.

With a deep, guttural growl, he reached down, fisted his fingers in her silken hair, and pulled her away from his cock. A second later, he had her on her back, her knees hooked over his arms, her husky cries filling his head as he buried himself about a mile inside her. Sweating, swearing, he pumped into her, slamming his hips against hers, driven by a savage, primal desperation.

She was impossibly tight, still a little swollen from the day before, but wet enough that he was able to get in every hard, blood-thick inch. Bracing himself on his knees, Kierland grasped her hips and pulled her over his spread thighs, working her on his slick shaft, the erotic friction so incredible he was ready to explode on the first thrust. But he bit it back, refusing to go over until he had her screaming and clawing at him, her face flushed, her lithe body convulsing with deep, clenching spasms of pleasure. He channeled all his violent, frustrating emotion into the act itself, riding her harder than he'd ever dared with another woman, his fingers digging into her hips as he pulled her into his powerful thrusts, but he knew how strong she was. Delicate and feminine and beautiful, but tough enough to take what he gave her.

She came again, her back arched with feminine grace as she convulsed around him in strong, clenching pulls, her damp hair spread out across the floor like a dark spill of liquid. Before she'd even caught her breath, Kierland had pulled out, turned her over and driven back into those hot, drenched depths, his arm wrapped tight around her hips, his left hand supporting his weight on the floor as he pumped his cock into her, going hard and deep with each lunging, hammering thrust.

Bracing herself on her bent arms, she said, "You were right. You do seem hungry tonight."

"Always," he panted, his breath coming in hard, sharp bursts. "Always hungry for you."

"But it's more tonight," she said in a soft voice, lowering her face over his hand and pressing her lips to his bruised knuckles. "You're...on edge."

"Sorry," he gasped, painfully aware of the heaviness in his gums that signaled the release of his fangs. He tried to gentle the vicious, grinding rhythm of his body as he forged into hers, but he was too far gone, the blistering, fiery burn of pleasure melting him down.

"I'm not complaining. Just...curious."

Heat climbed up his chest, burning in his throat as he said, "The dark."

"Dark?"

"Being so long in the darkness," he muttered,

curving himself over her, his lips moving against the tender skin beneath her ear as he spoke. "It affects the beast. Affects my control. Don't wanna scare you."

"You won't. Do whatever you need to, Kier. I'm not afraid of you. I know you would never hurt me."

Growling, he kept her impaled as he picked her up, putting her over the side of the high bed. "Hold on," he groaned, and then he covered her, his chest to her back, his arms braced on either side of her. His claws slipped free, ripping into the mattress and bedding, sending puffs of white fluff floating up into flickering firelight.

MORGAN COULD FEEL HIM getting thicker, heavier inside her, the breathtaking penetration stretching her impossibly wide. She wanted nothing more than to open her mouth and say things, tell him things, that she knew should never be said. The feeling stunned her, and she realized that this, right here, was why she'd been trying to pick a fight with him earlier. She'd known it was going to tear her open. After watching the way he'd fought for her against Micah Sabin, she'd bloody well known that if he touched her tonight, all her shields were going to come crashing down. She was wide-open to him, liquid and soft and aching, desperate for everything he could give her. For every hard, angry, beautiful part of him. She wanted to shower him with tenderness. Kiss and hold and love him so badly the need was like an aching, bleeding wound in her chest. She'd have done anything for him, gone anywhere with him, if he'd have only given her the chance.

But she knew that future wasn't being placed on the

table. Knew he viewed their time together as a means to an end, and so she bit her lip, choking back the words she wanted to tell him. Words that would lay her soul bare, giving him the power to crush and destroy her.

"Too much of the wolf," he growled, his body fever hot and slick with sweat as he pinned her against the bed with hard, hammering thrusts that jerked breathless cries from her throat. "Damn it, Morgan. I don't wanna hurt you."

"You won't," she gasped, the tears stinging her eyes born from emotion, rather than pain. "I love you like this, Kier. It's okay…stop worrying."

He made a raw sound, his claws digging deeper into the bedding as he rammed into her harder…faster, his hips pistoning that hot, massive shaft inside her. He slammed deep once, twice, shoving her body across the quilted bed, a harsh, guttural shout tearing from him as he started to come, his broad shaft jerking in thick, powerful bursts that filled her with searing heat. The breathtaking power of his release forced Morgan into her own shattering, screaming climax, the deep pulses of pleasure locking them together, their bodies steaming, chests aching as they struggled to drag in enough air. With a low groan, he retracted his claws and dragged her up onto the bed, pulling her against his chest as they lay on their sides. In the minutes that followed, Morgan realized that it was the quiet moments, the easy ones, that were truly devastating. Lying there beside him, listening to the heavy rhythm of his heartbeat, with his dark, delicious scent filling her head and his hot seed filling her body, was the most poignant, meaningful moment of her life.

Closing her eyes, she tried to soak up as much of the blissful sensations as she could, and quietly asked, "How can you do it?"

"Do what?" he grunted, while his hand smoothed its way down her spine, curving around her bottom.

A deep breath, and she carefully said, "How can you touch me the way that you do when it's only sex for you? Is it...are you like this with every woman?"

His hand stilled, and he rolled onto his back, his voice tight with strain as he shook his head and said, "No. Never. Not even close." Gruff, halting words that were scraped out of his throat. "It's you. You're... different."

Lifting up onto her elbow, she locked her gaze with his, seeing the caution in the pale green, and knew he didn't want to have this conversation. But she couldn't stop. She *had* to know. "Different how?" she asked.

He swallowed, and his breath rattled between his parted lips, his color high...his eyes shadowed with emotion. She didn't think he was going to answer, and then he slowly rasped, "Different in every way there is, Morgan. In every goddamn way that matters."

"I want to tell you something important, Kier." Her voice shook, and she could feel the uneasy tension quivering in his muscles. "But first, I need to ask you a question."

His auburn hair fell over his brow as he gave her a wary nod, waiting to hear what she would say.

"What would you have done if Ian had said yes?"

His eyebrow twitched, and he tore his gaze from

hers, staring up at the dark beams of the ceiling. "Honestly?" he grunted, his jaw hard.

"Please."

He lifted his hand, scraping his palm against his shadowed jaw, and muttered, "I'd have had to kill him. Even though I thought at the time that you were his last chance to do what was right, there isn't a chance in hell I'd have let him touch you."

A soft, shivery sigh of relief spilled from her lips, and she snuggled against him, her cheek pressed to the muscled warmth of his chest.

"I answered your question," he rumbled a moment later, the fingers of his left hand stroking the length of her spine. "So what did you want to tell me?"

Morgan didn't know if her confession would change anything between them. And she would still have her secrets. Emotional armor that would shield her heart. But she needed to tell him this one thing. Needed for there to be at least *one* truth between them. "I didn't...I didn't sleep with Ashe because I was ordered to."

There was a perfect stillness within his body, and then he shuddered, the tremor moving through his long frame like a rolling, ground-shaking quake. His breath became rougher...deeper, his voice a raw, guttural slash of sound. "What in the hell are you talking about?"

"The truth is that I've never taken an assignment from the Consortium that required me to use my body, and if they'd ever tried to force me, I would have quit in a heartbeat. And I certainly wouldn't have needed to do something like that with Ashe. He was more than willing to go after those bastards who killed Nicole," she offered in a quiet confession, her mouth trembling with emotion and relief. "I didn't need to sleep with him for his help or to make him more cooperative."

His reaction was instantaneous, his big hands gripping her shoulders, pushing her to her back as he loomed over her. "Why did you do it?" he growled, his dark expression revealing raw, visceral torment. "Jesus, Morgan. All these years, why have you let me believe a lie? What the hell were you thinking?"

"Once you made your assumption, I didn't see any reason to set you straight," she explained, taking a deep breath for courage. "And I think it was easier, somehow, letting you think the worst, Kier. Because you were right about me wanting you. I did. And I guess I felt that if you hated me, then it would make it easier to stay away from you. That I wouldn't ever be tempted to come begging for your attention and find myself humiliated in the process." A wry smile touched her mouth, and she added, "I just didn't realize that you would still be holding it over my head a decade later."

He shook his head a little, his expression dazed. "And now?" he asked, his voice thick. "Why tell me the truth now?"

"I've been pissed at you for a long time," she said in a soft voice, lifting her fingertips to the heated curve of his cheek, "but I'm...well, I'm not so angry now. And it would be good if we could be friends, when this is over. I'd like to leave the Watchmen knowing that I was on good terms with you."

KIERLAND SHOOK HIS HEAD, unable to believe the words he was hearing. She wanted to be friends with him? As in freaking pals?

*Christ.*

"Would that be so hard?" she asked, her small smile hitting the center of his chest like a physical blow.

"What's hard is keeping my hands off you," he muttered, pulling her under him. He half expected her to tell him no, that she'd had enough already—but she didn't. Instead, she sank her fingers into his hair and lifted up to him, licking into his mouth with a hunger that perfectly matched his own. They were both starving, desperate, as if they could feel their time together slipping away with each moment that passed by.

He kissed her harder, deeper, and began feeding his cock back into that deliciously hot, tender sheath, his hands touching every part of her that he could reach. He loved the lean play of muscle beneath his palms, her skin a sensuous assault on his senses. Everywhere he touched her she was smooth and soft and sleek, drugging him with pleasure, and he couldn't resist running his tongue over the damp patches of her skin. Beneath her ear. Across her shoulder. The curve of her breast. The inside of her elbow. He could have spent hours exploring her, making love to her. Days. Weeks. Years. It wouldn't matter how long he had; it would never be enough.

"You kill me," he groaned, pushing the damp strands of hair back from her face as he stared deep into her eyes. "So hot and wet and tight. I could stay in you all night, Morgan, and never get enough."

She gasped as he reached down and touched the swollen knot of her clit, rubbing in slow circles until he could see the pleasure haze in her eyes. He lifted his hand, wetting his thumb, then used it to rub that taut bud in tight, slippery circles.

He pushed up on his free arm, watching the way his cock stretched her, his ruddy skin slicked with her glistening juices, his breath coming in rough, ragged gusts. "You're so damn beautiful," he growled.

"So are you," she murmured, arching beneath him, and he caught the way she flicked a quick, greedy look at the vein pumping at the side of his throat. Pride roared through him, all but turning him inside out.

"Take it," he told her, turning his head to the side as he lowered himself over her. "Take as much as you need."

She groaned, touching the tip of her tongue to his skin, then sank her fangs deep, the hungry little pulls of her mouth shooting through his core, reaching all the way down to the head of his cock. He gasped for breath, grinding himself against her clit with each pumping thrust of his body as he drove himself into her, needing to get closer…deeper, until he was in every part of her. Even the ones where he didn't belong. Where he couldn't stay.

They came together, on a long, cresting wave that drained them both, his face buried in the curve of her shoulder, their bodies left panting and twined together, slick with sweat despite the chill in the air. Kierland knew he should pull away, but he couldn't, needing to soak up every moment of time with her that he could.

He hated that with each second he moved closer to

Kellan, he was also moving closer to the moment when he would have to tell Morgan goodbye. Their time together was slipping away too fast. He wanted to find Kellan, wanted to make sure his brother was safe....

But, damn it, there was a part of him that wanted just a little more time with the woman in his arms.

A part that didn't want to lose what he'd only just found.

# CHAPTER FOURTEEN

*The Casus/Kraven Compound*
*Wednesday, 2:00 a.m.*

"THE WOLF IS GETTING CLOSER."

Westmore's tone was conversational as he crossed
his arms over his chest in a casual stance, his shoulder
propped against the iron bars of the psychic's cell.
Most men would have found it difficult to sound so at
ease when conversing with a woman who was beaten
and chained to the floor, but the Kraven felt no pity for
the frail creature. He'd ordered Raine's beating late the
previous night, when his scouts had reported spotting
Kellan Scott traveling through the Wasteland in his
wolf form, heading straight toward the compound, no
doubt acting on some half-baked plan to steal the
Markers in their possession. The instant Westmore had
heard the report, he'd come to Raine, knowing she
would have seen the Lycan's approach with her powers.

Seen it...and kept the information to herself, which
had earned her this latest little punishment.

"I'm going to add the Watchman to my collection,"
he murmured, wishing she would lift her face so that

he could see her eyes. He was beginning to have an un-healthy obsession with that brilliant, unusual gaze of hers, and the knowledge made him frown.

"You no longer need him as a hostage now that I'm helping you with the maps," she whispered, her husky voice weak with hunger and pain. "So why take him?"

"You know the Markers are only good to me if I have them all," he replied. "I need the five that the Watchmen have in their possession."

A soft, brittle burst of laughter, and she shook her head, the metal cuffs circling her wrists scraping against the stone floor as she pulled her arms beneath her. "It's all just a waste of time," she told him, "because you're not going to win."

His eyes narrowed with outrage, and he silently wondered just what it was going to take to break her spirit. "You can't see the future," he seethed. "Only the past."

A trembling groan as she pulled her legs to her side, and then she said, "I don't need to be a seer to know what will happen in your war. Evil like you always makes a mistake sooner or later. Usually comes right around the time that your ego gets too big to control. The more you think you're invincible, the harder the fall."

"Bold words for a young woman whose baby brother is my newest plaything."

She stiffened in reaction to the soft words, trying to raise her torso off the ground, but her bruised, bloodied arms were shaking too badly, and he laughed quietly under his breath. "Let me tell you about this one Casus who escaped from Meridian last year," he murmured, enjoying her struggles. "His name's Gregory, and he has this thing for fingers. Crazy as a loon, but the guy could give lessons on good, wholesome torture. You couldn't imagine the things he's done. Things that I could so easily do to the rest of your loved ones."

"I've seen Gregory."

The words were soft, barely a whisper, and he was certain he must have heard her wrong. "What did you say?"

She took a deep, rattling breath, her voice a little stronger as she gritted her teeth and finally managed to push her body into a sitting position on the blood-covered floor. "I've seen Gregory. Seen you fail to capture him...and fail to kill him, as well."

A new edge of alertness sharpened Westmore's gaze, his fingers curling around the bars of her cell. "When? Where? Can you see where he is now?"

She lifted her chin, pinning him with her hate-filled glare. "Let my brother go," she told him, "and I'll tell you what I've seen."

Rage flooded his system, making him shake. "You think to negotiate with me, you little bitch?"

"I call it making a deal. And trust me when I say that you don't have any choice. Because I know what he has planned for you, and it isn't pretty," she whispered, the corner of her busted mouth curving the barest fraction as she gave him a cold, deadly smile. "If you don't want to end up just another one of his victims, Westmore, you'll give me what I want."

# CHAPTER FIFTEEN

*Wednesday evening*

ALTHOUGH THEY'D BEEN traveling through treacherous territory all day, they'd avoided running into any of the Carrington vampires, thanks to Ashe's knowledge of the area. After carefully navigating their way through a steep, rocky ravine that bordered the lands claimed by the Carrington nest, they were finally nearing the place where they'd be taking shelter for the night, and Morgan was again grateful for the chance to get out of the cold.

"Look down there," Ashe murmured, nodding his dark head toward the east, where the silvery gleam of the moon illuminated a small structure in the valley below, nestled amid a bower of fir trees. The cabin was one of several that were used by the Förmyndares when they traveled into the Wasteland, but it was only by chance that they'd found themselves near enough to use it, the "pull" of Kellan's blood that she was following thankfully leading them through this particular valley. "We should be there in another twenty minutes or so."

"Thank God," Morgan groaned. "My feet feel like they're going to fall off."

"And you need to eat," Kierland murmured at her side, the rough note of concern in his deep voice making her smile. After the wild, melt-your-brain-down orgasms he'd given her the night before, they'd caught a few hours of sleep, wrapped around each other like some erotic work of art. When he'd woken her, his dark voice whispering in her ear that it was time for them to head out, Morgan had stiffened with nerves, worried about how he would treat her after the things that had happened during the night. All the words that had been growled and whispered and confessed. It was with a startling rush of pleasure that she realized he wasn't going to take ten steps back and act like a belligerent prick. Instead, he'd been mellow, kind of quiet, lost in his thoughts, but…close. He'd stayed by her side, making sure she was okay, helping her when they had to make their way through tricky passages or across narrow, rickety bridges.

He'd even been less confrontational toward Ashe, who kept sliding her teasing, lopsided grins when Kierland wasn't looking, the I-told-you-so look in the Deschanel's brilliant gray eyes making her flush with color as she tried to warn him with her dark glares to cut it out.

"If you guys can get a fire started when we reach the cabin," she murmured, bracing her hand on one of Kierland's hard shoulders as he helped her down the last boulder, the thicket of trees spreading out before them the final obstacle before they reached shelter, "I'll heat up the cans of soup we brought. It's not much, but at least it'll be hot."

The Lycan flashed her a sexy grin, then moved behind her, taking up the rear as Ashe led the way down the narrow path that wound through the woods.

Morgan's mind wandered as they hiked deeper into the towering forest, shifting between worried thoughts for Kell and nervous misgivings about the state of her heart. She'd known that getting involved on a physical level with the gorgeous werewolf was going to seriously mess with her emotions, but she'd had no idea just how deeply she would be affected. Instead of it hurting when he walked away, it was going to rip a big aching hole out of the center of her chest. No way to avoid it. The damage was done. And yet, even knowing how it was going to end, she couldn't stop thinking about what it would be like the next time she got her hands on him.

She'd tried to come up with a way to explain the mad intensity of her need and her crazy, out-of-control emotions, but she couldn't. All she knew was that it went far beyond the surreal, mind-shattering ecstasy that he drenched her in, to something deeper…and infinitely more devastating. When he touched her body, he found his way to some sheltered, shadowed part inside of her that had been cold and dark and silent for years, but was now screaming at the top of its lungs, craving warmth and light and noise.

"Does it seem a little too quiet all of a sudden?" Ashe murmured, his low voice pulling her out of her internal thoughts as he came to a stop on the path before her, his dark head turning slowly as he stared into the murky depths of the forest.

Slick, icy fear shuddered through Morgan's veins, and she shivered, her lips trembling. "I have a bad feeling," she whispered, the uneasy sensation of being watched prickling at the back of her neck.

They each dropped the heavy packs they were carrying on the ground, and Kierland moved closer to her side, sliding a sharp look toward Ashe, who was lifting his nose to the air. "You scent anything?"

The Deschanel shook his head, his handsome face pulled into grim lines of frustration as he looked at them over his shoulder. "But I gotta admit, I'm suddenly getting that bad vibe, as well."

"There's something here," Morgan murmured. "Something close."

Before Kierland was able to respond, the forest exploded with movement. It was like something out of a movie, the perfect choreography of bodies soaring through the air, dropping from the upper branches of the trees to trap them on the path, dozens of pairs of silver eyes glowing with predatory fire in the moonlit shadows of the forest.

Kierland cursed something harsh and gritty, shoving her against a tree and planting his big, muscled body in front of her as they found themselves facing a feral nest of redheaded Deschanel vampires. Their lethal fangs were already fully distended, as well as their razor-tipped talons. And in the center of the group was Micah Sabin, his tall body still clothed in the same ragged, bloodstained clothes he'd been wearing the day before, a fresh bruise darkening one cheek, his chin and throat sporting streaks of dried, midnight-colored blood.

"Micah?" she gasped, peering around Kierland's broad shoulder. "How did you get free? Where's Juliana?"

"Juliana is probably back at our compound, wringing her hands like a good little girl, worried about what I'm going to do to her new friends," he sneered, the look of madness in his eyes even more pronounced than it'd been the last time they'd seen him.

"They just let you go?" Ashe asked him, keeping a careful eye on the surrounding vampires as he moved closer to her and Kierland.

The corner of Micah's mouth curled with a snide smile. "They didn't have much choice, considering I managed to get my talons around the throat of one of my cousins. She was a sweet little thing," he rasped, his chest heaving with the force of his breaths. "Poor Jules couldn't stand the thought of her getting hurt."

Bile rose in her throat, and Morgan had to cough before she could ask, "And where is the girl now, Micah? Is she okay?"

He flinched, his eyes tightening for a fraction of a second, and he shook his head as if to shake free of an unwanted memory. "I don't know where she is," he answered in a thick, broken voice, then shook his head again, that wild look of feral aggression washing over him once more. "It...it doesn't matter. What matters is that I found you. Been looking for you all bloody night and day."

"And who are your friends?" Kierland prompted, his voice deceptively soft as he slowly drew his gun from behind his back, while Morgan and Ashe did the same.

Micah sent Ashe a hard smile. "They're Carringtons. I knew, from what you told Juliana, that you were heading for the new Kraven compound. When I escaped, I made my way to the Carringtons and offered them a deal, since they're always desperate to get their hands on fresh meat. Told them that I'd share the meal, if they'd help me catch you."

"And now what?" Ashe growled, sounding every bit the deadly warrior that she knew he could be.

Jerking his chin toward Kierland, Micah said, "They get the two of you, and I get the woman."

"We won't let you have her," Kierland stated in a calm voice, but Morgan could hear the undercurrent of rage that roughened the edges of his words.

The vampire started to say something in response, then flinched, his brow pulling tight, as if with pain, the poison polluting his bloodstream no doubt ravaging his sanity, as well as his body.

"Micah," she murmured, keeping her voice soft…gentle, "you don't have to do this."

"You're wrong." His chest jerked with the heaviness of his ragged breathing, his skin clammy and pale. "I have to. I haven't been able to get you out of my head. You…you smell too good. I…can't stop thinking about it. Your blood. Your body."

"You *can't* have her," Kierland repeated, the low words carefully drawn out, as if he was speaking to a confused child. "I understand how you feel, but you can't have her, Sabin. She's *mine*."

"Not for long," Micah rasped, and as he signaled with his hand, the Carrington vampires attacked.

"Don't let them bite you!" Ashe shouted, firing off shots as the poisonous vamps rushed toward them. "Remember, they're contagious!"

Though they were each unloading a steady stream of bullets, there were too many wild-eyed, bloodthirsty monsters charging them. Both men were forced to engage in hand-to-hand combat, doing everything they could to keep Morgan protected behind them. When one of the poisonous bastards snapped at Ashe's arm, barely missing his powerful forearm, the handsome Deschanel went ballistic, his gun slipped back into the waistband of his jeans as he released his talons and began to rip out throats with deadly accuracy. It was a gruesome, blood-spattered scene, but Morgan didn't have time to be squeamish. Kierland had his hands full fighting off Micah and the rest of the Carringtons, and Morgan forced herself to stay calm as she aimed her Glock and took shot after shot, doing her best to help.

But it wasn't easy.

The feral, poisonous vampires reminded her too much of the ones who'd killed Nicole all those years ago, and she could feel the icy twinges of panic struggling to take hold of her. Fear swamped her system, perspiration dotting her upper lip, trailing down the side of her face, her lungs constricting. Catching sight of her panicked expression, Kierland started toward her, and Micah and the rest of the Carringtons took immediate advantage of the situation. With his back exposed to his enemies, they sprang at the distracted Lycan and mobbed him. Morgan screamed with rage as the group dragged Kierland away and disappeared into the darkness of the forest. She shouted for Ashe, but he was too busy fighting off his own attackers.

*Gotta do this myself. Can't lose him. Would rather die than lose him.*

With a deep breath, Morgan gripped her gun in both hands and set off running, thanking God every second of the way that she'd taken Kierland's blood, since she was able to follow the "pull" that led her toward him. They were dragging him deeper and deeper into the dense woods, the thickening darkness making it nearly impossible to see where she was going. Something snarled at her, rushing her from her left and she lifted the gun, firing her last bullet with a shot that nailed the vampire right between his silver eyes. He went down. And stayed down. Morgan knew the shot wouldn't kill him, but it was going to take him a hell of a long time to heal, and she hoped his ass was a frozen block of ice before he regained consciousness.

Ignoring the trembling fear scraping down every nerve ending in her body, she chained her infuriating panic into submission and kept moving, stumbling again and again as she followed the "pull" that led her toward Kierland. It was stronger than any other she'd ever felt, and it wasn't just centered in her chest. She could feel it burning in every cell of her body, her entire being focused on following him...finding him.

With a stifled curse on her lips, she pushed through a thicket of something sharp and thorny, and had to choke back a cry at what she found on the other side. Kierland stood in the center of a small clearing, arguing with Micah, while the Carringtons surrounded him, and she was out of freaking bullets! She had only one weapon left—the tiny glass vial, or "sparkler," that Gideon had left for Kierland in his apartment. Morgan had remembered to ask Ashe what it was for while they'd been hiking the day before, and he'd explained that it was a sort of bomb. Though not like any explosive she'd ever known. Specifically created to kill vampires, a "sparkler" created a blast of magic designed to annihilate any Deschanel within a twenty-foot radius. Gideon had obviously thought it was the perfect weapon to give them, considering they had been headed for the Wasteland.

Morgan could only pray to God that it worked.

Using her blood-tracking ability to determine Ashe's whereabouts, making sure he wasn't within the bomb's blast radius, she took a deep breath. Then she drew back her arm and lifted the "sparkler" high in the air, ready to slam it to the ground just like Ashe had instructed her to do. None of the vampires noticed, their focus on Kierland as he roared at Micah that if he had any balls, he'd stop hiding behind the Carringtons and fight him one-on-one. Micah shouted back, pacing from one side of the clearing to the other, and just as the Deschanel turned in Morgan's direction, he caught sight of her from the corner of his eye, his wild gaze zeroing in on the small vial she held in her hand. He might have been out of his mind, but he recognized the weapon. Just as the vampire turned to run, chaos erupted in the clearing, the Carringtons losing their patience and attacking Kierland, who looked like a thundering god as he took on all of them at once, his powerful body twisting and turning with a sinuous, predatory grace that would have been beautiful to watch, if she hadn't been so petrified for his safety.

Praying that the weapon would work the way it was meant to, Morgan threw the "sparkler" against the ground with all her strength. The glass vial shattered as it smashed against the forest floor, its sudden blast of heat hurling her through the air. She landed with a hard thud on her side, slamming her hip on a tangle of tree roots, her breath momentarily knocked from her lungs. Before she could pull herself back to her feet, Kierland was grabbing her up into his arms, his breathing shallow and rough as he locked her against his chest and tried to run. But he slowed after no more than a dozen yards, the strangest look carved into his rugged features as he staggered against a nearby tree, his hold on her loosening as his arms began to tremble.

"What's wrong?" she croaked, her hands clutching the front of his jacket as her feet slid to the ground. "Are you okay? Did they bite you?"

"No bites," he forced out through his clenched teeth, his irises glowing an unearthly green as he stared into her worried eyes. "Just got the wind knocked outta me. Go…go find Granger. Get to the cabin. I'll catch up when I've caught my breath."

Fear coiled through her insides as she registered how pale he was. "Are you crazy?" she cried, her heartbeat roaring in her ears. "I'm not going anywhere without you! Damn it, Kierland, tell me what's happened!"

"Don't argue with me!" he snarled, shoving her away from him. She stumbled back, falling to the ground as she tripped over another gnarled tree root. Fear solidified into paralyzing terror as she watched the color drain from his face, as if someone had pulled a plug and his blood was simply leaking out of his body. She tried to say his name, but nothing would come out, her throat choked, voice locked tight in her pounding chest. The flurries of snow that fell on her face and trembling lips were almost hot compared to the cold iciness of her skin.

"Morgan." The scratchy, whispery syllables fell from his stiff lips, and then he swayed, staggering forward onto his knees. She screamed, scrambling toward him, reaching him just in time to catch his heavy weight as he fell into her arms.

"What's happened? What'd they do to you?" she cried, but if he heard her, he gave no indication, his lashes fluttering as his eyes rolled back in his head.

"Ashe!" she screamed, gritting her teeth as she struggled with Kierland's muscled weight, trying to be gentle as she lowered him to the ground. "Ashe! Damn it, where are you?"

The Deschanel appeared out of nowhere, his clothes and face splattered with blood, his expression creased with deep lines of worry as he crouched down beside her. "Where are you hurt?" he growled, his terrified gaze moving swiftly over her kneeling body.

"I'm f-fine," Morgan stammered, her eyes flooding with the hot, salty burn of tears. "It's Kier. He's the one who needs help."

Ashe slid his gaze toward Kierland, his eyes widening with surprise at the sight of the Lycan sprawled on the ground. Two deep notches settled between the vampire's brows as he reached out, caught hold of Kierland's jacket and peeled back the dark fabric, revealing the shredded, blood-soaked sweater beneath.

"Oh, holy God," she sobbed, staring down at the bloodied mess of Kierland's torso. He'd been cut open across his stomach, the pour of blood from the gruesome wound already soaking into the ground beneath them, and as she lifted her hands to her mouth, she smelled the blood covering her skin. She must have been in shock, not to scent it before, because it was all over her skin, her clothes, and she realized why Ashe had thought she was the one who'd been injured when he'd first seen her.

She was covered in Kierland's blood. Drenched in it.

"What the hell happened?"

The snarl of Ashe's voice made her flinch, and she shook her head, trying to focus. But it was nearly impossible when her heart was shattering into tiny, fractured pieces inside her chest.

"Morgan! Damn it, talk to me. What happened?"

She wet her lips, forcing the hoarse words past her frozen lips. "There were so many vampires, and I...I started to panic. Kierland noticed, and he just turned his back on them in the middle of the fight, trying to reach me. They caught him, dragged him away. I...I ran after him, found them, but there were so many, and Kierland was trying to fight them all. So I used the 'sparkler' to get rid of them, but I must have been too late. They must have cut him open before the blast killed them."

"He has to shift," Ashe told her, deep brackets carved into the sides of his mouth. "It's the only chance his body has of repairing the damage."

She blinked, shaking so hard her teeth were chattering. "Will he b-be able to?"

With his elbow braced on his bent knee, Ashe blew out a rough breath and scrubbed his blood-spattered hand over his mouth. "Hell if I know," he grunted, "but we should get him to the cabin first. If he can make the shift, he's going to be down for the count for at least twelve hours or so."

Tears poured down Morgan's cheeks as she helped Ashe carry Kierland through the woods, the snow falling harder as they finally reached the cabin. He groaned when they laid him down on the rug before a rock fireplace, his lashes lifting, his pain-filled gaze struggling to focus on her face in the flickering candlelight.

"Don't...don't let Granger touch you," he moaned, his lips pulling back over his teeth as he hissed with pain. "Don't want him anywhere near you."

Kneeling beside him, Morgan pushed his hair back from his brow with a tender touch, her voice urgent as she leaned close to his face and said, "Kier, listen to me. I know it won't be easy, but I need you to shift."

"No," he groaned, his lashes fluttering. His lips turned gray, and a choked sob worked past the knot in her throat, her fingers trembling as she touched his cold cheek.

"Yes, sweetheart. You have to. You've been hurt," she whispered in a broken voice. "This is the only way you'll be able to heal."

He groaned again, closing his eyes, and she could feel him slipping away from her. Gripping his shoulders, she shook him a little, shouting, "Damn it, Kier. Shift! You have to!"

*"Can't."*

"He's fading," Ashe told her, his long fingers pressed to the side of Kierland's throat, monitoring his pulse.

"Like hell he is," she snapped, fury scorching through her system with such stunning force, she flinched from the burn. Pulling back her hand, Morgan focused on Kierland's beautiful, pain-ravaged face through the blur of tears, then slapped him as hard as she could, the blow striking against his pale cheek. He gave a low grunt, but nothing more, and so she slapped him again, harder, putting all her strength behind the blow. "Damn it, you're going to do it!" she growled, choking on her sobs.

"Morgan, honey, what are you doing?" Ashe's deep voice was thick with concern, and she clenched her teeth, knowing she must look like a mad woman.

"I'm going to piss him off," she gasped, slapping Kier again...and again, while her chest heaved with the choppy force of her breaths. "If he gets angry enough, he might be able to do it. To make the change."

"Jesus, Morgan." Ashe reached over Kierland's bleeding body and grabbed onto her wrists, holding her hostage in his grip as he gave her a thunderous scowl. "And he might hurt you by accident, if he's out of his mind with pain. Did you think of that? If he shifts out of anger, he's liable to kill you!"

"I don't care!" she shouted, tugging on her wrists. "I'm not going to lose him. Not now. Not like this!"

With a resigned sigh, Ashe released his hold on her and leaned back on his heels. Taking a deep, shuddering breath, Morgan pulled back her hand and smacked it against the side of Kierland's face again. Finally, his eyes fluttered open, glowing an even brighter shade of green, his lip curling as he glared up at her. He cursed something ugly and raw, demanding to know what she was doing in a slurry, pain-filled scrape of words, and she hit him again, even harder. Another hit, and his head shot back, his body jerking with a hard jolt at the same time his fangs began to descend beneath the firm curve of his upper lip.

"It's working," Ashe said in a low, gritty voice. "Keep going. But do it with your claws. You're running out of time."

Refusing to look any lower than Kierland's chest, knowing the sight of his blood-soaked body would only make her hysterical, Morgan released her short claws, held her breath, then raked them across the now flushed skin of his cheek, drawing crimson slashes of blood. A thick, guttural snarl ripped from his chest, and Ashe grabbed onto Kierland's wrists, pinning them against the floor as she choked back the bile in her throat and clawed him again.

Straining against Ashe's hold, Kierland's gaze locked with hers, the glowing green filled with pain and confusion and a primal, savage fury.

"I'm sorry," she whispered, tears streaming down her face as she clawed at his other cheek, her fingers slick with his blood. "I'm so sorry."

"We want him pissed," Ashe grunted. "Stop apologizing and do something else. Quickly, or it's going to be too bloody late, Morgan."

Kierland's eyes darkened with rage, his body trembling, the change in him so close Morgan could feel the power of the wolf pulsing from him in sharp, visceral waves that were blisteringly hot against her chilled skin. His furious gaze cut to Ashe, then back to her, and she suddenly knew what to do. How to push him over the edge.

Feeling like the cruelest bitch alive, she drew in another shuddering breath and leaned forward, putting her mouth at his ear as she said, "If you leave me, Kier, I'm going to run off with Ashe. I'll…I'll marry him. Be his mate. Have his children."

"It's working," Ashe rasped, struggling to hold down Kierland's wrists as deadly claws began surging through the tips of the Lycan's fingers, a rumbling snarl working its way up from his chest. "Keep going."

"I'll go to bed with him," she choked out, pressing her hands to his shoulders as she tried to help Ashe keep him restrained. Staring at the strong tendons in his throat, unable to face the look in his eyes, she hardened her voice and said, "I'll let him use me, however he wants. In any way that he wants. I'll let him take my blood when he's buried deep inside me, and I'll scream for him. I'll come for him. As many times as he wants me to. I'll—"

"Get back!" Ashe suddenly roared, shoving her so forcefully that she skidded on her side halfway across the room. Sitting up, she pushed her tangled hair out of her face, her eyes widening as Kierland's body began to shake with vicious, violent spasms, arching nearly a foot off the floor, his claw-tipped arms flung wide at his sides. He let out a stark, guttural cry, and his bones began to crack and pop and expand, clothes shredding as his skin darkened to a rich rosewood and thick, wine-dark fur spread over his shifting, healing physique, the change fully upon him now.

"For God's sake, be careful," Ashe muttered, and from the corner of her eye, Morgan could see the vampire backing slowly toward the door, while he kept a wary eye on Kierland's changing body.

"Where are you going?" she asked, using the back of her sleeve to wipe the tears from her cheeks.

"Considering what it took to get the results you wanted," Ashe offered in a wry drawl, "I think this is my cue to leave. I'll be keeping an eye on things outside, making sure nothing bothers us." He slid her a tight, crooked smile, adding, "You just make sure he doesn't come looking for me, angel."

And with those teasing words, the door to the cabin closed…and she was left alone with Kierland. The raspy, gritty sound of her name being whispered had her looking in his direction, and she blinked with wonder at the sight of his massive, wolf-shaped head turned toward her, his huge body trembling as he tried to push himself up on his arms.

"Don't try to move," she whispered, crawling toward him on her hands and knees. She was so shaky, she didn't trust her legs not to crumple beneath her. "You were injured, and we had…we had to get you to shift. You just need to rest now. Your body will do the rest."

He looked from her, to the rug, then back to her again, and cocked his head to the side, asking for what he wanted with drowsy, luminous green eyes.

A shaky smile touched her mouth, and she said, "Hold on a sec. I just need to get a fire started."

Morgan could feel him watching her as she fumbled with the matches, trying to light the kindling that had been left beneath the sturdy stack of logs in the hearth. As the flames began to smolder and spit, she turned toward him, her arms wrapped over her chest, and knelt at the edge of the rug, unable to stop staring. Despite having known Kierland for so many years, she'd never seen him in full "were" form before, and it was a mesmerizing sight. He was breathtakingly beautiful. Massive. Bigger than an actual wolf, with fur and fangs and a muzzled face, but a body that still retained shades of the man in the powerful arms and legs. He could have torn her apart with a single swipe of his terrifying claws, but she wasn't afraid. She knew he would never harm her. Not physically. Even when she'd slashed him with her claws, he hadn't attacked her. Would have probably let her kill him before raising his hand to her. She didn't understand, but she was too tired to figure it out. All she knew was that she wanted to be close to him, to watch over him.

Grabbing up the bloodied, shredded remnants of his clothes, she tossed them into the flames, then crawled to his side and stretched her body out along his. A low, satisfied sound broke from his throat as he rolled to his side, curving his long body around hers, and she stiffened with surprise as a startling truth occurred to her.

She was still in love with him.

She was still in *love* with Kierland Scott.

The strange, terrifying thought burned its way into her brain as she nuzzled her face against the warmth of his broad chest, her eyes squeezing tight as the hot rush of her tears soaked into his thick, silky fur. A part of her was terrified of what the future would bring, but as his strong arms wrapped around her in a tight, possessive hold, she couldn't help but be thankful for the miracle she'd been given that night. She hadn't lost him. It'd been so close, but he'd survived. He'd stayed with her…and God, that had to mean something, didn't it?

With a trembling smile on her lips, Morgan shoved her worries and fears aside, holding on to that fragile burst of hope with everything that she had, determined not to let it go…and snuggled down to sleep with her wolf.

# CHAPTER SIXTEEN

*Thursday afternoon*

KIERLAND OPENED HIS EYES TO the flickering embers of a crackling fire, surprised by how good he felt, while one nearly incomprehensible thought kept working its way through his mind, mesmerizing him with its meaning.

Morgan had come for him. Rescued him. And saved his life.

She was no longer lying in his arms, but he could scent that she was near...and that the vampire was not.

"Where's Granger?" The question came out as little more than a graveled croak, his throat as dry and scratchy as something that'd been worked over hard with sandpaper.

"He's running patrol around the cabin," she murmured in a soft voice, and he looked over his shoulder to find her kneeling behind him on the floor, a glass of water held in her hands. Pressing the glass to his parched lips as he rolled to his back, she gave him a tentative smile, then said, "I kept watch for a few hours in the middle of the night so that Ashe could sleep, and then we switched again."

"What time is it?" he asked, when he'd drained the glass, only just realizing that he wasn't in human form.

"Late afternoon," she told him, and he noticed that she was wearing clean clothes, instead of the ones that'd been stained with his blood. "You've slept for a long time."

Kierland watched her carefully through the wolf's eyes, and despite the fact that she'd slept in his arms, he couldn't help but be shocked that she looked so completely at ease with him in his "were" form. Although she had to know that he would never harm her, the fact remained that he was a predator, and Morgan was vulnerable enough to be seen as prey. "You're not…scared?"

A mysterious female smile touched her mouth, her voice soft as she reached down and stroked the side of his face with her fingertips. "No, Kier. I'm not afraid of you."

He could hear the wolf's voice in his head, guttural and raw as it made its demands. *Take her… Touch her… Claim her.*

Closing his eyes, he tried to block out the provocative temptation of her smile, that soft, warm look in her eyes, but all he could think about was how she'd saved his life. How she'd faced her fears to come after him, even when her panic had been crashing down on her. And then there was the visceral ache of hunger rushing through his veins, his mind consumed with exquisite memories of how perfect it felt when he was inside her. How wet and plush and deliciously tight it felt when she held him clasped within her body.

Kierland needed her against him, under him, surrounding him, with an urgency that shattered his self-control, but he could *not* allow himself to touch her like this. He *had* to change back, damn it, and he struggled to take command of the dark, primal hungers raging through his system, scraping him raw, as he forced his body into the shift that would transform him back into a man. But he lost the internal struggle before the shift was fully completed and pushed her to her back, covering her with the bulk of his larger, heavier form.

He was half-afraid she would scream for Granger or demand he get the hell away from her, but she did neither of those things. Instead, the beautiful little Watchman curled her hands around the back of his neck and lifted her mouth to his cheek. Her lips were exquisitely soft and cool against the burning heat of his skin as she pressed sweet, tender kisses to the places where her claws had cut across his face, though the wounds were already healed. "I'm sorry," she whispered, her voice cracking with tears as she lowered her head back to the rug, locking her watery gaze with his. "I was so scared you weren't going to shift. You were dying, Kier...I was watching you die...and it...it was killing me. I had to do something, *anything*, to keep you with me. But I'm so sorry that I hurt you."

"It's okay, sweetheart. I'm here... I'm fine. Because of you. I'm not going anywhere," he tried to murmur, his voice still too guttural, too much of the wolf in it for him to risk touching her. But he couldn't stop himself. Fur had melted into burning rosewood skin, his head returning to its human shape—and yet, he still sported his deadly claws, his body bigger than usual, taller and packed with thick slabs of powerful muscle, capable of crushing her so easily if he wasn't careful.

With his pulse roaring in his ears, his body aching with a violent wave of scalding lust and blistering need, Kierland braced himself over her, caging her beneath him, and rasped for her to take off her clothes. A warm flush burned beneath her creamy skin, her luscious, provocative scent growing stronger as she followed his rough command, her shields completely down. Catching her full lower lip in her teeth, she pulled her jeans and sweater from her body, the sight of her graceful curves and smooth skin ripping a dark, savage groan from his lips.

When her bra and panties were gone, and she lay beneath him naked and trembling with excitement, Kierland could only stare, mesmerized by the blinding, beautiful details, and the next thing he knew, his mouth was pressed to the lush curves of her breasts. His claws ripped gouges into the rug as he licked and suckled greedily at her deliciously pink, swollen nipples, loving their taste…their texture, then forced himself to pull away. Turning her to her front, he pushed the heavy fall of her hair over her shoulder, and reminded himself to take it slow…easy, while the wolf silently snarled that he needed to be in her *now*. He shuddered as he nuzzled the warm, silky skin on the back of her neck, her scent stronger in the damp strands of her hair. Beneath her ear. Behind her knees. Along the tender curve of her throat, where her skin was so fragile and smooth.

"Kierland, please," she groaned, arching against him. "I need you. *Please*."

There was so much fear, so much worry churning inside him, but he couldn't stop himself from turning her back over and spreading her beneath him, her legs sprawled explicitly wide, her tender little sex as glistening and pink as some delicate hothouse flower. With his breath coming in sharp, ragged bursts, he knelt between her sleekly muscled thighs, and greedily pressed his face against that most precious, intimate part of her, his mouth eating hungrily at her succulent juices, his tongue in heaven as he lapped and stroked and thrust inside her. She arched beneath him, her nails digging into his shoulders, her head flung back, a husky moan spilling from her open mouth as she started to come for him with strong, rhythmic pulses of pleasure, and he couldn't wait. Her breath sucked in with a sharp, startled cry as Kierland braced his weight on his left hand, retracted his claws and began feeding his cock into that tiny, narrow entrance, but she didn't push him away, didn't scream for him to get off. Instead, she reached up, cupping the hot sides of his face, and pulled him over her. The position forced him to go deeper, tearing another sharp cry from her lips as she touched her mouth to his, their torsos rubbing together in a steamy, sensual slide of skin against skin.

"Sorry," he gasped, bracing himself on his elbows as he tried to keep from pushing, shoving, terrified he was going to hurt her. "It's too much, damn it. You're too small."

"Am not," she breathed against his lips, the huskiness of her voice slipping up Kierland's spine like a smoldering lick of flame, curling around the backs of his ears, and he rolled his hips, another broad inch of his dark, vein-ridden shaft sinking inside her, spreading the tender passage impossibly wide. He knew he should get the hell away from her, but like a miracle, she was already getting wetter, slicker, bathing him in softness and heat. He sank a little deeper, his eyes nearly rolling back in his head at the intensity of it. Kierland had never, in his entire life, had sex when he was this close to his "were" form, and the sharpness of sensation just about killed him, not to mention the fear of just how far he could take this. He'd retracted his fangs, but they were still heavy in his gums, burning for release. He could so easily see himself opening his mouth, sinking those long fangs into the fragile slope of her shoulder, and making the bite that would forever bind her to him, body and soul.

Hell. It would have been so perfect, so right, if not for the fact that he was too much like his father, and she was a woman who would never truly belong to any man. One whose heart could too easily be given to another. She'd done it to him before. Wanted him, and then given herself to Granger. She would do it again. Would never be able to love him in the ways that he needed.

*Love him?* Oh, Christ.

He hadn't wanted it, but there was no hiding from it any longer.

No, the truth had become startlingly clear to Kierland, like a big neon sign blazing in his brain, and he flinched from the brightness. This burning, incom-

parable lust had always been there…and he hadn't
tried to see past it, too afraid of what he might find.
He knew damn well that some truths were better left
unknown, unexposed, because you never knew what
lies were the ones holding you together. The little half
truths that made it possible to get through each day.
Take them away, and there'd always been the chance
that he might fall apart. Crumble into pieces, or shatter
in some violent, rending act, like an explosion. Emotional overload, and God only knew that he sucked
when it came to handling emotions.

And now Kierland had to face the terrifying, gut-
wrenching fact that he was in love with Morgan
Cantrell. A head-over-heels, heart-ripped-open-and-
bleeding, worship-her-until-the-day-that-he-died kind
of love. The kind that could never be broken or
crushed. That would tie him in knots every minute of
every day, for the rest of his godforsaken life.

A warm, glowing spark of warmth hovered at the
edges of his consciousness, beckoning him, telling him
that this was a gift. A miracle. Something to be valued
and treasured and protected. But he couldn't do it.

No matter how badly he wanted to, he could *not* surrender to it, because it scared the hell out of him,
chilling him to the bone. And maybe, he realized, *that*
right there was why Granger had walked away from her
all those years ago. It was maddening to feel yourself
consumed by so much worry for another's safety, when
there were so many dangers in the world. Even without
the mountain of nasty, difficult issues that stood
between them, Kierland knew he would never be able

to get past the infuriating fear that something might take her away from him. Damn it, there were so many things that could go wrong. That could happen.

And as far as he was concerned, their current mission had become too bloody dangerous for her to remain in the Wasteland.

*But I want her,* the wolf snarled, seething with fury as it prowled the confines of his body. *I need her. We need her.*

With his jaw locked, Kierland struggled to block out that guttural voice as he straightened his arms, pumping himself into the cushioned, liquid depths of her body, forcing her to take him deeper...and deeper, and then she opened her eyes, and he almost flinched from what he saw as she stared up at him, locking her gaze with his. The soft gray swirled with too many emotions, like a window into parts of her that he knew better than to look at. He needed to rip his gaze away, damn it, but he couldn't. She had a lock on him, and she wasn't letting go.

Jesus. This was intolerable. He had to do something to set it right, while he still could.

Kierland could feel the blistering heat rising up inside him as he gritted his teeth, gripped her behind her knees, pushing them high and wide, and held her spread beneath him. Sweating and cursing, he drove himself as deep as she could take him, slamming his hips against hers, shoving himself into a scalding, explosive release, his body erupting with hard, visceral surges that made him feel as if he was spilling his bloody soul into her. His face was prickling with tiny pinpoints of hot and cold, his mouth shaking, his eyes burning with a suspicious sheen of moisture, and he started to turn his head, but she stopped him.

"No," she whispered, reaching up and touching the damp sides of his face with her fingertips, the fluttering pulses of her inner muscles telling him that she'd found her own release while he'd been crashing over the edge. "I just... It's so amazing...."

Reading the question in his eyes, she gave him a soft smile, then explained. "I just realized that you never look at me when you come. You always turn your face away. But it's so beautiful, seeing the wolf in your eyes, feeling your pleasure burning down on me. It's like I can see right inside you, Kier. I love it."

HE SHUDDERED, HIS THROAT working, but he didn't say anything. He didn't need to. Morgan could see the stunning emotions glistening in his pale gaze, could see the longing rushing through him, and it stole her breath. Melted her down, until she was a warm, boneless pool of love and desire beneath him, needing him forever...for always.

And then the fever-hot warmth of his gaze turned cold, something stormy and dark ripping through him, and he let go of her knees as he carefully began to pull himself from her body. "Damn it," he growled, his lip curling with anger. "I shouldn't have done that."

"Why not?" she asked, shivering from the look in his eyes as he slid her a quick, icy glance, then turned away.

"Too much of the wolf was still in me," he muttered, moving to his feet, his body changing before her eyes, completing the transformation to his human form. He found the clean set of clothes she'd laid out for him and, keeping his back to her, he started pulling them on. "Why don't you get it?" he grunted, his anger intensifying as he yanked on his boots. "I could have ripped you in two, Morgan."

"But you didn't," she pointed out in a low voice, reaching for her own clothes. "And I loved it, Kier."

"You didn't deserve it," he muttered, glaring down at her as he shoved both hands through the thick, tangled strands of his hair, his big, beautiful body all but steaming with frustration.

"Well, I happen to like all sides of you, Kierland. Not just the playboy one."

He gave a tight, bitter laugh, and lowered his gaze, his hands braced loosely on his lean hips in one of those rugged, purely masculine poses that pulled the gray cashmere of his sweater tight across his magnificent shoulders. "Let the beast out of its cage," he warned, "and who knows what will happen."

"I'm not afraid of your beast. Or you," she told him, pulling her sweater back over her head as she moved to her feet and fastened her jeans. "I'll take you both on, Kier."

"No, you won't." His voice turned hard, brooding, and another wave of chills broke out over the surface of her body. "Because you're leaving."

"What? The cabin?"

"No." He slid her a shuttered look, then stalked away, heading across the sparsely furnished room to stand before its lone window. "You're leaving the

Wasteland," he rasped, staring out at the twilight darkness of the afternoon. "I'll go on and find Kellan by myself. Ashe can take you back to England."

"What? What the hell are you talking about?" The hoarse, shocked words scratched against her throat, and she swallowed, feeling sick.

He braced one rugged hand on the frame of the window, the rage and tension vibrating from his big, muscular body striking against her like a physical blow, and she reached out, digging her fingers into the back of a nearby chair for balance. "This is too dangerous," he said in a hard voice. "Last night was proof of that. I want you out."

"Well that's too damn bad," she argued, furious with him for thinking he could toss her aside so easily. "Because I'm not going anywhere. And you need me to find Kellan."

The firelight gleamed against the auburn strands of his hair as he shook his head. "We're close enough now, I should be able to find him on my own."

"Maybe," she conceded, her voice thick. "But nothing's definite. You're willing to take that risk?"

A pause, and then he let out a deep, gritty sigh. "If it means getting you out of here, then yeah. I'm willing to risk it."

Morgan was so angry, she could feel the fury as if it were something more than an emotion. Something that was a part of her. A living thing coiling through her body, seething and twisting and shredding her insides raw. "So that's it? You're just done with me?"

"I should have never even started with you." His

voice shook, his tall frame shuddering, as if on the verge of something explosive. "Worrying about you always led to trouble. I'm not going to keep doing it, damn it. It stops here."

"I don't understand," she whispered, the soft words thick with confusion.

"I make mistakes because of you!" he snarled, turning away from the window to face her, his gorgeous face set in a hard, emotionless mask, while his pale eyes blazed with fury. "And Nicole paid the price for it."

"Nicole?" Morgan shook her head, completely stunned. "What in God's name are you talking about?"

"At the academy. I...I wanted you. But I couldn't let myself have you." He shoved his hands into the pockets of his jeans, his voice a dark, gritty slash of sound. "It screwed with my head, how badly I wanted you. I made unforgivable mistakes, because I let you get to me. I didn't want you hurt, and Nicole died because of it."

Morgan wrapped her arms over her middle, shaking so hard that her teeth were chattering. "I...I still don't understand."

He pulled one hand down his face and dropped his head back onto his shoulders, staring up at the ceiling. "I didn't want you to be a part of the attack that was ordered by the Consortium." His breath roughened, his Adam's apple moving beneath the corded stretch of his dark throat as he swallowed. "Not because I thought you were too weak, but because I couldn't stand the thought of you being in danger. Of anything happen-

ing to you. That was why I refused to attack with the
full unit of trainees. Instead, I took a few cadets with
me to take out the nest, but it wasn't enough, and the
bastards got away. They killed Nicole in retaliation."

Morgan couldn't believe what she was hearing, her
thoughts spinning as she began to piece together more
of the crazy puzzle that made up their troubled past.
"Kierland, you can't blame yourself. They were
monsters. It's not your fault they killed her."

Lowering his head, he locked his turbulent gaze
with hers. "She wasn't a random victim, Morgan. They
chose her because they'd recognized me. Because I
was the screw-up who let them get away." A tired,
bitter laugh that held nothing but anger and pain, and
he cursed something rough under his breath, his profile
stark as he turned his face to the side, staring at some
distant point on the wall. "She didn't deserve it. What
they did to her. And the last words we ever said to each
other were ugly as hell."

"You had a fight?"

"Yeah." Another low, bitter laugh slipped from his
lips, and he popped his jaw as he shoved his hands
back into his pockets. "She accused me of being 'emo-
tionally absent' in our relationship, and she was right.
It was the truth, because I was just using her to keep
myself away from you. The night they killed her, I
should have been there, but I'd left her alone. I left her
without protection because I was too damn worried
about you. I knew you were going to be at the drill that
was taking place in the woods that night, and so I was
heading there to keep an eye on you."

Her chest ached for him, her heart breaking at the pain she could hear vibrating in his deep voice. "Still, it wasn't your fault, Kier." Morgan wished he would let her come closer, but could tell that he wouldn't, and she didn't want to force him from the room. "What happened to Nicole was a tragedy, and I'm sorry that she suffered…that you lost her, but you can't keep blaming yourself for her death."

He snorted, the auburn strands of his hair falling over his brow as he shook his head and muttered, "Like hell I can't."

"If she loved you, and I don't know how she couldn't have, then she wouldn't have wanted you to feel this way. She wouldn't want you spending the rest of your life blaming yourself for what happened."

A heavy, breath-filled silence, and then he slowly looked in her direction, holding her stare, and she shivered from the raw force of his gaze. "Will you tell my why you were so determined to stay away from me?" she whispered.

For a moment, she didn't think he was going to respond, but then he blew out a rough breath, and his voice dropped as he answered her question. "Because I knew there could be something between us."

"And why would that have been so bad?" Her own voice was choked by emotion, her control shattering as she realized that this was it. That the next few moments were going to determine where they went from there. "Why won't you let yourself feel anything for me, Kier? Why did you fight it so hard? Was it because of my bloodline? Because you were ashamed of me?"

"Jesus, Morgan. Why would I be ashamed of you?"

"Then what is it? Because you can't claim that you ran off with Nicole because of my relationship with Ashe. I wasn't even with him when you started dating her." She wanted to yell at him, to shout and scream, but she could barely get out the hoarse, breathless words. "So what's the real reason? Because after everything we've been through, I think I have a right to know."

He lowered his head again, his chest rising and falling as he stared at a distant spot on the floor. "I come from evil, Morgan. From weak, nasty shit."

She blinked, stunned, not knowing what to think. "What are you talking about?"

"My father was a murderer." Rough, husky words, scraping against her skin. "A mean, jealous bastard who killed my mother during one of his rages."

"Oh my God." Kellan had told her that their parents had died in some kind of tragic accident when Kierland was a little boy, but that was all. "What happened? Was she having an affair?"

He shook his head with a sharp, abbreviated movement, and a muscle began to tic in his temple. "As far as I know, there was never another man. Hell, he was so over the top, the simplest thing could set him off. She probably smiled at the milkman the wrong way. Said hello to the postman. That was all it took with him." He drew in a deep breath, held it, then slowly let it out as he said, "I was there when it happened. I walked into the kitchen to ask if Kell and I could have some cookies, and she was lying on the friggin' floor at my father's feet, bleeding out. He looked at me, stared me right in the eye and told me to never love anyone. Said that it would rip a man apart. Then he tore his claws across his own gut and killed himself."

"And you think…" She couldn't get the words out, her mouth trembling.

He lifted his hand, rubbing at the back of his neck, a feverish rush of color burning in his face. "I had hoped that maybe…that maybe I wasn't like him. And I was finally starting to believe it. Then you walked into my class at the academy on your first day, and I knew that I was just like the bloody bastard. That was all that it took." He held out his right hand, his fingers spread, and watched the way it trembled. "You smiled at me, and I knew that I'd do anything—steal, murder, cheat—to have you. Keep you. Make you mine. And in the end, I knew there was the chance that you'd end up just like my mother. I couldn't…no matter what it cost me, I couldn't let that happen to you." His hand fisted, the dark veins thickening beneath his hair-dusted skin. "I *won't* let that happen, Morgan."

"Are you anything like him?" she asked, tasting the saltiness of tears on her lips that she hadn't even realized were falling. "Anything like the man that he was?"

He shook his head. Muttered, "I try not to be."

"Then what makes you think you could ever act like him? Just because he did something horrible doesn't mean that you—"

"I know that!" he cut in, his deep voice thick with frustration. "I'm not stupid. I know I'm not the same person. But I also know that every time Ashe looked at you back then, I wanted to kill him. Rip him apart

with my bare hands. And I still do." His chest shook
with a sudden burst of grim, breathless laughter that
held nothing but more anger and pain, and he slid
her another shuttered look from the corner of his
eye. "Maybe I have more of my old man in me than
you think."

"So then what you're saying is that you decided my
future for me, right?" She swiped at the tears on her
cheeks, surprised by the heat in her face, too much of
her own anger and worry and pain burning inside her.
"Without even giving me a choice?"

"Don't you get it? There was no choice!" he roared,
the harsh, guttural words slamming through the room
like a scalding force of energy, blasting against her.

Her hands fisted, her pulse roaring in her ears like
some kind of thrashing, destructive storm. "Damn it,"
she cried, her voice rising as she fought the urge to
cross the distance between them and grab him, locking
herself around him in a hold that could never be
broken. But it was an illusion. A dream. Because no
matter how tightly she gripped him, he would slip
away. No matter how desperately she struggled, it
wouldn't be enough. "Believe it or not, you don't
always know what's best for everyone!"

"I knew this was a bad idea," he growled, his chest
heaving with the ragged force of his breaths. "I
should have packed your little ass back on a flight to
England the second you stepped foot into that club on
Saturday night."

Morgan was so angry she wanted to slap him. Hit
him. Make him hurt, the way he'd made her hurt all

those years ago. The way he was hurting her now. But she couldn't do it, because she ached for him, too. As ridiculous as the idea seemed that he could ever physically harm her, she could see that he honestly believed it. That he didn't trust himself to be close to her. To care about her. Take a chance on her...

They both jumped as the cabin door suddenly banged open, and Ashe stepped into the room, his dark hair and clothes dusted with snow. Morgan shook her head a little, sending him a look that said *Bad timing,* but he let out a tight, tired sigh, and murmured, "Sorry, sunshine, but I've got news for the wolf."

Kierland turned toward him, his expression one of sharp, alert focus, and Ashe explained. "Your brother's nearby. I caught his scent while I was running a perimeter in the woods, and I followed it. Found him at a camp a few miles east of here. There were some Kraven on site, guarding him at gunpoint, but I masked my scent, so they never even knew I was there. They also had some redhead with them, who looked like she was running things, but she's human."

"Spark," Kierland muttered, his gaze darkening as he absorbed the news.

Ashe slid the Lycan a curious look. "Spark?"

"The human," Kierland told him, his voice cold...hard. "Her name is Spark. She's a Collective assassin."

"And one of the most heinous bitches you've ever met," Morgan added. "Was he—"

"Did you talk to him?" Kierland grunted, cutting her off.

The vampire shook his head. "No. But I put myself where he could see me. It looked like he recognized me."

"He probably did," she murmured. "He's seen photographs I have of the two of us together."

Ashe acknowledged the explanation with a slow nod, his piercing gaze moving between her and Kierland, and Morgan knew he was trying to figure out what had happened between them. His gaze finally settled on the Lycan, and he said, "I was going to try to get closer to him, but he warned me back with a look. He's not ready to be saved."

"That's too damn bad," Kierland muttered, heading toward his backpack.

"Wait!" she gasped, reaching out and grabbing his arm. "Just stop and think for a second. This is exactly what Kellan wanted to happen, Kier. You've got to let him do this his way."

He looked down at her with an arrested expression, a violent rush of color flaring across his cheekbones and the bridge of his nose. "You knew?" The soft words lashed with fury, and she flinched, watching his anger shape itself into something dark and raw as he ripped his arm out of her hold.

"Knew what?" she whispered, swiping her tongue across her lower lip.

"Do *not* mess with me, Morgan." He shook with barely contained rage, a muscle ticking in the hollow of his shadowed cheek. "If he's as close as Granger says, you would know."

She didn't want to lie to him—wouldn't—but she

knew he wasn't going to believe the truth. And in the end, her silence condemned her.

"What is this?" he sneered, cutting an ugly look between her and Ashe, who looked as if he wanted to take her into his arms and protect her from Kierland's anger, but knew better than to push his luck. "Have the two of you just been trying to screw me over?"

"No! God, you know that's not true," she said unsteadily, begging him with her eyes to believe her.

He ran his hand over the grim shape of his mouth, looking as if he wanted so badly to have faith in her, but was afraid to. "Then why the hell didn't you say anything?"

"Because, to be perfectly honest, I wasn't paying attention to where Kellan was last night." The quiet words shook with emotion. "I was too busy worrying about you. I didn't realize his 'pull' was so close until I woke up this morning. And then you...distracted me. I haven't had a chance to say anything. But I would have told you."

He just stared at her, his tall, powerful body rigid with tension, muscles hard and coiled, bulging as if he was going to explode into movement at any moment.

With a deep, trembling breath, Morgan forced herself to say the words she knew needed to be said. "We're not meant to stop him. You know that. We're meant to be here waiting, close by, when he comes out with Chloe and needs our help. But that's all. You have to have faith, Kier, because Kellan's not going to fail. This is too important to him."

"Yeah, well, it's important to me, too," he muttered, turning away from her.

"What are you doing?" she asked, watching as he knelt down on one knee and began searching through the weapons pack, pulling out two handguns and several rounds of ammo.

Without looking at her, he said, "I'm going after him."

"Didn't you just hear me? You can't!"

"Like hell I can't," he growled, moving back to his feet. He set the guns and ammo on the room's only table, then pulled on his jacket and slid everything into the pockets.

Trying to control the tremor in her voice, Morgan took a deep breath and said, "After all that he's gone through to get here, do you really think this is what he would want? You coming to his rescue? He has a plan, Kier. He's a grown man and a helluva soldier. Let Kell do what he thinks is right."

"He could get himself killed!" he snapped, turning around to face her.

"That's a possibility. Yes. That's always a possibility. But it's *his* choice," she argued in a husky voice, their gazes locked together in a fierce, explosive battle of wills. "Please, Kierland. For once listen to someone else and stop thinking you know what's best for everyone."

He shuddered with rage, but didn't say anything, and she could only shake her head, her shoulders weighted with disappointment as she realized nothing she said was going to make a difference.

"Have fun trying to talk some sense into him," Ashe muttered, a resigned note of disgust in his deep voice as he headed toward the door, obviously deciding that he'd heard enough. "I'll be outside if you need me."

The door closed behind the vampire, and Morgan waited for Kierland to say something, but he didn't. He just stood there, his body held in a tight, rigid stance, his big hands fisted at his sides as he stared at the door.

"Are you really just going to walk away and leave me here alone?" she asked, forcing her chin to stay high, when all she really wanted was to slink away into a corner somewhere and lick her wounds.

He cut her a dark, cold look from the corner of his eye. "You won't be alone," he muttered. "You'll have the vamp, same as always."

"God," she whispered, blinking against another frustrating spill of tears. "I've been so stupid, haven't I? I actually thought, after last night, that you were…that you might care about me. That we might finally have some kind of chance together. But you're never going to let that happen, are you, Kier?"

"Don't make this about us." He ground out the words, his eyes narrowing with rage. "This is between me and Kell."

"No." It was strange to hear her voice sounding so thin, so hollow, as if all the life had just been drained right out of it. "This is about *you*, Kierland. It's always about you."

He made a low sound in the back of his throat that sounded more like the animal than the man, the green of his eyes glowing with fury within the darkness of his face. "You don't know what the hell you're talking about, Morgan."

Her breath shuddered past her lips, the tears coming faster, in a hot, unstoppable rush as she wrapped her arms over her chest, trying to hold herself together. "I know I loved you, Kier. I loved you so much that I almost died when you introduced me to Nicole. I loved you so much that I hated you for being with her. And that's why I ran to Ashe. Because you broke my heart, and you didn't even know it."

"Damn you." His body shook with a hard, violent tremor, as if he was struggling to stay in control. He shoved his hair back from his face with shaking hands and snarled, "That's a lie and you know it!"

"It's not," she told him, shaking her head, unable to stop the flood of words as they came pouring out of her. "I'd spent months waiting for you to ask me out, and you never did. I thought you were just waiting for me to get a bit older, for my birthday to come around, and then…that was when I met her. When you introduced me to Nicole. I didn't…I didn't just lust after you, Kier. I loved you. And it broke my heart when you brought her to meet me. Like a slap in the face, which was what I'm sure now that you'd intended, so that I would know you were off-limits. So that I would leave you in peace. And your plan worked, because I went to Ashe that night. You just didn't know about our relationship until later, because we hadn't told anyone."

He appeared stunned. Frozen. Then he shook it off, his lip curling as he growled, "Why him?"

She swiped at the tears under her eyes with her fingertips, her voice trembling almost uncontrollably. "Because I knew he w-wanted me, unlike you. He wasn't afraid to admit it. And because he'd always been kind to me."

"Kind?" he snarled. "Christ, Morgan. He just wanted in your pants."

"You're wrong," she argued. "Ashe was a true friend to me, Kierland. I refuse to feel guilty about our relationship, because he's been one of the best, most loyal friends I've ever had. But the truth is that I ended up with him because you broke my heart. Because you were too afraid to take a chance on me. Because you thought you knew what was right, and you weren't willing to let anyone else have a say."

A heavy silence fell between them, the kind that stretched out and made the room vibrate with tension until she could barely breathe, and then he gave another hard shake of his head, his brows pulled together in a deep vee. "It doesn't matter," he muttered, hunching his shoulders as he shoved his hands back into his pockets. "I don't even know why we're arguing about it. Jesus. What's done is done. You fell in love with Ashe and forgot all about me. It was obvious to everyone that you were crazy about him. Devastated when he left you. Whatever you'd felt for me before, it wasn't as strong as that. So none of what you've claimed changes anything now."

He looked scared. Sounded scared. And it was that fear, she realized, that would always keep him away from her.

"So that's it, then?" she asked. "You'll still keep Ashe between us, because that's what suits you?"

"I'm not keen on being second choice," he grunted, his stony expression as hard as his tone.

"You'll only see what you want to see, won't you?"

He'd turned away from her, his hand already on the handle of the door. "He still wants you, Morgan." Deep, guttural words, rough with strain. "He obviously regrets walking away from you. Once I step aside, you can have what you want. What you've always wanted."

Staring at the rigid set of his shoulders, she fought for her voice, and finally managed to say, "You think you have it all figured out, but you don't know anything, Kier."

"I know you can't go back and change the past. I lost you, and I've learned to live with it."

"Of course you have," she whispered, and a choked, kind of broken-sounding laugh fell from her lips. Or maybe it was a sob. She was too destroyed to tell the difference, a strange, shivering tremor beginning in her chest that was threatening to spread through her entire body, breaking her down. "You don't need anyone, right, Kier?"

"What the hell do you want from me?" he demanded in a hoarse rasp, his shoulders shaking.

It hurt, she thought, giving your love to someone. Cutting a piece of yourself off and offering it to them. But even worse was the knowledge that it didn't matter. That they wouldn't *let* it matter.

"I want something I can't have," she muttered, giving him back the same words he'd said to her.

A low, gritty laugh, and he yanked open the door. "Trust me, Morgan. He's yours. You've wanted the vamp for years, and now you've got him. He won't walk away from you again."

"Wow. Congratulations, Kier." Impossible to hide the bitterness in her tone. Not that she tried. "Once again, you've got it all figured out."

The door had already slammed shut behind him as Morgan sank to her knees in the middle of the room. "Too bad you're always wrong," she said brokenly, and then she buried her face in her hands.

# CHAPTER SEVENTEEN

*Thursday evening*

KIERLAND CREPT THROUGH THE forest like a shadow, careful not to make a sound. He knew he needed to focus on the present, that he needed to stay sharp, and yet, he couldn't stop thinking about Morgan. About the pale, devastated look on her face when he'd turned his back on her in the cabin and walked away.

Christ. There were a thousand things he wished he'd said to her before he'd left, but he knew it was better this way. There was nothing she could say to change his mind. They would just keep hurling the same arguments at each other, getting nowhere, while Kellan's life hung in the balance.

With a gun in his right hand, Kierland lifted his left and rubbed at the ache burning in the center of his chest, while his gut felt like he'd swallowed a block of ice. It was impossible to describe the pain he'd felt when Morgan had told him she'd loved him all those years ago. But it didn't *matter*. He couldn't *let* it matter. Because the truth was that she'd gotten over him and fallen in love with another man. One who probably still loved her. And that was a risk he couldn't take—the fact that even if Morgan chose to be with him now, she might eventually change her mind and go running back to the vamp. Not with his father's blood flowing through his veins. No, he'd rather live with the pain ripping him to shreds for the rest of his miserable existence, than ever risk hurting her.

The winds were blowing colder, but he was thankful for the light snowfall that would make it nearly impossible for the Kraven to scent his presence. He'd been hiking through the woods for about twenty minutes, heading east, and although the weather was making it difficult for him to scent his brother, Kierland knew he was getting close. He could feel it, his senses telling him that it wouldn't be long now. He tried to clear his mind as he made his way deeper into the towering, shadowed forest, focusing on the mission...burying all the emotional crap that was scraping him raw—and then he caught the glow of a campfire flickering in the distance, and he knew that he'd found them. His heart began to beat in a hard, thundering rhythm, and he waited for the flood of relief he'd expected to feel at this moment. But it didn't come. Instead, he kept hearing Morgan's husky words as she'd begged him to listen to her.

*You have to have faith, Kier, because Kellan's not going to fail. This is too important to him.*

Damn it, he needed to get the bloody woman out of his mind. Now. Before he completely lost it.

He moved closer, stealthily silent, expecting to find sentries guarding the perimeter of the camp, but there weren't any. The Carringtons who had survived the fight the night before obviously hadn't warned Westmore and his allies about their presence, but then he supposed one couldn't really expect loyalty out of a nest of marked, poisoned psychopaths, no matter how much money had exchanged hands.

Hell, considering they were in the Wasteland, the deal might not have even been negotiated on monetary terms. For all they knew, Westmore might have offered the bloodthirsty vamps that "fresh meat" they were so keen on, and his stomach curled at the thought.

As he drew nearer, Kierland could see that a fire had been started in the center of a small clearing, and the Kraven were huddled around the flames for warmth, their voices rumbling in conversation. They were gossiping about two women that Westmore had in custody at his compound, referring to one of them as "the witch." She had to be Chloe Harcourt. When the men made a lewd comment about the one they called "the psychic," Spark, who sat removed from the group, looked up with an expression of disgust. "Pigs," she muttered, then turned back to her reading, her brow furrowed with concentration as she leafed through a small leather notebook.

And at the far edge of the clearing, about fifteen feet away from Spark, sat Kellan.

Kierland's heart clenched as he caught sight of the thick metal shackle around his brother's left ankle, the cuff attached to a heavy chain that was locked around the trunk of a nearby tree. They'd chained his brother to a tree, like a damn dog, and he choked back the feral rise of fury, wanting to launch an immediate attack against Spark and the Kraven, tearing their throats out with the wolf's deadly jaws.

Pulling in a deep breath through his nose, Kierland forced himself to stay calm as he assessed the situation. His brother looked exhausted, with bruise-colored circles beneath his eyes and grim brackets framing his mouth, his auburn hair now long enough to blow against the sides of his face. There was a feral edge to the look in his eyes, as well as the way he held his heavily muscled body, and Kierland knew that Kellan had been traveling in full "wolf" form. Taking the complete form of his inner wolf would have enabled Kellan to travel faster...and safer, than in his human or "were" forms, but there were consequences. Their kind didn't often take the complete shape of their beasts, but when they did, they gave more of themselves over to the animal...and could be dangerous as hell because of it. Their tempers were shorter, and their aggressive tendencies became more pronounced. Which meant Kellan would have to walk a very careful line when he finally found Chloe Harcourt, or he would end up scaring the hell out of her.

*Whoa. What's that? What do you mean "when" he finds her? Aren't you here to stop him?*

Cursing under his breath, Kierland scrubbed a hand down his face, and wondered if he was losing his mind. Not only was he having conversations with himself, but he was forgetting his entire friggin' purpose for being there. Which was to save his brother's ass, whether he wanted to be saved or not.

*Do you really think this is what he would want? You coming to his rescue? He has a plan, Kier. He's a grown man and a helluva soldier. Let Kell do what he thinks is right.*

He scowled at the whisper of Morgan's soft voice slipping through his mind, and moved until he was positioned directly across the clearing from Kellan. Kierland kept to the shadows, crouched behind a massive toppled tree trunk with a SIG Sauer in one hand, just watching, confident of the fact that Kell would sense his presence. He knew the bullets wouldn't kill the Kraven, since they could only be taken out with a wooden stake driven through the center of the heart, but the bullets would slow them down enough that he could get Kell out of there. A few moments later, his brother took a deep breath, and raised his head, scanning the shadowed edges of the clearing, his night vision far better than that of a human. Within seconds, his brilliant blue-green gaze locked with Kierland's, and he sent him a dark, uneasy look of warning.

Using a swift series of hand signals they'd devised when they were younger, while playing war on the sprawling grounds of their grandfather's estate, Kierland asked him if he was okay.

Kellan slid a surreptitious glance toward the Kraven and Spark, making sure no one was watching him, then braced his elbows on his bent knees, so that his hands were hanging loosely between his legs. Keeping his gaze on the others, he signed *Compound north. Thirty miles. She's called for backup. They're taking me in tonight.*

He waited for Kellan to look his way again, then found himself signing *You know what you're doing?* when he'd meant to warn him to get down, so that he could open fire on Spark and the Kraven. What the hell was he doing?

With his heartbeat roaring in his ears and Morgan's husky words still spiraling through his head, he watched as Kellan responded with a sharp nod, his eyes bright with determination.

*Okay,* he signed. *I hate it, but won't interfere. We'll monitor the compound. Then set up a rendezvous two miles south. If you're not out by next Friday, we'll attack. Just...get out of there as soon as you can. I don't want to lose you.*

Kellan grinned at him, the boyish, lopsided tilt of his mouth making Kierland want to throw back his head and howl. God, it hurt so much to let him go. But Morgan was right. This wasn't his situation to control. Kellan wasn't a child who needed him to make his choices for him any more.

Slipping away with a silent goodbye, Kierland felt strangely lost as he turned and headed back the way he'd come, like a compass that had suddenly lost its sense of direction. Something was happening to him, everything spinning out of control, his mind caught in a loop that kept leading back to one single, shining point of importance.

*Morgan.*

Christ, she'd been right. He *was* the one destroying everything, with his insane control issues and the stupid, blind fear that he couldn't get past. He was the

one who'd shoved everything into shit. He'd have
ditched it, the whole manic, screwed-up mess, if he
could. But he didn't know how. He was trapped inside
a prison of his own bloody making, and he was going
to lose her because of it.

Lose her? Hell, she was already lost. Gone. Driven
away by his miserable, prick-of-the-year attitude.

*Unless I go after her. Get down on my knees and beg
her for another chance.*

The urgent, fervent words echoed through his mind,
but he didn't know what to do with them. Yes, he knew
that he loved her. That he wanted her. That he would've
killed to have her. But where did that leave them? For
one, he was still scared shitless of what that love might
do to him. Of how it might get twisted and mangled
by jealousy, until he'd become as big a monster as his
father had been. And then there was the fact that she
hadn't told him she was still in love with him now.
Only that she *had* been. Before she'd run to Granger
and fallen in love with the vamp.

So what in God's name was he meant to do? He
couldn't just let her walk away...and yet, he didn't
know how to trust himself to be a part of her life, to
be the kind of man that she deserved.

*I need to talk to her. Tell her how I feel. Lay it all
out on the line, and let her help me. Give her the
chance to tell me what she wants, and help me figure
it out. Together. Without freaking out on her.*

It was terrifying as hell, the idea of opening up to
her and confessing everything that was inside him, but
at this point, what did he have to lose? He already

knew what his life was going to be like without her. Cold and pointless, until his bitterness had turned him into someone he no longer even recognized. He had to at least try, damn it. Who cared if he made an idiot of himself? It didn't matter. Nothing mattered, except for finding her and throwing himself at her feet.

Driven by adrenaline and desperation, Kierland started running, his legs pumping, picking up speed until he was racing through the moonlit forest, determined to reach her before she…

Huh. How strange. Just like before with Kellan, his brain derailed on him again, because his intended finish to that thought had been…*before she left with Granger and I have to chase her down, when all I want is to talk this out, so that I can make sense of what is happening.*

But it was a different track he found his mind traveling now. One that had him running harder, faster, his muscles burning as he pushed his body to its limits, a horrible sense of panic wrenching through him. He didn't know why, but he had the strangest sensation that something had happened. Something bad. It was impossible to ignore the cold suck of fear in his chest, in his gut, his entire being swamped with terror.

*Too late,* he thought. *I shouldn't have left her. I'm too late.*

Running as if the hounds from hell were on his ass, Kierland had already covered over half the distance back to the cabin, when he heard someone coming toward him in the opposite direction at an almost identical speed. He could tell by the scent that it was

Granger, the vamp doing nothing to mask his presence, and they both came to an abrupt, jarring stop the moment they caught sight of each other.

Granger's grim, shocked expression confirmed his fears that something had happened to Morgan. He could smell blood on the bastard—*Morgan's blood*—and something inside him cracked with a sharp, piercing pain that nearly staggered him.

"What the hell's going on?" he snarled, his beast punching against the confines of his body, as furious and as worried as the man. "I smell blood. Where's Morgan?"

"You've got to hurry," the Deschanel panted, his hands braced on his knees as he leaned forward, struggling to catch his breath. "I got her back to the cabin, but she's in trouble. Bleeding. We don't have any time to lose."

A red haze filled the Lycan's vision, and he fought to keep it together...to keep himself from sinking into the visceral, destructive burn of rage and despair. "What happened to her?" he growled. "Was it vampires?"

Granger shook his head. "Death-Walkers. The fool woman masked her scent and snuck out of the cabin to come after you," he muttered. "By the time I realized what she'd done and went after her, they'd already attacked."

"Oh, Christ." When the Death-Walkers hadn't attacked that first night, Kierland had foolishly assumed that the creatures hadn't followed them into the Wasteland. But he'd been wrong. And now Morgan had paid for his mistake. "How'd you find her if she was masking her scent?"

Granger curled his lip. "I could smell the Death-Walkers."

"Where are they now?"

The vampire shook his head as he straightened to his full height. "You won't believe it," he rasped, "but we have Juliana Sabin to thank for running them off. She's with Morgan now."

"Juliana?" he croaked. "What the hell is she doing here?"

"Micah managed to survive the blast last night and made it back to his compound. In one of his more lucid moments, he told Juliana what he'd done. She got her guards and started heading this way, to make sure we were okay. It was just blind luck that they found us when they did and were able to chase off those ugly bastards."

Knowing there was no time to waste, Kierland started running, only dimly aware of Granger keeping pace behind him, his entire focus centered on Morgan. He was sick with fear, his body cold, his thoughts tangled and twisted as he tried to wrap his mind around what had happened. They made it back to the cabin within a handful of minutes. He immediately rushed inside, not even sparing a glance at Juliana's guards, who were setting up a camp in front of the small structure. The scent of Morgan's blood was overwhelming, and Kierland broke out in a cold sweat as he moved in a numb haze toward the bed tucked into the far corner of the room. Morgan lay stretched out on top of a dark quilt, her eyes closed, her face and clothes spattered with blood. Juliana Sabin was sitting in a chair beside the bed, using a cloth to clean the blood from Morgan's

torn cheek. But the vampire rose to her feet as he and
Granger made their way across the room, murmuring
that she would be waiting outside if they needed her.

Walking to the side of the bed, Kierland stared down
at Morgan's pale, blood-streaked face through a
burning sheen of tears, his hands shaking, his heart
lodged in his throat like a boulder. He made a raw, fractured sound of rage as he looked over the slender
length of her body, unable to believe what he was
seeing. Her jeans and sweater were completely
shredded by claw and bite marks, her delicate skin
bloodied and bruised and torn open by those sick
bastards. The Death-Walkers had obviously been
toying with her, taking their turns attacking her. His
hands clenched into trembling fists as he thought about
how terrified she must have been.

"She's been unconscious since I found her,"
Granger rasped. "She's lost a helluva lot of blood, and
her self-healing abilities aren't powerful enough to
deal with the damage. Something has to be done."

Knowing exactly what the vamp meant by *something,* Kierland lowered his head and pressed his
thumb and forefinger over his eyelids, his facial
muscles pulled into a tight grimace. He wanted so
badly to be selfish and take what he wanted, but for
once, he needed to make this about Morgan. Not his
wants. Not his desires. But hers.

He couldn't ignore the memory of how devastated
she'd been when the vampire had broken things off
with her all those years ago. A pale, hollow ghost of
herself. Clearly, she'd been nuts about the guy. Which

meant there really wasn't any choice. If Kierland loved her, and God only knew that he did, then he had to do what was right. To hell with what it did to his own life. As Morgan had told him before, not everything was about him. What he wanted didn't matter. All that mattered was that she got what *she* wanted.

Cutting a narrow look toward Granger, he took a deep breath, then forced out the five fractured, guttural words that would permanently tear out a piece of his soul. "You have to bite her."

Kierland knew a Deschanel couldn't "make" a vampire. You were either born one or you weren't. But the males of the species could pass on some of their traits when they took a mate and bonded with her. It was done through a special serum that they carried in their genetic makeup. They would make a bite, inject the serum into the female's bloodstream and then nature would do the rest.

From the foot of the bed, Granger returned his stare with a piercing gaze, and asked, "Why me?"

"Because she loves you," Kierland conceded, the words vibrating with emotion as he moved his gaze back to Morgan, "and no matter how badly I want her, I'd rather see her live a long, happy life with you than a miserable one with me."

A heavy, breath-filled silence, while the heat of Granger's shocked gaze burned against the side of his face, and then the vamp quietly said, "You really do love her, don't you? I had my doubts that you had it in you, especially after today. But it couldn't be clearer now."

"What does it matter?" he growled, his pulse

roaring in his ears as he struggled to keep it together. Keep from falling apart. He could fall apart later, after Morgan was no longer bleeding out in front of him, as pale as a ghost. "All that matters is making the choice she'd make for herself, if she could."

"That," Granger rasped, "is how I know you're in love with her."

Forcing himself to move back a step, Kierland shoved his fingers through his windblown hair, his breaths coming in hard, ragged bursts as he shot a furious glare toward the vampire. "Christ, we don't have time for this bullshit," he snarled. "How and what I feel are irrelevant. All that matters is keeping her alive. So get your ass in gear and do it!"

With a rough sigh, Granger crossed his arms over his broad chest and said, "I can't. As badly as I'm tempted, I won't do that to her."

A dark, primitive sound tore from Kierland's throat, and he fisted his hands at his sides. "Damn it, she *loves* you!"

"As a friend, you jackass." The vampire jerked his chin toward him. "It's gonna have to be you."

"No." He shuddered, and took another heavy step away from the bed, not trusting himself to be near her. "That's not even possible."

Granger stared back, unrelenting. "Why the hell not?"

Rubbing his hand over his mouth, Kierland struggled to put his chaotic thoughts in order. "She can't be turned to a Lycan," he explained in a raw voice, "because she's already a shifter, which means that I can't change to 'were' form and pass the gene on through my bite. The only way I can give her the healing trait is by marking her. I'd have to bite her in human form, with the wolf's fangs. And because of how I feel about her, that would…bind her to me."

"Then do it," Granger grunted. "And before you waste more time telling me you can't, there's something I might as well go ahead and make clear right now. Morgan is the one who left *me,* not the other way around. She tried to make our relationship work, but she couldn't, because she was in love with you. And she still is."

Stunning bolts of shock skittered through his system, making his head spin, and he stumbled back another step. "You're lying," he said unsteadily, shaking, afraid to let himself believe. "I saw the two of you together. She was crazy about you."

A wry smile touched Granger's mouth, and he lowered his head, rubbing at the back of his neck. "She tried to be, but she couldn't get over you. She's been in love with you forever, and you've been so wrapped up in yourself, you've never been able to see it. But it's always been there." He lifted his head, a hard glint in his pale eyes as he blew out a ragged breath and went on, adding, "She loved you so much she almost died for you. And I'm not talking about tonight."

Kierland stared, something about the vamp's tone causing the tiny hairs to lift on the back of his neck.

Wearing a dark, primal expression of anger and disgust, Granger said, "How do you think we found the rogue nest of vampires that killed your girlfriend? While you were wallowing in guilt, drinking yourself stoned, Morgan offered herself up as bait. The plan went wrong, and by the time we found her, the vampires had already dragged her underground. They had her pinned down, all of them on her at once, and she was making the most god-awful sounds I've ever heard. Begging, screaming, pleading for someone to help her."

"That's why she doesn't like to be crowded by people," he croaked, his face misted with sweat. "Why she doesn't like to be in close spaces."

Granger nodded. "It's also part of the reason why she looked like she did when you thought I'd left her. She blamed herself for not being able to get over you, so that something between us could have a chance. But she was also still dealing with the trauma from the attack."

It was nearly impossible, but he finally managed to ask, "Did they...rape her?"

"No, but it was close." The vampire locked his jaw, his profile stark as he stared down at Morgan's blood-covered body. "They had her stripped, their hands and mouths all over her, but I got there just before one of them penetrated her. A second later, and it would have been too late. The bastard was already between her legs."

It took a moment before he could get his throat to work, too much fury and regret and guilt raging through his system, making him feel like hammered shit. "Why didn't anyone tell me?" he finally managed to rasp.

A low, bitter laugh, and Granger shook his head. "She begged us not to, if you can believe it. Said you had enough to deal with. And you were so out of it at the time, the others agreed."

He found himself moving a little closer to the bed,

his eyes burning with tears that he didn't even try to hide. "I can't...can't believe she would have done something like that."

"Not so hard to believe, considering how crazy she was about you." The vamp paused, then quietly asked, "Did you honestly not know how she felt?"

His throat shook so badly, Kierland could barely get the words out. "I didn't dare...hope. I was just... I couldn't..."

"You were scared."

For once, there was no judgment in Granger's deep voice, and he sucked in a sharp breath, then gave a jerky nod. "Yeah. Always have been when it comes to her." Hoarse, fractured words, rough with emotion. "I loved her, and it scared the hell out of me."

Kierland could see the past so clearly now that it hurt, like a wound that'd been carved into his heart. Could see what an idiot he'd been with a sharp, painful clarity that made him want to throw back his head and howl. Over the years, he'd built up an image of Morgan in his mind to help him stay away from her. But deep down, he'd always known it was a fraud. He hadn't sought out the truth, choosing to believe the rumors, as well as the lies he told himself, because it made it easier to keep his distance.

He'd been a jackass. And he didn't deserve her. But...he wasn't prepared to lose her, either. Which meant he was just going to have to spend the rest of his life trying to make it up to her. Trying to become a man who was worthy of her love.

He was still scared as hell of something happening

to her, and always would be. But he would suck it up and deal, because he got it now. Loving her meant surrendering to it all, even the fear, and fighting for what he wanted. Yeah, he'd probably be overprotective and possessive, but Morgan was strong enough to keep him in line. She was a beautiful, breathtaking goddess, and he was going to spend the rest of his life worshipping at her feet, thanking God for every moment that he had with her.

Moving between them, to the side of her bed, Granger reached down and gripped her wrist, checking her pulse. Fear burned in his pale eyes as he looked over his shoulder, locking his gaze with Kierland's. "If you don't do it soon," he said, "you're going to lose her."

He nodded, swallowed and started to move around the Deschanel, but Granger turned and blocked his way. "But make sure," the vamp warned him in a hard voice, his gray eyes glittering with emotion. "She'd rather go now, than be stuck with you for the rest of her life if you don't really want her."

"She's all I've ever wanted," he rasped, the husky confession scratching his throat.

"Then do this thing and make her right," Granger muttered, scrubbing his hands down his face. "Drives me crazy seeing her like this."

Feeling the strained bands of his jealousy beginning to snap, one by one, Kierland said, "You really care about her, don't you?"

Granger rolled his eyes and snorted. "I won't be trying to steal her away," he murmured, his tone dry, "so don't waste your time worrying about it."

"No…I just," Kierland swallowed, took a deep breath, then held out his hand and said, "thank you for being her friend. For taking care of her all these years."

Looking a little shell-shocked himself, the vampire shook his hand, cast another worried glance over his shoulder at Morgan, then pulled his hand down his face again. "Okay, then. I'm getting outta here. This is too much for me."

"Wait," Kierland called out, as Granger pulled open the door, an icy blast of wind whipping through the room. With one hand on the door frame and the other on the handle, the vamp looked back at him, and Kierland said, "There's still one thing I can't figure out. Why has she always claimed that you were the one who broke things off?"

A low laugh slid lazily from Granger's lips, and he smiled. "That was Morgan's idea. She didn't want to ruin my reputation. Always has been too sweet for her own good." His head tilted a little to the side, and his eyes narrowed as he said, "Just so you know, Watchman, I'll be keeping an eye on you, making sure you treat her right."

Kierland jerked his chin to acknowledge the warning, and then the door closed behind the vampire, leaving him and Morgan alone in the firelit room. With his heart pounding to a powerful, thundering beat, he walked to the bed and stared down at the woman who'd turned his entire world on its head from the moment he'd first met her. Things had never been right since, because he'd wasted so many years fighting the inevitable.

But not anymore.

Careful not to jar her, Kierland lowered himself onto the bed, bracing himself on an elbow as he lay down beside her. She didn't move, the rise and fall of her chest so faint, it was nearly imperceptible. The back of his throat burned, and he leaned over her, pressing his wet face to the exquisitely soft, chilled skin at the side her throat. He could feel her fading, drifting away from him, and his voice shook as he put his mouth to the tender shell of her ear and whispered, "I hope that you can hear me, sweetheart, because I love you. I should have told you today. Damn it, I should have told you a thousand times before, and I'm sorry for each time that I didn't. For every second that we lost. But...but I promise you that I'll never let you down again. I'll tell you every day, with words and the touch of my body and the way that I look at you. I swear you'll never have to second-guess or wonder how I feel. I'll be the most obvious bastard alive, and I don't give a damn how badly the others rib me about it. I don't care about anything but you. About spending the rest of my life with you and making you happy."

The fire in the hearth crackled as the Lycan drew in a deep breath and pushed her hair back from the pale, precious angles of her face. His heart beat faster as he pressed a tender kiss to the corner of her eye...the feminine curve of her jaw...the fragile column of her throat.

Then he released his fangs, whispered that he loved her and made the bite.

# CHAPTER EIGHTEEN

*The Casus/Kraven Compound*
*Friday night*

A STRING OF HOARSE, guttural swear words whispered past Kellan Scott's lips as he paced the confines of his cell. The Lycan had spent the past twenty-four hours in an interrogation room on the ground floor of Westmore's compound, where the Casus had done their best to find out why he'd traveled into the Wasteland. Between the violent beatings, Kellan had fed their assumptions that he was after the Dark Markers in their possession, careful not to show any interest in the whereabouts of the other prisoners. And it had paid off. Twenty minutes ago, they'd finally taken him downstairs, shoving him into one of the cold, barren cells that lined an entire wall of the compound's underground level. Although the iron bars on the front of the cells offered a clear view to those standing on the outside, the individual cells were separated by walls, making it impossible for the prisoners to see each other.

As he'd passed the first cell, Kellan had spied a slight female form sleeping on a narrow cot before they'd locked him inside the adjacent cell, and he assumed she was "the psychic" the Kraven had been talking about at the camp on Thursday night. All the other cells were empty.

Chloe Harcourt wasn't there.

Kellan could detect the lingering scent of a female Merrick in the empty cell on his left, which told him that Chloe had been staying there. But where the hell was she? Her faint, mouthwatering scent was a gut-wrenching reminder that he had somehow just missed her despite all he'd been through. He tried to hold on to his reason and his faltering hope. But it wasn't easy. Three days earlier, he'd been bitten by an infected Deschanel. Although he couldn't pass the poison on to another, it was slowly spreading through his system, and he couldn't control the tension in his aching muscles, his body flashing between extremes of hot and cold.

"Damn it," he snarled, under his breath, terrified that they had taken her someplace with the intention of hurting her. That she was scared and alone. He crossed his arms tightly over his chest and tried to still the shivers that shook his spine while sweat trickled down the sides of his face. "Where the hell are you, woman?"

"They haven't harmed her," someone murmured, the soft, raspy voice coming from the cell where the psychic had been sleeping. "They've taken her to be examined by a doctor."

Wedging himself into the right front corner of his cell, Kellan wrapped his hands around the iron bars, the metal cold against his fevered palms. "Why a doctor?" he asked in a hoarse voice, careful to speak quietly enough that they wouldn't be overheard by those upstairs. "What happened to her? Is she hurt?"

"She's weak, because her awakening Merrick half is starved for its first feeding," the female whispered. "Westmore refuses to allow anyone to touch her, because he's saving her for someone named Calder. So they're going to try to give her the blood she needs intravenously. But it won't work."

"I know," he rasped, stunned by the knowledge that Chloe's awakening had already begun. "When are they bringing her back?"

Silence, and then a soft reply. "Soon."

"Who are you?" he asked, his unsteady words rough with fury as he thought of the things the Kraven had been saying about this young woman. Their crude jokes about the torture and abuse she had suffered since being captured.

"My name is Raine," she told him, "and you've already figured out why I'm here. I'm Westmore's pet psychic."

"If you're psychic, can you see the future?" he asked, swallowing against a dry throat. "Can you tell me what's going to happen?"

"I'm sorry," she murmured, "but my powers don't work that way. I can only see the past and the present. But from what I've seen, I can tell you that something bad is coming. A Casus named Gregory is on his way here to destroy Westmore."

"Gregory's an asshole," Kellan muttered, curling his busted lip as he leaned his damp forehead against the cell's cool iron bars, "but if he wants Westmore, he's welcome to him. His attack may even serve as a diversion and give us a chance to escape. I'll find a way to get both you and Chloe out of here."

"I'm afraid it won't be that simple."

"Why not? What do you see?"

"This Gregory wants more than just Westmore," she explained, the quiet words edged with exhaustion and pain. "Even if you escape here with the witch, you won't be free. Not while Gregory still lives."

"Oh, shit," he groaned, understanding what she was trying to tell him. The Casus bastard wanted Chloe, too.

Kellan's gut twisted with dread, and he prayed that Kierland was nearby, knowing they were going to need his help when they finally escaped. With Chloe's awakening draining her strength and the poison twisting through his insides, there was no telling what kind of shape they would be in when they finally made it out.

"Can you see my brother?" he asked in a low voice. "Is he okay?"

"I can see him, and he's fine. Anxious to get you out of here, but willing to play it your way." It almost sounded as if she was smiling as she said, "There's quite a lot that he wants to say to you."

Kellan gave a soft snort, knowing Kierland had to be furious with him. "Yeah, I'll bet there is."

"He's not angry with you," she whispered. "Not anymore. He's terrified for your safety, but he's thankful that you brought the female Watchman into his life. There were a few…complications, but he's determined not to lose her. In fact, he's already claimed her with his bite."

Shaking his head, a slow smile curved Kellan's battered mouth, and he sent up a silent word of thanks to whoever might be listening. Despite the hell that he'd survived and the challenges that lay ahead, it felt good to know that he'd actually gotten something right.

After all these years, his brother finally had his woman.

# CHAPTER NINETEEN

*The Sabin Compound*
*Saturday evening*

TWO DAYS AFTER KIERLAND had bitten her, Morgan still hadn't regained consciousness.

Kierland would have been terrified, if Juliana Sabin hadn't assured him that it was completely normal for the healing process to take a little time. Having never intended to claim a mate, he'd not paid much attention to the more intricate rules that applied to the act, and it drove him crazy that he didn't know what to expect. Yeah, he'd known the basics. But he couldn't help worrying that he'd done something wrong. Did it matter that she hadn't been conscious when the bite was made, or that she'd already lost so much blood? He constantly berated himself for not sinking his fangs into her the moment he'd made it back to the cabin on Thursday evening, but he'd been so certain that Granger was the one she wanted....

After he'd gone outside to let them know the bite had been made, Juliana had invited them back to the Sabin compound. Kierland had accepted the offer, wanting to keep Morgan in as secure a location as possible, especially with the renewed threat of the Death-Walkers hanging over their heads. The female Deschanel had also graciously offered the use of her room, and she came to check on Morgan often, even helping Kierland to bathe and dress her in a clean T-shirt, so that she would be more comfortable when she finally came to. And Ashe stayed with her for hours at a time, his grief and concern carved into the grim lines of his handsome face as he sat at Morgan's bedside, holding her slim hand in both of his. Kierland had thanked the vampire again, and had even shared some quiet conversations with the man he'd expected to hate for all eternity. But it was hard to hold a grudge against the cocky bastard when Kierland was starting to like him so much. Ashe had even agreed to join in their fight against the Casus, just as soon as he'd managed to track down his brother, and Kierland had told him that he'd be damn appreciative for their skills on the battlefield.

The only thing they hadn't talked about was the "family trouble" Ashe and Gideon were dealing with, but Kierland knew better than to push. He'd made it clear, though, that if they needed his help, all they had to do was let him know.

Even Micah, who had been chained inside his room since his return to the Sabin compound, had expressed his concern for Morgan's welfare. Although the poison continued to send him into his mad bouts of rage, Juliana had told Kierland that there were times when Micah seemed at peace with his confinement, relieved to be somewhere that he couldn't harm anyone. Despite their continued searches for the young vampire that Micah had taken hostage when he'd last escaped, she hadn't been found. The Sabins feared the worst, terrified that Micah, who claimed he couldn't remember what had happened to his cousin, had actually killed the girl.

On several occasions, Kierland and Ashe had tried to question Juliana about the reason for her family's confinement within the Wasteland, but she'd refused to answer, claiming the subject was still too painful to discuss. While Kierland was content to let her keep her secrets, Ashe seemed unable to contain his frustration. He constantly started arguments with Juliana, until she'd begun to leave the room whenever he came to visit Morgan.

For the most part, though, Kierland had simply spent his time alone with the female who was now his mate, holding her in his arms, praying to every higher power he could think of that she would wake up and come back to him. His bite had healed the physical wounds that the Death-Walkers had made, but it was the ones he couldn't see, that were buried inside her, that scared him most. And yet, whenever he'd start to worry that the trauma of the attack had been too much for her, he'd remind himself that she was the bravest, strongest woman he'd ever known, and hold her more tightly, whispering in her ear, telling her that she *had* to come back to him, because he couldn't live without her.

And then, exactly forty-eight hours from the time that he'd bitten her, she finally opened her eyes.

Kierland was lying on his side, with Morgan's head cradled in the crook of his left arm, murmuring to her while he stroked his fingers along the delicate arc of her cheek. And the next thing he knew, she was staring right back at him, her beautiful gaze locked with his.

"Thirsty," she groaned, and then she shocked the hell out of him by nuzzling into the curve of his shoulder…and biting his throat. She sank her fangs deep, pulling on his vein, and the scalding burn of pleasure nearly turned him inside out. His fingers curved around the back of her skull, holding her against him, and he went rock hard, the need to get inside her so intense, he thought he might actually die if it didn't happen.

But first, they needed to talk. And Christ, he needed to make sure that she was okay. That she wasn't in any pain.

She drank deeply for almost a minute, each evocative pull against his vein making him shiver and gasp, the pleasure an exquisite blend of erotic sensations. And then she made a low sound, and pulled away, the back of her hand pressed to her rosy mouth as she stared up at him through huge, startled eyes. "Why did I just do that?" she whispered, the quiet words hoarse with embarrassment.

"I'm not sure, sweetheart." A grin twitched at the corner of the Lycan's mouth, and he was too bloody happy to hold it back. "But I'm not complaining."

She blinked, a delicate flush burning across the bridge of her nose. "I just took your vein, Kier, as if I had every right to it!"

"I know," he rumbled, and it was impossible to disguise the rich satisfaction in his tone. Lifting his hand, he pushed a few silken strands of hair from her face, then ran his thumb over the worried grooves that had settled between her brows. "What do you remember, honey?"

"Not much," she whispered, her gaze growing distant as she sank into her memories. "I know I left the cabin to go after you. I was worried you were going to get hurt. Then I remember smelling the Death-Walkers, and..." She blinked again, and a little shudder ran through her body. "They bit me, didn't they?" she asked, staring deep into his eyes.

"Yeah, and it was pretty bad. But Ashe and Juliana Sabin got you back to the cabin, then Ashe came after me." Taking hold of her hand, he pressed the tips of her fingers against the side of her throat, where a faint bruise from his bite still lingered, the skin there burning hot to the touch, and her eyes went round as he said, "You were in rough shape, until I made this bite right here."

"You...marked me?"

Kierland nodded, watching as she studied the proud, possessive look on his face, and her mouth began to tremble. "Oh, God," she gasped. "How could you?"

He went perfectly still, his voice a little tight as he said, "That wasn't exactly the reaction I was hoping for. I thought..." He paused, choosing his words with care. "Isn't that what you wanted?"

Tears glistened in her eyes, the shimmering wash of liquid making his stomach cramp with dread, until she admitted, "Of course it's what I wanted. I'm in love with you! But...was it what *you* wanted? Or did you just do it to keep me alive? Because I'd have rather you let me die than be bound to me when you don't...when you're not in—"

"Morgan, honey, just shush and listen to me for a moment," Kierland said with a tender smile, pressing his mouth to her petal-soft lips. He pushed his fingers into her hair, shaping his hands around her skull, and pulled back just far enough that he could hold her gaze. "I didn't bite you just to keep you alive. I did it because I can't live without you. Because I don't want to wake up one single day without your body next to mine. Because I want to grow old with you, and build a life with you. Once this bloody war is over, I want to take you someplace and keep you there for days, weeks, until we've made a miracle and our baby is growing right here," he told her in a husky voice, lowering his right hand so that he could rub her belly with the flat of his palm.

"Am I dreaming?" she whispered, clutching onto his shoulders, and then her eyes went comically wide. "Oh God, I didn't die, did I? That would be so typical! Get everything I've ever wanted, then find out that I've croaked...and none of it's real."

"You're not dreaming." A crooked smile touched his mouth, and he kissed her again, saying, "You're very much alive, sweetheart. And you're also very, *very* loved."

"I am?" she murmured against his lips.

"You are," he rumbled, pulling back to see her face. "And you're also a beautiful little liar."

"Oh." Pulling her lower lip through her teeth, she asked, "Which one did you find out about?"

Holding her close, Kierland told her about the talk he'd had with Ashe, explaining how the vamp had told him the truth about their past relationship, as well as the horrific attack she'd suffered at the hands of the rogue vampires. Then he explained how they'd come to be at the Sabin compound, recounting the events from Thursday evening, and his voice shook as he said, "After I left Kell and started making my way back to you, it scared the hell out of me, thinking that I might have lost you because I've been such a jackass. That I might have to go through life without you. It's... That's something I *can't* do."

"And your father?" she asked, pushing his hair back from his brow. "That doesn't worry you anymore?"

He took a deep breath, and quietly explained, "I'm jealous of everything where you're concerned. Of every man who looks at you. Of the air that you breathe. The clothes that touch your body. But the difference is that I love you, Morgan. And that love is more powerful than anything else. I would never hurt you or betray you."

Her eyes went hazy with memory, and she whispered, "I remember something from Thursday, after the attack. I could hear you arguing. You tried to get Ashe to bite me."

"Because I thought you still loved him. That he was the one you really wanted." He swallowed, working to push the words past the knot in his throat. "And that's all that mattered to me. That you lived and were happy. If being with Ashe would have done it, then I would have gotten down on my knees and begged him to do it. But he…he said that you weren't in love with him."

"He's right." Soft, husky words that made heat crawl up his chest. "I'm not, because I'm in love with you."

"Yeah, he said that, too." Cupping the side of her face in his palm, Kierland caught the glistening drop of a tear with his thumb, and there was a rough note of urgency in his voice as he said, "Don't join The Guard. Come home with me. Work with me. Live with me. Put me out of my misery and make me whole, Morgan. Do that, and I swear I'll worship you in every way that there is, until the end of time. You'll be a queen. *My* queen. I'll— "

"I couldn't care less about being a queen," she murmured, cutting him off, a provocative gleam sparkling in her eyes. "I just want to be yours, Kier."

"You always have been," he groaned, running his hand down the graceful curve of her spine, until he was cupping her bottom, pulling her against the burgeoning ache of his erection, his cock getting harder, thicker, by the second. "I was just too terrified to admit it."

"And now?" she gasped, arching against him.

"Now the only thing that scares me is losing you."

"And what about Ashe?" she asked, sounding worried. "Because he'll always be my friend. I can't… I couldn't ever just turn my back on him."

"I wouldn't expect you to," he rasped, his hand slipping along the back of her thigh, to her knee, and he hitched her leg over his hip, thrusting against her. "And I trust you, Morgan. Nothing can change the way I feel about you."

"And the panic attacks? Because, well, I could be a liability," she explained unsteadily. "I'm still...broken, and I don't know that I'll ever be able to not...to control the panic. It makes me weak."

"Like hell it does," he growled, hating that she felt that way about herself. "I don't know of any other man or woman who could have survived what you did and still gone on to be a Watchman and a helluva soldier. You're a miracle, Morgan, and I'm so damned proud of you."

"You are?" She blinked, looking...shocked. "You always said, back at the academy, that you couldn't stand any kind of weakness."

Kierland winced. "God, I was just being a cocky jackass, spouting the same bullshit I'd grown up hearing at home. But the truth is that it's our weaknesses that make us whole, that make us complete, and even the toughest son of a bitch has them."

With a wry smile, she said, "You don't."

"Do, too," he argued, his voice thick with emotion. "I'm holding my weakness in my arms, angel. The fear of anything ever happening to you... Christ, it drives me insane just to think about it. And I still don't understand how you could have put yourself at risk the way you did with those rogues."

She lifted her hand to his face, lightly stroking the shape of his brows as she said, "It was an easy choice, really, because I knew you were going to get yourself killed if we didn't do something. And I couldn't let that happen."

"Just promise that you'll never put yourself at risk

like that again," he muttered, pressing his lips to her forehead, "because I would die if I lost you."

"THEN WE HAD BETTER MAKE sure you did it right," Morgan whispered, her heart so full of love, she didn't know how she kept it all inside. "You know, the whole claiming thing. Just to make sure."

His eyes gleamed with predatory fire as he twisted his hand in the soft hair at her nape and pulled her head back. "You wear my mark, Morgan." His voice was a dark, intoxicating rumble of sound. "Trust me, angel. I did it right."

"But we'd better make sure," she said huskily, completely dazzled by the smoldering look of love-drenched lust on his face.

"You're still healing!" he growled, his color rising, as if he were burning with fever. "Christ, don't tempt me."

Nipping his chin, Morgan reached down and popped open the top button on his jeans. "If you don't get inside me, Kier, I'm going to get rough with you."

"Damn it, Morgan. Wait—"

"No," she gasped, undoing another button. "I've waited forever for this. I want to know how it feels to have you staring down at me, with your body buried inside mine, as you tell me you love me. Don't make me wait any longer."

"Hell, I can't deny you anything," he groaned, his hot, powerful hands stripping off her panties and T-shirt. Morgan helped him rip his own shirt over his head, and then he was settling over her, his weight braced on his left arm as he opened his mouth over a sensitive nipple, his tongue stroking her…licking her, while using his right hand to shove his jeans over his hips. And then he was inside her, the feeling of rightness so intense she cried out, dissolving in a long, shivering release, his mouth finding hers…and he kissed her as if he was starved for her. As if he wanted to eat her alive. They made love with a primal, passionate intensity that was so much sweeter for the breathtaking emotions burning between them, their mouths feeding off each other with long, drugging kisses that tasted of happiness and hope and hunger.

*"Mine,"* he breathed against her lips, nipping her with his teeth, and she clenched around him, milking his cock with lush, greedy pulls, desperate for everything he had to give her.

When their ragged breathing had finally slowed, she asked, "What happens now?" She pressed her ear to his chest, listening to the steady beat of his heart as he lay on his back beneath her.

"We need to monitor Westmore's compound," he told her, his deep voice rich with satisfaction. "Wait for a signal from Kell. I'll give him 'til Friday, but that's it. After that, I'm finding some way to get him out of that place, even if I have to dig through miles of ice to do it."

"Fair enough," she murmured. "Are we going to contact Quinn and the others?"

He stroked his hand through her hair, saying, "Ashe is going to head out tomorrow and track down Gideon, then come back here to help us against Westmore. He's also going to call Quinn for me and let him know what's happening. If Quinn and the others are determined to come and help, like I imagine they will be, then Ashe will meet up with them and lead the group back here."

"It's so strange, hearing you talk about Ashe." She grinned and pressed a kiss to his warm chest. "It's like the universe has been knocked out of whack or something."

"Yeah, well, I owe him a lot for being there when you needed him."

Morgan's grin got bigger as she raised her head, locking her gaze with his. "I told you he wasn't such a villain."

"We won't be picking out best friends' bracelets anytime soon," he drawled, a lopsided grin kicking up the corner of his mouth, "but, yeah, he's not so bad."

"You know," she whispered, "when you grin like that, it just makes me want to attack you."

Heat gleamed in his beautiful green eyes, but he frowned, his voice rough as he said, "I don't want to wear you out."

She lifted her brows. "Then give me what I want so I don't have to fight you for it."

"Morgan," he groaned, his voice catching as she reached down and wrapped her hand around the hot, rigid length of his cock. "Damn it, you're killing me."

"I feel incredible, Kierland. Better than I've ever felt. But I'll feel even better with you inside me again," she told him, stroking him with a slow, possessive grip. *"Please."*

He cursed, growling husky, sexual words about how

crazy she drove him...how much he wanted her... craved her, as he pushed her to her back again and settled himself into the cradle of her thighs. Her lips curled with a slow, satisfied smile as he fit himself against her, forcing his cock inside the slippery, clutching depths of her body. He pressed his open mouth to hers, licking his way inside, and pushed himself deep...deeper, the muscular wall of his chest rubbing against her breasts. A rough, guttural sound slipped from his lips as he pulled back his hips, then thrust back inside with a slow, heavy lunge that arched her back, her hands gripping onto the hot, sweat-slick surface of his shoulders.

Then she shivered, choking back a muffled sob, and he lifted his head, staring down at her, a stricken expression tightening his features the instant he noticed the tears in her eyes. "Damn it, did I hurt you?"

"No!" she gasped, locking her legs around his lean hips when he started to withdraw. "It's just that...I'm so scared, Kier. I'm terrified you're going to wake up and suddenly change your mind."

"Aw, angel. That's never going to happen," he told her, taking her hands and threading his fingers with hers. "God, Morgan, my life has been hell without you, and I know I have so much to make up for. So many mistakes. I've wasted so much time that I could have spent with you, because I've been an idiot and a jackass, but I'm not going to be one anymore. I'm just... I'll be whatever you need me to be."

"Mine," she said breathlessly. "All I need is for you to be mine."

"Always. I promise. I couldn't ever be anything else."

"Then bite me again," she whispered, smiling up at him. "I want the chance to enjoy it this time."

"Bloody hell," he growled, already opening his mouth over the curve of her shoulder as he buried himself deeper within her body. And then she couldn't hear anything except for the pounding of her own heart. The roar of her pulse.

As the ecstasy swam through her system, Morgan closed her eyes, giving herself up to the beauty of the moment. To the blistering warmth and pleasure and limitless expanse of love that surged inside her.

Then Kierland pulled his fangs from her shoulder, nuzzled his way along the shivering column of her throat…and whispered a soft, husky question in her ear.

With perfect trust in her heart, and tears burning in her eyes, Morgan threw her arms around his neck and said, "I thought you would never ask."

\* \* \* \* \*

*Be sure to watch for the exciting conclusion
to this trilogy, coming out in November.
And now for an exciting preview of
Kellan's romance,
TOUCH OF TEMPTATION,
please turn the page.*

WITH ONE HAND shoved in his pocket, Kellan Scott scraped the fingers of his other hand through his hair and struggled to remember his mission.

*Find the witch.*

*Protect the witch.*

*Rescue the witch.*

Unfortunately, nailing the witch's beautiful little ass to the wall wasn't anywhere on the agenda. Didn't matter how tempting she was. Because even without the poison he'd been infected with slicking through his veins, he wasn't fit for her to wipe her freaking shoes on, much less trust with her body. She was a stunning, white-hot goddess with a shy smile and endearing blushes, and he was...well, he sure as hell wasn't a god. At the moment he was even more animal than man.

Which meant he had to keep his filthy paws *off* the delectable little Chloe Harcourt.

But it wasn't going to be easy. Big, thick-lashed eyes stared back at him, the silvery gray edged by a darker ring of charcoal that added an exotic touch to her ethereal, delicate beauty. She was too pale, the bruise-colored smudges under her eyes growing darker, and his insides twisted with guilt. Damn it, she needed blood, but it was too dangerous. His beast was too close to the surface.

And it wasn't like blood alone was going to ease her suffering. As an awakening Merrick female, she needed blood...*and* an earth-shattering orgasm.

"This is wrong," he groaned, wincing at the raw, gritty sound of his voice. "Damn it, you don't wanna do this, Chloe. Trust me."

"Please, Kellan." A vivid blush burned beneath her smooth skin, and he could tell how much it was costing her to ask him for something that was so intimate. "I'm...starving."

A sheen of sweat broke out over the surface of his skin, despite the freezing temperatures in the cell.

"If you don't help me, I'm afraid of what I'll do," she said unsteadily. "I *need* you."

Though he'd used every ounce of his strength to hold on to his fraying control, it was those last three words that broke him.

Cursing and shaking with lust, Kellan crossed the distance between them, wrapped one arm under her bottom and lifted her clear off the ground as he shoved her against the wall. His free hand closed around the nape of her neck, holding her still as he covered her mouth with his, licking his way past those plush, petal-soft lips, seeking the silken warmth within. She was delicious. Mouthwatering. Addictive. He used every last ounce of willpower to give her the time to decide whether or not she wanted to go further, but the instant she flicked her tongue against his, he was gone.

"Please," she gasped, her slender fingers tangling themselves in his hair as she fought to pull him closer, her legs wrapping around his waist. *"More."*

With a deep, guttural growl, Kellan lifted her higher…and gave her exactly what she'd asked for.

## *GLOSSARY OF TERMS*
## *FOR THE PRIMAL INSTINCT SERIES*

**The Ancient Clans:** Nonhuman races whose existence has been kept secret from the majority of humans for thousands of years, their abilities differing as widely as their physiology. Some only partially alter when in their primal forms, like the Merrick. Others fully transform, able to take the shape of an animal, similar to those who compose the Watchmen.

These are but a few of the various ancient clans that remain in existence today:

<u>The Merrick:</u> One of the most powerful of the ancient clans, the Merrick were forced to mate with humans after years of war against the Casus had decimated their numbers. Their bloodlines eventually became dormant, dwelling within their human descendants, until the return of the Casus and the time of their awakening. In order to feed the primal parts of their nature, the newly awakened Merrick must consume blood whilst having sex. Characteristics: When in Merrick form, the males have fangs, talons, flattened noses

354 GLOSSARY OF TERMS

and massive, heavily muscled physiques. The females have fangs and talons.

*The Awakenings:* Each time a Casus shade returns to this world, it causes the primal blood within one of the Merrick descendants to rise within them, or awaken, so that they might battle against their ancient enemy.

*The Buchanans:* One of the strongest Merrick bloodlines, the Buchanans were not only the first of the Merrick to awaken, but they also each possess an unusual power or "gift." Ian has a strange sense of premonition that comes to him in dreams, Saige can "hear" things from physical objects when she touches them and Riley's telekinetic powers enable him to control physical objects with his mind.

The Casus: Meaning *violent death*, the Casus are an immortal race of preternatural monsters who were imprisoned by the Merrick and the Consortium over a thousand years ago for their mindless killing sprees. Recently, however, they have begun escaping from their holding ground, returning to this world and taking over the bodies of "human hosts" who have dormant Casus blood running through their veins. The escaped Casus now prey upon the newly awakened Merrick, feeding on their flesh for power, as well as revenge. Characteristics: When in Casus form, they have muzzled faces, wolf-shaped heads, leathery gray skin, ridged backs and long, curved claws. The males have ice-blue eyes, while the females have eyes that are pale green.

*Meridian:* The metaphysical holding ground where the Casus were imprisoned for their crimes against the other clans...as well as humanity. Although it was created by the original Consortium, no one knows where it's located or how to find it.

*Shades:* Because of their immortality, the Casus can't die in Meridian. They have simply wasted away to "shades" of the powerful creatures they once were, which is why they're forced to take human hosts once they return to this world.

The Deschanel: Also known as vampires, the Deschanel are one of the most powerful of the ancient clans, rivaling the strength of the Merrick and the shape-shifters. Although duality is a common feature among many of the clans, the trait is especially strong within the Deschanel, whose very natures are a dichotomy of opposites—of both darkness and light—which makes them complex friends...and dangerous enemies. Characteristics: Pale, pure gray eyes that glow after they've taken a blood feeding. Despite their power and strength, they move with a smooth, effortless grace that is uncommon among human males of their size. They also have incredibly long life-spans, until such time as they finally take a mate.

*The Burning:* The body of an unmated Deschanel male runs cold until he finds his mate. The phenomenon is referred to as being "in heat" or "burning," since his body begins warming from the moment he finds her.

*The Förmyndares:* As the Protectors of the Deschanel, it is the duty of these warriors to destroy any threats to the vampire clans.

*Nesting Grounds:* Ancient, sprawling castle-like communities where Deschanel family units, or nests, live for security, which are protected by powerful magic that keeps them hidden from the outside world. The grounds are located throughout Scandinavia and other parts of Europe.

The Witches: Although there are many witch clans still in existence, their powers vary greatly from one clan to another.

*The Mallory:* A powerful clan of witches whose diverse powers were bound by a curse. Because of the centuries-old curse, they now magnify the emotions of those in their presence to extreme levels.

*The Reavess:* A clan of witches who can communicate mentally with those in their families. They access their considerable power through the use of spells, and will bond their true loves to them through sex. They are also able to assume the traits possessed by their mates during "joining."

The Regan: An aggressive clan responsible for hunting several rival clans to near extinction. Characteristics: long noses, pointed ears and deeply cleft chins.

The Kenly: A mountain-dwelling clan nearly hunted to extinction by the Regan. Characteristics: short statures and large, doelike eyes.

The Feardacha: One of several ancient clans that resides in Ireland. They are extremely superstitious, believing that the dead should never go unchecked. As a precaution, they tattoo pagan symbols on their hands and arms, believing the symbols will draw to them any evil souls that manage to escape from hell, so that they might kill them once again. Characteristics: tattoos, mocha-colored skin and pale green eyes.

The Vassayre: One of the more reclusive clans, they seldom come out of the underground caves where they dwell. Characteristics: dark markings around their sunken eyes.

<u>The Shape-shifters:</u> A richly diverse, powerful collection of clans whose members can take either the complete or partial shape of a beast.

*The Prime Predators:* Consisting of the most dangerous, predatory animal species, they are the most aggressive breeds of shape-shifters, well-known for their legendary sex drives and their unquestionable devotion to their mates. In order to claim a mate, a Prime must bite the one who holds their heart, marking them with their fangs while taking their blood into their bodies. They are also known for their incomparable skill as warriors and their strong healing abilities. Examples: the tigers, jaguars and lycanthropes.

*The Lycanthropes:* Also known as werewolves, they are formidable warriors who can actually change humans to their species with the power of their bite if they are in wolf form. However, in order to mark their mates, they must make a bite with their fangs whilst still in human form.

*The Raptors:* One of the rarest breeds of shifters, the Raptors are known for being ruthless warriors and possessive, utterly devoted lovers. Although they do not completely shift form, they are able to release powerful wings from their backs that enable them to fly, as well as sharp talons from their fingertips for fighting.

*The Charteris:* Dragon shape-shifters who possess the ability to control fire, and whose bodies burn with a dangerous heat when making love to a woman who holds their heart. It is believed that no pure-blooded Charteris are still in existence.

**The Archives:** The records that belonged to the original Consortium which are believed to hold vital information about the ancient clans. Though the new Consortium has spent years searching for them, the archives have fallen into the hands of the Collective Army.

**The Collective Army:** A militant organization of human mercenaries devoted to purging the world of all preternatural life. In an ironic twist, the Collective Army now finds itself partnered with the Kraven and the Casus, in exchange for information that they believe will enable them to exterminate the remaining nonhuman species.

**The Consortium:** A body of officials composed of representatives from each of the remaining ancient clans, the Consortium is a sort of preternatural United Nations. Their purpose is to settle disputes and keep peace among the differing species, while working to hide the existence of the remaining clans from the human world. Over a thousand years ago, the original Consortium helped the Merrick imprison the Casus, after the Casus's relentless killing of humans threatened to expose the existence of the nonhuman races. The council fashioned the Dark Markers in order to destroy the immortal killers, only to be murdered by the newly created Collective Army before they could complete the task. Years later, the Consortium re-formed, but by then its original archives had been lost...all traces of the Dark Markers supposedly destroyed during the Collective's merciless raids, which nearly led to the destruction of the clans.

**The Dark Markers:** Metal crosses of enormous power that were mysteriously created by the original Consortium, they are the only known weapons capable of killing a Casus, sending its soul directly to hell. They also work as a talisman for those who wear them, offering protection from the Casus. Although it is unknown how many Dark Markers are in existence, there is a set of encrypted maps which leads to their locations. The Watchmen and the Buchanans are using these maps to help them find the Markers before they fall into enemy hands.

> *"Arm of Fire":* Weapon mode for a Dark Marker. When held against the palm, a Dark Marker holds the power to change one's arm into an "Arm of Fire." When the cross is placed against the back of a Casus's

neck, the flame-covered arm will sink into the monster's body, burning it from the inside out.

*The Encrypted Maps:* When Saige Buchanan discovered the first Dark Marker in Italy, she found a set of ancient maps buried alongside the cross. The maps, which lead to the hidden locations of the Dark Markers, had been wrapped in oilcloth and preserved by some kind of spell.

**The Death-Walkers:** The demented souls of clansmen and -women who were sent to hell for their sadistic crimes, and who are now managing to return to our world. It is unknown how to kill them, but they can be burned by a combination of holy water and salt. Driven mad by their time in hell, they are a formidable force of evil, seeking to create chaos and war among the remaining clans simply because they want to watch the world bleed. Characteristics: Although they retain certain traits from their original species, each of the Death-Walkers has cadaverously white skin and small horns that protrude from their temples, as well as deadly fangs and claws.

**"The Eve Effect":** A phenomenon that affects various breeds of shape-shifters, causing them to be drawn to certain females who touch the primal hungers of both the man and the beast. If a male falls in love with one of these females and bites her, she will be bonded to him as his mate for the rest of their lives.

**The Kraven:** The offspring of female Deschanel vampires who were raped by Casus males prior to their imprisonment. Treated little better than slaves and considered an embarrassing symbol of weakness, the Kraven have been such a closely guarded secret within the Deschanel clan that the Watchmen have only recently become aware of their existence. Although their motivation is still unclear, the Kraven are working to facilitate the return of the Casus. It is also unclear as to why they are working with the Casus to gain possession of the Dark Markers. Characteristics: They are believed to have long life spans, and their fangs can only be released at night, causing their eyes to glow a deep, blood-red crimson. They can also easily pass for human, but can only be killed when a wooden stake is driven through their heart.

**The Wasteland:** A cold, desolate, dangerous region that was created by powerful magic, where exiled Deschanel "nests" or family units are forced to live once the Consortium has passed judgment against them. Protected by spells that make it invisible to humans, this vast region "shares" physical space with the Scandinavian forests surrounding it.

**The Watchmen:** An organization of shape-shifters whose job it is to watch over the remaining ancient clans. They are considered the "eyes and ears" of the

Consortium. They monitor the various nonhuman species, as well as the bloodlines of those clans that have become dormant. Prior to the recent Merrick awakenings, the most powerful Merrick bloodlines had been under Watchmen supervision. There are Watchmen compounds situated around the world, with each unit consisting of four to six warriors. Characteristics: Physical characteristics vary according to the specific breed of shape-shifter.

# REQUEST YOUR FREE BOOKS!

## 2 FREE NOVELS
## FROM THE SUSPENSE COLLECTION
## PLUS 2 FREE GIFTS!

**YES!** Please send me 2 FREE novels from the Suspense Collection and my 2 FREE gifts (gifts are worth about $10). After receiving them, if I don't wish to receive any more books, I can return the shipping statement marked "cancel." If I don't cancel, I will receive 3 brand-new novels every month and be billed just $5.74 per book in the U.S. or $6.24 per book in Canada. That's a saving of at least 28% off the cover price. It's quite a bargain! Shipping and handling is just 50¢ per book in the U.S. and 75¢ per book in Canada.* I understand that accepting the 2 free books and gifts places me under no obligation to buy anything. I can always return a shipment and cancel at any time. Even if I never buy another book, the two free books and gifts are mine to keep forever.

192 MDN E4MN  392 MDN E4MY

Name _____ (PLEASE PRINT) _____

Address _____ Apt. # _____

City _____ State/Prov. _____ Zip/Postal Code _____

Signature (if under 18, a parent or guardian must sign)

### Mail to **The Reader Service:**
**IN U.S.A.:** P.O. Box 1867, Buffalo, NY 14240-1867
**IN CANADA:** P.O. Box 609, Fort Erie, Ontario L2A 5X3

Not valid for current subscribers to the Suspense Collection
or the Romance/Suspense Collection.

**Want to try two free books from another line?**
**Call 1-800-873-8635 or visit www.morefreebooks.com.**

* Terms and prices subject to change without notice. Prices do not include applicable taxes. N.Y. residents add applicable sales tax. Canadian residents will be charged applicable provincial taxes and GST. Offer not valid in Quebec. This offer is limited to one order per household. All orders subject to approval. Credit or debit balances in a customer's account(s) may be offset by any other outstanding balance owed by or to the customer. Please allow 4 to 6 weeks for delivery. Offer available while quantities last.

**Your Privacy:** Harlequin Books is committed to protecting your privacy. Our Privacy Policy is available online at www.eHarlequin.com or upon request from the Reader Service. From time to time we make our lists of customers available to reputable third parties who may have a product or service of interest to you. If you would prefer we not share your name and address, please check here. ☐

**Help us get it right**—We strive for accurate, respectful and relevant communications. To clarify or modify your communication preferences, visit us at www.ReaderService.com/consumerchoice.

MSUS10

# RHYANNON BYRD

| | | | |
|---|---|---|---|
| 77448 | TOUCH OF SEDUCTION | ___ $7.99 U.S. | ___ $9.99 CAN. |
| 77423 | EDGE OF DESIRE | ___ $7.99 U.S. | ___ $8.99 CAN. |
| 77399 | EDGE OF DANGER | ___ $7.99 U.S. | ___ $8.99 CAN. |
| 77367 | EDGE OF HUNGER | ___ $6.99 U.S. | ___ $6.99 CAN. |

*(limited quantities available)*

| | |
|---|---|
| TOTAL AMOUNT | $ _____ |
| POSTAGE & HANDLING | $ _____ |
| ($1.00 FOR 1 BOOK, 50¢ for each additional) | |
| APPLICABLE TAXES* | $ _____ |
| TOTAL PAYABLE | $ _____ |

*(check or money order—please do not send cash)*

To order, complete this form and send it, along with a check or money order for the total above, payable to HQN Books, to: **In the U.S.:** 3010 Walden Avenue, P.O. Box 9077, Buffalo, NY 14269-9077; **In Canada:** P.O. Box 636, Fort Erie, Ontario, L2A 5X3.

Name: _____
Address: _____ City: _____
State/Prov.: _____ Zip/Postal Code: _____
Account Number (if applicable): _____

075 CSAS

*New York residents remit applicable sales taxes.
*Canadian residents remit applicable GST and provincial taxes.

## HQN™

We *are* romance™

**www.HQNBooks.com**

PHRB0510BL